ZOTOV

EL DIABLO

MAGIC DOME BOOKS

El Diablo
Published by Magic Dome Books, 2018
Copyright © Zotov 2018
Cover Art © Andrei Ferez 2016
English translation copyright ©
Irene Woodhead and Neil P. Mayhew 2018
All Rights Reserved
ISBN: 978-80-7619-012-2

TABLE OF CONTENTS:

Part One. Cine Pornografico

Part Two. Cine Patriotero

Part Three. Cine Commerciale

Part One

Cine Pornografico

B uild my fear of what's out there
And cannot breathe the open air
Whisper things into my brain
Assuring me that I'm insane

Metallica, *Welcome Home (Sanitarium)*

PROLOGUE

Lima, capital of the Republic of Peru
October 14 1931

T HE OLD TELEPHONE rattled, jumping up and down on the bedside table. Miguel groped for it in the dark, then swatted it like a fly with a blow of his hand.

Contrary to his expectations, the phone didn't shut up. It continued to annoy him with its repeated buzzing which sounded like a snoring man having rust poured down his throat.

Miguel struggled to rub his eyes. What was going on, dammit? He reached out, feeling for the receiver, and brought it blindly to his ear.

"Speaking."

"Excuse me, Señor Capitan," the phone wheezed.

"You have any idea what time it is?" Miguel said, swelling with spite.

"Yes, Señor Capitan. It's four a.m. May the Virgin Mary and Jesus himself be the witnesses of my apologies, but I was told to wake you up on the orders from Deputy Minister Juarez. He demands you arrive at Plaza Mayor ASAP. This is an emergency."

"And what's up there?" Miguel asked, suppressing a yawn.

"I've no idea, Señor. We've had a driver sent to get you. The car should already be waiting by your front door."

Miguel hung up without saying goodbye.

He sprang from his bed. A dull light bulb under the ceiling lit up a closet which the hotel keeper had the audacity to call a furnished room. A well-worn bed, a wash stand, a faded bedside table, a stone floor (especially welcome in this constant heat), a writing desk (which, judging by its age, must have been left behind during the conquistadors' retreat) and a portrait of El Presidente on the wall, generously embellished with the dried bodies of mosquitoes. Luis Sánchez Cerro stared wearily into the semidarkness of the room, lips pressed tight, his epaulettes resembling large unwashed dishes on the faded photo.

Miguel splashed his face with some icy-cold water. Yawning mercilessly, he buttoned up his tunic.

He walked down the loose steps which groaned their death throes underfoot. That bastard landlady of his had the cheek to ask fifteen sols a month for this dilapidated box of a "hotel room" on the third floor of a 17th century colonial shack.

The car's motor was already chugging away below. Predictably, a Ford and a rather ancient model at that. Could anything new come out of this country?

A familiar young driver courteously opened the car door. Miguel slumped onto the worn back seat, immediately transported to another planet: one that smelled of cheap two-centavo cigars, with a magazine picture pinned to the dashboard, a cracked windscreen and a missing rearview mirror. It was a good job the driver was sober — something that didn't happen very often in Peru.

The car sped off, racing through the empty city.

"Do you know what happened, Señor?" the driver tried to strike up a conversation.

"It's none of your fucking business," Miguel snapped.

The driver subserviently shut up.

The Ford turned off toward the Barrio Miraflores, bypassing a coconut grove and a row of dark yellow morisco houses with their columns, tiled roofs and tiny carved balconies. The sound of the ocean surf lulled him to sleep; the car's rocking motion felt like a cradle. Unwittingly Miguel closed his eyes and didn't even notice himself dozing off.

He had the same dream he'd always had in Lima ever since he'd first arrived here. It had already become some sort of tradition.

American and Japanese warships, packed into Vladivostok harbor like sardines. The clouds of explosions hanging in the autumnal sky. The screams and the sounds of weeping and cussing voices that hung in the air. It felt like true pandemonium. The whole world seemed to be there: respectable merchants, their beards quaking with fear; petrified young girls in school uniforms; ladies in threadbare furs.

That was the early-morning scene of October 25 1922 during the evacuation of General Dieterichs' troops from Vladivostok. Rumors spread, one more terrible than the next, about the Japs' treachery and their alleged retreat from their positions. The Bolsheviks were expected to enter the defenseless city within an hour.

With shouts of "Get back, motherfuckers!" the Americans fended the panic-stricken people off with their bayonets as the crowds stampeded for the last ships, even though the night before, the most beautiful girls in Vladivostok had parted with their virginity in the sailors' cabins, paying for their right to be the first to step on the life-saving gangplanks. The whole surface of the water was littered with the contents of smashed suitcases, clothes and children's toys floating side by side.

Miguel had been one of them that day, a puny blond lad of about twenty years of age with a pallid freckled face. *'Allow me to introduce myself, ladies and gentlemen: Second Lieutenant Mikhail Martynov'.* He'd been wearing a tattered army greatcoat, with a Nagant revolver in his hand and a crazy look in his eyes.

Good God, how long had it been... he could still clearly remember the moment when the ship had finally set sail, packed to the brim with fugitives. And as the gray strip of the shore began to widen, he'd realized he'd never return to his home city.

As he'd stood on the deck that day, he'd vacantly put the revolver's barrel into his mouth and licked it. The taste of gun oil assaulted his tongue. He'd said a prayer, then silently cussed as he pulled the trigger with all the determination of youth.

The click echoed in his ears like the tolling of a funeral bell.

Of course. There hadn't been any rounds left in the cylinder for a long time. The Tsarist White army had been completely depleted of ammunition during the prolonged campaign.

What a young idiot he'd been then. He'd then spent years in Tokyo gutters — without money, in lice-ridden tatters, subsisting on one cup of rice in three days and sleeping rough under the bridge next to drunken prostitutes. He quickly realized that his Spanish was of no use there whatsoever and began dreaming of getting to Spain which was prohibitively far away.

Three months later, he found a job as a deckhand on a rickety old tub which was taking some Japanese migrants to Peru.

That's when Mikhail Martynov had become Miguel Martinez.

He got himself a Peruvian passport, then made a quick career from ordinary cop to criminal investigator. He finally had a roof over his head, never mind it that was only an old shack but, excuse my French, only generals could afford the good life on their salaries in this country. How many of his fellow officers had either gone on the bottle or shot themselves; some of them were now shoeshine boys in Tokyo and Shanghai while countless others had become horse-cab drivers in Harbin. He'd been one of the lucky ones...

"SEÑOR? Excuse me, Señor, but we've just arrived," the driver had already opened the car door and was shaking him awake.

Reluctantly Miguel climbed out of the Ford. His head felt leaden; he was falling asleep as he walked. He reached into his tunic pocket for a small wad of pressed coke leaves and blindly sent it into his mouth.

Great stuff. It may have numbed the tongue and tasted like a cross between bay leaves and peppermint, but it gave you a real boost.

In just a couple of seconds, he felt fresh as a daisy. His mind had cleared, his eyes could focus, his body sensed the chill in the air. Where had they brought him to?

These were some rundown back alleys behind the pretentious Plaza Mayor. He'd been here many times before. Murders were common in nighttime Lima. The city thrived on them. Knife fights, shootouts, rapes and drunken brawls... very nice.

The sunrise was long in coming. Miguel headed for a group of men with flashlights who froze in the gloom between the skeletal remains of houses.

A beam of light flashed straight in his face.

"We're very happy you're here, Señor Capitan."

Hearing the voice had finally awoken Miguel to the fact that something bad must have happened. Up until then, he'd thought it just a bad joke... but if the deputy police minister had arrived at the scene in person, there must have been a reason for it.

He brought two fingers up to his kepi in salute. "Good morning, Sir."

The Deputy Minister Juarez, a squat overweight balding half-breed (like half the local population, he was an explosive mix of the Quechua Indian and Spanish colonials), looked rather out of place in a civilian suit and a fedora. *He would have looked more impressive hunting jaguars with a spear in his hand,* Miguel thought lightheartedly in Russian.

The deputy minister brought a handkerchief up to his head and wiped his brow. His lips were shaking. Miguel's reckless cheerfulness vanished, replaced by an uneasy anxiety.

The two of them stood in a small clearing between an ancient colonial *casa* and an abandoned church. The old priest had died almost a year ago and a new one hadn't yet been assigned.

ZOTOV

Miguel cussed as his shoe got stuck in the viscous mud. Juarez lowered his flashlight.

All the remaining drowsiness had now cleared from Miguel's head. His shoe was colored a deep cherry red.

"It looks like the murderer bled her to death," the deputy minister said. "It's like a lake here. All the grass and tree roots are soaked in blood. The rest you'll see in a minute," he stepped aside, giving way.

The police photographer's camera flashed, imprinting the scene on Miguel's retinas. A girl, dressed in a lacy cream-colored dress puffed up with petticoats almost medieval in their style, the sort women still wore in the areas bordering Bolivia. Her thick black hair was meticulously coiffed, her eyes wide open — as was her mouth with just the tip of her tongue showing. Her face resembled a crimson mask: someone had covered it with blood, painting it like a fence around a peasant's hut. Her arms had been tied behind the trunk of a thick tree, her body positioned on top of its roots. A wash tub stood by her feet; judging by the dirty-brown streaks covering its bottom, it must have been used to collect the blood.

He shouldn't have been so cross with Juarez. This was indeed an emergency.

Miguel walked over to the body. The cops parted, letting him through. Blood squelched underfoot.

"When did you find her?" Martinez asked,

peering at the dead face.

"Two hours ago, Señor Capitan," a young corporal said in a stifled voice, trying not to look at the victim. "You know how old people can't sleep at night sometimes, don't you? They just take their dogs for a walk or something. It was one of them who found the Señorita. You can't imagine how quickly he ran to the police station. At first we wanted to untie her but... as soon as we touched her we decided to call an officer. He told us to contact his superiors. And his superiors called you, Señor."

Miguel crouched in order to get a better look at the dried blood on the girl's cheeks.

A faint pleasant aroma hung in the air. How strange. Normally, a murder victim stinks like a dead animal at an abattoir. And this... he couldn't quite place it. It smelled like perfume but sweeter... more delicate.

He reached out and touched the girl's arm, pulling it toward himself, then recoiled as the body gently leaned toward him with a soft rustling sound, like a pillow.

Martinez touched her arm again, gently pressing the skin.

Something crunched inside. How interesting. The murderer had professionally removed every bone from her body, then stuffed it with aromatic herbs, painted her face with her own blood and brought it to the slums behind Plaza Mayor about midnight. He must have drained her of blood prior to that (aha, there was a lacerated wound on her throat), then used some of it as decorating material and dumped the rest of it on the ground.

This wasn't going to stop at the Deputy Minister's level. Very soon El Presidente would know too.

Her eyes were framed with four glittering lines pointing in different directions. Miguel nodded to a cop to bring his flashlight closer. He'd been right: it was gold dust, hence the shimmering.

Oh, great. The guy had some sick imagination. Miguel didn't for one moment doubt the fact it had been a man. He'd already solved three serial killer cases in the past in different Peruvian cities, including the Trujillo Predator — a baker who'd strangled four street whores. But those were rather narrow-minded people with no imagination whatsoever who'd collected their victims' body parts as souvenirs following the mothballed example of Jack the Ripper.

This was something different. A very specific approach. This girl wasn't a well-ridden priestess of the high street, the kind he'd encountered already in Vladivostok. She appeared to be no more than fifteen, a mere schoolgirl.

So what would our murderer's profession be, then? A surgeon? A taxidermist? A crazy artist? In any case, it made no sense for Miguel to linger here. The body (or cynically speaking, the stuffed bird) had to be sent to the station for further investigation. It was hard work trying to examine it in this weak light.

It didn't look as if he'd get any sleep tonight. Nor the next night, most likely.

Miguel rose to his feet.

The sound of surf came from the ocean. The girl, painted with blood and stuffed with aromatic herbs, looked like an expensive doll in the first sunrays, similar to those that Miraflores-based rubber tycoons gave to their spoiled little daughters. The gold streaks around her dead eyes were dazzling.

Miguel reached into his pocket for his cigarette case. With a bow, the cop offered him a lighted match.

Miguel's head disappeared in clouds of bluish smoke. Tobacco was excellent here, much stronger than the Russian home-grown *samosad*. The only thing he couldn't get used to was the local brew, *pisco*, and there was no way he could get vodka here, not even from smugglers.

Red parrots shuttled between palm trees, squawking. What was he doing here, at the very edge of the Earth?

Martinez stepped toward the Deputy Minister, then swung round.

The nails.

The dead girl's fingernails had been different.

He walked over to her and took a closer look, bringing her hands to his eyes one after the other.

Her left hand had the long, sensitive fingers of a piano player. Her right-hand fingers were short and knobbly.

Miguel cussed in Russian, investing all his fury into two snappy words.

This time he spent a good ten minutes examining the body before he finally returned to the Deputy Minister.

Juarez raised his blood-shot eyes to him.

Miguel waved his hand at the tree to which the girl was strapped. "I'm afraid, this is gonna be fun, Señor."

The Deputy Minister raised a quizzical eyebrow. "What makes you think so?"

"She was put together from several bodies — at least four, by the looks of it. The murderer took his time creating this doll. It looks like he might want to open a toy shop."

Seagulls squawked hysterically over the ocean. Dark clouds concealed the sky. A powerful gust of wind from the shore threw up grains of sand which stuck in the teeth of early-morning passersby. A storm was brewing.

CHAPTER ONE

VINTAGE

October 14 2015
Location unknown

HAVING ARRIVED on the scene as the promise of a new world wonder — the mixture of a childish dream and medieval magic — the film industry had quickly degraded to the state of a mediocre dumb-entertainment option. By the early 21st century, it had already grown into a fat kraken whose tentacles reached into any available space, forcing its way out of the tiny movie theaters and taking over the world which had willingly succumbed to its dominance.

Take a look around yourself. Movies are everywhere: in our offices and lounges, in front of our airplane seats and on our smartphone screens. They reach their fine predatory earbuds into our brains, focusing our eyes on the images they want us to see. We've been reduced to a state of blind zombies, the obedient slaves of a colorful world of make-belief.

Movies have been absorbed into the bloodstream of every living being on planet Earth. We can't be a hundred percent sure anymore whether it's us living our real lives or whether it's someone else filming a movie of them. As any priest will tell you (maybe in not so many words), God is the film director of our Universe, which makes us a bunch of underpaid extras in His latest blockbuster.

But I digress. Time to start this show.

The lights dim. The celluloid rustles in the projector.

Ladies and gentlemen, please remove your 3D glasses. You won't need them: the movie's rather old. Everybody got their popcorn? Make yourselves comfortable and try to disconnect from the rest of the Universe in order to hear these two people speaking.

They're walking toward you gingerly, groping their way in the pitch darkness. You can hear the sound of their footsteps from afar: a soft and predatory feline gait interspersed with a timid clatter of stilettoes on the cemented floor.

Like a tiger stalking a young deer. Or is it the other   way   round?

[MALE VOICE] Please don't. The electricity doesn't work here. There's a candelabra here somewhere.

[FEMALE VOICE] Why doesn't it work?

[MALE VOICE] It's a very old basement. I don't think there's electricity in it at all. It's been empty for ages. Nothing lives here, not even rats, can you imagine? This is my underground world. The rusty pipes, the smell of a rotting mattress, the rustling of crumbling old magazines, the crunching of broken bottles underfoot... This is the music of my solitude. You understand, my girl, don't you? The symphony of salvation.

[FEMALE VOICE, unhappily]. Sorry to be so rude but this place is a mess! It looks like a BDSM torture chamber.

[MALE VOICE] That's how I need it to be. This way I can hear it when they finally get to me.

A match strikes. A weak uneven candlelight sends the trapped shadows darting in horror across the walls. The floor is heaped with half-rotten women's clothes and colorful underwear, some filthy red leather corsets and stockings. The dark lair of a grim monster who doesn't leave his den for months at a time.

[MALE VOICE]. Yes, this is my bed. I sleep here too. That's why I chose this ruin in the suburbs. No one ever pays any attention to it. I get out once a day, to get some food and see what's going on. I don't have to hide. I don't paint my face with camouflage, if that's what you think. Still, even once a day is once too many. I need to bring my outings to a minimum, otherwise it might end very badly. Very. They don't for one moment stop hunting me down."

[FEMALE VOICE, echoes] I know.

[MALE VOICE, coughs]. Finding something suitable to eat is a problem. There's no decent food here! I'm sick to death of cucumbers, bananas and whipped cream. My stomach is in tatters. I'm getting jumpy like a wild animal. Whenever I manage to doze off, I dream of those awful streets flooded with neon lights. Me cowering behind trash cans from the floodlights searching for me... encircling me, baring their teeth as they close in...

The shadows flitter. Obeying a sudden bout of sympathy, she raises her hand, about to stroke his cheek. He recoils from her touch.

[FEMALE VOICE] Sorry, sorry, sorry, I'm so sorry. I keep forgetting...

[MALE VOICE, gasps]. It's not your fault. Nothing to do with you. Where was I? Yes, the horror of it all. The City's divided between several groups, you know that, don't you? There're certain twilight zones where the likes of me disappear like melting snow. We never hear from them again. I'm sick and tired of never having any money because the City lives in a subsistence economy. I can't afford even the barest of necessities. I have one last candle left. Once it burns down, I might need to-"

[FEMALE VOICE shakes, breaking]. But from what I heard, the convent...

[MALE VOICE] Maybe. I have no choice, do I? Even though the convent is the craziest place in the entire City. No one stands a chance there. Have you any idea who inhabits it? If you meet a couple of Black Habits in the street — or three even — you still have a chance of escaping. Or, if push comes to shove, you can work it off. But the convent is jam-packed with them. There're at least a hundred of them in there. That's death. They can sniff you out the moment you approach its walls; you can hear them laugh, a disgusting laughter, sort of carnivorous. No male has ever come back from there. Even their skeletons have never been found. Me, I've been in there twice.

[FEMALE VOICE] *Twice?!*

[MALE VOICE] Well, what do you want? I need more candles. It's no fun sitting in the dark, it's sorta spooky. Tomorrow I'm going there again. You know why, don't you? It's my only chance of survival. I've been here for way too long. I've learned to survive in your world without money or food — and no one knows what it's cost me! I've been forced to show up in the City's most dangerous streets, knowing *they* could suck the life out of me drop by dwindling drop. They're constantly hungry, those creatures, regardless of their age. The Checkered Skirts are only merciless during their springtime hunting periods; but it's the Black Habits who are the real monsters. You never know who you might come across: they're masters of disguise capable of putting even the most vigilant of townsfolk off their guard.

[FEMALE VOICE, with regret]. I used to help them. How awful... I didn't know what I was doing. You opened my eyes to their true nature. I wish you good luck — I won't go to bed before I hear from you, I swear. Don't fall for their charms. The Black Habits' voices are sweet like those of sirens, it's all too easy to forget oneself listening to their songs. Sometimes they used me too to lure passersby to the convent walls. I'm so ashamed of it.

A little light flickers on with a typical hissing sound as one of them lights a cigarette.

[MALE VOICE] Stop beating yourself up. That was meant to happen. Before I came to your world, I too used to think of it as heaven, everything a red-blooded man could wish for. I used to think things like these could only happen in a teenager's wet dream — or in places like Cuba although there you'd have to pay. Whatever. I couldn't have even imagined I'd be stuck here cowering in a basement, hungry, exhausted and totally wasted! I thought... doesn't matter, sweetheart. I used to think lots of things, none of them too decent. Instead of coming to heaven, I'd been given a one-way ticket to hell. Never again will I ever ask for a dream to come true. Because they do come true only to devour your life with demonic laughter. Had I believed in God, I'd have considered my fiasco a punishment for my sins. Do you think I'm crazy? Life amongst monsters prays on my mind which shrinks in panic, inch by desperate inch...

[FEMALE VOICE, hopeful]. Are you sure you've chosen the right place? Old women say, there're some old-school settlements only a couple of hours' drive away. They have those cute 1970s cottages, very pretty, and the air there smells of milk and fresh hay. Nothing too complicated, everything's pretty natural. If they catch you, they finish you off quickly. They don't torture you to death. The locals are a happy bunch. They're not into any BDSM stuff.

[MALE VOICE, sighs]. I know. It's called vintage mode. In vintage mode, the entire ordeal lasts from twenty seconds to a maximum of five minutes. It's not that bad, even if they attack you in bulk. But... I can't get there, can I? From what I hear, the journey is too perilous. I don't even want to tell you what kinds of neighborhoods it crosses. Have you ever heard about the "tough illegals" neighborhood?

ZOTOV

I knew you haven't. When they play, they kill for real. In my world, a video of this kind costs eighty thousand bucks. There's so much dirt here... so many perverts, mutants and predators. How come I knew nothing about it before?

She looks him in the eye. Their lips almost meet.

[FEMALE VOICE] Let's change the subject. You seem to be nicer... and calmer when you're telling me about your world.

[MALE VOICE, heaves a sigh.] Oh. Can you imagine I didn't really appreciate it? Now I go to bed every night hoping that I might wake up and realize all this was only a dream. Dream my ass! Every morning it starts all over again. And the thing is, I *know* I'm not asleep. If I die here, I'll die for real. It's a real Freddy Krueger nightmare.

[FEMALE VOICE] Freddy what?

[MALE VOICE] Forget it. He's just a horror creature from my world. You have the likes of him too in some neighborhoods. He's an incredible, unbelievable killer who visits his victims in their dreams. He pierces them with his steely claw and they die for real... what a lot of bullshit. I'm stuck here now and I've got no idea what to do. Luckily, I met you. I never thought creatures like you existed in the City. They might, theoretically, but they don't.

[FEMALE VOICE, pensively]. If your theory is correct and we're just an artificial embodiment of other people's fantasies, why not? Didn't you say that even in your world virgins are difficult to come by?

[MALE VOICE, agrees eagerly]. Absolutely! Not at your age, anyway. Funny, isn't it, there're plenty of fourteen-year-old virgins around but if you want to find a twenty-four-old one, you've got your work cut out for you. And even those who are are mainly fakes, courtesy of plastic surgery.

[FEMALE VOICE] Well, I'm not exactly innocent, either. Here, virgins are preserved for very special kinds of games. Did you say that our world is based on a mere dozen scenarios which keep going round in circles, repeating themselves? You might be right. I'm quite experienced at certain things. I've taken part in BDSM orgies and seen things that would make the most seasoned of City whores shrink in horror even though it might not involve penetration. Would you like me to tell you? Having said that... no, not a good idea. You'd better tell me how you got here. I'll listen to you. I won't interrupt you, I promise.

THE WEAK CANDLELIGHT expires. In the thickening darkness, the two converse in whispers

ZOTOV

— but the audience can hear them. For the umpteenth time, he describes in every detail how he came to the City while she shrieks weakly in fear and suspense.

In the absence of light, all the camera shows is a black square. The man explains that very soon he'll go hunting in the convent; the girl sobs, sympathetic. Their relationship is just as erotic as it is innocent. She wants to touch her new friend but is reluctant to do so even in the dark... because she already knows his reaction to touch.

The two seem to be perfectly safe. No one can find their secret hiding place. They're alone in the basement, just as the man said.

Still, he's wrong. There's at least one other man watching their secret meeting from a considerable distance. He doesn't exhibit any emotions neither does he show any animosity.

He just watches them. He's been doing it for quite a while.

CHAPTER TWO

The Convent

October 17 2015
The vicinity of Sex City

T HE PICTURE ON the movie screen becomes blurred, apparently filmed by a primitive 1960s handheld camera. The audience boo their disappointment. Someone whistles. A man in front rises from his seat and leaves the theater, cussing under his breath and slamming the exit door in protest.

He shouldn't have been so impatient. Soon after he leaves, the picture comes back into focus, showing a close-up of a twenty-year-old nun, her hands pressed together in an ecstatic prayer. She casts anxious glances around her cell. She's a lousy actress but the audience doesn't seem to mind. This isn't the Academy Awards, anyway.

SISTER NATHALIA had discovered something was missing almost straight away. It wasn't that difficult even. Only a moment ago, there'd been two fat bunches of wax candles lying on the oak table on both sides of a carved malachite box. Now the bundle on the left was gone.

The nun emitted a guttural groan. The audacious theft could only mean one thing: that quite a few of the sisters would be forced to miss the midnight orgy in the refectory. And she'd be the one to blame as usual.

The nun darted toward the window (which was the only possible escape route for the impudent thief) and looked out.

The sight had immediately cheered her up, inspiring her more than any prayer could have done. The thief — a real flesh-and-blood male of about thirty years of age — was scrambling down the drain pipe, clutching his trophy in his teeth. He was dressed in filthy tattered jeans and a threadbare T-shirt.

The thief seemed to be in a hurry. Deep down she could understand him.

Nathalia bit her plump lower lip, trying not to scare her prey away. Wasn't it great? It had been a year since the last city dweller had walked willingly into their trap. This had made her day. All she had to do now was warn all the other sisters, and then-

And then, as if on cue, the stranger looked up.

Their eyes met. Seeing the young nun in her body-hugging habit, the stranger must have realized what kind of fate he was facing. With a stifled cry (his teeth still closed tight around his trophy), he let go of the drainpipe and dropped down, desperate to reach the ground as soon as possible.

Seeing him fall, the nun pressed her hand to her own mouth in panic, pleading and praying. Heavenly forces must have heard her: the lucky thief collapsed onto a plantation of raspberry bushes which rebounded under him, preserving his body intact.

Nathalia made the pious sign of the cross and hurried to peel off her hated habit.

"A maaaaaaan!" she wailed like a Banshee, sticking out of the window naked. "A man in the convent! In the name of God, sisters, *don't let him escape!*"

Her screaming must have reached the stranger's ears as he barged through the raspberry bushes into the garden, leaving the shreds of his T-shirt on the thorns.

Nathalia grabbed a camera from atop the malachite box and took a snapshot of the stranger's firm buttocks. She could use the pic later to relieve her solitude during one of her nightly self-gratification sessions.

She unlocked the door and darted down the stairs. She had to be quick before everything was over. If the sisters were truly hungry, no amount of shouting from the abbess would delay their orgy, in which case Nathalia might only get the stranger's cold corpse to play with. It had happened before.

ZOTOV

Quite a few times, in fact.

The stranger raced past the dead apple trees like a cheetah, heading toward the slimy convent gates of gray stone. Considering his adrenalin rush, vaulting over them wouldn't be a problem for him. And then he'd be as good as gone...

He would have been. Only he didn't get the chance.

A sharp snapping metallic sound pierced the air. The bushes by the wall parted commando-style, releasing two nuns, focused and determined. The one who'd happened to be in front — a plump gingerhead in a white headdress — cocked her gun, pointing it at his stomach. Despite it being an old single-shot hunting rifle, it still looked threatening enough.

"Be careful," the one next to her whispered, a dark-haired woman with lips painted a bright bloody red. "Make sure you don't hurt anything vital. The Abbess will go mad if he can't do his job. She'll have us flogged and lock us up in the cellar. It's too important, you understand it honey, don't you?"

"I do," the gingerhead said through clenched teeth. She blew a strand of hair out of her eyes and addressed the stranger, "You'd better surrender, dude. You're staying here anyway. No one has ever escaped the Black Habits. If you move, I shoot to kill. Then one of us will rape you until you're dead. Or both of us, depending on how long it takes you to die. You knew very well where you were heading."

The stranger didn't appear surprised. It didn't take a brain surgeon to see that his chances were slim. His face was covered with a two-week's growth of stubble, his body reeked of sweat (he hadn't washed for three days prior to his foray), his face was streaked with dirt — but nothing seemed to repel them. His dark-brown eyes, his high cheekbones, his well-defined muscles and the stench of a cornered wild boar — all this was plenty to arouse them.

This was the convent, the monsters' den notorious in the City, the birthplace of bloodcurdling legends. Apparently, about a year ago a seventy-year-old illegal migrant had come to its gates and asked for a drink of water in his halting, broken accent. There was nothing left of him afterwards.

Step after tentative step, the stranger kept backing off in search of an escape route until he stumbled over a tombstone.

A cemetery. The Black Habits had corralled him into the cemetery.

He bit his lip in expectation of his agony. Panic clenched his chest. The tombstone was old and crumbling, one of about thirty similar ones. Who had they been — burglars? Adventurers? Lone travelers? All of them at some point in the past had been lured here by the tempting songs of those virginal sirens... Each of them had entered the convent walls oblivious to his fate, to never come out again. All of them had been sexually worked to death.

What was it the wise Giovanni Boccaccio had said in his Decameron? "While farmers generally allow one rooster for ten hens, ten men are scarcely sufficient to service one woman."

One woman! Here, there were at least fifty of them.

The sound of their triumphant giggling sliced through his ears. The black habits encircled him; the gingerhead clutched her rifle, licking her lips in carnivorous anticipation.

Slender hands with sharp nails reached out to him. A couple of the more impatient nuns had already stripped down to their lacy underwear. The vigilant Sister Nathalia stood in the first row, stroking her breasts (and not only them). Her thighs were just a tad too plump for his taste.

"In the name of our Lord, sisters, clear the way," a stern voice said.

The nuns hurried to part their ranks, letting through the Mother Abbess.

The stranger gave her a wary look. The Mother Abbess was a stout woman of about forty-five years of age, her 5D bra size almost as scary as her attire. An SS officer's cap crowned her head, complete with skull and crossbones; a jacket of black riveted leather hugged her ample chest; high red boots reached to her thighs. A short riding crop enlaced her wrist. He could have bet his bottom dollar that before taking the veil, she must have worked in the local medieval BDSM quarter.

The woman caught his haunted gaze and flashed him a victorious smile.

"You're thinking in the right direction," she said sarcastically. "All these men had their own agendas — but they had forever remained our guests. You look quite healthy and fit, stranger. You're not as exhausted as some of them were. You might last a month, I'm pretty sure of that. We'll feed you a diet of walnuts and honey to make sure you're able to satisfy my sisters for as long as you can."

She turned a haughty head toward the restless, impatient crowd. "I have the first night. All the others, draw lots for your turn."

The stranger cast a desperate look up at the sky. The convent's golden domes loomed over him as if preparing to collapse on top of him and squash him under their weight.

The women closed in, licking their lips and exchanging encouraging slaps. He could sense their hot breathing; he could see the droplets of saliva on their lips.

Today was their day.

Or so they thought.

A gunshot thundered. The redhead dropped her rifle and screamed, pressing her hand to her bleeding shoulder. Her dark-haired friend (wearing nothing but a pair of lacy crotchless panties) darted to pick up the rifle but collapsed next to it, bleeding profusely, as the second bullet hit her thigh.

ZOTOV

Shrieking weakly, the half-naked nuns froze in terror as the stranger raised his Makarov semi-automatic.

"There's no way you're fucking me," he said, waving the gun from side to side. "I've plenty of rounds to kill at least twenty bitches like you. I've nothing to lose, you know that, don't you? Are you prepared to die right here, right now? Do you realize you'll never be able to indulge your carnal desires ever again?"

The crowd fell silent, even the wounded. He could hear birds chirruping in the garden.

The nuns froze in blank dismay. It would have been stupid to meet their own deaths now, denying themselves all the perverted carnal pleasures which had been the reason for their taking the veil in the first place. By the same token, it seemed like a real shame to let this full-blooded male go. A real living man whose arrival held the promise of thirty explosive nights. Few of the sisters were capable of forgetting it, reverting to the solitary pleasures of carrots, cucumbers and other garden-variety substitutes. In the five minutes they'd spent chasing the man, each of them had already possessed his body in her mind at least once — a few of them twice and even more.

The stranger pointed the gun at the Abbess' forehead, aiming for the silver skull on her SS hat. The woman gulped. His hand was shaking but at this distance, there was no chance he would miss.

"Let me go," the stranger said through

clenched teeth. "I'll kill you all, I swear."

It didn't take the Abbess long to make up her mind. It might be easy to play a hero in the movies — but when you're looking down the barrel of a real gun, you become much quicker on the uptake.

The Abbess reached into the holster hanging from her hip and produced a remote control. At the press of a button, the convent gates creaked slowly open.

That was the end of their hopes. The nuns hugged one another, sobbing.

"Piss off, you wanker," the Abbess hissed. "We'll meet again, I promise."

"Go and plant some more carrots," the stranger retorted, grinning. "You'll need some tonight."

ONLY WHEN HE'D PUT a good three miles between himself and the convent, did Oleg breathe a sigh of relief. He'd been bluffing all along. His Makarov had only one round left. Had the nuns called his bluff, he might have had to shoot himself instead.

Just think he'd allowed himself to be caught so stupidly when he'd nearly escaped!

For the first time in the six months of his stay in Sex City, he'd been granted the chance to escape this Catch-22 situation. He had an important meeting the day after tomorrow... and he fully intended to capitalize on it.

Oleg secreted both bundles under his shirt (one containing the candles he'd stolen simply to divert their suspicions, the other containing the true goal of his perilous visit) and headed for the highway to hitch a ride back to Sex City. Here, money had no value — but his bleeding skin ripped by raspberry thorns might arouse one of the women drivers enough to accept his offer to pay in kind.

Disgusting, he knew it. Still, he had no option. Time was an issue.

FURIOUS, THE ABBESS went back upstairs to her cell to change for evening mass. As she laced up her corset and slid on her silk stockings, she was choking on her tears. They'd missed such a chance!

That's false economy for you. Never mind. Tomorrow she'd have cameras installed on the walls to make sure no newcomer could escape. It might take some time though because lesbian installers weren't easily available (and no man fitter would go anywhere near their place).

The sisters were so upset she'd even had to cancel the carrot orgy. She also had to order more candles to replace the missing ones.

But did it justify denying herself one final nighttime pleasure? Not really. That wouldn't be right.

As soon as the mass was over, Sister Nathalia went upstairs to the Abbess' cell. Her face puffy from all the crying, she knelt and offered the Abbess the malachite box.

Shaking with excitement, the Abbess blew a breath, readying herself, then swung the lid open.

Her pupils dilated. The Abbess sank her nails into her cheeks and screamed in horror.

The blasted thief!

THE CAMERA FOLLOWS Oleg who stops a yellow Honda cab. The muted picture closes in as he fakes a smile, discussing something with a girl in the driver's seat: a long-haired braless blonde in an unbuttoned white shirt, her skirt dangerously short. Suppressing a grimace of disgust, the man climbs in. The girl laces one arm around his neck and presses his head to her chest as she steers away.

Some distance away from the car, the wilted grass parts. A man scrambles to his feet, a tiny figure in a large field, and watches the departing Honda through a pair of binoculars.

Then he turns to the audience.

The celluloid freewheels.

CHAPTER THREE

The Doll Maker

Lima, the Republic of Peru
October 17 1931

BEFORE EVERYTHING else, had he ever had such an opportunity, he would most definitely have explained his position to the public. He had absolutely no criminal intentions in doing what he did. The police should stop trying to come up with theories which only betrayed their own illusions regarding his work. Ditto for the newspapers.

Everything he did, he did in the name of love.

Yes, love. No need to grin so cynically. Love did exist. It controlled this world bogged down by laziness and malice, cladding darkness in robes of light. Great love, the kind that only visited man once in the course of his useless little life.

For a love like this, he too would have broken his own ribs and dug deep into his own chest, ripping his own heart out in order to present it — a throbbing clump of flesh and blood — to the object of his veneration. He could swear by the hair of the Virgin Mary that his intentions were holy and sacred. Had they not been, would he have submitted himself to the kind of tribulations he now had to suffer?

From what he'd heard, murderers enjoyed the agony of their prey. If newspapers were to be believed, their victims' death throes even aroused them. How terrible, how blood-curdling. He'd never experienced anything of the kind. He was fully aware of what he was doing. He knew this was illegal. But unfortunately, he had no choice.

You couldn't resist love. Nor fight it. You could only go down on your knees and serve it in almost-religious elation.

A SNAZZY CABALLERO stopped at the crossroads and glanced at his watch.

In a clatter of hooves, a horse-driven cab rolled past, its drunken driver hollering a ribald song.

The man's contemptuous gaze followed the cab, a bitter smile playing on his lips. Jesus, this country was a real hole. In Europe, there were automobiles everywhere these days, not a horse cab in sight. But here you could still see peasants riding astride their llamas. He had to watch where he was going to make sure he didn't step into steaming piles of shit. And it was everywhere like this here! Nothing but filth, dirt and heaps of refuse. Could you believe that Francisco Pizarro, the legendary conquistador who'd founded this city in 1535, originally called it La Ciudad de Los Reyes — The City of Kings?

Still, it wasn't for nothing the man had chosen to live in Barrio de Chino. It wasn't about the money even: a seedy place like this offered plenty of opportunities to remain unnoticed.

The Chinese janitor stopped raising street dust with his broom and bent his back in a ceremonious bow, "Good evening, Señor."

"Good evening."

The squat pagodas of the local China Town looked exotic amid the Spanish churches of yellow stone. The red Chinese roofs with upturned edges looked as if they'd been nailed to the colonial houses and tiny trellised balconies.

The road was littered with dried-out fallen coconuts. Stinky Guanako llamas with matted hair walked around; baby pigs basked in the roadside mud. Chinese symbols on red paper lanterns swayed in the breeze. The unwashed bodies of local whores reeked of cheap self-made perfume; the stench of corn oil mixed with the effluvia of animal farms. Most locals kept pigs which they'd slaughter in the morning when you had to leap over pools of blood trickling from everywhere. The pigs would scream a single monotonous note, drowning out all other sounds.

Which was a very good thing. He too had some screaming noises to conceal. Only in his case, they weren't pigs.

Quite the contrary.

The man winced. Oh, yes. He did it for love. For a love heavenly and eternal, the likes of which had never been born amid lowly humanity. He could speak about it for hours at a time until his throat became dry and rasping. Then he'd have a drink of water and continue his inspired soliloquy.

As he walked, he looked down at his own reflection in a pool of dirty water. He looked way too dandy for this area. The bespoke suit, the alpaca shoes, an English fedora hat... He'd bought his suspenders in Paris. Wasn't he getting too reckless? Smart dressers like himself were bound to attract unwanted attention.

Still, you couldn't surprise the locals with a rich dandy who'd steal into their dark alleys searching the company of black girls or wishing to relax in an opium den. Apart from the month of August, Lima was a rather hot place but this awful sea breeze forced him to wear warm clothes even at night.

Never mind. Once he was finished, he'd take his beloved one as far from here as possible: to New York or maybe even Paris, to drink champagne and shine in high society ballrooms. She was older than him, more intelligent and definitely more experienced. And he would do all it took to make sure he didn't disappoint the love of his life.

He walked past the statue of Confucius marking the red-lanterned entrance to a restaurant and turned off into a side alley. His snazzy shoes slipped on the cobblestones covered in fish scales. The stench of rotten fish hung in the air. Holy Virgin Mary, the things that happen in this quarter...

Finally, he came to the right door secured with two padlocks.

The key squeaked as he unlocked them and darted inside, barring the door behind him.

Just in time, dammit.

A hoarse, wheezy wailing came from the dark depths below, a woman's sobbing voice,

"Help! Someone! Please help me! In the name of Jesus! Somebody help!"

It looked like his doll had somehow chewed her way through the rag that had gagged her and was now screaming her head off. Women were strange creatures. Their survival levels were extremely high. Using men as material for his dolls would have been much easier: men were weak creatures who didn't cling to life so desperately. With women it was much more difficult. She must have ripped the gag with her teeth and spat it out. He should have thrown her into the pit next to the others to keep her company. But he'd thought it a waste of time and effort; he'd wanted the damsel to be fully ready for his arrival.

And what was he supposed to do with them from now on? If he gagged them too tightly, they might choke and spend several extra hours hanging there, forcing him to get rid of all that useless flesh.

And the contents of their veins? To satisfy the love urge, blood had to be absolutely fresh.

Never mind. Let her wail. He'd padded the outside walls with plenty of rags. She could scream all she wanted, no one would hear her.

Still, it never hurt to be careful.

The funny thing was, the stupid girl wasn't thinking logically. Did she really hope to get out now that she'd seen his face?

Yeah right. Hopeful idiot. The likes of her would pray for a miracle rescue even as the guillotine blade slid down toward their necks.

Like a child, really. Hoping for the nightmare to end the moment she closed her eyes. Thinking the monster wouldn't be under the bed when she woke up the next morning.

... He'd hung the girl up at the far end of the slaughterhouse before he'd left. A taut chain pulled her hands toward the ceiling so she could barely stand. Her shins were chained too to make sure she couldn't kick him.

Seeing him, his victim screamed again, this time in bitter desperation. He smiled sympathetically at her.

Yet another step on the precipitous staircase to love. She was only fifteen. Having said that, at this age most Indian girls have had two or three children already. Swarthy skin, dark eyes holding the promise of witchery, the glossy sheen of her body drenched in sweat. He kept her naked: the filthy rags that her kind wore made him nauseous.

ZOTOV

The attire of his future doll should smell of fresh flowers.

The horrified prisoner watched as he undressed. When he had nothing left on but his underpants, she started screaming and wailing again. Stupid cow. Preserving her virginity was the least of her problems now.

But of course all these girls had been raised in dumb sheep-like obedience to Catholicism. They couldn't possibly think of anything else.

True, he didn't enjoy what he did. But really, his guest's behavior was annoying. She kept screaming on one monotonous note. His ears were hurting. And what did she hope to achieve?

Completely naked, he stood in front of her.

The girl wasn't screaming anymore, she was croaking. Poor animal. Yes, he had to force himself to view them as such because it would be unbearable to realize he had to do such things to human beings. But as long as he considered them as part of the animal world, he could take it.

If you thought about it, all those innocent schoolgirls, children or married ladies walked past butchers' shops every day, ignoring the sight of the shop windows hung with poor dismembered creatures, their legs, heads and even hearts. They didn't seem to be too affected by all the gore, did they?

For him, too, his victims were like... like well-washed pretty little pigs. Would the pig really think he'd removed his clothes only to defile his body by copulating with it? God forbid.

He was free from sin. He was saving himself for the love of his life, elated and pure, the kind that man only experienced once in his lifetime. Jesus his witness, he wasn't even experiencing an erection which was something any man was supposed to have at the sight of a naked woman.

Finally, the doll had screamed herself voiceless and stared in horror at his blue and red tattoos.

He reached into a chest in the corner and produced a stone box. In it lay a dagger, its blade fashioned of dull grey rock glass.

He tried its edge with his fingernail. Good. Sharp as a razorblade.

He was soaked in sweat. The air in the basement was hot and close. A few burning candles added to the feeling, creating the impression he was a turkey in the oven.

He took in a wheezing lungful of air, exhaled and walked over to the girl. She stared at the glinting blade, her body shaking uncontrollably.

The monster took his time as he looked over her. His gaze paused on her breasts.

Exactly what he needed. The barely formed breasts of an adolescent, their nipples so dark they appeared almost black.

"Please, Señor," the prisoner begged. "Please don't hurt me."

His brows raised ever so slightly. "Of course," he said in a warm, paternal tone. "Don't be afraid, my girl. I promise I won't hurt you."

In one swift thrust he buried the blade to the hilt in her left eye, ripping through the brain tissue.

She died instantly and painlessly. He wasn't some street lowlife; he always kept his word.

Gushing blood, thick and hot, spurted onto his face and weapon hand. He stuck his tongue out and curiously tasted it as he waited for the victim's convulsions to subside. They lasted for about twenty seconds after which he slowly, millimeter after painstaking millimeter, drew the dagger out of the eye socket.

He'd have to discard the head, anyway. The girl's features were too crude for his ideal creation. But her chest was nothing short of perfect. He'd been truly lucky with her.

He carefully wiped the blade with a cloth and returned the dagger to the stone box.

He couldn't have chosen a better place than this slaughterhouse. Its slimy walls were black with pigs' blood, the heavy stench of rot blocking your nostrils, the surrounding gloom barely dispersed by the candlelight... awesome, truly awesome.

Time to get to work, anyway. The dolls' parts could keep for a long time but still he preferred them fresh.

The murderer unscrewed the handcuffs. The girl's body slumped to the cement floor. He walked over to the basement's far corner and soon returned with his tools: a hatchet and a hand saw. He wasn't at all looking forward to what he had to do next even though he should have gotten used to it by now.

He'd already ordered the necessary plants to be delivered. Normally, he'd had it done for him but this time he'd had no choice. The aromatic herbs from the foothills of the Andes would have to make do this time but in the future, he would need special plants possessing a very specific aroma. The doll had to be stunning, that was the whole idea. Unfortunately, it wasn't very often you came across a young Señorita who complied with every standard of beauty.

Sadly, such was women's nature. No justice on earth!

With the precision of a surgeon, he clenched the saw in his hand and prepared to make the first incision.

AFTER ABOUT AN HOUR, the murderer — tired and covered in blood — had packed the part of the doll he needed into some soft fabric (which became immediately sodden and blotched with dark crimson) and walked downstairs into his secret room. The slaughterhouse owner must have used it to cure meat, judging by the remaining tubfuls of brine which were perfect for preserving dolls' parts.

The door into the room was wide open. This was his lair; he had no one to fear down here. He'd taken his time preparing this place, including the "reception room" with the handcuffs under the ceiling, the "hotel" for the damsels, the "storeroom" and even a "recreation room" with a telephone line which had cost him an arm and a leg in bribes. It couldn't be helped, unfortunately. You couldn't do completely without a telephone these days: give it a few more years, and this rattling coffin-shaped device would become the main means of communication between people, he was pretty sure of that.

He leaned over the edge of the tub and peered into the brine.

So what did we have now which could make a complete set? A head he'd already obtained, with beautiful (albeit now dull) azure eyes which were extremely rare among native Peruvians. The hair was dark but he couldn't help that. Once he'd shampooed the blood away and curled the tresses with curling irons, it would look gorgeous. The chest he now had... a good pelvis and attractive hips...

Oh yes. He could now put together a new doll. He'd already bought some coarse thread. This was going to be a painstaking job.

He decided against taking the new victim's blood. He already had plenty. Two large tanks surrounded by heaps of ice stood by the tub, full to the brim with thickened red liquid. He had everything he needed. Time to put his pretty girl together.

Just think of all the work! He had to sew her together, then dress and paint her — and he had to do all of it by hand. It would take him the whole night — and then he'd have to wait for the plants which would arrive by the morning at best.

Still, the result was going to surpass all expectations. He was sure of it. He'd take an icy-cold shower now, drink a cup of strong mate and get busy creating art.

HAVING DROWNED the bag containing the girl's body parts in a brine bath, the murderer went to the shower. The cold water struggled to wash away the caked blood, tricking down the faces of the tattooed creatures and mixing with red streaks. It was an eerie feeling, having one's ablutions where the butchers had once removed the traces of dismembered pigs.

He'd have to get rid of the girl's remains. Either he'd have to discard them or move them over to the "hotel". That was another problem. Taking them to the dump site was too risky. And the "hotel" was currently a bit crowded.

He heard the rattling of the telephone over the noise of the shower. He walked downstairs and picked it up with a badly washed hand.

"In the name of love," a faraway voice said.

"Truly so," the murderer replied. "In the name of the only love, forever and ever."

His face lit up with the naïve dreamy smile of a child looking at candy.

CHAPTER FOUR

The Journal

A basement on the outskirts of Sex City

DARKNESS IS PIERCED by a single spot of light. A man is sitting cross-legged on the floor in one of the corners of a shabby room. Not on the floor actually (bare concrete can be quite cold): he's perched upon a heap of dirty rags.

That's irrelevant, anyway.

A large sheet of cardboard rests on his knees, table-like. A fat school notebook bound in oilcloth lies on top. The man is writing something quickly with a ball pen.

The picture quality is very low, grainy and out of focus with a greenish hue, the way they show infrared footage in action blockbusters. The theater audience begins to voice its disappointment. Finally, a woman in front says that the bad picture quality is part of the story.

The camera closes in, showing the uneven lines of handscript on a page illuminated by one of the candles stolen from the convent.

LET ME tell you this: you've no idea. Really. You must be thinking this is all bullshit. Well, I kid you not. You can't grasp the entire scope of this nightmare before you get here. At least I didn't.

Why do people keep diaries, might you ask? The answer is pretty obvious: they must have no one to talk to which in turn forces them to vent on paper. Which is exactly my case. If I do speak my mind, everyone in this world — and in my own — will think I'm a mental case. I've only shared my secret — a very abridged version of it at that — with one person in the whole City.

It could be that the entire thing is only a delusion, the product of my feverish mind. From the very start, I had this funny feeling I must have gone nuts. And you know what? — I wish it were so. It would have been the best-case scenario. At least in this case I could have stopped seeking meaning in everything that's happening around me.

At other times, I just wish I could drop dead, as simple as that.

Allow me to introduce myself. My name's Oleg Smolkin. I'm still far from retirement age (I've just turned 32, to be precise). I sell smartphones for a living. I'm that guy who walks over to you in the shop and says, "Hi, how can I help you today?" Ninety percent of you will reply with a nice equivalent of "Fuck off" while the remaining ten percent won't even mince the words.

ZOTOV

Not that it matters, anyway.

I can almost see you cringe. A grown-up man in his thirties working as a sales rep... oh please, do me a favor. It's not as if you're surrounded by oligarchs, either. I sell smartphones for a living, so what? It's not like I intend to run for the presidency or aspire to become the CEO of Microsoft. At least I know how to sell you a phone. I even have two spacious apartments in Moscow, both of which I inherited from my grandmothers. Being a sole grandchild is an excellent thing, I tell you. I live in one and rent the other one out to pay for my travels.

I'm passionate about traveling. I have a five-year old Kia Rio in decent condition but which does occasionally break down though.

I wouldn't call myself popular with women but I've been having this relationship with a girl called Vicky for the last couple of years. Not a relationship even, just an on and off thing, you know what I mean. We'd see each other for a couple of months, then split up again. Vicky isn't happy with my job. She thinks I lack ambition. Her idea of a man is a bodybuilder marine TV star doubling as a dildo and ATM machine. Someone she could show off in the company of her friends.

That night, I was going to take her out to watch some Hollywood flick but predictably, we had one of those petty arguments and fell out. It had happened quite often just lately. I had problems at work too: the boss had taken me to task for bad sales results and threatened to fire me for the umpteenth time. So you can imagine my state when I'd finally gotten back home.

I opened the fridge, took out the chunk of serrano ham I'd brought from Spain and hacked off a few slices, washing them down with some beer, then helped myself to a good shot of White Horse. If anything, it made me feel worse. I'd been quite looking forward to some normal love-making. Idiot woman.

I was so pissed with her that I put on some porn — Swedish, I think — and fell asleep in front of the screen clutching the remote (what did you think I was clutching?)

The light dims briefly, then comes back on with a flash. The man looks directly at the camera.

When I woke up... it was crazy. It was the stuff that normally only happens in fairy tales. The adult kind, if you know what I mean.

I was lying on my back in a blossoming meadow. A stunningly beautiful girl sat astride me, stark naked, moving rhythmically.

My first thought was, I must still be sleeping. What else was I supposed to think? This just had to be an adolescent wet dream. My last doubts had dissipated when a second girl — a brunette with an impossibly ample bosom — crawled out of the undergrowth and asked if she could join us.

Yes! Sweet lord, yes, please!

ZOTOV

It all ended too quickly (Sorry about that. It just felt too good.). The ladies lost all interest in me, scrambled back to their feet and walked away swaying their delicious hips, not even bothering to get dressed.

Gradually I began to come round. I seemed to be somewhere out of town, wearing the same stuff I had on back home: a T-shirt and a pair of blue jeans. Which pointed to the fact that I was still asleep.

Well, who was I to complain? So far, the dream had been excellent. I'd thoroughly enjoyed the experience.

I ambled around the meadow for a while until I came out on a highway. I noticed a bus shelter nearby, went there and waited for a bus. The conductor was a pretty woman in a blue uniform that didn't conceal the absence of her panties. She made it clear to me that the fare was paid in kind.

That wasn't a problem. I paid my dues to her on one of the shabby back seats, then, obeying some impulse, asked to stop the bus on the central avenue of an unknown city.

You'd think I should have put two and two together by then. Only I hadn't.

The city looked like one large red-light district.

Peep shows. Porn theaters. Strip tease bars. Newsstands carrying erotica magazines. The funny thing was, all of it was free.

And the girls... no, I hadn't yet worked their nature out yet.

They immediately recognized a newcomer,

sensing me like wolves sniff out an innocent lamb.

I couldn't work out what was going on. All the females around me only wanted one thing which was myself. After the third copulation right in front of a crowded café (the people didn't seem to mind at all — on the contrary, they surrounded us, encouraging us and clapping their hands), I got a funny feeling there was something wrong there.

My fourth time didn't impress. I'd been feeling so confused I'd asked a girl (a school student in a checkered mini skirt) for a cigarette. She offered a swap. Later, I realized that the Checkered Skirts were the most dangerous and insatiable of them all.

I felt sick. My head began to spin. I slumped onto the sidewalk and asked some passersby to call an ambulance.

It arrived suspiciously fast: a fully equipped resuscitation vehicle manned by two slender nurses with nothing under their skimpy lab coats. I panicked and jumped out of the van, skinning my leg raw in the process.

Limping, I barged into the local police station. Predictably, I walked in on a full-blown orgy between the officers and detainees. I fled the place like an idiot before the female officer could handcuff me to the bars and have her way with me.

I fell asleep under an oak tree, adamant that all this had been a mere hallucination.

Some bastards must have laced my beer with a mind-altering drug. Tomorrow it would be over.

Still, once I'd awoken, I saw with horror that

ZOTOV

nothing had changed. Everything was the same: my throbbing injured leg, the couples prowling around in search for more partners, and Sex City glittering its neon lights atop a high hill. At the time, I didn't know its name yet.

By the end of the first week, obeying the animal instinct of a hunted beast, I finally found shelter deep within this basement, desperately trying to escape the greedy stares of all the horny women, from the Checkered Skirts to the forty-year old crones with schoolgirl-style pigtails.

Then I finally realized what must have happened.

I'd been teleported into a porn movie.

Preempting your questions, no, I've no idea how it happened. All I remember is falling asleep in front of the TV, beer in hand, then waking up here. In the movie. Which didn't give me much room for speculation.

Theory number one: I'd gone off my trolley. Theory number two: I was in a porn movie. In either scenario, trying to fight it was pretty pointless. A nutcase believes his delusion to be true. And if I wasn't a nutcase, so much the worse because I wouldn't be able to stay sane here for much longer.

Porn is basically fairy tales for adults. What I didn't know was that this was more of a horror story — a dark, blood-curdling gothic nightmare.

At first, you'd think what could possibly be better than having all these women lusting after you? Isn't it what they call paradise?

Gosh was I wrong. Reality couldn't have been farther from the truth.

You don't believe me? Very well. Sit down and have a good think: how much sex do you need on a daily basis? Three times, okay. Possibly four. And then what?

In order to survive in Sex City, you need to have sex every three hours. It's not about your body needs anymore. You have to eat, pay a bus fare, rent a hotel room — and all this has to be paid for in kind. The women in this world are horny bitches drunk on their own lust who are always ready to make out, whether it's in the street, in the office, in an elevator, a car, an airplane...

I'd lasted a week before I was too scared to go outside at all. This world is different. If they catch a burglar, they don't call the police, they make him shag the house owner. Schools are the most dangerous places to which you should give a wide berth: teachers there are beasts, not to mention the hordes of teenage students drunk on their own imagination.

The local hospitals seem devoid of antibiotics or bandages even but they're packed with hot doctors and nurses. This is the whole idea of studying medicine here, simply to have plenty of fun in hospital beds.

Here, plumbing is a job for male models, fit and handsome with heaps of long tousled hair. As for female models, in order to get on all those glossy covers, they have to have sex with the advertisers

ZOTOV

first.

Having said that, it's the same thing in our world, isn't it? Here, the most beautiful girls are only too happy to sleep with janitors, cleaners, street bums and entire football teams the moment they meet them, enjoying every moment of such a promiscuous lifestyle.

What else? The local women absolutely love anal sex. Hotel chambermaids' services are included in the room price. You can never find a vacant toilet cubicle as someone is always making out there. Sex shops have fitting rooms. The point of a wedding is to allow all guests to have their way with the happy bride. `

Oh yes, babe. This is our Sex City.

I've been here for six months already. I'm a survival expert.

The city is divided into districts. BDSM, amateur porn, Swedish Private Studio *productions (which were instrumental in my coming here),* Maximum Perversum, *the neat streets of the German* Das Ist Fantastisch *and the delicate French suburbs overgrown with ivy. In five hours' drive from here were located the 1970s Wild West settlements complete with ladies in shorts and cowboy hats, with hair in rollers and bushes that had never seen a razor in their lives. According to my helpful lady friend, that's where all the exhausted men tend to escape to. True, those women are just as demanding and indiscriminate, but at least the scenes in those videos used to be shot in just one take which means*

I won't have to suffer for longer than forty seconds or so.

Are you laughing? Funny, isn't it? I'm not surprised. The guy got himself sent to some sort of carnal paradise where women would have sex with all and sundry — and he's cowering in an old basement burying himself under heaps of old rags?

Yeah right. I suggest you check out their BDSM quarter when you have a chance. After staying there for a week, even the most die-hard copycats of leading male porn stars like John Holmes or Rocco Siffredi are reduced to childlike tears.

The worst thing is that this ephemeral world of imaginary sexual freedom is gruesomely real. As I already told my lady friend, one can so easily die here. Funeral processions pass my basement virtually every week, complete with black-clad attendants and pallbearers. Normally, they don't even reach the cemetery as gangs of love-crazy women attack the unfortunate male creatures, cornering them.

That's what they are here: creatures. Not men. Just some rightless, exhausted, overused meat.

Meat! Oh... sorry. I can't think straight. I'd have given everything for a slice of steak. Preferably rare. As I already told my lady friend, food here is obnoxious, badly cooked and devoid of even the most basic of spices. I'm not surprised: the local restaurants serve as love-making joints, with customers only ordering drinks simply to keep up

ZOTOV

appearances.

You can't imagine how I'd have loved to sink my teeth into a juicy orange, splattering everything around with its sweet bliss. But how are you supposed to find it? All you can see is cucumbers, carrots and bananas. I HATE THEM. Especially the abundance of bananas. You don't need to ask why, do you?

I've forgotten what an apple tastes like. I could try and get some sausages, I suppose, but they're hard to come by, you need to know the right people and even then they're likely to be plastic stage props. Chocolate and whipped cream are the local staples. Another six months of this diet, and I'll be diabetic. What a nightmare of a life. Can someone tell me please how to get out of here?

The man stares directly at the camera and grins.

During my first long sleepless nights I used to think this must have been my comeuppance. I remember reading a very clever thing once, "You can jail any man at all for ten years and deep inside, he'll think he knows why". That's so true. I have lots of sins. I used to lie, fornicate, overeat, successfully covet my neighbor's wife (repeatedly and in all kinds of positions), and fuck knows what else. I've never been to church, come to think of it. But now, for some weird inexplicable reason, it occurred to me that my sins might somehow be absolved if I started a new life free of vice.

It's a bit like the passengers on a nose-diving plane who all start to pray, regretting their wrongdoings and promising the Lord to mend their ways. Then, once the plane has safely landed, they happily forget all about it. As in, "Jesus, that was really stupid of me!"

Here too I started by confessing my sins like a good boy. I prayed passionately every night in my basement, addressing the black void. Because if I had nothing at all to hope for, that would have been too horrifying for words.

After about a month, I lost all hope in God and started looking for alternative ways: anything at all as long as I could get out of here. I ventured into the most dangerous snuff-movie districts where they murdered people on tape. I sneaked into the medieval porn streets; it's so hilarious to watch those actresses in cumbersome 18th-century robes with their silicon boobs and waxed private parts.

Talking about silicon — this particular material is nothing short of a God here. The surrounding 1970s villages hate this 1990s innovation with a vengeance, calling the Sex City girls "rubber dolls". Apparently, hippy-era actresses (complete with natural boobs and full bush) attacked the city suburbs quite a few times in the past, pillaging and plundering and putting entire streets to the torch. In the end, the city dwellers managed to stand their ground, using the latest-generation vibrators as weapons.

Oh yes, the city keeps growing new districts

as porn evolves in synch with humanity. Who would have thought that a hundred years ago the Private *and* Vivid Colours *districts didn't even exist! The city dwellers enjoy guided tours of the local mountains to see the settlements of illegal retro porn makers. I went on one of them too, just to see those funny black-and-white naked Victorian ladies.*

Pointless. It was all in vain.

Still, at the very moment when I lost heart, realizing I must have been destined to perish in this abyss of lubricants and naked bodies, I saw a glint of hope. I came across this girl in the Perverts Quarter... she claims she can help me. All I have to do is find some very important artifacts.

You'd think I'd be happy but I'm not. If anything, I have a bad feeling about it. I keep getting this idea that I'm in grave danger. Don't ask me why. I have this watched feeling all the time. Paranoid, I know.

THE CANDLE STUMP is about to expire. The man leans over the page in his lap, almost touching it with his forehead as he hurries to finish his writing.

The camera moves back. Now the audience realizes why the picture was so amateurishly grainy. A strange man is sitting in front of a computer screen, watching the basement scene — apparently through some camera secreted in there.

The man turns. His face is hard to discern in the dark. All we can see is his eyes glistening with a cold, wolfish glow.

CHAPTER FIVE

The Artist

Lima, the vicinity of Plaza Mayor
October 20 1931

MIGUEL LABORIOUSLY munched on a new helping of coca leaves which tasted tart and unpleasant on his tongue. But at least his head began to clear.

He'd had virtually no sleep for the past week. He couldn't afford to. The news of the discovery of a human doll — sewn masterfully out of the dead bodies of four different girls and lying in a pool of blood in the center of Lima — had predictably shaken even such a hardboiled cynic as El Presidente. The Deputy Minister Juarez had been summoned to the palace where El Presidente promised the man to personally put him up against the wall if the inquiry showed no progress any time soon.

He was only joking, of course, and everyone knew that. The worst thing El Presidente was capable of was having his political opponent wrapped into a carpet and thrown into the sea in the deep of night. With politicians, one could get away with this sort of thing — but not with the police which had become El Presidente's main bastion of support after the coup.

Miguel sipped some boiling-hot water to get rid of the taste in his mouth.

He set the cup back on his desk and didn't even hear the sound in the surrounding cacophony of lunchtime clinking and clattering. Meal times were just as sacred in Peru as the fruit of the Virgin Mary's loins. Their police station resembled a busy middle-class café. Two fat men in black uniforms were busy stuffing their faces with *ceviche*, the dish of raw fish in lemon juice. Ignoring forks, they used their fingers to pick up pieces of fish from their plates while Felipe, the police photographer, rattled his spoon in his coffee cup munching on a piece of lemon cake. Lomez the medical examiner was pedantically slicing a roast guinea pig: a local delicacy known here as *cuy*. Ever since his arrival from Russia, Miguel had been struggling with his aversion to this exotic delicacy and tactfully but adamantly declined any offers of it.

He took a second look at the two pages of typescript in front of him. A stack of glossy unedited photographs lay on the desk. According to their investigation, over thirty girls aged 14 to 17 from predominantly poor families had gone missing in Lima and its suburbs within the last month.

No one had paid any attention to it. Here, people disappeared all the time. With a good dozen children in every family, no one was going to report a missing daughter to the police. If anything, it meant one mouth less to feed. She could have run off with a lover, or joined a traveling circus, or was so fed up with never having any money that she'd simply added to the ranks of local prostitutes. Virtually none of these disappearance cases had been filed with the police. The Quechua Indians took a philosophic view of these matters: if you lost a child, the best thing you could do was to have another, especially because Quechua families tended to have children every year.

At least thirty missing girls.

They'd just found four of them: sewn together into a doll stuffed with aromatic herbs from the foothills of the Andes and painted with a mixture of blood and gold powder. Their bones and internal organs had been removed and the entire crime scene had been covered in blood.

Which meant that the murderer would have to get rid of the girls' remains, including their skin and all the spare body parts. On Miguel's orders, the city cops were now rummaging through the local dumps, combing through the coastline and carefully interrogating hundreds of red-light district regulars.

Apparently, no one had seen anything. As in, thirty Indian whores had been kidnapped, big deal. Nothing to write home about.

ZOTOV

Miguel took another swig of boiling water, feeling the coke flaking in his mouth.

The doll maker was definitely trying to send a message — not just to Miguel but to the rest of the world as well. He wanted to make a name for himself. That little was pretty obvious: the guy had to be a born actor who savored the newspaper clips he'd laboriously collected, reveling in his secret celebration — because these days, newspapers could speak of nothing else.

Butchers live for fame. Jack the Ripper used to send letters written in blood to the police, enclosing bits of his victims' flesh inside. Dr. H. H. Holmes, an intellectual who'd become the first serial killer in the history of the US, was believed to have murdered as many as two hundred people in Chicago during the 1890s — and he'd loved nothing better than to read newspaper articles about himself. He then used to send angry anonymous letters to the newspapers, pointing out that "they'd got it all wrong".

Then there was Joseph Vacher, a Frenchman, a monster with half his face paralyzed who'd raped and murdered eleven boys and teenage girls in the period between 1894 and 1898 (he primarily targeted young village shepherds). Already in prison he asked his warders to read newspaper articles describing his murders to him out loud, openly enjoying his notoriety.

This must have been the same mechanism. Like a seasoned theater diva, the killer carefully prepared his every entrance on stage, making it as dramatic as possible, complete with applause, music and fireworks.

The question remained, who he really was.

Miguel half-opened his eyes watching a gecko on the wall.

The killer was definitely an artist — but an amateur in his new trade. Professional taxidermists would have gone about the task differently. Still, if anything, it added to the gruesome attraction of his work. A lot of effort and dedication had gone into this particular doll. Miguel had no doubts that the Artist (which was the moniker the press had given the killer) had already had plenty of practice in other areas. He must have tried to become a painter or a sculptor even, only to have met with merciless rejection both from critics and art school experts.

What would normally happen next? The man would be reduced to a loner, bitter and unappreciated, bent on proving his genius to the world in some other art. Just like that wildly popular German politician whose naïve childish watercolors had failed to impress his tutors. What was his name now? Albert, Adolf? Whatever.

And now the Artist was preparing to create his masterpiece. The greatest work of his lifetime. He'd do it with a jeweler's precision, meticulously putting it together and enjoying his handiwork. So what if a few girls died? It didn't matter to him: firstly, because he was a nutcase and secondly, because since when did artists care about human life? A real artist didn't feel aroused by the sight of his naked model: to him, she was just another inanimate object not different from a leg of ham. In the old days of hand-written books, scribes used vellum for their most precious illustrations, which was made of lambskin. Had the lambs' fate really bothered them?

Miguel drew in the hateful smell of ceviche. He'd have given anything for a hearty bowl of good old cabbage soup, piping hot, preferably with a shot of vodka. What kind of retarded backwater was this? You couldn't find a Russian restaurant here for love nor money.

Miguel couldn't cook to save his life: a descendant of one of Russia's oldest noble families wasn't supposed to know how to do this sort of thing. Because that's what he was, yes sir! After all these years he still didn't have a place of his own, surviving on sandwiches and making do with hired love at 2 sols an hour.

Having said that, when was the last time he'd actually done the deed? He was completely put off life — or whores, for that matter. Come to think of it, why did Russian men even go to the whores? It wasn't just about alleviating the tension. A Russian man needed to get drunk with the girl, then start singing songs and pour his heart out to her, telling her all about his treacherous ex and his fucked-up life. A Russian whore is a born shrink. But here in Peru he had no one to drink with — nor talk to, for that matter. The local *chicas* didn't know a word of

Russian.

Never mind. No good whimpering. He had a job to do.

So it looked like the killer could be an artist, bitter and unappreciated, who might have been denied the possibility to exercise his art. He must have been lying low in the pitch dark now, smiling and watching his audience's reaction to the spectacular show he'd put on, awaiting a standing ovation and flowers thrown at his feet.

And as for the missing girls... you didn't have to be a mind reader. They were either already dead and turned into doll parts, or he was hiding them somewhere alive. To keep such a vast number of victims you needed large empty premises somewhere in the outskirts.

Miguel had already sent cops to all the abandoned warehouses. If the truth were known, he really should check out all of the neighboring villages — but where was he supposed to find so many men? Especially because their work standards left much to be desired... when it came to shirking, the Indians beat even Russians with their proverbial laziness. They'd have their breakfast, pray a little, discuss the matrimonial problems of Don Pedro next door, pray some more, eat some more, then look around themselves and finally get to work, reluctantly and half-heartedly. Miguel had lost count of the times when he sent a cop on an important mission only to find him hours later in a Plaza de Armas café drinking his "pisco sour" and flirting with Señoritas.

"What are you doing here?" Miguel would demand.

"I'm sorry, Señor Capitan, I've only popped in for a moment. The day is so hot..."

The Russians weren't that different but at least they got drunk and picked fights *after* work. In the morning, a Russian would take a dip in an icy-cold stream, gulp a glass of pickle brine to cure his hangover and off to work he'd go, his head clear, his eyes sober and innocent like those of a heavenly dove. But here... the local combination of questionable work ethics and unceremonious curiosity was driving him up the wall.

Now too, their janitor — a puny Indian called Enrique — was standing by his table tilting his head to one side at an impossible angle studying the pictures of the victim. Back at home tonight he'd probably burst with pride telling his family how he'd been helping investigate major crimes and ordering those useless police bastards around.

With an anxious swish of its tail, the gecko disappeared.

"Excuse me, Señor?"

"What do you want?" Miguel asked, not even trying to conceal his annoyance with the man.

The Indian's filthy finger poked a glossy picture. "What do you know about this?"

Miguel rolled his eyes. One more word, and he'd kick the desk out of his way and give the bastard a good thrashing.

"Yes, Enrique. That's exactly what I'm busy with now. Four girls have been murdered. And if you-"

"Oh no, Señor!" the janitor interrupted him. "That's not what I'm talking about! Do you know what kind of tree this is?"

"Why, what is it?" Miguel deigned to ask.

"It's a magnolia," the Indian said softly.

"Thank you so much for this lesson in botany," Miguel said sarcastically. "Feel free to speak to me whenever you wish to mess with my work."

The janitor's withered face darkened with embarrassment and indignation but he didn't get the chance to reply.

The station's flimsy front door swung open, pushed from the outside. The Deputy Minister Juarez stood in the doorway, drenched in sweat.

It took Miguel a moment to realize that the fat little man was scared out of his skin. His legs were shaking.

"El Presidente's gonna kill me," the man croaked. "We've found another doll."

CHAPTER SIX

The Quarter of Horrors

The southern edge of Sex City
Early morning

T'S DARK. Two girls walk under the incessant drizzling rain, groping their way in the intermittent red lights. One wears light makeup and a short dress over revealing black fishnet tights. She's so graceful and light-footed she seems to be walking on air.

The other one stomps along heavily on her muscular legs like a draught horse, her feet in downtrodden shoes constantly giving way under her. Her head is wrapped in a fluffy shawl concealing most of her face, her two huge scared eyes blinking above the fabric. A comical disguise indeed — but men in drag are one of porn's staples, especially if one remembers Thai lady boys.

The street is busy with garishly painted women who follow the two with their stares, their pale faces and blood-red lipstick reminiscent of the

Joker.

The picture is blurred and grainy, the sound unstable, creating the impression we're watching an ancient videotape unearthed by a curious teenager in his parents' wardrobe. The audience watch the unfolding scene curiously as they munch on their popcorn.

OLEG TRIED TO CONSOLE HIMSELF by the fact that at nighttime, the risk was far less than usual. Not because it was any quieter here at night, oh no. Being in drag didn't help him much: if anything, it made him look like an old woman who'd long reconciled herself with a constant five-o-clock shadow.

But at least now he had an ally on his dangerous journeys, a girl serving one of the rarest and most perverted of Victorian vices.

Her name was Joan, and she lived in the smallest district of the whole of Sex City which served as a virgins' retreat. Her specialty was introducing men to all kinds of erotic fantasies without inviting them to her main lounge. Most of such girls were fakes, starting with the notorious Traci Lords and ending with Chasey Lain immortalized in the title song by the Bloodhound Gang.

In this world, too, the local prototypes of our world's stars led celebrity lifestyles which defied any fan's attempt to get anywhere near them. But their fake virginal properties were nothing like the real thing which was a caste in itself.

He'd met Joan accidentally as both waited in line to get Cicciolina's autograph. At the time, a desperate Oleg had been trying everything in order to get out of the city. Slim with closely cropped hair, Joan had won him over by admitting she couldn't have sex with him straight away for two reasons: firstly, because she was a virgin and secondly, because they fell short of the obligatory six-men requirement.

Now they walked side by side without saying a word to each other, stepping over puddles of rainwater.

"Actually," Joan said without looking at him, "do you really need porn in your world so much?"

The question caught him unawares. "Well," he drawled, biding for time, "I suppose so. We need it to... to unwind?"

"Can't you unwind with each other?"

Oleg heaved a sigh. "It's complicated. For ages, people loved spying on each other. When I was in the porn museum in Amsterdam, the guide told us about the mini orgies organized by the aging Roman Emperor Tiberius in front of his throne: two patricians per one matron or two matrons per one patrician. He was too old to participate even if he'd wanted to but he still loved watching them. Apparently, very soon the Emperor's palace couldn't contain all the onlookers so they started offering similar shows in special establishments all over Rome, Athens and other ancient cities known as *lupanars*. In medieval brothels, especially in Venice, peeping on mass orgies through a hole in the wall cost three times more than spending the night with three women — and they had to fend off high-ranking clients with a stick! And once the movie industry came about in the early 20th century, it immediately started offering early black-and-white erotica flicks. Finally, the worldwide legalization of pornography had ushered in the golden age of sex industry. We had an old joke: you pay a hundred bucks for a night with a woman, two hundred for peeping on two unsuspecting strangers making out and three hundred for peeping on the peeper. Because that's what we are, peepers. We used to have a TV show... what was it called now? Wasn't it *Big Brother?* Anyway, they placed a group of people under constant surveillance and followed their every step. All the quarrels, the fights, the innuendos... their rankings went through the roof!"

Joan stopped, trying to take it all in. "That's absurd. Why can't your men sleep with women themselves? Why do they need to watch others do it? That's pretty unnatural, isn't it?"

'Well," Oleg began slyly, "I suppose life is just too hard. You never have time for anything in Moscow, let alone dating. In your world, it's easy. Anyone can come over to anyone and offer a quick jump. You can't do that in our world. Any lady worth her lady parts will whack you in the face with her handbag — and ladies' handbags are heavy these days, what with all the iPhones, iPads and makeup bags they stuff in them. You need to date her properly, take her out and give her flowers, pull the wool over her eyes..."

Joan raised a quizzical eyebrow. "Do you use wool in lovemaking?"

"That's not what I meant. All I want to say is that when you're broke with payday still five days away, you can't really play a Casanova. And this way you come home, grab a beer, switch on an XXX video and you're all done in ten minutes."

"Meaning?"

"I'd rather not explain."

They kept walking. Oleg squeezed his eyes to shut out the red light, trying not to look around himself. He had a nagging feeling that he could be found out at any moment. Even though his drag was quite believable, at least from a distance, a hungry female wouldn't care. To add insult to injury, all of them were bisexual here which made the prospect of his disclosure ever scarier.

To borrow the women's clothes for him, Joan had had to visit her XXXXXL lady friends from the *Maximum Perversum* district. The attire made him feel awful, forcing him to sashay like a circus camel. How could drag queens even enjoy this? His feet were pounding; those heels were killing him. The padded bra had rubbed his skin raw. The thong which he wore on Joan's insistence ("What if you have to lift your skirt?") was stuck in some indescribable recesses of his fleshpots.

"Does that mean that you find watching more

enjoyable?" she returned to the subject.

"You really should come and live in our world before you talk," Oleg snapped. "It's easy for you to say we're all nutcases. It's not so simple. We live in an era when twenty-four hours a day is just not enough. Between Facebook, Twitter, Instagram and all those games and series... Ever since they introduced free Wi-Fi in the Moscow metro, no one's looking at each other any more. Guys and girls all sit glued to their tablets and smartphones. Nobody has time for anything, let alone to start a relationship. Why would you need it? If you're so desperate, you can always indulge in some virtual sex without even having to get away from your computer screen. Or put on a *Das Ist Fantastisch* video and watch some good-looking people doing some professional sexobatics and getting good money for it. But actually doing it to a real woman? By the time you get home from the office, you're dead on your feet; all you want is a good night's sleep. The sheer thought of having to shave and get dressed again, then pay for a hotel room... I don't think so."

She stopped, staring at him open-mouthed. "Are you all fucking nuts?" her voice rang out loud and clear.

"Well," Oleg faltered, clumsily shifting his feet like a horse.

Joan dismissed his attempt. They continued in silence.

Can you stoop any lower, Oleg pondered as

they walked. The worst kind of porn starlet accuses me of a dissolute lifestyle! And that's not even the worst thing about it. How I'd love to know whether I've indeed gone mad. Or can this be really happening? What if I'm in a coma right now, exploring the nooks and crannies of my overwrought mind? Having said that, if all my gray matter has to offer is porn memories, I should have stopped watching it a long time ago.

He pulled the shawl over his head and prayed soundlessly, addressing all the gods he'd ever heard of.

They walked along some lethally dangerous streets past the school buildings that harbored some of the most predatory females in the entire city. The buildings were easily recognizable: they were the film sets of *Little Girls Blue*, the German *Mädchen Internat* and a plethora of less-known flicks, Russian as well as foreign. The girls' greedy eyes glowed behind the fences, searching the crowd for any males. But compared to the convents, these institutions at least offered you a slim chance of escaping.

From what he could have surmised from the flicks produced by the German *Magma* studio, schoolgirls preferred to hunt in large packs of five and more: they found it easier to ensnare their prey that way. The girls' hands were young and weak which meant he stood a chance. But if they were joined by their more experienced teachers schooled in all sorts of sciences, that meant sure death.

Schools had other advantages compared to the convents. They were equipped with male staff serving their municipal labor duty: all those cooks, guards and PT teachers who acted as lone martyrs drawing the female passion to themselves. So in schools you stood a fair chance of not being screwed to death although the experience itself was horrible to say the least. The institutions belonging to Private Studio had turned into a sadistic arena of every kind of cruelty imaginable, their students resembling purebred horses glistening with oil, their waxed bodies sporting multiple piercings. Truly they were the mutants of this new era!

And what about the *Russian Institute* by Marc Dorsel? Did French parents even realize why they brought their daughters to these kinds of closed schools? Judging by Dorsel's movies, the girls were all suffering from nymphomania.

Even when they'd finally left the school district behind, it didn't bring Oleg any relief. Because what opened up before him was the fairy tale district with its medieval attires, cobbled streets and Disney-style castles.

Oleg shrank his head in his shoulders. He'd already heard enough about it. Luca Damiano's Snow White was the worst nymphomaniac that had ever trodden planet Earth, so you shouldn't really ask what she does in her spare time in the company of the prince and all seven dwarves. Her stepmother was just as bad, with Cinderella prowling the midnight streets searching relief from her concupiscence.

As for the local adaptation of *Pinocchio*, don't even ask. Apparently, a wooden nose can be used in all sorts of ways.

Oleg shuddered, recognizing the next setting as the American version of *Alice in Wonderland* where the angelic little girl had had it with the entire cast — the King, the Queen, the White and Red Knights and even the-

A girl's figure stepped in their way.

It just had to be Alice.

Things were taking a very bad turn.

"What're you doing here all by yourselves?" the girl smiled. "Come and join us. The crowd is awesome."

Joan's fragile shoulder shoved Oleg aside. "You're from another story," she said matter-of-factly. "He's mine. I caught him myself and I'm having him for the night. I don't practice gang bangs since high school."

"Come on, don't be greedy," Alice moaned, losing her panache. "I haven't had sex since lunchtime."

"I haven't had sex for twenty-four hours!" Joan snapped, her pupils dilating. "You've any idea what it's like? Can you even imagine the gravity of it? I'm close to losing my mind! My brain is melting."

Their attacker seemed to be taken aback. Still, she refused to surrender so easily. "*Twenty-four hours?*" she muttered in amazement. "How is it

possible? They told us in orgy lessons at school that the female body can't survive without sex for longer than seven hours. That's how Nature made us in order to-"

"Exactly," Joan unceremoniously pushed the girl aside. "I'm close to death. It'll take us another ten minutes to get to my place and another three hours to restore my depleted reserves. You can wait if you wish, if you're not too desperate."

"Nah," Alice replied, not even trying to conceal her disappointment. "I'll find myself someone. It's not often you see a girl refusing a good party but if it's a question of life and death, so be it."

She disappeared into the drizzle.

Oleg heaved a breath of relief. "Thanks," he said, deeply grateful. "You saved my bacon."

"You're welcome," Joan replied sternly.

Finally, they left the quirky towers and crinolined ladies behind. A new district lay ahead, shabby and crumbling, with pitted sidewalks and vandalized bus shelters plastered with colorful bank advertisements offering payday loans.

Oleg stopped, shaking all over, as he recognized the familiar ruby letter M indicating a metro station.

This was Moscow. Great lord, this looked identical to the suburb where he used to live. Was he... was he back home?

Joan turned round. "I'm sorry," she said softly, noticing his dismay. "This is what you'd call an amateur porn district. It belongs to indie filmmakers from all over the world. It's very possible that this particular block is inhabited by your compatriots. Do you recognize it?"

"Yes," Oleg replied reluctantly. This momentary flicker of hope had left him drained. "That's exactly the kind of set our amateurs use. Cheap hostels, prefab houses, clumsy rip-offs of *PickupGirls* and such. Those guys don't have Private Studio's budget. They use the cheapest girls they can find, usually well-worn prostitutes working at railway stations, so no wonder their quality suffers. Still, there's something very endearing about it. When you watch a Private video, their girls are groomed and waxed to an inch of their lives, their hair, legs, makeup all out of this world and cup sizes to match, perfect from their noses to their fannies. And as you watch it you begin to realize that none of these creatures would ever go anywhere near you. You just can't afford any of them. The fact that they're being serviced by some plumbers with the physique of Schwarzenegger is some consolation, I suppose. And then you watch someone who's your typical girl next door in badly mended panties and hair which could use a shampoo. All of us had sex with them at some point, a quick bonk in the back yard or at home, petrified that your parents might walk in on you. That's the kind of fuzzy nostalgia these videos give you when you watch a plain girl without makeup being used without as much as a by-the-by and recreate your own youth and your first timid kiss, the feeling of a cheap bra under your clumsy fingers..."

"Don't get carried away," Joan interrupted him. "We're nearly there."

The crumbling prefab buildings had already given way to squat huts. The smell of fish and fried noodles hung in the air. They were still in the amateur district but this location wasn't exactly Russian.

Grabbing his hand, Joan dragged him into a narrow side lane. Here, the houses almost met, the washing lines on their balconies hung with lace stockings. They had to grope their way in complete darkness.

I wonder what it's called? The Sex Horror Quarter? Plenty of those around. Films like Jamie Gillis' Dracula Sucks or Joe d'Amato's Porno Holocaust. There's even been a porn version of The Walking Dead just lately. I hope none of them jump at us from around the corner. First they'll bonk you, then they'll devour you.

With Oleg's every step, his heels sank deep into the mud with a crunching sound. Could they be human bones? True, he had a gun in his handbag but what good could it do? He had one slug left. So it was either shooting the first female who approached him, hopefully a Black Habit or a Checkered Skirt. Or... he could always point the gun at his own temple.

It might actually be a better option. He was

exhausted beyond belief. He didn't want to fight. He just couldn't take it any longer. At least he'd die for real.

As for Joan... well, she belonged here. This was her world. She didn't know any better.

A door creaked on its ancient hinges.

Joan pulled him inside. The lock clicked.

A stale smell of dust hung in the room.

Darkness closed over them.

THE PICTURE ON THE MOVIE SCREEN now shows a perfectly black square of absolute darkness. The speakers fall silent. All we can hear is the rustling of the scratched old film in the projector.

The audience is frozen in suspense. They've seen enough horror movies to believe that this pause is the filmmaker's intention. In a moment, ghastly music will start playing, cut short by spooky howling. Some hysterical woman in the audience might scream.

The theater falls silent. No one's munching on their popcorn. No one's ripping soda tabs.

And... now...

But nothing happens.

Nothing at all.

CHAPTER SEVEN

The Apprentice

Lima, El Agustino District
October 20 1931

THIS TIME the Artist had left his doll between the walls of the two monasteries: the old and the new. This was a much more elaborate work, much better made than its predecessor.

Miguel lingered, mechanically admiring the creature, then forced himself to stop.

Blood squelched underfoot. He was already getting used to it. This time the murderer had soaked the whole place in it: he must have had at least four gallons.

The girl he'd put together was stunning. He must have used at least six bodies to produce it. She was dressed in a robe of heavy burgundy velvet (a theater curtain?), and guanaco sandals. Silver bangles shaped as snakes hugged her wrists.

But the main thing was, this doll was frozen in a silent dance. She stood pressing the flat of one hand against the wall while touching the top of her head with the other, slightly setting the elbow aside. A seductive smile played on her lips. Her mouth had been sewn shut, its corners stretched. Her eyes had been poked out and replaced with gemstones: an emerald for her left eye socket and a piece of quartz for her right. In the first rays of the rising sun, the doll's macabre eyes glistened with foreboding.

The Artist had fashioned her head out of two halves, with a scar encircling her forehead as the murderer had transplanted a scalp of gorgeous hair onto another victim's skull.

Predictably, her hands were different too, her nails painted black on her left one and scarlet on her right. One look at them was enough for Miguel to realize they'd been painted with venous and arterial blood respectively.

Just like in the first case, the doll's face had been painted red.

The murderer had used the gold powder here too, but its application was different. He'd fashioned it in slanted shapes reminiscent of crescent moons, three on each cheek. Her breasts were pushed up in her cleavage — most likely, using some kind of support inside. Her legs, too, belonged to different bodies; the sandals were handmade.

This Artist was a Jack of all trades, whoever he was. He'd killed ten girls in the course of one week, with at least another twenty held as prisoner.

Provided they were still alive.

Just like the one before it, this doll too had been stuffed with some sort of herb emanating a delicate but strong aroma. Something painfully familiar. He had to check it out.

The cop standing next to him gasped when Miguel unsheathed a knife from his belt.

The police officers around him turned away, whispering prayers. Miguel realized that what he was doing was considered sacrilege here: the desecration of a corpse. Still, time was an issue: he couldn't afford having the body taken to the lab.

Gingerly he sliced through the thread keeping the doll's lips shut, then used the tip of the knife to prize her mouth open.

The murmur behind his back had grown to a rumble. He disregarded it though.

This was the very reason for such low crime solvency rate here. Whenever you found a dead body, you had to first pay your respects to the deceased by sprinkling the corpse with some holy water; then you had to present your condolences to the next of kin and pray together; and as for having an autopsy performed, that was the equivalent of having the body raped.

He didn't mind. He had nothing to lose. He was Russian — and by no means a Catholic, which in the local system of beliefs made him a brother to Satan himself.

A sweet scent wafted in his face.

Something white showed in the doll's mouth.

ZOTOV

A sudden breeze tugged at it, showering the air in front of the blood-smeared face with magnolia petals. The blossoms of Magnolia Amazonica have a particularly strong and harsh smell when they open — so strong that those unaccustomed to it can suffer bouts of vertigo, and children can faint if they approach the tree.

So this time instead of herbs the doll's chest and stomach had been stuffed with flower petals.

Miguel took a step back and gallantly gestured to the police photographer to approach. Felipe stepped forward and tipped his hat to him, then unhurriedly pointed his camera at the body. The flash blinded Miguel. The photographer was a born artist, his entire act a ballet dance.

Miguel unhooked his tunic collar, gulping lungfuls of fresh air. The magnolia scent had already given him a headache.

Now. The doll had been placed in a narrow back lane in the rather unpopular El Agustino district, in the vicinity of the monasteries and the palm grove. At night, the place was pitch black and absolutely deserted, not a streetlamp in sight. Which meant that the murderer had to use some sort of light to bring the body here and position it as intended. Which must have taken him a few hours at least.

It wouldn't have been wise for the Artist to transport the body and the lamps in a horse-drawn cart. He was short of time, not to mention that a loaded cart would have attracted the attention of the few nighttime passersby — he was bound to have come across a few. He couldn't have hired a taxicab because that too meant unwanted witnesses.

Which meant that the murderer must possess an automobile.

Finally, some good news. The fact of owning a car considerably narrowed the circle of potential suspects. Lima was no Paris: here, only very rich people could afford an automobile.

By the same token, rich meant well-connected, therefore such a suspect would have enough clout to brush the whole thing under the rug. He'd simply grease all the right palms, then pull the wool over El Presidente's eyes by coming up with a scape goat, most likely some illiterate peasant boy from a fishing village. Peru was no Russia, but here too money decided everything.

Which meant he had to find the Artist as soon as possible, then just kill him there and then, using the perennial excuse of "shot while resisting arrest". Piece of cake.

Still, he had a bad feeling about it. One shot might not quite cut it. Too many movements for a lone killer. To kidnap thirty girls, lock them up somewhere, slaughter them, cut them up, make a doll, dress it, get rid of the victims' remains, bring the doll here and position it as intended... the killer had to have accomplices.

He was bound to have an apprentice.

The killers had to be at least two. Probably

more: a true maestro always has a small clique of students at his beck and call. It's almost a prerequisite to genius.

Trembling with excitement, Miguel reached for a cigarette from his old Russian wartime cigarette case.

The flash went off again, spreading the stench of gas. The cops pulled their caps deeper over their eyes, trying to escape the sea breeze spattering them with brine. The Deputy Minister kept casting Miguel imploring stares, almost begging him, while keeping a safe distance.

Miguel gave him an encouraging smile, then borrowed a torch from a cop and meticulously searched the crime scene.

Nothing. No tire prints. Could this be why the killer had poured so much blood on the ground? It could dissolve any prints, turning them into mud on the bed of gravel. There was no way he could track anything here.

Stepping squeamishly around the pools of blood, he walked over to the Deputy Minister. "I might need your help, Señor."

"Anything you want," Juarez hurried to reassure him.

"The killer is a rich man," Miguel explained. "And he's not alone. The doll was taken to the crime scene in a large, spacious automobile. We need to run a check on everyone who own American or French cars in the country. The German ones are too small. The Artist transported the bodies in something that's expensive and respectable. I want you to have the police force compile a list of all car owners. Then I'll find a way to check the cars' insides without hurting their owners' dignity. You know what I mean, don't you?"

The man nodded eagerly.

"Next. You can't drain victims of this amount of blood in an average town house. He needs to keep it somewhere, too. Which means we need to find out which of the respectable car owners also own large slaughterhouses. In any case, we need to act quickly. The Artist keeps at least twenty more girls captive. Which means that he can erect yet another doll in the city center any moment if he wants to... and what if he sets it up by the gates of El Presidente's palace?"

Juarez' dark cheeks erupted in crimson spots.

Which was exactly the reaction Miguel had been trying to provoke. He'd been known among his wartime trench comrades for his talent to drive people to a nervous breakdown.

"Absolutely," Juarez mumbled. "I'll give orders straight away. Anything else?"

Sure, Miguel thought. I'd like a new apartment just like yours, a fivefold salary raise and to have the Bolshevik government overthrown in Russia. This latter can't happen too soon as far as I'm concerned.

"Oh yes please, Señor," Miguel touched the peak of his cap. "Could you be so kind as to help us take the doll to the station? I can't really call it a dead body, seeing as it's comprised of various parts of six cadavers. So basically, I need some transport. Also, could you please get some tarpaulin and have the crime scene covered, then post a couple of cops next to it? We don't need any prying eyes here today, especially not the press."

Juarez hurried to nod.

With a mental chuckle, Miguel realized that he must have resembled a spoiled jazz singer setting the conditions for her tour contract: ten bouquets of white roses, unlimited amounts of soda water of her favorite brand, a hotel room for her Siamese cats and a permanently full bathtub at a certain temperature.

Well, this particular investigation had the equal power of turning him either into Lima's police chief (yeah, dream on) or into a traffic cop banished to the dusty streets of the one-horse Trujillo town in the north, depending what exactly he managed to uncover in the course of his investigation. Miguel had witnessed quite a few cops disappear after they'd meddled with things they hadn't been supposed to uncover.

Then again, in this particular case the Artist's notoriety had played against him. El Presidente himself had taken an interest in the affair, demanding the murderer be caught. An entire squad of American tabloid journalists had already disembarked in Lima, their poisoned pens at the ready. The families of the local elite had begun to evacuate their own daughters from the city. In this atmosphere, the killer's money was unlikely to help him sweep his crime under the proverbial carpet. He had to be indecently rich to successfully pull it off. But... who said he wasn't?

Miguel climbed back in the car. The driver gallantly closed the door and whisked him back to the station.

...HE MUST HAVE dozed off at his desk. The janitor's tactful cough awoke him from his slumber, followed by the clatter of a tin bucket and the splashing of water.

Miguel opened his eyes. Enrique gave him a timid smile, clenching a filthy rag.

A bolt of lightning flashed through Miguel's mind. 'Magnolia... Why did you ask me if it was magnolia?"

The old Indian's face changed. He stood up straight and flung the rag in the bucket. "Are you sure you want to know, Señor?"

Miguel nodded.

"Very well. In that case, I'll be happy to receive you in my house tonight. Now I need to work."

Miguel dropped his head on his folded arms and dozed off again.

He dreamed of a New Year's Eve ball in Vladivostok all those years ago where he, in his brand-new second lieutenant's uniform complete with sabre, was dancing with the happy Vera

ZOTOV

Anokhina who'd closed her eyes in the sweet anticipation of a kiss. Much later, after the Revolution, Vera would have to work as a prostitute in one of Harbin's most notorious brothels. Like most of the Russian aristocracy, she'd had to flee the country with only the clothes on her back.

But that would happen much later...

Miguel smiled to his dream, oblivious of the Indian janitor peering intently at his face.

CHAPTER EIGHT

The Artifact of Creation

Sex City
Amateur Porn District

C ANDLES. Lots of candles.

At first the audience suspects a trap: they've already worked out that candles are luxury goods only available in convents and other cult institutions of the porn world. Still, on second thoughts they realize that the place has the authority to use them.

Wallpaper peels off the dirty drab walls plastered with faded pin-ups from American porn magazines. A round wrought-iron chandelier hangs from the ceiling, grinning its broken teeth of expired candle stubs.

The camera focuses on a furrowed old face in the semi-darkness, blurred tattoos covering its sagging cheeks, chin and forehead. It's a woman sitting with her legs tucked up under herself, her eyes staring vacantly at the door.

ZOTOV

The camera zooms in.

Now the audience can see that the woman's eyes are glass prosthetics. She's blind. Her matted gray hair falls onto her stooped shoulders as she leans forward, feeling in front of her with her gnarled fingers.

This could have been a good horror movie opening, the only things missing are the grim music and the shaky camera. Just then a dark cello piece begins to play — probably, to stay true to the tradition.

THE WOMAN [in a calm level voice]. "You're late."

JOAN [curtsies]. "Forgive us, Great Mother."

OLEG [surprised]. "You even have a Great Mother here? I just love it! Excuse me for asking, but can an ancient crone surpass young sweet ladies in their art? What's so special she has to offer that would draw the local men here like moths to a flame?"

GREAT MOTHER [removes one glass eye, exposing an empty eye socket]. "How about this?"

OLEG. "Sweet Lord!"

GREAT MOTHER. "Yes, stranger. Have I answered your question?"

OLEG [suppressing a bout of nausea]. "Quite, Great Mother."

GREAT MOTHER. "Good. I know that you came from another world. And no, you're not crazy. Your head is throbbing with horror. I can sense it, just as I can sense thousands of questions which have all perished in the depths of icy silence. Let me tell you now: I have no intention of answering them."

OLEG [shudders]. "That's very nice of you."

GREAT MOTHER [calmly]. "You're not the first one to teleport here. At the time, it came as a complete surprise to me that our city had been summoned from the abyss of oblivion simply as an impersonation of your movie world. You can watch it from outside as you switch on a TV or visit a movie theater. Some of you came here accidentally, which must have happened to you too. The mechanism of this isn't quite clear to me. There's only one thing I know: you can arrive here by accident but you can't escape... not if you know about a couple of conditions."

OLEG [gasps]. "What conditions are they?"

GREAT MOTHER. "You should be grateful, young man, that you haven't yet discovered the gay districts. You may be wary or even afraid of women now but no one has ever come back from there alive. So if you believe in some gods, it's about time you thanked them."

OLEG [gulps and clears his throat]. "Shit. I should thank God, you're dead right there."

GREAT MOTHER. "I suppose that will have to suffice. Your people have always been economical with their gratitude because they don't realize the severity of their circumstance. Your survival skills are remarkable, stranger. Normally, your ilk don't last a month. Some die of sexual exhaustion within the first few weeks. And you've lasted six months! Did you bring me what you visited the Black Habits for?

JOAN's young voice joins the conversation, "Yes, Great Mother."

GREAT MOTHER's voice rings with respect, "Impressive. You're brave, stranger. Many have ventured into the convent to fetch it but none have yet come back. Do you have it with you? Give it to me. Now."

The girl looks into the man's face and nods.

The camera focuses on Oleg's hands untying a small canvas bag. With a reverent bow, he hands the Great Mother a transparent object, holding it with both his hands. The blind woman reverently touches her forehead to it.

GREAT MOTHER. "The Lingam of Creation! The first dildo of our world, made by the Black and White Goddess of the oldest porn film ever. She crafted it from quartz fused with rock glass and bestowed on it the ability to heat itself up, reaching the required temperature in seconds."

OLEG [modestly]. "No comments. I'm glad you like it."

GREAT MOTHER's voice quivers. "The Goddess used it to please herself before the arrival of the first men[1]. This is a holy artifact which still remembers the touch of her flesh... The convent stole the precious relic and claimed sole ownership of it, using it to reward especially lascivious sisters... Thank you for retrieving it from the thief's room — and thank you, Joan, for suggesting it to him. By bringing me this, you can consider my services as been paid in full. I will banish you from this world without asking anything in return. O Great Goddess! I can sense the warmth of the holy

---

[1] The very first porn film was made in 1899 and indeed portrayed a young girl indulging in self-gratification. Having said that, its precedence is often disputed by another film which is now preserved in Amsterdam, featuring an Harlequin and two Columbines.

glass..."

JOAN's voice fills with hot, passionate force. "Me too, Great Mother! Oooh..."

OLEG [in alarm]. "Excuse me! Let's finish with me first. Then you can do what you want with it."

GREAT MOTHER [grudgingly complies]. "Very well. The Lingam of Creation will make it even easier than I thought. In fact, it's the only thing that bonds our two worlds together. Still, we will need other things like gels, spices and ashes necessary to perform the magic ritual. Mind you, I can't guarantee the outcome that you desire! According to the legends about the Black and White Goddess, the power of the sacred rod might be too strong. Once I perform all the sacrifices, I'm not sure if I'll be able to calculate its energy correctly. I will teleport you but you might die in the process. Think well now. Would you rather die or would you stay here?"

OLEG [unflinchingly] "I'd rather die."

GREAT MOTHER's voice rings with respect. "So be it, my guest. Fortune seems to favor you. You were lucky enough to survive. You found the one who treated you with compassion. You've procured the artifact which has become the undoing of hundreds of men who died trying to retrieve it from the convent. You made your way through the Thai amateur porn district which is truly unchartered and inaccessible. You even managed to navigate the horrendous school district. It might be that the powers of Darkness have taken a liking to you, in which case the ritual might go smoothly. Joan, I'm going to tell you now what you need and where you can get it from. Tomorrow night I'll teleport him. Don't look so happy, stranger. Nothing to celebrate yet."

OLEG [sourly]. I'm not celebrating anything."

GREAT MOTHER. "Good. Now hurry and bring me some ashes and spices. Aren't you surprised, stranger, that we can all understand each other without knowing any languages?"

OLEG. "Not at all. In my world, no one bothers to translate porn."

WITHOUT LETTING the Lingam of Creation out of her shaking hands, the old woman begins to instruct Joan who leans over the candle writing the items' names in a notebook. The scene has reverted to black and white — probably to symbolize the ancient nature of the recovered artifact.

The Great Mother focuses on the item as if she can see it, warming her fingers on its mystic glow. Joan nods, listening to her explanations. Oleg smiles to his own thoughts.

ZOTOV

They then leave the house and close the door politely, finding themselves back in the same dark alley. Joan rummages through her handbag, producing a pack of condoms, a set of porn cards, a bottle of aphrodisiac and finally, a pack of cigarettes.

Oleg curiously watches her light up and blow out smoke. "You're very much like us in certain respects."

"Are we different, then?"

"Oh yes. You don't get sick because in your world, hospitals aren't intended for treatment. I haven't seen any people with pets because here, animals serve a different purpose. I haven't been to that horrible district and have no intention of ever doing so. All your advertisement is about sex... actually, here we're very similar. In my world, they put naked women on everything, even removal van services. They advertise vacuums with posters portraying a seductive blonde and a catch line, *Sucks like a five-dollar whore!* The other day I saw a workwear catalog with a picture of a topless girl and some road workers hugging her breasts with their tarpaulin gloves. That's exactly what I was telling you about: we're drowning in an ocean of virtual sex, to the point where we don't want each other anymore. You know what I'm gonna do first thing once I'm back in Moscow? Even though I'm completely drained by now? I'm gonna fuck Vicky. Had I been with her that night and not in front of that stupid TV watching that stupid porn, nothing would've happened."

Joan pounds her fist against a wall, squashing out her cigarette.

"You okay?" Oleg asks.

"I'm fine. You and I are gonna have one hell of a day tomorrow. I can't get the teleportation potions on my own. You'll have to go to the city center with me. Anything can happen there, you understand that, don't you? Be prepared to be more accommodating if needs be. Try to get some sleep when we get back home. You need to build up some strength. You'll need it, I tell you."

Oleg heaves a sigh. "And you... do you really like it here?"

"What do you mean, do I like it? As they say in the Russian district, you don't choose your motherland. This is my home. According to you, your world is better. You have different foods and entertainment. You even have your own use for Coke bottles: you *drink* out of them! Still, in our world sex is a natural habitat. Everything is geared toward it. Personally, I'm not very happy I might never have proper sex with a man because a virgin here only has one alternative... or two, rather, but it's irrelevant. We wake up experiencing an animal craving and go back to bed unsatisfied, having to resort to masturbation. Sex is our nourishment; our race can't exist without it. I don't understand what you mean when you're saying that we're only puppets obeying every tug of the film director's strings. Or as one very well-hung black guy said in that new TV sex show, "All the world's a stage, and all the men and women merely players."

"Actually, it was Shakespeare who said that."

"Shakespeare? Sounds familiar. Doesn't he live in the Fairy Tale quarter? Or somewhere in the Medieval District? That's right. He wrote some wonderful plays, very touching. Especially *Romeo and Juliet*. It's so romantic, especially when the Montagues and the Capulets finally reconcile and the show ends with a gorgeous orgy where the beautiful Juliet is being..."

Oleg erupts in a dry, defiant cough. "Stop it."

"Okay."

"Sorry. I shouldn't have started. I had no idea that-"

"Don't apologize. I don't give a fuck. We need to go. Tomorrow is going to be one hell of a hard day. And we still need to go back through the Fairy Tale Quarter and past the schools with their packs of hungry Checkered Skirts. And you never know what that horny idiot Alice might come up with. We need to hurry. We don't want to disappoint the Great Mother."

THEY DISAPPEAR into the night. The cameraman focuses on their silhouettes in the moonlight: a confidently striding young girl and an awkward camel of a woman staggering in her stilettoes. The audience digs deep into their respective popcorn buckets, waiting for the figure of the mysterious onlooker to appear.

He doesn't. The man and the girl disappear into the darkness as the camera zooms out, revealing the entire panorama of the amateur porn district. A tense, sinister music begins to play. Still munching on their popcorn, the audience white-knuckles their armrests, impatient.

Much to their disappointment, nothing happens. Just like before, the screen goes dark.

CHAPTER NINE

El Diablo

Lima, Barrio de Chino
October 21 1931

TERESA WAS SCARED too. The whole murder thing gave her the shakes. It had only been a week since the first of those abominable dolls (Lord have mercy upon us!) had appeared in the city squares, and by now the streets were now nearly empty! Lima, this ancient Ciudad de Los Reyes, was pregnant with dark rumors about the contents of the stuffed girls' stomachs.

So how was she supposed to earn a living? Her clientele had shrunk to a mere pittance. Gone were the tipsy rich daddies; other women's husbands stayed dutifully at home; even schoolboys didn't seem too eager to spend their painstakingly saved pocket money on a grope of her cleavage. What were they all afraid of? It wasn't as if the Artist used male bodies to make his blood-curdling creations.

But no, men had been the first to lose heart. Teresa could walk the streets all she wanted these days but no amount of seductive smiles could tempt them. And she wasn't some useless opportunist, oh no Señor, she was a hard-working woman. She charged two sols an hour or five for the night, and may Jesus be her witness she made it worth the client's money. She wasn't like some of her other sisters in trade who'd lie staring at the ceiling waiting for their customers to get it over with, so that they could finally get up, smooth out their skirts and go back out onto the boulevard. Teresa had been doing it for a year and a half and was always giving it her all, groaning and screaming and scratching the client's back.

It wasn't for nothing she'd been dreaming of becoming an actress when she'd been little. Even though bodily pleasures gave her nothing but physical pain, her men were always pleased and always paid her extra, sometimes twice her usual rate. And every time Teresa received a payment, she always put a bit aside for a rainy day because she knew only too well that girls didn't last in her line of business. She, too, would end up selling octopuses at the pier... provided she didn't croak the way Anna Maria had the other day, jumping into the sea because syphilis had eaten her face away.

The night was so dark and grim. And she had to work.

Teresa cussed and immediately covered her mouth in fear. Lord Jesus could see and hear everything... he could see her too, a swarthy Quechua girl of seventeen years of age, slightly plump with a pretty and gentle childish face, clad in a white dress she'd made all by herself.

Surely sweet Jesus could send her a rich client tonight? Even though it was none of his business, Teresa still needed to eat every day without dipping into her piggy bank. Wretched cops! What did they think they were doing? Couldn't they just catch that stupid Artist and let an honest girl hook a man?

A tipsy old Chinaman staggered past her.

"Señor? Please? How about a little love?" Teresa grabbed the man's sleeve.

The Chinaman freed himself from her grip and stumbled off without saying a word.

What kind of times were these? Love wasn't worth a dime. Would she have to go to bed hungry again? Having said that... how about those two dandy boys celebrating?

Teresa slid under the weak glow of a red Chinese lantern. "Are the Señors looking for company? They won't be disappointed!"

The two stopped, eyeing her. They were way too young, almost the same age as herself — the likes of them usually didn't have much money in their pockets. Unless they were some spoiled rich mommy's boys spending their pocket money on whores: Teresa had seen quite a few of those.

One of the two — a pale youth with blood-shot eyes — walked over to her and lifted her chin with his commanding fingers.

His pallid complexion untouched by the sun betrayed a descendant of the Spanish conquistadors. His ilk were all rich. Finally she was in luck.

"So what can you do?" the spoiled brat asked nonchalantly.

"Anything you wish for five sols," Teresa blurted out. "And then some."

The pale youth turned to his friend who gave a dismissive shake of his head. His face was concealed by a scarf.

The pale youth took his hand away with a little smile. "I'm afraid my amigo isn't in the mood tonight. Sorry, my precious. Some other time, maybe."

Having waited for the two brats to retreat a safe distance away, Teresa spat out a hearty dose of the choicest Indian expletives. Oh, well. This seemed to have been a sign. It looked like she might have to make do with a corn cob and a tiny piece of cheese for her dinner.

Time to go home.

Teresa plucked up her skirt and began leaping over the rain puddles.

Her room was at the other end of the district, a mere fifteen minutes' walk. Actually, that was where she used to take her clients, her bed the only piece of furniture she had. As for washing herself, she could always do that in the sea which was only a stone's throw away.

ZOTOV

She could already see the hotel — although if the truth were known, "brothel" would be a much more accurate description.

Teresa took an absent-minded step and landed her shoe deep into the mud. Cussing like a trooper, she stopped, studying her shoe in the weak lamplight.

A large shadow rose before her.

Someone grabbed her throat from behind with one hand, pushing a piece of thick cloth into her mouth with the other.

Don't breathe, Teresa told herself. Her mind was fading, overcome with terror. She struggled, trying to wriggle herself out of the stranger's clutches. She managed to kick his knee cap quite successfully a couple of times but he didn't even budge as if it hadn't hurt at all.

Teresa floundered in his arms, squirming like a snake while the man's steely fingers closed harder on her neck. Her vision darkened. Instinctively she parted her lips and took a convulsive gulp of air.

Her mind and body collapsed into a black void.

WHEN SHE'D COME ROUND, she had no idea how much time had elapsed.

She squealed at the top of her voice. Someone elbowed her ribs hard, shutting her up.

Teresa couldn't work out where she was. Her eyes were wide open and still she couldn't see anything. She reached out and felt something moist under her fingers — someone's lips?

Immediately she received another whack in her ribs, much harder this time.

"Shut up, you stupid cow," a female voice hissed next to her ear. "No good you screaming."

"Who are you? Where am I? What's this place?" Teresa blabbed, unable to stop.

All she heard was sobbing around her. Several other girls who seemed to stand very close to her were wailing and whimpering, their desperate sobs louder with every second.

"Shut up!" the voice hissed. "Don't you remember? He'll come back soon."

The crying stopped as if on cue.

"Where am I?" Teresa repeated in Quechua, hugging her bare shoulders.

"*Estamos en la casa del Diablo,*" the voice replied mournfully in Spanish.

Even though the news had done nothing to cheer Teresa up, at least it had confirmed her suspicions. She was standing stark naked in pitch darkness next to seven or eight other women, packed like sardines in a small stone cell. Coupled with the fact that she'd been kidnapped in the street, chloroformed and brought here in the dead of the night, it could only mean one thing. Both she and all these other girls were the future parts for the Artist's macabre dolls.

What body part was he going to cut from her? Would it be her head or her legs?

The stench in the cell was overpowering. It

looked like the girls were kept here 24/7 without allowing them out to do their thing. The place reeked of stale urine, feces and blood. The pungent smell of fresh blood.

"So what's the point in keeping quiet, then?" Teresa said, surprisingly calm. "If he's gonna kill us all anyway? Just so that you know, his name is the Artist. He cuts up people and uses their bodies to make sculptures. He takes legs from one girl, arms from another, a head, a pair of breasts, then he sews them all together. We won't survive, anyway. At least if we scream, someone might hear. What could be worse than what the Artist is going to do to us?"

A croaking laughter came from the dark. "You're one smart bitch, aren't you?" said the sarcastic voice of the woman who'd spoken to her first. "What would we do without you? Praise be to the Holy Trinity that you've come and enlightened us! So that you know, we've been here for quite a while. I've been here for three weeks already and my turn hasn't come yet. Guess why? Because I keep my head down, that's why. I'm doing it because I've no intention of croaking in this rathole. I hope I last until the cops catch the motherfucker. He brought me here with some other girl. She was screaming her head off like you can't imagine. Called for help for hours, the idiot. We very nearly went deaf down here. So naturally he came back and took her. After a while we heard her scream some more. Then she went quiet. He came back and threw that thing down to us... it was all wet and slimy. Well, pretty face, guess what it was? *He'd skinned her alive.*"

"What have you done with her?" Teresa asked timidly, immediately regretting her curiosity.

"What do you think?"

The girl's back erupted in cold sweat. Dear Lord, what kind of monsters she was with! "But-"

"Oh, give me a break. You have no right to judge us. He doesn't feed us. At all. Once a day he lowers a bucket of water down here and we lap it like dogs. That's what we are now, dogs. There's nothing human left about us..." the girl broke down, sobbing.

Teresa shook uncontrollably, struggling to keep herself in check. This didn't sound good. Even if she avoided the killer's knife, her own hunger-crazed ilk could devour her alive. They'd already tasted blood and raw meat.

Teresa knew only too well how low a human being could stoop.

The sound of pounding footsteps came from a distance.

The girl next to her stopped crying. A large hand reeking of sweat covered Teresa's mouth.

A tense silence hung in the room. The girls had almost stopped breathing.

A blinding beam of torchlight assaulted them from above.

The prisoners huddled together like a flock of sheep. They squeezed their eyes shut, shielding themselves with their hands.

"So what do you think?" a question boomed, echoing from the stonework.

"Honestly, I've no idea," the other one replied.

The first man spoke in a soft, singsong manner; the other one staccatoed every word he snapped.

"I bet you haven't," the first man's voice rang with sarcasm. "You're the genius, the poet. I just serve evil as its humble assistant. Who else would you dispatch to the local villages to buy up magnolia petals from stinking peasants? That's the answer to your question. I appreciate your trust in me, my kind Señor."

"You've said it a thousand times already," the other man chuckled. "That's not what I think. It's our fault we hadn't thought about the flowers earlier. That's the only reason I had to ask you. Look at me: I'm not moaning even if I had to spend all night dismembering bodies. So let's stop arguing about whose job is bigger. It's not what matters now. We've barely just started and already we can't find good material. Just look at this one!"

The torch beam moved to Teresa's left.

"All we can use is the top of her skull. And what do you want us to do with the rest? Throw it back down or bury it? We have too many offcuts as it is, my friend."

The two spoke as if they didn't even consider the girls human, calmly discussing how exactly they were going to cut them up. Even peasants had more respect for the animals they were about to slaughter. They felt sorry for them — probably because such animals were given human names. Back home in the village, Teresa's parents used to have Fernando the boar and Felicia the pig, enormous like you can't imagine. Teresa used to love them so much. She'd been crying when the two had been slaughtered for Christmas. Her father had averted his eyes as he'd left the pigsty, his arms covered in blood up to his elbows.

And to this man, girls weren't even pigs — not insects even, just some inanimate objects whom he could discuss with contempt. Like a tailor who'd come across a filthy piece of fabric just as he was about to cut a new suit of clothes, indignant that he'd have to wait until it was washed.

To these two, they were nothing but faulty material.

"Did you say offcuts?" the other man sneered. "Hope you didn't forget that they're my responsibility too. I'm the one who does your dirty work for you. I find the models and clean up afterwards. You don't seem to be bothered by the fact that Lima is teeming with cops now. There's one on every corner. And you expect me to keep bringing new ones as if nothing has happened? It's just plain dangerous, my friend. If I get caught, we won't be able to complete what we've started. So let's try and work with whatever we have available, okay? It's the best I could do."

Teresa squinted, struggling to make out his

face, but couldn't. The creature lurked in the shadows enshrouding the light: needle-sharp teeth, a black tongue licking the swollen lips... that was all. She couldn't see his eyes behind the weak flickering of the torch.

The rest happened quickly.

A rope noose, flung from above by a skillful hand, entwined the neck of the girl who'd claimed she'd been here the longest hoping to survive until help arrived. The two began hauling the victim up; she croaked and wheezed grabbing at the noose with both hands.

Judging by the sound, the killers forced the girl onto the floor. The torchlight moved, allowing Teresa to see the silhouettes of the two men on the ceiling. Both seemed to have long hair. One was tall, the other stocky.

"Have you got the bucket?" the other man asked.

The first man chuckled. "Absolutely. You're the inspired artist here, amigo. I'm only a filthy butcher. The item you're looking for is here. Take the artifact and just do it."

Overhead, the trapped girl croaked, trying to wriggle herself free as she clung desperately to life. Judging by the position of the shadows on the ceiling, she was kneeling with her head pulled back by the noose.

The first shadow removed its clothes and bent down, then stood back up, holding something that resembled a knife blade. The Artist's body swayed as he began singing a song in the Quechua tongue.

The other shadow joined in. They weren't really singing but rather howling like hungry wolves at the Moon. The dialect was strange: Teresa could barely make out a few words.

The girls in the hole stopped groaning, as if falling into a trance. Even the victim stopped croaking.

The song stopped abruptly.

With a sideways swing, the killer sliced through the girl's throat. Jets of blood hit the empty bucket with a cheerful patter: a sound familiar to Teresa since childhood when her Mom used to milk the cow.

The girl's body arced; her feet pummeled the floor.

The killer's assistant let go of the rope. The girl slumped to the floor, her nails clawing the concrete. Her wheezing died away.

The servants of the House of the Devil bent over the body, studying it closely.

"Shit," said the snappy voice. "Just as I thought. Why did we even have to keep her? We can use the blood, I suppose, but all the rest is unusable. I know you don't like it when I say that but pray tell where you managed to find such trash?"

"In the port," the other replied reluctantly. "That's why I kept her all this time. I thought she might lose some weight and you could use her. Now

ZOTOV

I can see it was my mistake. I normally collect them at night and what with the lighting here in Lima, you can't really see what you're taking. In any case, we're not losing anything. A bucketful of good blood is always useful."

He kicked the body hard toward the edge of the hole. The dead girl's hair hung over the trap's edge.

"Dinner, Señoritas," the killer laughed. "It's a very generous helping today with all the trimmings. And if you're not hungry, you can always enjoy your ex-friend's company, can't you?"

He kicked the body again. The corpse dropped down onto the girls' heads. Teresa shrieked, feeling the victim's hand on her face — the very hand which had covered her mouth only ten minutes ago. The hand was still warm.

But that wasn't what had scared her. A hungry growling echoed through the hole as the other prisoners began ripping the body apart with their nails.

Teresa leaned against the wall, choking on her own vomit.

"Please don't take offence," the other man said with unexpected meekness. "We are friends, not rivals, aren't we? The problem is, I'm desperate to put a new model together right now. But unfortunately, I don't have a head. Whatever we have in stock isn't worthy of my queen's amazing body. So allow me to disagree with you: we can't settle for less than the best. This way, we'll never become successful. Love requires the best of everything. Let's take another look, if you don't mind."

The torchlight approached, illuminating the women's mouths smeared with red. Teresa squeezed her eyes shut from the sight and whispered a desperate prayer. Lord, please, please...

"Wait a sec," the second man sounded surprised. "We've completely forgot this one. It's good, isn't it?"

"I brought her in an hour ago," the first one said grimly. "You have a very short memory."

"Sorry. I completely forgot. Pointless keeping her here. Get on with it."

...The noose jerked around Teresa's neck so hard it almost snapped. She croaked and wheezed just like the girl before her, trying to slide her fingers under the rope. Her tongue stuck out, her face was flooded with tears.

The servants of the Devil were smart, whoever they were: you can't fight back when you're being strangled, your fingers are too busy clutching at the noose to try and claw the killer's eyes out as you're struggling for just one more gulp of air.

She knew what was about to happen but wasn't going to ask for mercy. Not because she was proud: she wasn't. They were going to slaughter her like a pig, anyway: guests at the Devil's party can't expect him to show mercy.

ZOTOV

By the time they'd hauled her out of the pit, Teresa was only half-conscious, aware of only one weird thing: the skin on her neck didn't feel sore. The rope was made of silk. The bastards had thought of everything, cautious not to damage the future dolls' body parts.

They lifted her, forcing her to her knees just like they'd done with the girl before her, and pulled her head back with the rope. A booted foot sank into her back, preventing her from moving.

Her eyes flooded with tears, Teresa tried to make out the face of the man before her.

He was stark naked, his chest and shoulders covered in tattoos. A strange knife blade made of gray-tinted glass glistened in the dull torchlight.

"Perfect," the man said to his invisible accomplice standing behind the girl's back. "Lord Jesus, I've never seen such perfection. We've been really lucky. I might need to touch up a couple of things but overall... excellent! Just think that you chose her by accident with nothing but a quick glance and your gut feeling to guide you — and what a result! I'm all shaking, I just can't wait... Hold her well, I need to be really precise. We shouldn't ruin such a pretty pelt."

The pit below was filled with slurping sounds and the crunching of bones.

Then Teresa recognized him.

She lunged at him with inhuman force. Neither the tattooed killer nor his accomplice keeping her on the leash had expected anything like it. She leapt at the naked man, clawing his cheek.

A heavy blow landed on the back of her head.

Her torturer hadn't even tried to dodge her attack; he just stood there smiling in her face.

Teresa's vision darkened. Her tongue slurred as she struggled to speak.

"Good blow," the Artist said to his accomplice. "It didn't leave a trace. What a crazy bitch! Okay, I know how we're gonna do it. Unfortunately, we can't strangle her, it's against the rules, you know. We have to shed some blood. Don't worry, I'll be careful."

Teresa collapsed onto her side. He knelt next to her and swept her hair away from her ear, wrapping it around his hand.

The girl's one bloodshot eye watched the play of light on the gray blade, flat and razor-sharp. Jesus our Savior, why was the knife made of glass?

"In the name of love," the first voice said.

"The one and only," the other voice continued, "may it be with us forever and ever."

The tattooed man lowered his hand. Teresa's world exploded in a cascade of crimson.

CHAPTER TEN

The Portal Guide

The outskirts of Sex City
Late at night

WE'RE BACK in the abandoned basement dimly lit with the two stubs of the remaining convent candles. The man is crouching over his black notebook, surrounded with heaped-up junk.

He looks up from the page and stares into the camera. A blissful smile lights up his face which is finally devoid of the hopeless grief.

He stares forward into space, his eyes half-closed in anticipation. The audience falls silent. A female movie goer suppresses a sob and reaches into her purse for a crumpled handkerchief.

The man on the screen lowers his head and writes laboriously in a schoolchild's halting hand,

I JUST HOPE this is my last diary entry. Tonight I might regain my freedom and return to my world.

EL DIABLO

Only a few hours left. Honestly, I just can't believe it. My hands are shaking; you can see it yourself by all the ink spots and erratic lines. Is it possible I might go back to our wonderful universe where you risk being knocked out for propositioning a strange girl on the street?

Only now do I realize how good my old city is. There, you can go safely to a mall and use their restroom without fear; you can take a cab or even walk into a sex shop without the risk of being confronted by half-naked shop assistants in lacy underwear.

What an utter bliss.

I can't even tell you how I dream of seeing Moscow again. Oh the delight of walking into one of the seedy bars of its working-class suburbs where they'd kick your teeth in for as little as a sideways glance at someone's girlfriend. How awesome is that?

Oh yes, this is exactly what I'm going to do once I'm back: I'll walk over to a strange woman at a bus stop and ask her, 'Fancy an orgy, babe?' Then again, I shouldn't overdo it. Something like this might land you in jail for fifteen days[2]. Should I just pinch her backside? That's probably a better idea. At least that way you can feel the crack between our two worlds. If I did it here to some local girl, she'd be

---

[2] Fifteen days in jail: the shortest Russian jail sentence usually applied to hooligans and peace offenders

*out of her panties in seconds, followed by her best
friend, while all of the bus passengers would get
busy watching, their hands living a life of their own.*

*That's something that gave me the shivers
today. Joan and I had to venture into the very thick
of it: the Sex City's business center which is the
heart of local porn life. I had to wear my own male
clothes: firstly because I don't really look like a girl
and secondly, if they found me out, it would have
been much worse than any orgy as the entire district
is packed with gay video district spies.*

*Great Lord! I knew what to expect and I
prepared for the worst. We took a taxi to the center:
an old English black cab from the British amateur
dogging porn videos which are apparently very
popular in London at the moment, the ones where
mild-mannered British gentlemen shag refined
British ladies during their morning jogs. Mild-
mannered being a bit of an exaggeration, of course,
but that's the genre for you.*

*Joan, God bless her, managed to find a cab
with a male driver which are almost extinct these
days. He was already so exhausted by having to
accept his fare in kind that he was only too happy to
give us a free ride. The moment we got out in the
center, Joan grabbed me and dragged me into the
City of Vice before even the cab's door had slammed
shut.*

*Oh wow. I hadn't been in the monster's jaws
since the day of my arrival. Here resided the
prototypes of our modern film studios: Private,*

Magma, Moli, Wicked Pictures, Evil Angel, Ribu Film and Videorama. Like any megalopolis, Sex City needs an administration to function properly. This isn't some 1960s anarchist squat. They have everything for real, even a Mayor: a dark-skinned girl who likes to appear in public carrying a whip and wearing a leather corset and a pair of enormous platform shoes. They have their own malls and supermarkets (offering the same old choice of bananas and cream), their own teams of burly firefighters and even their own janitors — admittedly naked, their brooms fashioned out of old-age vibrators.

It's true though that their firefighting services receive a lot of complaints as they skip work too often, responding to calls from nymphomaniacs. Every time some such desperate housewife calls them up, the entire team is stuck there until they receive a call from another one, 24/7 with rare breaks to grab some sleep and a bite to eat.

As we walked, I had this eerie feeling we were locked in a cage with tigers. None of the women around us were wearing a bra (which were considered dated in Sex City) and were devoid of body hair like nuclear attack victims — but with plenty of peroxide curls. Covered in cosmetic oils and rattling with all the piercing hardware, they zero in on you, targeting you in the crowd.

I can tell all the types by now. Housewives: look like photo models, all of them under 30 and each sporting enormous breast implants. Their houses seem to be in a permanent state of disrepair because they keep calling plumbers, car mechanics, TV repairmen, and the aforementioned long-suffering firefighters.

Chambermaids: they wear starched white aprons and the only time they turn on their hoovers is to drown out the sounds of their own groaning.

Businesswomen: bespectacled and in drab gray suits, they await their prey in offices where paperwork is only a pretense and all the desks and copying machines are used in a number of quite inventive ways, none of them to do with actual office work. Secretaries in those offices have never made a single cup of coffee for their bosses or visitors but can be very savvy in taking care of said bosses and visitors' other needs.

Holidaymakers: covered in beach sand, pale and constantly wet, their skin in permanent goosebumps from sea water, their bikinis in tatters from too much rough handling. Oh, and did I mention pole dancers? Young dentists' and gynos' assistants with doll's faces, wearing nothing under their lab coats? Talking about which, all Sex City inhabitants have disgustingly bad teeth because their dentists have no idea how to treat them: they're too busy pleasing the actual patients. All the gynos here are men, their eyes red from constant lack of sleep, their faces a hue of vampire pale, teetering on the brink of sexual exhaustion. They'll give you a thirty-second vaginal check while an average orgy with the patient and the doctor's assistant might last about an hour.

EL DIABLO

Who did I forget to mention? Oh yes: the naughty cheerleaders in their skimpy skirts. Prison guards (who are exclusively female in male prisons): burly and stern in horn-rimmed glasses and armed with riding crops and truncheons. They often form packs with policewomen; both are constantly aroused and doubly dangerous.

I heard the sound of their truncheons as we walked but I wasn't afraid. Whatever happened today, tomorrow I'll be home.

Joan walked next to me, her arm hooked through mine, her face dark but purposeful. What was she thinking about?

There's no way I can find that out.

I was beginning to doubt my own intentions. Was I really going to leave her here, in this den of vice and wickedness? Yes, I know I sound like a Jesuit monk. You should come here and try to live in this hellhole a couple of weeks like I have — that'll quickly teach you some chastity.

Thoughts crowd my head. As soon as I escape this place, I might leave for that Valdai friary for a few weeks. Then again, I might not. I told Joan a lot of BS about having sex with Vicky but the truth remained, I wasn't even sure I'd be able to look at naked women anymore. The moment one of them reached her hand out to me, I might run away with my tail between my legs.

So here I am, describing it all to you, weaving words on paper while too scared to ask myself point blank: why don't I take Joan along? Is it only because Vicky's waiting for me back in Moscow? Of course not. I've been missing for at least six months by now. She's probably hooked up with someone else waiting for the results of the half-hearted police investigation.

So what prevents me from taking Joan with me? Is it because we both understand she doesn't belong in our world? Even though I'm pretty sure we might be quite compatible in bed. With time I might even get my libido back. She possesses a double virtue: not only is she a virgin but she's also an expert in the art of love.

But even so, what kind of future do we have? Bringing her to our world would be a little like inviting a savage cannibal to an Apple presentation in New York. She's never even heard of Moscow. To her, it's perfectly normal to go with the first guy who winks at her or to offer a blow job to a supermarket greengrocer in exchange for a nice firm cucumber. This world has no idea of fidelity; why would they, if a bride habitually makes out with her entire wedding guest list, then continues to seduce all of her husband's male friends while he openly screws all her cheerleader friends and nannies in front of her? If I took her with me, I might one day walk in on her in the company of our plumber and she wouldn't even feel guilty because that's how they pay for plumbing services here.

Of course I've grown very attached to her — but she'd be better off here. Taken out of her habitual environment, she'll be a bit like a rare

*endangered animal which might die in the safety of
a zoo within months, unable to survive in captivity.
What's the point in living if an hour of free love can
pay for anything you want? It's not that we're so
much different. It's not as if sex can't buy you
anything in Russia, from iPhones to cars and
designer bags, but at least there it's not so explicit if
you know what I mean. I'm yet to see a porn movie
where a girl would have done it in exchange for an
iPhone. It's just the way it is: porn is an escapist
fairy tale as opposed to crude reality.*

    *So I'm very sorry, Joan, but I'm not taking you
with me. I'm leaving on my own.*

    *As we walked, I asked her something that
had been bugging me for quite a while. How come
their society was made up of predominantly
desperate women? It's not the only kind of porn, you
know. Where's all the virgin-seducing, violent stuff?
Where're all the dominant males ripping clothes off
scared young blondes?*

    *That's when she finally told me. Apparently,
there're two cities in this world. Two countries, even.
This place, including some far-off convents, is
dominated by nymphomaniacs while the mountain
republic Sex Land is ruled by macho men.*

    *The two countries are in a state of a
permanent war with each other, accusing their rival
of all the crimes under the sun. Both have their fair
share of deserters and turncoats who appear on
local TV in brief 5-minute news breaks between porn
movies, telling the audience about the blood-curdling*

horrors unfolding in the enemy city. I remember one such story about the death of a nerd male student, a willowy bespectacled creature who fell prey to an uncontrollable female mob. The audience gasp in fear and admiration, sometimes secretly envying the victims.

These parallels between our world and theirs never cease to amaze me. I know this kind of unbridled sexual fantasy might sound grotesque to you — but you have to agree that we too get screwed by everybody and their grandmother: our bosses at work, the government, and even TV presenters.

Enough of that. At the moment, philosophy is surplus to requirements.

So basically, Joan and I just kept walking until we came to the right address.

This is a very special district. It provides very special kinds of rituals, some of which might make one's blood freeze. Like when it's twenty women on one man — the procedure otherwise known as "reverse gangbang". I don't think anyone has ever survived it. At least I remember seeing those series back on earth which featured a new man in every episode. This is the center of all sorts of mass indulgencies — swingers, masked balls, you name it. Arguably the most dangerous district in the entire city. Even male deserters from Sex Land don't venture here: the unnamed graves in the local cemetery could tell you many a blood-curdling tale.

Unfortunately, this was the only place where we could get the items necessary to bring me home.

EL DIABLO

As a sales manager, I know perfectly well that commerce needs large numbers of people in order to prosper. And naturally, we had to pay in kind.

Our first point of call was a tiny seedy shop next to a swingers' club which sold various relics, including the kind of ash we needed.

The ashes of a man who'd once teleported here from another world, the shopkeeper told us.

My blood ran cold. So this was the kind of future that awaited my body if I stayed! They'd burn it for souvenirs and rub my ashes into... never mind.

As I was busy in the adjacent room paying the shopkeeper on her velvet-upholstered bed, her naked twin sister knocked on the door as if by mistake. Here, you just don't refuse a ménage a trois: it would look suspicious. Then some cousin or other stumbled into the room, followed by an auntie who'd come out of the shower apparently in search of a towel...

At that point, I broke. I asked them to let me use their bathroom and fled.

Then we went to a nearby street stall to buy the gel made from virgin's tears. It was quite costly, too: the stall vendor turned out to be a Marquis de Sade aficionado who got her kicks by pinching me. She gave me five lashes, drove a needle under my fingernail and finally threatened to strangle me. I suffered in silence, praying she didn't make me jump her.

And finally, a nun's bone. This latter cost me an arm and a leg (literally) because a savage forest

ZOTOV

nun is a powerful beast very difficult to catch. They kill banana pickers in the jungle by attacking them in prides, then exhaust them with their animal lust which renders them almost immortal. 'Almost' being the operative word. I can't help admiring the anonymous unsung hero who'd managed to nail this creature to death: he must have been a demigod with virility to match. That's how he'd acquired this valuable trophy: a forest nun's skeleton. You could live off it for at least forty years simply swapping its precious bones for food.

This time they charged me what I feared the most, which was a reverse gangbang. That put my trip back home in serious jeopardy. I hadn't yet recovered from paying for the ash.

But I was a sales manager, wasn't I? Dealing with difficult clients was my job. True, I might not have been in the best shape initially so that some of the women began complaining, accusing me of selling them damaged goods — but I got out of this brilliantly by dividing the girls into pairs. In the end, they were too busy with each other to take any notice of me. What bliss!

And now my trip is coming to an end.

I've got the artifacts. Time for me to go and see Joan one last time.

Honestly, it makes me sad. Still, there's nothing I can do about it. It just wasn't meant to happen.

THE MAN FINISHES the last sentence and rises. He

picks up the notebook, slides it into a large bag, slings the bag over his shoulder and walks out of the basement, holding the burning stub of the last remaining candle. The camera follows him.

The person watching him switches off the computer screen and turns anxiously, looking around himself. The audience still can't see his face which remains in the dark. His lips part in a smile. The man slams on a fedora hat and disappears behind the door as the camera follows him, filming him from behind.

We watch him get into a black car parked by a white mansion. He turns the ignition key. The motor roars to life as the car speeds away.

THE CAMERA SWITCHES to the Great Mother's hut deep in the quagmire of the amateur porn district.

For the next fifteen minutes, the bewildered audience have to listen to the frogs' croaking. Finally the observer appears by the door — he must have left his car in some side lane nearby.

He knocks on the door. The blind woman opens and touches his face, studying it. She smiles as she recognizes him and gestures him to come in.

The man disappears inside.

CUT TO BLACK

AN HOUR AND A HALF later, the two tiny figures of Oleg and Joan approach the hut from the same side lane. They too disappear inside for a long time.

ZOTOV

As the audience loses all hope, the hut windows flash with a bright green light. A blue flame escapes the shattered window panes. Someone screams. We can hear a weak groan, followed by a growling noise and the smashing of furniture.

A powerful explosion swallows the hut.

 END OF FILM SPOOL

CHAPTER ELEVEN

The Scent of Death

The northern suburbs of Lima
October 21 1931

THEY HAD TAKEN a car to travel the first half of their journey. Then they'd hired a cart pulled by humpbacked cows as the car couldn't make it any further along the mud track flooded by last night's rain.

It probably takes Enrique at least a couple of hours to get to work every day, Miguel finally realized as his body was jolted by all the potholes. He probably lives like a dog too. It's a miracle they haven't yet had a revolution here. This is so like Russia in a way. We too used to party like there was no tomorrow. All those audiences with the Tsar, trips to Paris, spa vacations in Baden Baden and the ten-ruble lobsters at Ustinov's restaurant... But before you know it, it was 'Down with the

Tsar!', torched mansions burning, their owners pitchforked, Tsar's army officers thrown into the frozen river alive...

His heart clenched. When he'd first arrived in Japan, a lot of his friends didn't even want to unpack their suitcases. "We'll make quick work of the Bolsheviks," they'd said.

Well, well. He'd been here in Peru for over ten years now. He might stay here for the rest of his life for all he knew.

Miguel turned to Enrique whose dark Indian face was impassive. The janitor stared into space as if hoping to see something in the dusk.

"Watch out, Señor," the man said. "There's a nice big bump in the road here somewhere."

As if in confirmation, the cart jumped so hard that their teeth chattered.

They were heading for Corpus Christi, a mountain village to the north of Lima.

We have so much in common, Miguel kept thinking. Fancy calling a village after Christ's body! But Russians do it all the time too. We too have our fair share of villages called after all sorts of religious holidays: Christmas Cross, Epiphany Gate, Apostle on the Hill... we even have a Jerusalem somewhere in Siberia, in the vicinity of Khabarovsk... from what I heard, they've renamed it the Stalin Collective Farm now. And here you have Christ's Body, Holy Cross, Holy Savior... it might be a bit too zealous but that's how they like it. Not that I believe in this kind of piety. In Russia too, our supposedly God-fearing nation spent their every waking hour praying and fasting, but it didn't stop them from burning down every church in the country mere months later.

"Here we are, Señor."

Miguel jumped effortlessly from the cart. His feet sank deep into some soft substance. He looked down and cussed. Of course. This was the choicest manure one could find.

Enrique suppressed a smile. "Mind your step, Señor. We're poor people here."

He took Miguel under his arm and switched on a flashlight. They waded through the mud and pools of rainwater past peasants' huts for a while, lighting the way with the torch beam to avoid any cow pats.

Finally, they came to a steep cliff edge. The janitor gestured Miguel to stop and lifted his flashlight, pointing it upwards.

Miguel looked up and startled. They were standing by the trunk of a huge old tree. Its tangled mess of gnarly roots resembled the arthritic fingers of an old woman. Black leaves rustled overhead.

he familiar sickly sweet scent was so strong here that Miguel's head swam. He accepted a handkerchief from the janitor and pressed it to his nose.

"This is Magnolia Amazonica," Enrique said calmly. "It mainly grows in the north although they do plant it in cities just for the looks of it. You've heard of piranhas, Señor, haven't you? The fish, I mean. They can make quick work of a buffalo and pick his bones clean within seconds. But if you take them home and put them in a fish tank, they'll forget their murderous nature so you can put your fingers in the water and they won't even bother. These monsters with needle-sharp teeth will be perfectly happy eating fish food."

He paused. "This tree, Señor, grows in the very depths of the Amazonian rainforest where it's pitch dark even during daytime because the tree canopies are so thick they block out all the sunlight. You can tell this tree by all the dead insects and little animals — frogs, small snakes and other critters — that litter its roots. The tree's blossoms produce a strong scent which knocks them senseless and kills them. My grandmother used to tell me that the magnolia feeds on them. It's a hunter tree which kills living things and sucks their dead bodies dry... watch your step, Señor."

The flashlight's beam pointed down.

Miguel recoiled. The tree's roots were littered with the dead bodies of hundreds of mice, spiders, little birds and forest roaches. Even as they'd died, they had stubbornly kept crawling toward the deadly tree, lured by the sweet aroma of its beautiful but poisonous blossoms.

"So you see," Enrique said, nonplussed by his reaction. "But if you plant them in the city, they lose their deadly properties and the scent gets much weaker. If you pardon me, Señor, planting a Magnolia Amazonica on Plaza Mayor is the same as having a cat's balls cut off. He'll still look like a cat but he won't be the same if you know what I mean. But there's something else too, something bigger than that..."

The janitor fell silent, then continued, "Why did none of you, big city bosses, notice this little detail that all of the dolls had in common? The question is pretty self-explanatory, really. You're a foreigner, Señor, and as for all the others, they're not interested in Indian culture. I'm only a small man who officially believes in our Lord and Savior Jesus Christ and his Holy Virgin Mother Mary. But before Catholic priests ever set foot in this land, we used to have our own name — the Quechua — and our own country, Tawantinsuyu. Then the white gods came astride their terrible horses and razed our country to the ground..."

Miguel struggled to suppress impatience. And anger.

To come all the way up here, first in the car and then in a cart, only to receive a quick botanical excursion followed by a lecture on the ancient Peruvian Inca Empire? That wasn't worth it to say the least.

He knew everything about the predatory Magnolia Amazonica, anyway. And as for the Inca Empire, he could lecture anyone on it himself, thank you very much. From what he remembered, Tawantinsuyu had been founded in the 12th century: the most powerful empire in South America which had stretched from Chile to

ZOTOV

Columbia, rivaling only the Aztec Tenochtitlan and richer that all the European countries combined. In 1532, the Spanish conquistador Francisco Pizarro had conquered it without even breaking a sweat. During the Battle of Cajamarca, he'd defeated the Incan army, killing seven thousand Indian warriors with only two hundred of his own men and without a single casualty.

Impossible, you say? Please. The Spanish had four cannons and twelve harquebuses. The sight of all the smoke and fire, the sounds of gunshots and the bodies of fellow Quechua warriors torn to pieces by the volleys must have wreaked havoc among the Indians. The final attack of armor-clad knights on horses (which the Incas believed to be submarine monsters) had sealed the Indians' defeat.

Two hundred men bringing a country of ten million population to its knees — you wouldn't think it was possible, would you? Apparently, it was. The Incan Emperor Atahualpa had surrendered, promising Pizarro to fill one of his three prison rooms with gold and the two other ones with silver. The Indians then spent three months collecting the gold all over the country and another month melting it into ingots. The total weight of gold came to just under six tons.

But the moment Pizarro had received the ransom, he loaded it onto ships and sent them back to Seville and Santo Domingo. The Spanish king was to receive one-fifth of the booty as some primitive form of profit tax. Those unheard-of masses of gold had triggered an incredible inflation all over Europe.

Pizarro hadn't kept his word, after all. Emperor Atahualpa was accused of plotting a conspiracy and sentenced to be burned at the stake. In a travesty of clemency, Pizarro then had the sentence changed to death by garrote. That was more or less what Miguel could remember about the whole thing.

"Thank you, Enrique," he said, tactfully suppressing a sigh. "I think I've heard about the Incas before. Let's cut the history lesson, okay? You'd better tell me about this tree here. How can it possibly have anything to do with the Artist?"

The janitor smiled and shook his head. "All in due time, Señor," he reached into his pocket for a pack of cigarettes and offered it to Miguel.

Miguel nodded, knowing that the Indian might view his refusal as an insult.

He struck a match. Both of them lit up. The tobacco smoke took the edge off the sickly magnolia smell.

The moon had risen. The tree looked even more sinister in its light; gnarly and Grimm-Brothers grotesque, it seemed to reach out its dry contorting branches toward the two men who stood there watching it.

Miguel choked on the smoke and burst into coughing.

"Everyone knows about Emperor Atahualpa,"

ZOTOV

Enrique said. "And about the roomful a gold he had ready for the treacherous Spaniards. What few seem to remember is that Atahualpa wasn't the lawful ruler of Tawantinsuyu. The previous Emperor, Huayna Capac, had justly divided his kingdom between his two sons, leaving the South and the city of Cusco to Huáscar and the North with Cajamarca to Atahualpa. But Atahualpa had other ideas. He wanted to become the sole ruler of the Incan land. He started a bloody war with Huáscar which lasted three years. Neither of them could prevail — until at a certain point the power balance changed drastically. Huáscar's army literally disappeared overnight, vanishing into thin air. The victorious Atahualpa entered the capital city and had his brother executed in the most horrific way. Still, his triumph didn't last. Only a year later, he himself was killed by the Spanish. Pizarro had a new king enthroned: the teenage Manco Inca Yupanqui. He must have thought the young emperor to be a perfect puppet ruler for the Spanish crown who'd be obeying Pizarro's every command sending him as much gold as said crown required. Pizarro hadn't dared to run for Emperor himself — he only had two hundred men, don't forget, against the countless Incan thousands. Indeed, the new monarch started off by following his orders until two years later when the invaders discovered he was an excellent actor who'd only pretended to have taken their side. In command of a hundred thousand-strong army, Manco raised a rebellion against the Spanish even though, according to the conquistadors themselves, there hadn't been even five hundred well-armed warriors in the whole of Tawantinsuyu. They besieged the invaders in Cusco and set the ancient Incan capital city on fire until the Spanish were surrounded in the main square."

The Indian paused, frowning, then continued,

"According to Pizarro, all those archers and swordsmen who'd joined Manco's army didn't speak any language at all. They were always silent, their lips tightly pressed together. It was these mysterious warriors who'd wiped out Pizarro's army at Ollantaytambo and forced his Indian allies to flee the battlefield. All hope seemed to have been lost for the Spanish: they were seven hundred against a hundred thousand. But just at that moment, luck swapped sides again. A miracle had happened: soon after the Ollantaytambo defeat, a Spanish squad left Cusco under the cover of the night and launched a surprise attack on Manco... and they won. Manco escaped into the mountains. All eyewitnesses seem to be adamant that each of the five hundred Spanish knights which had left Cusco that night had somehow transformed into ten men, turning the small squad into a host of invincible ghosts. Funnily enough, soon Pizarro's fabled luck changed again as his army was defeated by another conquistador Diego de Almagro who'd easily taken the weakened city. Don't you think it's amazing?

ZOTOV

Starting with Atahualpa himself, there's a distinct pattern we can follow when a certain person enjoys a period of the most amazing luck for no reason whatsoever. It may last for a year or a few months — or a few days even — until finally Lady Luck turns her backside on her protégé forcing him to fall from a great height. Interestingly, Diego de Almagro didn't escape this destiny, either, as he was beheaded in Cusco. And three years later, Francisco Pizarro himself was assassinated in the course of a coup d'état. History had gone a full circle."

A heavy pain pierced Miguel's head.

The blurred spot of the moon quivered in his eyes. His temples pounded. His tongue rasped his dry mouth. His saliva tasted thick and honey sweet.

Miguel dropped his cigarette in the grass and rubbed his eyes. "You're not what you say you are," he forced out. "Who are you? A janitor wouldn't know the words to tell the history of Peru the way you just did! And what happened to your Quechua accent? You speak Spanish like a university professor!"

Enrique smiled again: not a grin but rather the predatory, fang-baring scowl of a wolf watching his prey. He pressed down on Miguel's shoulder.

Miguel slumped obediently onto the heaped-up animal bodies by the tree roots.

The cigarettes. The janitor must have laced them with something.

"You're right, Señor," Enrique said softly. "I

have another life which most people don't see. But please allow me to finish. You won't regret it, I assure you."

Miguel chuckled. "Do I have a choice, Mister Professor Cleaner? Can I have another one of those cigarettes, please? It's not as if I have anything to lose."

"I want the Artist found," Enrique said. "It's in our mutual interests, trust me. Please accept my sincere apologies for the long story but without it, you wouldn't have been able to grasp the essence of it. These days, all the Quechua are good Catholics and obedient children of our Mother the Roman Church. But in times of old, the Incas used to have so many gods we couldn't even remember them all. Whenever the Tawantinsuyu Empire conquered other nations, it added their gods to the existing pantheon. Our head god Viracocha married Mama Cocha, the ocean goddess, who bore two glorious children: Inti the Sun and Mama Killa the Moon. Later, we rather stupidly sacrificed the first white men to Viracocha but at the time, we used to worship him just as we worshipped his children and also the stars which used to protect our livestock and forest game. Our emperors were officially considered the sons of Inti and Mama Killa and had the mixed blood of the Sun and the Moon running in their veins. We worshipped Illapa, the great god of thunder and lightning, and offered flower garlands to Chasca Coyllur, the patron goddess of young maidens. We danced by the altars of the magnificent Huanacauri, the god of the rainbow — the rainbow which you can still see on the Incan flag — and offered our respects to the stern Paricia, the god of floods. The coca leaves which I can often see you chew in your office are the body of Kuka Mama, the goddess of health, while cooked maize is the symbol of Mama Sara, the goddess of corn. Gods didn't differ much from humans: they too were constantly fighting. That's how Viracocha had become their leader, by defeating a host of smaller deities in a cruel and bloody war."

He paused. "When the first Spanish missionaries had arrived, they were stunned by the similarities of our legends with the traditional Catholic story, so they used them to illustrate their point when converting entire tribes wholesale. Look, they'd say, Illapa is none other than the fiery Prophet Elijah; the floods sent by Paricia are part of the Deluge and Viracocha is our Lord and Savior... you have the same gods, they'd say, only that their names are different! You won't be renouncing your old faith by converting to Christianity! What difference does it make to you, they'd say, whether you put a stone statue or a crucifix over your altars? White people's gods are exactly the same as your own. Well, we allowed them to sweet-talk us into it... and we forgot our own past."

As he spoke, Miguel threw his head back, staring into the starry sky.

He offered his face to the light of Chuqui

Chinchay, the patron star of jaguars which pointed its predatory rays at Urcuchillay, the star of llamas and sheep. Nearby, the brilliant Machacuay shone through the misty veil: the patron star of snakes.

"You're an Incan priest," Miguel finally mumbled through the fog filling his head.

Enrique shrugged. "You could say so, I suppose. My father was the tribe priest which is a hereditary position with the Quechua. I studied law in Spain — but about the time I graduated, my father had gone missing. I had to go back home to become the Faith Keeper. But who would hire a lawyer who spends his spare time studying ancient lore and performing pagan rituals? A couple of centuries ago, they'd have had me burned at the stake. I found it easier to get myself a menial job. An illiterate janitor won't attract any unwanted interest. My father used to lord over this part of the world but even he spent his mornings selling lake fish at the market to cover up for his real activities. Even now, a good hundred years after the Holy Inquisition had the last man burned at the stake in Mexico, there'll be plenty of people only too happy to torch my house and the whole village. I don't like it. I wear my crucifix hung with ancient Quechuan charms; I pray to the Lord and perform our old rituals — all because I'd rather live in peace with Jesus and Mary without offending our old gods. I think they can live very happily together."

"My... sympathies..." Miguel struggled to get his tongue around the word. "But now... tell me...

what the hell... does this tree... have to do with..."

The priest laughed good-naturedly. "And you really think you would have understood it without this brief introduction to our history? I haven't finished yet. My people used to worship lots of things: mountains and cliffs, caves and even big rocks, believing them to be sacred pieces that had once broken off the sky. We called them *huaca*. There're over three hundred of them in the vicinity of Cusco alone, and plenty in Lima as well."

He paused. "The Artist's first victim was found on a *huaca* hill that had been the object of worship long before Pizarro founded La Ciudad de Los Reyes. It's topped with a magnolia tree which still emits a weak albeit deadly scent. According to Incan mythology, this was one of the first of the many passages leading to the dark dungeons of Uku Pacha, the world of the dead and the unborn. Apart from the tree, the area was completely deforested already in the 18th century; and now that the hill lies at the center of a giant city, the magnolia tree has lost almost all its power. But in days of old, priests from all over Tawantinsuyu used to come here to offer precious gifts to the tree."

Gradually Miguel's head began to clear. "So that was a... *sacrifice*?"

Enrique took a deep tug on his cigarette and nodded rather nonchalantly. "Of course. I'm surprised the police didn't realize it. They immediately jumped to the conclusion this was a serial killer job. Having said that... it could be both. It could be some sick attention seeker who just happened to be a follower of the cult so ancient that even the Incas themselves feared it, not to even mention the conquistadors who had all the passages to Uku Pacha blocked with earth and rocks."

The priest gently supported Miguel, helping him to his feet. "Follow me. I need to show you something. Just please, don't make any noise whatever you see, no matter how surprised you are. I'll explain to you later."

They walked past the adobe huts of the Indians until they came to a larger building. Tar torches burned bright by the entrance, spitting cascades of sparks.

Miguel staggered as he bent under the low entrance, still weak from the strange herb his cigarettes had been laced with. He entered a large hall and froze.

A totem pole towered at the center, topped with a carved head of some beast. All around it, strapped to the pole, girls clad in white hung listlessly in their tethers. Their cheeks were painted crimson; their long hair touched the floor as their heads bobbed from side to side. Their white robes were covered with dark spots.

A large bowl stood at the foot of the totem, filled almost to the brim with blood.

"You fucking bastard!" Miguel swung round, closing his hands around Enrique's throat.

ZOTOV

The old Indian didn't resist. Miguel sensed the muzzle of his own gun being pressed against his stomach. The old bastard must have pulled it out of the holster while Miguel had been sitting barely conscious by the tree.

"What did I say?" the priest's voice sounded bored. "I'll explain to you later."

Dozens of shadows slid from the walls toward Miguel.

Part Two

Cine Patriotero

There has been much killing
There will be much more
The medicine man is dancing
He's calling us to war
Hatchets sing with pride
Let the white men die

Manowar, *Spirit Horse of Cherokee*

CHAPTER ONE

The Worse World

Somewhere in the dark void of uncertainty

THE SCREEN is dark. All the audience can hear is a wheezing breath, followed by gasping and coughing.

Gradually the picture comes into focus, revealing a bird's view panorama of a city. This time the camerawork is excellent — not an amateur job but professional digital footage taken from several angles. The picture gains depth and color, revealing a skyline dotted with billowing plumes of smoke.

The camera descends onto a small forest glade nearby and focuses on a man lying in a fetal position on the grass. His eyelids begin to twitch. A few women in the audience gasp and dissolve into sobbing.

...OLEG CAME ROUND. Warily he opened one eye, afraid of what he might see. A twig topped with a bright yellow blossom swayed in front of his face.

ZOTOV

He turned round. Another twig prickled his cheek. Grass. Dry grass.

He shook his head. He seemed to be lying in a wilting meadow. Judging by the yellowed grass and the leaden sky pregnant with cold rain, it must have been sometime in the fall.

The field stretched all the way to the horizon, dotted with brownish haystacks. Behind him rose a forest of fir trees and what looked like silver birches, judging by their white trunks.

Haystacks. They were probably meant for livestock — cows? If they had cows here, it meant they had beef, too, and most definitely milk.

He'd escaped the porn world, after all. He'd made it.

Oleg squeezed his eyes shut, remembering what had happened in Great Mother's hut. It was dark when Joan and he had entered it. Which made sense: why would a blind woman need light?

The witch had then asked if they'd brought the remaining artifacts. Hearing their affirmative, she checked the items by feeling them and bringing them to her nose. Finally, her lips parted in a smirk. She warned them once again that she couldn't guarantee the result, then began preparing for the ritual.

The actual ceremony had lasted but a few minutes. The old hag produced a python from a wooden box. That came as no surprise as snakes had been widely used in the porn industry ever since Cicciolina who'd employed them already in the 1980s for rather unorthodox purposes (no pythons had been harmed in the making of her films).

With an accuracy remarkable in a blind person, the old woman cut the python's head off and drained the blood into a bowl. She ground the nun's bone in a mortar and added it to the blood, following it with the ashes of Oleg's unlucky predecessor. Her every movement confident and precise, she stirred the mixture, then transferred it to a brass brazier at the center of the room. Moving in small cautious steps, she headed out of the room, warning them she was about to fetch the Lingam of Creation.

That was the last thing he could remember relatively well. Had he glimpsed a green glow of someone's eyes in the corner? There was a figure — a shadow which stepped away from the wall. He could still sense the icy touch of the creature's hand in his own. A blinding flash of blue light, followed by darkness.

Oleg struggled to his feet.

He had to find people. Anyone. He had to find out where he was.

A deep humming noise vibrated through the air. Oleg looked up and froze.

Nine airplanes flew low in combat formation, the undersides of their oblong wings sporting black crosses encircled in white.

Oleg followed them open-mouthed. A sharp pain pierced his head as he began to realize the terrible truth.

Please, Lord, anything but this, he prayed, frozen in terror. You can't do this to me... to us.

Still, God seemed to have had other plans for Oleg that day.

A large group of people walked out of the forest: at least a hundred men of all ages from twenty to forty. Clad in helmets and field gray uniforms, they moved in lockstep, their polished boots splattering the mud.

Their tunic sleeves were rolled up, their hands clutching black machine guns with long clips. They laughed, talking to each other in the brusque language which Oleg had learned to recognize since childhood. He made out the familiar words and phrases: *Achtung!* and *Noch einmal*, with the addition of a brief *Ja!*

Mesmerized, Oleg stared at the approaching soldiers. He wanted to scream but predictably, his throat only produced a weak wheezy sound.

The uniforms were Wehrmacht. The soldiers were German.

Where the hell was he now?

The sound of a hammer being cocked came from behind his back.

Oleg closed his eyes. In moments like these, you were probably supposed to say a prayer but all he could remember was the sweet smell of a freshly-baked Easter bread.

"Who the fuck are you?" a voice behind him demanded in Russian. "Hands up!"

Russians. Dammit. This was even worse. They were probably some kind of local collaborator police or SS troops.

Obediently Oleg put his hands in the air.

A gun butt was poked at his neck. "Turn round."

Oleg obeyed. A tall soldier in a faded pre-1943 Soviet uniform stood in front of him, pointing the bayonet of his battered 19th-century rifle at his chest. He was freckled and jug-eared, blond hair peeking from his side cap.

"Jerry?" the soldier asked.

"Do I look like one?" Oleg snarled. "Can't you see I'm Russian?"

"Not the way you're dressed, no," the man replied in amazement. "What's with the blue pants? They look like you dragged them through a hedge backwards. Is this a shirt? And why are there foreign words on your shoes?"

"It says, *Adidas*," Oleg explained. "It's the name of the shoemaker. He was German."

He immediately bit his tongue but the soldier beamed.

"Aha! You took them off a German, did you? Did your regiment get surrounded? Or are you wearing these duds on purpose? There's nothing wrong with stripping a dead German, just don't mention this to them commissars. You know very well that looting is strictly forbidden in the Red Army. If they find out, they'll put you against the wall first and ask questions after."

ZOTOV

A weak but important suspicion stirred in Oleg's heart. The soldier looked too *picture perfect*. Oleg seemed to have seen him many times before. The boy's freckled face looked as if he'd just left the makeup artist's room. His hair was perfectly styled, his cheeks still bearing the traces of powder...

Oh, no. It couldn't be.

The German speech sounded very close to them now.

The Wehrmacht group was almost within reach. Now Oleg could clearly see their dark shoulder boards framed with white and the silver eagles spreading their wings on the men's breast pockets.

An officer walked haughtily in front of them, pushing the grass aside with his riding crop.

"Run," Oleg whispered. "They can't see us yet."

"Why?" the soldier asked. "Who do you want to run from? What's the big danger?"

"But the Germans?"

"You mean them guys over there?"

"Of course."

"Jeez man, you've completely lost your marbles."

"You might be right," Oleg said weakly. "I think I've gone mad."

The young soldier raised his rifle and took a nonchalant aim. "It's a minute job. Piece of cake."

He pulled the trigger.

The world slowed down.

Oleg watched the slug leave the muzzle unhurriedly, spitting a tongue of fire and a cloud of smoke. At a speed of no more than a few yards an hour it headed for the Germans. After some considerable time it finally pierced the officer's head, splattering blood all over his peaked cap.

The Nazi performed a few rather funny moves, kicking his legs in the air, until finally he floated down onto the grass.

All the other Germans froze in mid-air too, moving languidly like the Bolshoi ballet dancers, then floated down to the ground, their bodies freezing in the most improbable positions. Blood squirted out of their agonizing mouths, its perfectly rounded crimson droplets flying in all directions.

This is slow motion, Oleg realized, horrified. The favorite trick of all bad war movie directors.

The show stopped.

Dead bodies heaped up where the Germans had just stood. Not a single survivor in sight. The young soldier nonchalantly ejected the still-smoking spent shell case.

"This is impossible!" Oleg croaked, losing what was left of his sanity. "You've just killed a whole company with one shot! They didn't even get the chance to see you!"

The soldier slung his rifle over his shoulder and began rolling a cigarette. "I've no idea," he said in earnest. "It's just the way it is. The Germans aren't good soldiers, as simple as that. They don't even bother to duck. They just barge right in on us, shouting their German words, and that's when we shoot them down. They're pissheads, too. Back in Stalingrad, we once spent a week in a fortified house fending off Jerries. They lost five hundred men to each of ours! I'm surprised they still have soldiers left! They sent tanks and whole SS regiments against us, you wouldn't have believed it if you hadn't seen it. And the house's commander, you know what he did? He drew our gunners' fire to himself — so that they made mincemeat of thousands of Jerries. The guy died like a hero... That's how it is here, brother."

"Wait a sec," Oleg said. "Why didn't the Jerries use their own artillery against the house?"

"Search me," the soldier replied cheerfully. "There's no rhyme nor reason to any of it. They might not even have artillery, you never know. And they're stupid like you can't even imagine. Sometimes they can't notice obvious things in combat, just like they didn't notice us right now. Don't you think it strange these dimwits ever made it to the Volga? Never mind. 'Nuff shooting the shit. Come with me to Stalingrad, I'll report you to our company commander, Comrade Soldier. Be careful with him though, he's very short-tempered. He might just have you shot, end of story."

Staggering on his rubbery legs, Oleg followed the happy soldier. He'd scratched his head raw, trying to stop the thoughts from escaping. He was shaking all over.

This was ten times worse than pornography.

He'd been transported to a war B-movie.

As the two unhurriedly approached the city, the ear-shattering sounds of explosions grew closer. The Dolby Surround systems did a good job amplifying the cacophony of machine guns and the howling of bombers zeroing in on their targets.

WHEN THE TWO are reduced to two tiny dots on the horizon, the camera returns to the clearing piled up with dead bodies.

A man walks out of the forest, clad in a plain canvas shirt and pants. He's carrying something around his shoulders — some sort of big sack or other.

When the man reaches the impromptu open-air burial, he stares at it in confusion, then gingerly lays his sack on the ground and begins to unbutton the Wehrmacht officer's collar.

The camera focuses on his hands, groomed and delicate.

CUT TO BLACK

CHAPTER TWO

The Unborn

The northern outskirts of Lima
October 21 1931

INDIANS CLAD in gray clothes (which was why Miguel hadn't noticed them earlier) dragged Miguel off Enrique and forced the detective to his knees. One of them reached for a machete which had been leaning against the totem pole but the priest motioned him to put it back.

Enrique crouched next to Miguel,

"Is it true what they say, Señor, that you come from the North? How strange. They say that the Northerners' temper is just as cold as their weather. Just like the Patagonians from Argentinian ice fields: they first offer their enemies something to eat and only then slaughter them. But you're so impulsive, just like my late wife, may she rest in peace. Thank God I relieved you of your revolver, otherwise you'd have shot first and then asked the dead bodies to show their IDs. Do approach me calmly, I beg you. This is the answer to your questions."

Without turning his head, the priest snapped a few curt words in Quechua.

The Indians let go of Miguel. He scrambled to his feet and staggered toward the sacrificial altar.

They were handmade dolls. A dozen dolls tied to the totem topped with the head of a mysterious beast.

Impulsively Miguel leaned down and pressed his forehead to a doll's face. It was as cold as ice.

Just think he'd taken them for dead bodies. They were only intricate masks made of bleached pig skin which resembled that of a human. Their Indian clothes were painted with blood — which undoubtedly had come from pigs' veins, too.

The aroma of the magnolia tree beckoned and intoxicated him. The idols' lips were so inviting.

Miguel struggled to suppress a sudden desire.

The doll stared back at him with her dead painted eyes. The unknown master's art was incredible — her gaze seemed to be following him around the room.

"People were killed for these kinds of jokes before," he said bitterly.

The priest laughed softly. "No reason to get so jumpy. Then again, I understand. Too many dead bodies this week: no wonder you misunderstood the setting. I'm sorry. So do you know the main point of the Incan religion? I personally find it quite quirky. According to our ancestors, evil has the same right to exist as does good. Don't you think it's logical? The Devil is God's creature too. Which was why both the Incas and the Aztecs wanted to make sure they were on good terms with the powers of evil just as they were with good and kindly gods. I still respect this philosophy by offering blood to the evil overlords. Granted, we don't gut people alive anymore; we just perform a symbolic recreation of the old ritual. Who said that the patron demon of caves requires a human sacrifice? A pig sounds just as good. They say that you should offer the god the best you have — so that's exactly what we're doing. A human life costs nothing these days — but you pay a lot of money for a good boar. My tribe can only afford pork on big holidays. So I really don't think the powers of darkness would so terribly mind receiving a good escalope instead of a dead virgin. I know I wouldn't."

"Why are you doing this?" Miguel asked him point blank. "You don't look like an idol worshipper."

The priest raised both hands in the air. "Oh yes, I am, Señor. I already told you I don't for one moment doubt our gods' existence. I'm sure you can have it both ways. There's a Catholic church downhill in the village; and topping the hill is the magnolia tree and its clandestine sanctuary guarded by twenty warriors. You know what the problem is with you Christians? You stick to your belief in an ethereal being which floats on the clouds and doesn't even bother to communicate with you. Only once did it send its messenger instructing you to await His second coming. Now the Incan gods, they've always lived with us. Actually, why am I telling all this to you? You can see it for yourself."

He reached into his robes and produced a fistful of seeds which he hurled into the fire.

A thick purple smoke filled the hut. Pressing his hands to his nose and mouth, Miguel hurried to the exit but was stopped by the silent guards' crossed machetes.

Resistance was pointless. Accepting his fate, he took a deep chestful of smoke.

WHEN MIGUEL OPENED his eyes, he found himself standing in the mountains next to a heap of giant black rocks. He struggled to breathe: apparently, the altitude was quite high.

Two men in medieval knights' armor staggered out from behind the nearest boulder, rattling and clattering like a string of tin cans.

Miguel shrank back but they didn't seem to notice him. They were busy dragging a dead woman by her legs. Her head bobbed on the rocks, her long hair trailing along the ground. The blood from her slit throat had poured all over her face. Her rolled white eyeballs stared out of the crimson mess.

The two knights spoke to each other in loud

voices but the Spanish they used was different from the language Miguel knew, very dated with lots of Latin words in it.

Luckily, he used to learn Latin at high school so he managed to grasp the gist of their conversation.

"You think this is the last one?"

"We'll see in a moment. Francisco said we need thirty of these pagan girls."

With a swing, they hurled the body onto a heap of corpses already piling up by an old magnolia tree which towered over a rocky drop. One of the knights climbed the mass of dead bodies and began counting the heads. He had to do it twice, then cussed through clenched lips,

"Bastard! Two more we need. You know Francisco, he'll skin us alive. Go back and fetch them."

The second Spaniard grumbled his discontent but chose not to argue.

An hour and a half later, he reappeared, dragging two sobbing Indian girls no more than fifteen years old. The first knight was waiting for him while munching on a rather juicy apple. On seeing the girls, he cheered up.

The other Spaniard threw the girls to his feet. Still busy chewing, the knight pierced a girl's throat with his sword, pulled it out and buried it in the other girl's chest. Without taking his eyes from his agonizing victims, he heaved a sigh of relief, smiled and finished off his apple.

"All done! Now let's go and report to Francisco. We've done what he told us to do: kill all Indian females."

"And rightly so," the other one replied. "Pagans don't deserve Christian clemency, not after the blood bath of Ollantaytambo. Every night I pray I wake up the next morning without a knife sticking out of my throat. What a place! Even twelve-year-old brats raise their fathers' weapons against us."

Their voices died away as they began climbing back down the narrow path.

From where Miguel stood, he could clearly see the skyline of a large ancient city encircled by a wall built with identical stone blocks. He could make out the familiar rainbow colors of the Indian flag fluttering on top of a tower and the red serrated cross against the white background – the so-called "Burgundian cross" which looked remarkably like two crossed saws – topping a neighboring spire, the flag of the Spanish army and all Spanish colonies in Latin America, Peru included. He could hear the dry crackling of rifles and the booming of cannons raising little clouds of white smoke into the air.

Oh, no. Groaning, Miguel clasped his head with both hands. This had to be a mirage – a hallucination. And still the Spaniards didn't seem to notice him as if he was watching the scenes from another dimension.

The familiar sounds of clanging steel similar to those he'd heard two hours ago awoke him from his dismay. Two more knights appeared on the path. One was older with a graying goatee typical of the era. He must have been about sixty, judging by the deep lines furrowing his gaunt face. The other was a fit young man, red-headed with no facial hair. They were leading about a dozen bound Indians, including an old man wearing a headdress of eagle feathers.

On seeing the dead girls, the Indians stopped in their tracks, exchanging the exclamations of terror. Cussing, the two conquistadors used their swords to push them toward the magnolia tree.

"Are you sure that's what Manco did?" the older Spaniard asked the priest, casting wary glances around to make sure no one else was watching.

Staggering, the old Indian nodded. "Si, Señor."

"Very well," the knight grumbled. "In that case, go ahead and do what you promised. Otherwise I swear by our Savior's blood I'm gonna disembowel your entire family in front of you and make you eat their guts so that's the last thing they see in this life."

The younger conquistador was shaking. "Francisco, in the Lord's name, don't do this! Do you really want to stoop to these pagans' level? We've come to bring Christ's word to them! We're here to bless the pagan lands with the holy cross, not to appease the devil! Remember what the preacher said? Satan's honey is sweet but those who eat it are left with a bitter aftertaste."

"Shut up, Juan!" the old knight spat a dark blob of saliva at the rocks. "Jesus can't help us here. How do you think this traitor Manco got hold of a hundred thousand finest soldiers overnight? Whoever had conjured them up for him, his name wasn't Jesus, trust me! You and I, our days are numbered. There's no end to more pagans coming. Very soon they'll decorate their filthy altars with Castilian flesh! If only the Devil agrees to help us, I'm gonna strike a deal with him. Any sin can be absolved, you know that, don't you? So let's get on with it, brother. We've got a whole lot of Indian bitches to gut. Mercy will have to wait till better times."

A *brother*? But of course. The older knight must have been Francisco, Pizarro's bastard son. His mother had been a young orphaned servant in a convent when the future conquistador general had seduced her, earning Francisco the moniker of El Ropero – the "housekeeper's son". And the younger knight must have been Juan, Pizarro's illegitimate son from another servant girl Maria Alonso. The brothers' lowly status was often ridiculed at court which must have prompted the two to enroll in their father's overseas conquest.

Miguel watched the two knights with bated breath as they began ripping through the dead girls' bellies (the older one moaning about his armor being too heavy and awkward for the job). They seemed quite accustomed to the gruesome task — even the young one — and worked with all

ZOTOV

the energy and knack of seasoned butchers.

From the many accounts of the Peru invasion, Miguel remembered reading about the conquistadors dismembering Indian bodies and feeding them to their dogs. According to the chroniclers, the Spanish often had Indians brought along on their journeys as "canned food" for their dogs.

How did that 16th century letter go? "Please lend me a quarter of your pagan to feed my dogs, and I'll repay you later..."

All covered in blood from the gory task, Francisco finally nodded to the old Indian priest,

"Now it's your turn. You should work as fast as you possibly can."

The Indians set to work. For the following four hours, they kept building dolls under the old priest's guidance.

Finally Miguel could get a glimpse of what the Artist's work might have been like, albeit not as meticulous. The Indians stuffed the bodies with the sickly-smelling herbs, filled their bellies with magnolia petals, then crudely sewed them up.

There were two things that puzzled Miguel, though. Firstly, none of the victims had been dismembered. And secondly, their murderers hadn't painted their faces red neither had they collected their blood to water the tree roots with. Blood flowed freely at the Indians' feet and they didn't even seem to bother.

Having completed the blood-curdling ritual,

the Indians stood around the tree in some sick parody of a sacred ring dance. They hung their heads as if peering at something by their feet and started chanting a gloomy song in Quechua. Every time they completed the chorus, they stomped one bare foot, raising cascades of blood in the air.

It was completely dark now, the torches in the two knights' hands casting an uneven glow on the sacrificial scene. The older one was as cool as a cucumber. The younger one looked jittery even though you could see that it wasn't the fact of the mass murder that bothered him but the realization of his own sin and devil-worshipping.

The singing stopped.

The Indians broke their circle and walked over to the cliff's edge – all of them but the priest, that is. They closed their eyes and sang glory to Uku Pacha, asking it to accept them.

Then they jumped down.

The old priest didn't move. His eyes shut, he continued chanting his blood-curdling song.

Francisco didn't bother to acknowledge the Indians' death. Juan, however, made the sign of the cross.

"I have a bad feeling about this," he began.

"Shut up," Francisco interrupted him again. "We've got nowhere to expect help from. This godless dog has told me that Manco has sacrificed three hundred girls already. Well, I'm gonna kill five hundred in just one week! Who do you think their pagan god will listen to and obey? You and I, we're both illegitimate bastards. Our mothers were washerwomen for noble folk. Where would we have been now, had we not been smart enough to hitch a ride on fortune's coattails? You and I, we both had to claw for our titles and riches. You shouldn't forget there're only seven hundred of us here! The pagans have already recovered from the initial shock. Now they know we're not gods from above. They know we can be killed. No more of that "Viracocha's divine sons" shit. If you can't handle it, just grin and bear it like I do."

The old knight gave the priest a shove. The Indian opened his eyes.

"Do you think that my gifts to spirits are generous enough?" Francisco asked.

"Well enough," the Indian replied, painstakingly enunciating the Spanish words. "Those who descend to Uku Pacha without gifts, never come back. They get killed by the toxic vapors. But one who is generous will earn the honor of the underground gods' attention. It's just that... are you sure you want to go there, beardy? Manco the great Inca had spent but three hours in Uku Pacha but once he re-emerged, he wasn't human anymore. Because the underground world does change people, and even the worst of our nightmares cannot describe the extent of this change. The Unborn Ones might have granted Manco an army of ghosts but do you have any idea what he was forced to offer them in exchange? The passages between the worlds of Uku Pacha and Kay

Pacha are unlocked and unguarded. In order to enter, all you need to do is offer a bloody sacrifice. Still, a great many people who'd lost their wealth and power chose to die in poverty rather than disturb the Unborn Ones. Manco had lost his mind. He must have thought that if Viracocha hadn't helped him, he had to beg the underground monsters for help. But you're just as stupid as Manco was, beardy! You're making a bad mistake which will cost you your life. Manco never spoke about the creatures he'd encountered in the depths of Uku Pacha. You have any idea who you're up against?"

Juan's hand shook as he made a frenetic sign of the cross.

Francisco turned pale. "I don't care if it's Satan himself," he wheezed. "I-"

The old priest chuckled. "Satan! You really think he's the worst that can happen to you? The kinds of creatures that inhabit Uku Pacha have the Devil himself serve them hand and foot; he fetches their breakfast of sweet potatoes and fills their pipes with the best tobacco. Those men who sought the company of the dead returned complete strangers; some of them perished never to be heard from again. This isn't a scary bedtime story that kids seem to love so much, beardy. Uku Pacha lures people in. There're certain places – like caves, brooks, crevices and even deep wells specially dug for this purpose; to enter them, all you need to do is offer a sacrifice. Don't you feel scared when you see the Great Inca change whenever he commands his ghostly army? His eyes don't even have pupils, so flooded are they with gloom. I heard him howl at night – the sound makes the blood freeze in your veins. I know. Please don't do this."

Predictably, Juan didn't look happy at the news. "Don't you remember, Francisco, how we went down what we thought was a silver mine?" his voice broke. "There was nothing inside but heaps and heaps of human bones. The walls there were furrowed with nail marks from the still-alive victims who must have been trying to climb back up. And you want us to kiss Lucifer's ass? But that would make us no different from these pagans!"

A steel blade whooshed through the air.

The old priest's severed head rolled over the rocky ground. His body slumped, gushing blood.

Francisco cussed, lowering his sword. He used his free hand to give Juan a hearty smack across the head.

The magnolia branches lit up, illuminated by the fanciful glow of thousands of lightning bugs.

"I'm going down, you idiot," Francisco said. "With or without you."

"Go ahead," the young man said. "I'll wait for you here until next sunrise. If you don't come out, I'll go back to my men. The battle at Cusco is in full swing. They're desperate for more soldiers."

The old knight heaved a sigh and cussed heartily but good-naturedly, calling his young brother every name under the sun. Then he swung round and began his descent down the crevice gaping by the magnolia's roots.

From that point, Miguel lost any sense of time. He watched Juan wedge his sword between the rocks hilt up and pray passionately. After a while, the young man fell asleep. When he awoke, he unwrapped a piece of cooked pork and asked the Lord to bless his food, then ate it.

Isn't it shocking, Miguel thought (by then, he'd already gotten used to the fact that he'd somehow traveled four hundred years back in time without any need for either food or drink). *Just think that these deeply religious, noble people used to slaughter Indians like cattle in their thousands without flinching. Having said that, didn't the Spanish think that pagans didn't have souls? At least not until they began converting them to Christianity.*

As he so thought, Juan made the umpteenth sign of the cross and began chanting psalms, casting forlorn glances down the crevice.

Finally, a loud rattling noise came from below: the sound of steel grating against rock.

Francisco reappeared instantly as if he'd been hiding behind a boulder wishing to scare his young brother with a "Boo!"

Juan shrank back. Francisco stepped toward him into the bright torchlight.

His face was different now. He was still Pizarro's eldest son – but not quite. He looked at least ten years younger. The gray in his hair had disappeared. Gone were the deep lines that used to furrow his face. His eyes had a wolfish glint. Overall, his entire bearing was that of a beast rather than a human.

He smiled, baring two rows of unnaturally long, large teeth. Juan shrank back further. The man who'd re-emerged from the fissure was not the same as the one who'd entered it a few hours ago.

"Thank God you're alive!" Juan exclaimed. "Tell me! Did you see the Unborn Ones?"

"Yes, Francisco replied. His voice too was different. "I didn't like them though so I didn't enter into any deals with them. I made an agreement with someone else. It's gonna be fine now, brother. Everything's gonna be all right. We'll keep Cusco and defeat the pagans. The victory will be ours. I have their word on that. A great miracle indeed!"

Juan peered anxiously into Francisco's face. "Who did you speak with?"

The beast who used to be his brother bared his teeth in an icy grin. "Why should you care? The main thing I was told is that our offerings aren't enough. They want one more sacrifice and they want it now. I'm sorry, brother."

He charged at Juan, knocking the young man off his feet. The two knights rolled down the slope.

Miguel couldn't see much in the dark but he could hear the sounds of fighting. He glimpsed a hand picking up a rock. A thumping sound. Someone wheezed. Another thump. Silence.

The darkness enveloping Miguel rippled, falling apart into wisps of purple haze. The fortress on top of the mountain began to dissipate. The clouds dropped from the sky toward the ground.

CHOKING AND GASPING, Miguel convulsed on the hut floor in a bout of coughing. At first he thought he might spit his lungs out as new spasms flooded over him the moment the previous one subsided.

The Indian behind him closed his fingers around his neck and forced a clay mug to his lips, full of obnoxious-looking murky liquid. Miguel took a desperate gulp. Strangely enough, he felt better. Back in his days as an exemplary Russian officer, he used to drink much worse. Hell, he used to get drunk on stuff which could make a grown bull faint from the smell alone. Still, this swill which tasted of swamp weeds, frog slime and snake guts was more overpowering than even denatured alcohol[3].

"Is Señor Capitan sufficiently impressed?" Enrique asked calmly.

"Not really," Miguel replied, mimicking the Indian's composure. "It's not as if I saw something new to me. You threw a handful of seeds into the fire – probably something like our nightshade or opium maybe whose smoke can trigger powerful

---

[3] Denatured alcohol: a potentially lethal low-quality spirit intended for industrial use only, which has poisonous, bad-tasting, foul-smelling or nauseating additives to discourage recreational consumption.

hallucinations. After that, you just told me a lot of fairy stories while I was watching them unfold in my imagination. Have you ever been to the motion pictures? This plot device is actually very common in films. One person urges another not to do something stupid – like, *please, just don't go there, please!* — but the other one does it anyway, then returns looking a bit funny. He might even have fangs like Bela Lugosi's Dracula. Have you seen Frankenstein? It was in the theaters just a few days ago. Boris Karloff is one hell of an actor."

"No. I didn't get the chance."

"That's what I thought. All I want to say is that I got your message loud and clear, Enrique. If one character disobeys another and enters an underground cave in order to perform a bloody ritual, chances are he might return bringing something stronger than a bucket of popcorn. Thanks for the guided tour, anyway. I need to get back to the station. Oh, and a couple more questions. Why didn't the conquistadors make dolls in order to appease the unborn, the way the Artist does? And what prompts him to soak the entire scene with blood, especially the magnolia roots?"

Without saying a word, Enrique laid his hands on Miguel's shoulders and led him out of the building. Outside, a cart pulled by four horses awaited them, driven by a gloomy-faced, mustachioed Indian.

"This is my nephew," Enrique said. "He'll take you back to your car, Señor. As for your questions, let me just tell you that after Francisco and all of his brothers had been murdered and his arch rival Don Almagro beheaded, the Viceroy of Peru Pedro de la Gasca had all the wells, caves and crevices filled in, destroying all the passages between Kay Pacha, the world of the living, and Uku Pacha, the world of the dead and the unborn. De la Gasca was a priest, after all, who thought that both the Incan emperors and his own fellow conquistadors used those passages to gain access to Hell in order to sell their souls to the Devil. That was hundreds of years ago. Since then, all the rocks and earth have merged together, blocking the passages completely. There's no way the Artist can get to Uku Pacha the way the ancient Incas did. It's impossible. So he tries to think of more intricate sacrificial rituals."

Enrique paused, remembering. "According to the legend, the first Incan emperor Manco Cápac, the son of the God Viracocha, had arrived from the world of the dead by the foothill of Tampu Tocco, "the tawa of many windows". But he didn't have enough servants, so he decided to summon an important official from the world of the dead. According to the Spanish chronicler Pedro Sarmiento de Gamboa, Manco Cápac had a great many noble maidens killed all over Tawantinsuyu and had four dolls made out of their body parts. And for their bait to be even more attractive, they soaked the earth in the girls' blood. Now you have all the answers, I hope. Good night, Señor. See you in the office."

Miguel fell asleep almost as soon as the rattling cart left the Indian settlement. Then a perfectly clear thought pierced his drowsy brain:

The Artist hadn't been trying to get to Uku Pacha. That wasn't why he'd performed his sacrificial rituals.

He was trying to summon someone to our world.

But even this discovery failed to keep him awake.

CHAPTER THREE

Popcorn Wars

The war-ravaged ruins of a city which
looks suspiciously like Stalingrad

THE MOVIE SCREEN shows a crude underground bunker – basically, a dugout. The camera focuses on the weak glint of a candle. The cameraman indulges himself by slowly zooming in on the flame to reveal its many layers: blue one moment, bright yellow the next.

A whistling noise comes from above, followed by a heavy thud. Earth showers from the dugout's ceiling. A soldier picks up a sheet of lined paper from a makeshift desk and shakes it over the floor, then blows on it to clean away the dirt. That done, he licks his ink pencil and bends over his writing, trying to make out the lines in the weak light. The camera moves behind him, showing the back of his close-cropped head and the faded shirt stretched tight between his shoulder blades.

A gramophone is playing Glenn Miller. The

ZOTOV

soldier presses hard on the pencil, covering the paper in neat rounded handwriting.

WHY? Why did it have to be me? Just my luck, isn't it? I can't sleep at all at night, wondering if I should have stayed in the world of porn instead. At least there I knew how to survive. It may have taken me six months but in the end I was quite at home there. If it ain't broke, don't fix it, or so they say. Why did I have to escape? Didn't the Great Mother warn me in her ancient wisdom that I could check out any time I liked but I might never leave? And I, the model Muscovite idiot that I am, believed Moscow to be the only possible end destination! I really thought she'd beam me back up where I belonged.

Yeah right. So instead of going back to the real world, I found myself in another one of those sick movie places. Only this time it's the world of bad war movies. Dear Lord, why? What have I done to deserve this?

Because war B-movies are worse than any amount of porn, amateur included.

Before, I didn't give a damn about all that bullshit they were shooting. All those red-carpet Oscar-winning big shots — they might just as well have lived on planet Mars while I was perfectly happy watching my bit of porn in the comfort of my lounge. What is porn, anyway? It's basically sterilized love. They dutifully document all the technicalities which make it look rather like the workings of a factory tool complete with piston, lubrication and lots of shiny little parts. Forget love: this isn't about passion even. Actually, passion is a feeling in its own right which can be more powerful than love; it can ignite and incinerate you before you even know it.

But that's irrelevant. Our modern war movies are pure unadulterated porn: a lot of emotionless technicalities and pretty pictures devoid of soul. That's what I call them: popcorn wars. I'm not surprised at Stalingrad*'s 12+ rating[4]! It's not a movie but a fast-food kid's meal where a war is served as an airbrushed magazine cover. All those sweet girl soldiers in pristine fatigues, with their cute upturned noses, freckled cheeks and elaborate hairdos (of course they have hot irons in the trenches), running to and fro with snow-white bandages tending to the soldiers' wounds while evoking the most platonic feelings in them. They're constantly either singing or crying, then dying dramatically at the climax of their Great Love for a bigger effect.*

The Germans just love killing these pretty daydreaming chicks in war movies these days. I met one such girl last night. I barely had time to say hello when she was already dead as a doornail, sporting a sniper's bullet through her heart.

Mind you, these movie girls just can't shut up.

---

[4] *Stalingrad*: a 2013 Russian war film directed by Fedor Bondarchuk which received a lot of negative reviews for its "airbrushed" portrayal of the war.

ZOTOV

They absolutely have to say something even after a
dumdum bullet crashes through their forehead.
They'll profess their love to you, lament their
untimely demise, then tilt their pretty little heads to
one side and freeze with their eyes staring into
space. My girl took my hand and uttered "Farewell,
my love" before finally kicking the bucket.

Jesus H. Christ! How do they manage to film
such a lot of bullshit?

Some directors like it pretty while others prefer
their war graphic. Filthy crazed characters sitting up
to their ears in their own shit – I've seen my fair
share of them here too. Soldiers who attack enemy
positions without any ammo, apparently hoping to
club Germans to death with their rifles or even spade
handles, then die in their droves instead.

And talking about Germans! All they do is
yawn, listen to classical music, file their nails, shave
and generally lead a very languid lifestyle which
makes you wonder how this bunch of wannabe drag
queens could once have been considered the best
army in Europe.

Makes you wonder, really. In the long-gone
days of the USSR and the iron curtain, Russian film
directors had somehow managed to produce brilliant
work in spite of their measly budgets and
Communist pressure. But the moment the USSR had
collapsed and those same directors were finally
freed of all their constraints, financial as well as
ideological, their respective talents suddenly turned
sour. Apparently, if you give a creative artist enough

180

freedom and money, all you get back is a pile of crap. Don't ask me why. It's just the way it works. Some of them tried to film their own "vision" of the war which was pure BS of course because they have no idea what a war was like. Others tried to please the mass audience which resulted in airbrushed anachronistic drivel for preteens.

Also, this place here seems to be all about Stalin. His images and statues are everywhere. There're songs and even oaths praising his name. From what I remember, the Soviet-era war films generally never mentioned the guy at all. And here his portraits are even in the latrines! Once Nikita Mikhalkov had landed an Oscar for his Burnt By The Sun[5], *everybody and their auntie jumped on the bandwagon and plastered their movies with Uncle Joe's pockmarked face.*

But do you know what really drives me crazy here? It's all these people looking alike. And you know why? Because they're all played by a handful of actors who feel obliged to grace every movie and TV soap in existence with their presence. That's not the way to do it, surely? If ever I manage to escape this nightmare, I'm gonna find them, and this is what I'm gonna tell them: "Give it a break, man! No one's gonna sue you if you say no to an occasional script!"

---

[5] *Burnt By The Sun* (1995) – "A moving and poignant story set against the corrupt politics of the Stalinist era" (IMDB)

ZOTOV

Another explosion shakes the dugout, triggering more dirt drifting to the ground. The soldier moves his lips, mouthing something.

Ah, there's one more thing I find funny here, apart from all the squeaky clean girl soldiers who die the moment they meet you. No one cusses here. Whether it's a direct hit or an open wound, the only thing you hear is "damn!" or maybe "shit!" if you're lucky. You can hear more cussing in my office during lunch break. Also, they're constantly drinking vodka which gives you the impression that entire armies from privates to top officers are permanently sloshed. Things keep falling from the sky, like burning aircraft, bombs and paratroopers. Did these things really happen daily regardless of the army's location?

You have to give the Germans their dues though: they're remarkably obstinate, attacking our positions every hour on the dot. Luckily, there isn't much they can do. Our guys are used to it by now. They just climb out of the trenches and have a bit of a shootout, not even bothering to aim their guns because Germans promptly drop dead anyway. There's also an occasional hand-to-hand which is just harmless fun, really. I've been in three of them already. The Germans are so feeble even a ten-year-old child can blow them over with a feather. They put on a great show when they go for you, glaring and baring their teeth as they fire their Schmeissers from the hip (even though it's the least accurate way

*of shooting), barking something in their guttural
language. They do present a danger for the girls
though, so that's what you should be doing, saving
the girls. Otherwise it's just a joke.*

*Our Russian guys are way smarter than the
Germans. We're much more chivalrous. Much more
merciful. We're amazing, period.*

*Most of these Nazi bastards are terrible
lowlifes. Still, recently we've been coming across
some nicer specimens which show some rudiments
of honor, mercy and integrity. Apparently, it's a
recent fad, portraying the Nazis as actual human
beings. Which makes it easy to forget that some of
these merciful people used to smash Russian babies'
heads against concrete walls while others burned
their victims in extermination camps without
showing the slightest remorse. In the summer of
1942, these cheerful sanguine guys in their field-
gray uniforms with rolled-up sleeves were happily
advancing toward the Volga, reducing entire Russian
regiments to blood-drenched mincemeat, and here
we are now, portraying their miserable agony at
Stalingrad, poor little darlings! You really think we'd
have earned the same honor had the Nazis won the
war? Like fuck we would, excuse my French. There's
no other way of putting it.*

Not that filmmakers give a shit.

*Private Petrov – the young soldier who found
me – is by no means an underpaid extra. He may be
playing a bit part but he definitely has plenty of lines
to memorize. He's been here for quite a while and*

ZOTOV

lost 746 girls already. One of them he misses quite badly: a Ukrainian brunette from Kiev with whom he only managed to exchange a couple of kisses. This morning he asked me when I was going to stop mourning the girl I'd lost and get myself a new one.

I told him I wasn't interested. After my near escape from the porn world, these things just don't matter to me anymore. I do hope Joan's alive though, my little virgin. You never know, she might be somewhere here too. I get this feeling at times; I can sense her presence.

But where can she be? From what Petrov told me, there're loads of towns in the area, big and small, both in the mountains and out in the valley. That's apart from Stalingrad and some sort of German-controlled Citadel.

Luckily for us, Russia isn't the only country which makes bad B-movies. Not just war-themed, either. All those spaghetti westerns, British Carry On spoofs, slapdash flicks, horror films with cardboard monsters, not to mention failed sequels to old box-office hits apparently made under the influence of intoxicating liquor.

So Joan could be anywhere. She might have ended up on the Titanic or in the latest remake of The Mummy. Alternatively, she could be in trouble now, desperately trying to escape the Twilight vampires. Or she could be entering the predatory depths of Jurassic Park.

Just please don't tell me she ended up in Pearl Harbor. I hope not.

EL DIABLO

The fact remains, I've no idea where to look for her but still I've got to find her. She did her best to save me, so now I'm obliged to do the same for her. Not that Private Petrov would appreciate my platonic intentions. It's a good job he hasn't got Comrade Stalin's face, otherwise I would have already defected to the Germans.

I remember watching war films – real war films – when I was little. That was truly scary stuff. Come and See, Ivan's Childhood, Ballad of a Soldier, The Dawns Here are Quiet[6]*... Today's war movies can't scare anyone – they're just a mixture of airbrushed guts and gore. And you can't even tell them they know jack about war because they'll start moaning about their creativity being compromised.*

I just love it. You take 50 million bucks of the taxpayers' money, then tell them you're about to make the ultimate film about the ultimate war, therefore you don't give a damn about how it does in the box office. Because you're a freakin' artist! The difference between the real Wehrmacht and today's movie Germans is the difference between a torture rack and a Christmas bauble.

Earlier today, I snuck out into some German-occupied territories (in disguise, naturally) and what did I see? Same old, same old. Same German Shepherds pulling on their leads, same blond clones in dubious uniforms barking the inevitable "Snell!".

---

[6] Several of Russia's award-winning war films

ZOTOV

Some of them have a vocabulary of a dozen words which is plenty for today's war movie: Achtung, Halt, Partisanen, Kaput, Sieg Heil, Sehr Gut, Ja ja, Volkswagen.

According to Petrov, Russians normally don't take prisoners unless they manage to lay their hands on some top German brass complete with eye piece and riding crop. Those actually understand Russian although they're too conceited to speak it. German soldiers are a different story: they can't speak their own tongue, let alone Russian. You ask him about his unit's location but all you get is "Gut, gut!" You smash his face in with a rifle but all he says is "Sieg heil!" Animals.

Oh, one more thing I forgot to mention. In his version of Stalingrad, Bondarchuk must have thought it politically incorrect to shoot at Germans while they were collecting water from the river. According to him, "Even wild beasts don't attack each other at water holes." He should be watching more Animal Planet, especially the program where a crocodile assaults a thirsty zebra by the water's edge. Here too, I saw a herd of Jerrys standing by the river shuffling their feet like cows in need of milking, waiting for their leader to signal them to start drinking. It drives our Russian guys up the wall but shooting is strictly forbidden.

They should be grateful that Bondarchuk didn't think of a "Banana Truce" (seeing as he'd apparently read The Jungle Book). Trust him to make Russian and German soldiers pick some *tropical fruit in an African jungle. You think he wouldn't have done it? I bet he would. He could always blame it on artistic license. He could say this was his vision. You can explain anything away with a "vision". Russian and German soldiers are all clean-shaven (apparently, Gillette runs regular promotions in the trenches) and squeaky clean (never mind that in reality they were lice-ridden and only had one hot wash in six months). Their girlfriends are sexy and groomed to perfection. A toy war, a pretty picture painted by numbers.*

Still, as Petrov told me in strict privacy, this was nothing compared to what was happening in Berlin. One morning, its grim black-and-white denizens had woken up to discover they were in Technicolor[7]! Martin Bormann got himself a pink nose; the swastika flag fluttering over the Reich Chancellery turned out to be red and black; and the air defense gunners staring up in the blue sky wore the uniforms of the finest field gray.

Apparently, Hitler was in such a state over this discovery he very nearly jumped out the window. His aides grabbed him by the legs just in time. You'd think it was the perfect moment to launch an offensive and smoke the cheeky bastard

---

[7] The author alludes to the Russian 1970s black-and-white TV saga *The Seventeen Moments of Spring* telling the story of a Russian secret agent in the wartime Berlin. In 2009, the series was colorized, to mixed reactions as the audience complained that the film had lost a lot of its original atmosphere.

but alas! the taking of Berlin is the only epic scene missing in the entire body of Russian war movies. So in the end, we let it drop.

Private Petrov is coming in a moment to take me on one of his water-fetching missions. And when the dawn breaks... you never know, he might actually help me to get to the nearby city. Provided I manage to convince him I'm not trying to desert in which case he might just shoot me on the spot, end of story.

He wasn't really surprised to find me there. According to him, there were others here before me – funny people in stupid clothes with tiny walkie talkies, who spoke Russian kind of weird. You can't believe how happy I was. I asked him where I could find them. He laughed and said that his unit sent them up against the tanks just for kicks, with one grenade between the three of them. No one has heard from them since. Later, I ventured into that field and found a squashed iPhone trampled into the ground. Great. Just shows you the kind of BS we've been filming for the last twenty years.

I've got to stop writing now. Soon we'll venture out into the night to face explosions and tracer bullets. No idea if the next city is any better. At least this one doesn't have any commercial breaks.

THE SOLDIER LAYS the pencil down. The camera moves outside, showing a friendly plane limping through the air as it's coming in on a wing and a prayer. Then it zooms out, revealing the panorama of a battlefield engulfed in smoke. The smoke is rather thin though: just a cheap budget computer animation. A leaden-gray Zeppelin hovers high in the sky, sporting a swastika on its side. No one seems to wonder what it's doing here: it looks good, that's the main thing. The audience can hear bursts of gunfire; the smoke dissipates, revealing Nazi soldiers advancing in extended formation, their German Shepherds straining at the leash.

The camera moves to the outskirts, showing a squat Wehrmacht officer in a peaked cap who strides past the bombed-out buildings casting anxious glances behind him. He clenches a Walther handgun in one hand; the other is closed tight around a slender young woman's neck.

A patrol stops them: two field gendarmes on a motorbike, with brass *kettenhunde* plates on their chests. The officer points at the woman, then waves in the direction of the town gates.

One of the gendarmes shakes his head, speaking in a low voice. The audience have to strain their ears to catch a few words: "*Brigadeführer... Befehl... Nein...*"

The officer shrugs and shoots both: one in the head, the other in the chest. The girl opens her mouth wide but the audience can't hear her scream. The two disappear behind the ruins.

The camera focuses on the dead gendarme sitting askew on his motorbike. Blood trickles down his fingers, dripping onto his Schmeisser.

The audience dissolves into gloomy whispers,

ZOTOV

hugging their popcorn buckets. They can't wait to
see what's going to happen next.

CHAPTER FOUR

The Apprentice

Lima, the Republic of Peru
October 24 1931

GREAT MOTHER MARY, he was so tired! Let's face it, he was destined to always play second fiddle. Sad but true. The Dandy was the brain behind the whole thing, the idea machine, while he, the Apprentice, was only a tool to bring his magic to life by doing his dirty work for him. His job was to find good-looking models, choose the spare parts for the dolls, get rid of all the offcuts and cover up their tracks.

He wasn't complaining, no. The Dandy had always been like this, ever since school. He'd been the one in control of their childhood friendship. But now everybody in the slums envied the Apprentice: his old friend hadn't forgotten him, he visited the slums in his posh shiny car, saying hello to all the neighbors and enjoying the company of his old school friend.

ZOTOV

You had to give the Dandy his due: he might be as rich as they come but he'd never shunned his down-on-his-luck friend. He used to pay the cops off whenever the Apprentice got caught in a knife fight and always made sure his friend's parents were provided for whenever the Apprentice was doing time for petty theft. So even though he was often on the receiving end of his slum friend's jokes, their friendship was perfectly kosher. The Dandy was a natural leader which was more than the Apprentice could say about himself. Despite the difference in their height and social standing, they still got on very well together, thank you.

The only disagreement they'd ever had was three years ago when they realized they couldn't continue loving the same woman. They just couldn't. Now that was tough. Their slum friends used to laugh at their infatuation, at least until the Apprentice had thrown a few punches around. The others didn't need any encouragement and promptly shut up.

Love had stricken them both like lightning from the sky.

Being a man of letters, the Dandy might have winced at the simile but the Apprentice loved a flourish in his speech. They spent nights roaming the streets drunk on their love, writing poems and singing serenades (after which their neighbors called the cops thinking someone was torturing cats). Neither of them was jealous because both knew perfectly well the object of their desire would never notice them. They were but dust on the toes of her shoes, two conceited nincompoops thinking they could be worthy of her divine perfection. The two friends had suffered in silence; no one around them had noticed the pain of their bleeding hearts or the occasional manly tear on their pillows.

And so it went on until the Dandy stumbled upon an Idea.

If the truth were known, he'd always been into this sort of thing. There'd always been somewhat of a risk-taker in him. Not in the serial-killing way, you understand. The Dandy wasn't much of a womanizer — but he was absolutely crazy about all those ancient rituals. Many a time had he tried to summon Satan. He did it by the book, drawing the pentagram, reciting Our Father back to front and soaking the floor in the blood of sacrificial cats and chickens. Satan didn't give a shit. Somebody else might have given up and forgotten the whole thing but not the Dandy. He banded together with a group of like-minded rich boys and took them on an archeological expedition. Some hobby! Perfect for spoilt young men who aren't afraid of soiling their groomed little hands.

Personally, the Apprentice didn't give a damn about all those dark tunnels, temple ruins and ancient Incan palaces. You just don't think about this sort of thing when you bust your hump from dawn till dusk to earn three-quarters of a sol just to buy some corn cakes. But the Dandy would have given all the corn cakes in the world for the privilege of digging out the dusty pieces of some broken statue of an ancient god. No points for guessing his pedigree – like father, like son, as we say.

That's when the Dandy started wondering what had possessed the Spanish Viceroy to have all the caves and crevices filled. The old bastard had even ordered the draining of certain brooks! And once the Dandy had heard about the undoing of all the Inca emperors and Pizarro's conquistadors, he couldn't think of anything else.

He spent three months digging – and when he came back, he was a changed man.

He said to the Apprentice they needed to talk. And when he spoke, he spoke calmly without any of his posh airs and graces. All he said was: he knew how to solve their problem.

They sat down and had a drink, then the Dandy told him his plan. He spoke in a frozen voice, calm and deadpan serious without a shadow of a doubt.

At first, the Apprentice laughed at his suggestion — but the Dandy said they should try and see.

The only thing that worried the Apprentice was the method they were going to use. Still, the Dandy was adamant it couldn't be done any other way. The creature they were about to summon was capable of fulfilling any wish – surely it could give them the object of their desire on a silver platter. But unlike the Satanists with their black masses, a cat or a chicken just wouldn't cut it.

This kind of creature wanted a human sacrifice as payment, and it only accepted women.

This detail hadn't surprised the Apprentice. He knew that a duck always tasted better than a drake; a chicken was far better than a cockerel and a sheep made a better roast than a mutton. But as for the killing part...

Predictably, the Dandy wasn't going to soil his dainty little fingers. Once again the Apprentice had to do his dirty work for him.

And still he agreed, even though he was rather skeptical about the whole thing. He didn't want to waste a human life without any gain but the Dandy insisted and somehow the Apprentice found it hard to say no.

He wasn't afraid of getting caught: it wasn't often that they arrested murderers in Lima. In order to arrest a murderer, you needed to find the body first, and hiding bodies was something all slum dwellers knew how to do since infancy. The local police had been created to serve El Presidente and shoot at strikers; they wouldn't even notice a single slut missing in an alleyway, especially if you picked a rather dark alley and a rather ugly slut.

And that was exactly what they did. They went one night to Plaza Mayor where the Apprentice grabbed the first whore he'd chanced upon and covered her mouth with a clothful of ether, then brought her to the address the Dandy had given him.

ZOTOV

Despite his experience, the Apprentice still felt sick whenever he thought about the things he'd done that night. Cutting her throat hadn't been enough for the Dandy who demanded the Apprentice carve her up like a piglet. All the while, he stood next to him watching and telling him what to do, covering his face with a cloth. He told the Apprentice to drain her blood into a bucket, then pointed where to place her heart and her bones...

At that point, the Apprentice himself was about to puke but the Dandy didn't give a damn. He even spared his beautiful ancient knives for the job. They were amazing, their charcoal-gray blades smoky from the tip to the hilt. According to the Dandy, he'd discovered them in the ruins of Cusco temples. They were made of rock glass: the only material which could be sharpened much better than even the best steel. Those were the knives Incan priests had used to slice in one practiced motion through prisoners' chests, offering their still-beating hearts on a platter to the Great God Viracocha.

Still, it wasn't Viracocha the two friends wanted to talk to. That's what the Dandy had told him: he could ask whatever he wanted and the creature would do it.

Very well. So they carved the slut up the way the ritual demanded and dumped whatever was left of her in a brook. The Apprentice made a wish.

The next morning he got up real early to help his parents dig up their vegetable patch before going to work. And just as he'd started, his spade hit something. An old clay jug with about thirty gold Spanish doubloons in it, from the times of the God-fearing Viceroy Fernandes de Castro[8], may he rest in peace. If you converted it to today's money, that was one hell of a lot of dough.

And the jug had a picture on it: a black head of some beast with fiery eyes and two big horns. When the Apprentice saw it, he wrapped both his arms around the jug and slumped onto the ground. At first he'd thought it was the Dandy's prank. The bastard knew about his parents' garden and must have buried the jug there himself. But... no. Oh no, sir! That spoiled little brat wouldn't have slaughtered a living breathing human being just to play a trick on him.

That's when the Apprentice knew they were on the right track. Once they'd managed to contact the awesome entities of Uku Pacha, they would help the two friends to win their loved one.

The Apprentice wasn't too bothered about his own future. Their love would choose one of the two of them; the loser would have to leave the country in order not to stand in the way of the winner's bliss.

Two days later, the Apprentice dismissed his last doubts when the cart driven by his father fell

---

[8] Viceroy Fernandes de Castro ruled Peru between 1667 and 1672

off a cliff. Papa had survived by a sheer miracle — he'd managed to grab on to a tree branch overhanging the abyss — but he'd broken both legs.

Now everything had fallen into place. The terrible dwellers of Uku Pacha had made it clear that even though the Spanish had buried them deep underground, they still accepted sacrifices. The unborn would happily drink the blood offering, then dutifully do what they'd been asked to.

He'd been lucky. Normally, those who asked the underground creatures for assistance didn't live long. The unborn would soon claim their souls and make off with them, spiriting them away into the rocky chasms of Uku Pacha. Like they'd done with the Emperors Atahualpa and Manco and with the great conquistadors Pizarro and Almagro.

You had to give the Dandy his due though: he'd thought of it too. He'd warned the Apprentice that the loser would have to willingly give the solemn vow of *mutelma*, accepting his miserable fate. Then let those underground dwellers come and search for him all over the world if they think they can!

The Apprentice had unhesitantly accepted the proposition. This was an honest offer. If their love chose the Dandy, it would break his heart — but he wasn't going to fight over her. Her choice was sacred; you can't win love by force. He'd have to leave. He might go to Chile or Bolivia — or maybe even to the United States of America — and wait for his nemesis to strike. He had little doubt it would.

Still, it wasn't over yet. You never know, Lady Luck might just for once turn away from her pet the Dandy. He was too gentle, too spoiled, way too weak without his money. If push came to shove, do you think he'd be able to work for a handful of rice? Because their love had a certain standard of lifestyle — she was rich; she wouldn't want to downsize her needs.

Not so the Apprentice. She could count on him. He'd rob people in broad daylight for her. He'd kill and torture them. He'd do anything to ensure she rolled in luxury.

If the truth were known, he was much more popular with women than his dandy friend who still didn't know the pleasures of a woman's cherry. What was money, after all? It was just some crumpled paper, amigo. A woman could sense a hot macho in him, an alpha male who could sink his teeth into the scruff of her neck and carry her into his lair to mate with her. That's what girls like in men — not some scruffy bits of wrapping paper decorated with the picture of the sun[9].

So the Dandy could dwell in anticipation of his victory all he wanted. It isn't over until the fat lady sings. They still had to face the final battle. And once the Apprentice had won, he'd get down on his knees and offer his true love his heart.

---

[9] The name of the Peruvian currency first introduced in 1863 is "sol", meaning "sun" in Spanish. The watermarks on the banknotes depicted the sun too.

ZOTOV

Still, it was no easy route. If only he'd known the extent of all the suffering! He wasn't sorry about the girls, no. No one had ever felt sorry for *him*, so why would he start walking around sympathizing with strangers? But it was a lot of hard work. You had to gut them, bleed them, wash them, place them into the tubs filled with brine... it was a long sweaty job.

The Dandy helped him, of course; sometimes he took over from him completely — like the last time the Apprentice had had to leave to get some magnolia petals. Still, all those spoiled sissies did more harm than good.

Admittedly as a taxidermist, the Dandy was tops. He had a natural talent for art: his work entrapped your heart, there was no other way of putting it.

The Apprentice stepped back and tilted his head, openly admiring his friend's latest creation.

Teresa stood in front of him as if still alive, staring at him with a haughty smile on her lips, forbidding like the Snow Queen. Her cheeks had an icy blue glow: the Dandy had mixed blood with crushed violets. What a poet.

In this the Apprentice agreed with his friend: they needed to be more open to experimentation. The inhabitants of Uku Pacha didn't suffer boredom gladly. They wanted variety. The only requirement was that the doll had to be impossibly beautiful, empty inside and enveloped in perfume. From what he'd heard, magnolia was the underground demons' favorite scent.

It was incredible how similar the Spanish and Quechua religions were. No wonder they got merged so quickly. The Virgin Mary was in fact Pacha Mama, the mother of all living things in the Incan pantheon. Viracocha who'd risen from the dead was none other than Jesus himself. And Uku Pacha...

Uku Pacha was hell, the difference being that the Christian faith said nothing about the unborn (according to it, all dead babies became angels) while the Incas knew a lot about them. The unborn were doomed to dwell in the underground tunnels away from sunlight. Blind and without a hope of ever escaping the darkness, they were the most frightful demons one could imagine. Those were the kinds of creatures the Dandy had appealed to and who'd already shown their power to the Apprentice by granting him the gold.

Very soon — very very soon — the demons would resolve the dispute between the two old-fashioned lovers and would grant their lady's love to one of them.

He didn't need more. Gold was a great thing; he'd made good use of it but selling his soul for money wasn't wise. The unborn were worse than bankers: they would always get their pound of flesh. Despite the deal's terms, the demons were never short of clients: people of today were just as happy to part with everything they had for the promise of a momentary triumph. Isn't it so?

ZOTOV

Anyone would willingly lay down his own life for the opportunity of ruling the country for a few brief months. It wasn't for nothing the Spanish had blocked all the passages to Uku Pacha. The place was pure hell.

The Apprentice couldn't take his eyes off Teresa's dead face.

Oh yes, sir. She may have been a slut but still she'd been a beautiful woman.

Just think that they'd chosen her by pure accident. She could have survived had she not offered herself to the two friends as they walked to their slaughterhouse in Barrio de Chino. It had been the Apprentice's idea. Just as they'd walked past the girl, he'd thought she was actually a decent choice. They could take her with them and get a better look at her later at their leisure.

And that's exactly what they did. The Apprentice ran ahead and waited for her in a dark alley, then pressed an ether-soaked rag to her face. Easy.

You should have seen her eyes when she'd recognized the Dandy. Had they all been so sweet and cooperative, getting rid of their bodies wouldn't have been half as taxing.

That was the third doll. They only had one left to make. They had a deadline to meet.

He'd already warned the Dandy that the Russian cop was hot on their heels — a seasoned detective with lots of solved crimes to his name. The Dandy had chosen to ignore it. If you listened to him, the police wouldn't dare to touch him. They were sure to look for some serial killer, a new Trujillo Predator. A human sacrifice? — Please. The thought would never cross their minds. This wasn't Haiti, you know. We were all good Catholics here.

Let them think so.

Still, they really should get rid of El Ruso before he got to the gist of the matter. Having said that, the Dandy had been right. El Ruso had very little time left.

Because the party was about to begin.

And once the party was over and the undead had arrived, the Russian cop's investigation would become pointless. The winner would take his love on honeymoon while the loser would die a terrible death, one way or another.

The Apprentice glanced at his watch. Two a.m. It was time to set the doll up.

Whatever had happened to the Dandy? There was nothing to fear, of course: the Dandy would never grass his friend up to the cops. But if he got himself arrested, the Apprentice would never be able to build the last doll on his own. He didn't know how to sew it up or paint it — which meant he'd never win the demons' attention. He'd have to forever watch his love from a respectful distance, gritting his teeth as she'd smile at other men and bestow her kisses on them.

That shouldn't happen.

Anxiety flooded over him. Where was that idiot now? Shouldn't he call him at the slaughterhouse? The Dandy could spend days there just pondering over the dolls' parts preserved in brine.

Fucking *artist*. He was enough to drive a man mad.

He heard a soft knocking at the door. A familiar code.

One-two-three. One-two. One-two-three. One-two.

The Apprentice smiled. Talk about the devil.

Oh, the sweet night of wonders. They were about to present the unborn with their third doll.

CHAPTER FIVE

The Realm of Mayonnaise

Glitz City
A movie set of modern Moscow
60 miles from Stalingrad

THE CAMERA pans around a beautiful summer city in Technicolor. Sparkling fountains spout jets of water; young women walk around eating ice-cream. The screen is full of sharply dressed people who seem to be happy with their lot. Their hair is done by the best stylists; their broad smiles reveal excellent unfilled white teeth. Many laugh; some even dance around as they walk.

As if by accident, a broad-shouldered blond man waltzes past the camera. His orange scarf looks a bit weird in the hot weather, but the camera focuses on it nevertheless.

Here, all the young men appear to be handsome and all the girls stunning with their permed curls and impeccable makeup.

ZOTOV

The camera zooms in on two men sitting on a bench next to the VDNKh Fair. Both are wearing Red Army uniforms but passersby don't seem to pay much attention to them. They probably think a war movie is being shot nearby.

The movie audience chuckles as they've already worked out what's going on. Some woman or other whispers in her friend's ear, sharing her ideas about what's going to happen next. The audience shushes her, and she continues to watch the film stone-faced as if she doesn't give a damn.

PRIVATE PETROV doesn't stop casting astonished looks around. He cusses (in the best style of today's Russian war movies which prohibit profanity but allow cutesy euphemisms in the vein of "I don't give a flying monkey" or " or "for crying out loud!") while making repeated signs of the cross.

Talking about which, all the fake Russian soldiers on the Stalingrad movie set wear crucifixes and hang their trenches with icons as religion seems to be the latest Russian movie fad.

"I didn't even know that things like these existed," Petrov says in his soft backwater drawl. "Don't get me wrong: we've had guys who've been past here on recons and they told us all these things. But I thought they were bullshitting."

"I thought so too," I tell him in all honesty. "Even though I'd heard about this city a lot."

In actual fact, the Moscow of commercial movies does resemble the real thing, but not quite to such a degree. For instance, it has a hundred times more adverts than its real-life counterpart.

A girl joins us on the bench and flashes us a smile. Remembering my experience in the world of porn, I'm quite wary.

"Have you tried the famous Malve mayonnaise?" she asks. "I find it really delicious! I always put it on salads without having to worry about putting on weight!" she jumps up, spins around and sits back down. "So light, so soft and so wonderful! And it's made with quails' eggs! It's divine!"

I heave a sigh and give her a stern look. "You sure you're all right, lady?"

"Of course," she says, nonplussed. "And you know why? Because I always put Malve on my salads which provides my brain with all the necessary vitamins. That's why..."

Crack! In a flurry of silk, the girl disappears over the back of the bench. Private Petrov — who has no previous experience with advertising — has just given her a hearty whack with his gun butt. Not very glamorous but definitely effective.

Do you think that helped us? As if. Along comes another one: a fidgety guy who starts yelling into my new soldier friend's ear:

"Okay, Google!"

Private Petrov turns into Lot's wife with shock. That's when the guy in the orange scarf returns wearing a pair of shades. He swings round and heads toward us in the mechanical heavy gait that only exists in slow motion.

Of course. This is a modern Russian movie which, if you took out all the slow-mo bits, would only be half as long.

"Hi there," orange scarf says, approaching us. "Have you heard of our cell phone provider's new plan? It offers unlimited Internet access. Imagine all the opportunities offered by its incredible speed!"

A gunshot. The guy slumps to the tarmac. A wisp of gray smoke rises from Petrov's rifle barrel.

The Google guy chokes mid-word, drops to the ground and crawls away from us like a crab.

I've no idea how to react to this. On one hand, I've just witnessed a murder. On the other hand, I'd always wanted to do something like that, hadn't I?

Petrov cocks his Mosin's action. The spent shell case clatters to the ground and rolls away.

"That's him shut up," Petrov says with a peasant's candor. "What an idiot. I just had to smoke the bastard. There's a war going on and he was attracting too much attention."

The passersby don't even turn to the sound of the shooting.

That's modern Russian cinema for you: its main purpose is to cram as many brand names into the scene as they can, and to hell with the story.

Here too, the story seems to be a bit enigmatic.

It starts to rain. The girl's skirts cling to their

bodies, rain dripping off their soaking hair. They turn to their lovers and start kissing. The fountain jets rise even higher.

I get the impression that these are not even human beings but grinning celluloid mannequins. In modern films, the ability to act is surplus to requirements — as numerous Russian directors' children have successfully proven. All you do, you create a collage with a couple of popular faces, a lot of adverts (because a film has to pay for itself even as it's being made) and a bunch of bum special effects plagiarized from Hollywood. That's the extent of it. Oh, and also a pinch of patriotism to be able to cream off some government funds.

With a screeching of brakes, a dilapidated old Volga shoots through the sky, leaving a smoky trail in its wake. It just has to be Black Lightning[10]. In a nearby café, beer-drinking patrons turn to the camera with frozen smiles, showing off their green beer labels.

Yet another guy sits down on our bench (what kind of a sick conveyor belt is this?). Unshaven and wearing a tattered padded jacket — the kind typical of Russian peasants — he seems to be trying to pass for a street bum. Still, if you take a closer look, you can see that his padded jacket has a Karl Lagerfeld logo on it. His stubble reeks of

---

[10] *Black Lightning (Chernaya Molniya)*: a 2009 Russian superhero movie

ZOTOV

Paco Rabanne and has been trimmed by a professional stylist. It doesn't take a brain surgeon to work out his dubious sexual orientation. Although nobody dares utter anything about such things nowadays, do they? Heterosexuals are a rarity these days, especially in the movie industry.

"Rasputin Vodka," the hobo announces, staring into space. "The best there is. You might ask what's so special about it? It's made with the softest spring water and…"

"Do me a favor and shoot him, will you?" I ask Petrov without turning.

"Please don't," the seasoned advertiser reacts promptly. "I'm going, I'm going."

He shoves the bottle into his pocket and disappears into the moving throng.

Petrov shakes his head in disbelief. "Listen up, brother, where are we, in God's name? What kind of country is this? China?"

"Not quite yet," I reply, grinning. "It might be, in another fifty years."

"Why are they always trying to sell us something? First mayonnaise, then beer, and now vodka?"

I can't tell him the truth, of course. If I do, he'll kill me first, then shoot himself.

Not far from us, a girl puts her hand in the air and sprays herself with some deodorant or other, looking so languid as if she'd just danced the lead in *Swan Lake*. But of course. She's using Regina Ultra Dry. Back at work, we always used to have a good laugh about this commercial. First a guy runs out of an elevator, apparently unable to stand the smell of stale sweat. At the end of the commercial, he gives the girl flowers at a corporate party. It's as if someone has told him, "Do you remember that sweaty chick in the elevator, the one that smelled like a rancid polecat? Well, she doesn't honk anymore. Go and congratulate her."

The only thing that's worse are the middle-aged broads who seem to keep big bottles of fabric softener in their handbags at all times. Had this been the case in real life, the rape ratio would have dropped considerably. All you'd have to do is bash the pervert over the head with the bottle and it would take him some time to come round again.

"Well, how can I explain it to you, bro... I know this city like the back of my hand. The gist of its existence is to give exposure to certain brand names."

"Whatcha mean?"

"Oh yeah, you're from a different movie, aren't you? In brief, in order for this world to prosper, it has to push all sorts of products to the public. Like mayo, vodka, butter, cars, chewing gum, you name it. Without it, film producers would earn a lot less dosh. That's why they keep hawking all kinds of junk, relevant or not, while the movie itself takes second place. All they care about is getting their pound of flesh from the sponsors and breathing a sigh of relief. Like, that's it, they've earned it so they don't give a toss about how many people actually go to see the movie. And you know, it's kinda good job we made it here. Other places are much worse. Like *Six Degrees of Celebration*[11], for example. We've simply forgotten how to make movies- er, how to build cities these days. They're either erected by yesterday's promo gurus who used to shoot toothpaste adverts, or by some artsy idiots who don't give a hoot about the bottom line. They hassle the government for funds, divvy them up between themselves, then happily report that they've invested their heart and soul into the revival of the national product."

I paused. "Russian art is a bit like Russian cars. We've spent the last twenty-five years inviting expert marketers to advertise our sad rides with the help of everyone from the President to porn stars. We've spent gazillions on foreign managers but the fact remains, our cars are still like a bag of nails. It's the same with movies. Why bother shooting quality work if you get paid anyway?"

Private Petrov sets his rifle aside and reached over to feel my forehead. "I'd be damned if I understood anything," he admits. "All this talk about dosh, porn stars and marketers. What the hell are sponsors? I should have looked after you a lot better. How did I miss you getting shell shocked? You've got a fever, that's why you're a bit

---

[11] *Six Degrees of Celebration* - currently, "the most successful non-animated film franchise in Russia" (Wikipedia)

delirious. You need to go to the sick bay. Here, have some water."

As he fusses over me, unscrewing his flask top, I curse my luck in the choicest of f-words. If I was fated to end up in these worlds of silver-screen dreams, why couldn't I have landed somewhere really interesting, like *The Game of Thrones*? Imagine this: me on horseback, larger than life and twice as ugly, surrounded by White Walkers and slashing them with my sword while egging on my warriors to slay the evil...

Oh. What am I even talking about? What horse, what sword? What me? They would have studded me with arrows within the first five minutes, mauled me, then sent me to the Wall. Or just hung, drawn and quartered me for a change.

Shit. I'm the loser to end all losers. I can't do anything. I can't make a career for myself; come to that, I can't even land myself a good movie.

I take Petrov's flask and pour some water over my head. "I think you're right," I tell him. "It must have been one of Jerries' shells. It exploded just by my ear. Okay, I'll go and see the quack but first we need to decide what to do next."

"That's it, bro," he replies. "I'd love to know too. We came here under a hail of bullets. You said you really needed to get here. And now we're sitting round eyeing up girls and having all sorts of innuendo. What if the Jerries have launched another attack while we've been hanging here? So come on now, make up your mind a bit quick."

ZOTOV

I want to tell him that we defeated the Germans quite some time ago but I know it's pointless. They're stuck in their world destined to repel the Wehrmacht's attacks for centuries to come. This is the crux of their existence. They die, then resurrect for new battles like the Vikings in Valhalla[12].

I rack my brains trying to work out where to look for Joan. In the real-world Moscow you might amble along to your local citizens advice bureau and ask for her address. But I'd be damned if I know if these bureaus exist in those modern Russian movies. Plenty of other things here: a bunch of catwalk queens, lots of advertising, a few voiceless singers and giftless actors. Chic restaurants, expensive boutiques, unpleasant millionaires, plastic girls and a handful of ubiquitous leading men playing all the main parts. Same old, same old.

"Let's take a cab," I finally suggest. "They might know her address."

We head for the taxi rank with the inevitable billboard advertising their services. All the taxi drivers are handsome young men with distinctly Muscovite accents.

Talk about screen perfect.

"Where to?" one of them asks: a red-haired guy with a typically Russian bulbous hooter.

---

[12] An allusion to the author's other bestselling novel, *Moskau*.

"Chief," I say, "you know of a citizens advice bureau nearby?"

"Eh," he looks up, thinking. "I think there is one not far from the Belorussian Station."

I gave a decisive nod. "Let's go. If you find it, I'll make it worth your while."

I'm bluffing, of course. We don't have any money. Where would we have gotten it from? If Petrov has any on him, it's either a few reichsmarks he's taken off a dead German or some period Stalin rubles. Neither will do us much good here.

The cabbie shows no surprise at the sight of Petrov. Apparently, he's not the first Stalingrad soldier to make it here. The driver starts up the motor, and we head off down a wide boulevard.

"So what do you think about my wheels?" the driver smiles. "She's a Brokeswagen Crash. Listen how quiet the motor runs! It's no gas guzzler. She starts up first time, you've just seen it yourselves. It's our special offer today for only 700,000 rubles."

"Shut your face," Petrov enunciates.

"Got it," the driver replies with professional sangfroid. "Don't shoot, bro."

"I ain't no 'bro' of yours, you billboard bitch," Petrov turns away.

I still can't work it out. Unlike the porn world where everyone sticks to their own camp, the various locations of the B-movie world seem to interact with each other. Which is understandable: in the porn world, any such visit might result in a slow painful death from sexual exhaustion. But here, they seem to come into contact quite often — connected by trade, maybe? After all, they do need to sell their mayonnaise to someone.

We speed along the traffic-free boulevard lined with billboards enticing us to buy tasteless gum, drink watery beer and take money from loan sharks.

Finally, the car brakes by some building sporting the old Soviet emblem. The building, however, is quite new and smelling of fresh paint. Yeah right. These kinds of offices always look brand new in our movies. It's a good job I haven't ended up in some gory action movie, the likes of *Cargo 200* or *Leviathan*. I wouldn't have liked it, that's for sure. When we Russians make an action movie, it makes you wish you'd never been born even before the opening credits are rolled. It's so depressing and hopeless, complete with junkies, skinheads, alcoholics and corrupt officials, all of them drunk as skunks, everything dying, nothing but screwing, bribery and filth.

Here, however, it looks hunky dory. All kinds of bespectacled official-looking men with briefcases traipse up and down the building's corridors, mingling with girls in severe-looking two-pieces and ugly pumps the sight of which might stir one to write a Greek tragedy in three acts.

The cabbie kills the motor with a care and turns to us. "That'll be eight hundred rubles, please."

I linger, expecting Petrov to resolve the

problem with the help of his rifle but his reaction defies logic.

"You've got a cheek!" he snaps and scoops a bunch of old paper money from his pockets, so large they look more like tea towels than banknotes. "Will you take Soviet money or what, you old leech?"

"No problem, Comrade," the driver nods impassively. "But unfortunately, there is no exchange office within walking distance, so I suggest we play it down to earth and use the black market rate: fifty of our rubles to one of your Stalin ones."

"You're not asking much, are you?" Petrov voices his indignation. "A month ago, Sergeant Annushkin from the army recon boys was here, he told us they'd been really eager to change them at one to sixty."

"And I need something out of it as well, don't I?" the driver replies logically. "I'll have to waste time going to the exchange office and filling in all the forms. If you'd have paid in reichsmarks, that would have been totally different. Collectors always pay a good price for them. But we've got Uncle Joe's money up to our eyeballs."

"But why is the exchange rate so high?" I ask. "The Stalin ruble was almost the same as the dollar."

Both Private Petrov and the cab driver stare at me in surprise.

"You sure you're all right, mister?" the cabbie

asks. "Think how much Stalin's ruble used to buy at the time compared to how much our ruble is worth now! That's a really shitty exchange rate. We have guys shuttling to Stalingrad and back, buying up weapons and military uniforms for criminal gangs. We even have guided tours for foreigners. And given its buying capacity, your Stalin ruble should cost at least three hundred of ours. It's just that there isn't much to be had in Stalingrad. The choice is poor and all the shops have been destroyed."

"Once we push the Germans back, we'll rebuild again," Petrov replies cheerfully.

We're already climbing the steps to the citizens' advice bureau when I suddenly realize I don't know what to actually ask them. "Hi, I'm looking for a girl called Joan, petite with cropped hair, we were shooting a porn film together." Is that it?

Never mind. No need to panic. I'll just play it by ear. This is a movie, after all; here, miracles are commonplace. Here, the good guy never runs out of bullets; he never dies from mortal wounds and always rescues his lover. Even though I'm not sure I was a good guy, I have no choice, anyway.

We enter the building. How strange. There's not a soul inside. Just now there was a bunch of civil servants coming in and out and now all of a sudden the place is deserted, only the wind whistling through the corridors, sending loose paperwork and empty plastic files flying through the air.

Talk about *Silent Hill*. Could this be a portal to some domestic horror movie?

All three lockets of the information desk are empty and unmanned. Where is everybody?

I feel the barrel of the 19th century rifle pressed against the back of my head.

"*Du bist schon hier?*"[13] Petrov asks someone I can't see.

He speaks German freely without any trace of an accent. As if it's his mother tongue.

"*Ja,*" a voice replies from inside the locket. "*Hast du ihn hierher gebracht?*"[14]

"Alles in ordnung," Petrov laughs behind me. "Kamerad, ich komm' ja gleich."[15]

He takes a swing at my head with his gun butt. The world goes blank.

THE CAMERA PANS DOWN from above, from the prospective of an old rotating fan on the ceiling.

We can see a soldier wearing a Red Army uniform. He's facing a man who's kneeling in front of him pressing a hand to his head, blood trickling through his fingers.

A side door next to the locket opens, letting

---

[13] Are you here already? (German)

[14] Have you brought him here? (German)

[15] Comrade, I'm coming right away" (a line from a Lili Marlene song)

out a petite girl with short cropped hair. Her hands are tied behind her back. A Wehrmacht officer in a field-gray uniform and peaked cap is shoving her along with a pistol in her back.

The audience gets the scary impression that the film is about to end and the closing credits are about to roll.

CHAPTER SIX

Blood and Flowers

Lima, the Republic of Peru
October 26 1931

C OKE DIDN'T HELP him anymore. Miguel spat the wad of black and green chewed leaves with disgust into an overflowing ashtray, paused, then reached for a fresh bunch.

His desk was piled high with photos in manila envelopes, stacks of witness statements, dusty tomes borrowed from Lima's Historical Library, as well as a number of the inevitable dirty cups in which he brewed the leaves.

The kettle spouted a flow of steam. Miguel poured some boiling water over the coca leaves.

Three dolls. Three dolls already.

El Presidente was predictably furious. Deputy Minister Juarez had been dispatched to the station to "monitor the course of the investigation". From now on, the fat Indian was sitting at the desk next to his, casting him imploring glances full of trepidation.

Juarez had every reason to be fearful. If he was sacked, the world and his grandmother would turn their backs on him. His wife was of white descent which had a prestigious edge to it; she'd drop him like a lead balloon — and all of his property must have been in her name. Sometimes, having a top job is not such a good thing because when you fall from grace, it really hurts.

Come to think of it, how many presidents had Miguel outlived already? Luis Sánchez Cerro was already the sixth one this year. First it was Augusto B. Leguia in 1930 who was overthrown by General Manuel Ponce Brousset — who'd only lasted two days before being ousted by Sánchez Cerro. In March 1931, Sánchez lost his battle to Ricardo Arias who only ruled for four days, replaced by Gustavo A. Jiménez whose term was only six days before finally losing out to David Samanez Ocampo. The latter had reigned as a stand-in president until October 8th when Luis Sánchez Cerro had regained his dictatorship.

No wonder Miguel's head spun with all the political musical chairs. Here, coups d'état were just as frequent as the rains. In this respect at least, Latin America was so much like Mother Russia, if you disregarded the climate, the siesta and the pisco.

Still, all this was irrelevant at the moment. They had to come up with a solution to the Artist problem ASAP before the mysterious killers had it their way. Had he known which particular Uku Pacha demon they were trying to summon, he would have been less insecure... or would he?

Back in Russia, they exorcized demons with a crucifix, prayers and holy water — and also silver in certain cases, such as to banish red-lipped vampires rising from their coffins. Here, things were much easier with the unborn: nothing could kill them, period. Nothing at all. There was no record of Incan chronicles depicting battles with the mysterious underground dwellers. No songs about brave knights capable of slaying multitudes of monsters with their hands tied behind their backs.

After his escape from Vladivostok, Miguel had no faith in anything anymore. He didn't even wear a crucifix anymore; he had no icons in his house neither did he now pray every night like he used to. Logically, he should have stopped this religious nonsense altogether, including all the Incan mumbo jumbo about demons and the colorful trip he'd had in the village of Corpus Christi. After all, this was South America, baby. The place had so many hallucinogenic herbs and berries that you could pluck any fruit from a nearby tree, take a bite and see yourself flying off to the Moon.

But still. The Artist was trying to *summon* the unborn. He was trying to bring them *up here*. Which meant that he believed in them in the same fanatical way as the Inca Emperors and Spanish conquistadors had.

ZOTOV

This may be a cliché of every pulp murder mystery, but if you wanted to catch a murderer, you had to start thinking like him. And that wasn't easy. There were far too many ravines and deserted mines around town, their collapsed tunnels all leading to Uku Pacha. You couldn't post a police officer next to each and every one of them. There was no way you could locate the exact spot to where the killers would take their fourth doll.

In any case, how did they transport them? Miguel had already done everything humanly possible. He'd left no stone unturned. He'd had all the cars in Lima meticulously (and inconspicuously) checked. No traces of blood anywhere. No smell of Magnolia Amazonica, nothing.

Still, Miguel had little doubt that the dolls had been delivered to the crime scenes by car. So he'd turned his attention to taxicabs. Who in Peru could afford hiring those prohibitively expensive vehicles? — only the richest of the rich, including North American tourists. The rest of the population was perfectly happy with horse-drawn cabs.

And what if the car belonged to some get-rich-quick countryside landlord? Then it was probably parked up in some dilapidated barn buried deep under heaps of straw. In which case, Miguel could forget ever finding it.

DEPUTY MINISTER JUAREZ was on the phone with his wife and son. He'd called them seven times already, complaining about his miserable situation and bad luck. The cops in the room maintained a tactful silence.

Miguel took a picture from the desk and peered close at the last doll. He understood why this time the Artist hadn't had to compose her out of four or six girls' bodies. The seventeen-year-old prostitute Teresa Chamorro, may she rest in peace, was a purely angelic creature. It hadn't taken the police long to identify her, thanks to her sisters in trade from the red-light district.

They'd found her in a cave on the outskirts of Lima. A beautiful face, painted with blood mixed with crushed violets. This was the Artist's new touch. Gold-covered cheeks. The empty boneless corpse stuffed with countless magnolia petals. Ever since the night spent in Enrique's village, their smell followed Miguel everywhere.

Enrique himself had disappeared, by the way. Gone without a trace. Miguel didn't have the time to find out what had happened to him.

He downed the cold coca brew in one gulp (the way he used to drink shots of vodka) and pulled one of the dusty tomes on the desk toward himself. Leafing through the pages faded with time, he immersed himself in the text.

"Uku Pacha is the kingdom of the dead, the unborn, and evil gods. There's never any light there but all of the creatures of the netherworld can easily find their way around in the dark. From time

immemorial, the Incas have offered sacrifices to the demons to ensure good harvests or summon rain, leaving potatoes, corn alcohol, and pieces of guanaco meat in the underground tunnels.

Even the seasoned conquistadors were horrified by the dark rituals held by the Incas to appease the Uku Pacha beasts. Anyone could turn to them with their ugliest and most despicable desires, like a dream to possess their own sister or murder their own father — or to usurp power leaving a trail of dead bodies in their wake. The underground dwellers never let you down. The only thing they wanted from you was human sacrifices, as numerous as possible.

If Inca mythology was to be believed, the spirits of stillborn children were the ones most commonly supplicated. These belonged to the most repugnant class of demons in the whole of Uku Pacha: eyeless with a gaping mouthful of razor-sharp teeth on their withered infantile faces. These abominations were constantly thirsting for blood and were prepared to do anything to obtain it.

According to eyewitnesses, in order to ensure the victory of the Emperor Atahualpa over his brother, Incan priests threw the bodies of hundreds of young girls into ravines on a weekly basis. If oral tradition were to be believed, these demons hated all living beings and even sometimes attacked silver miners in the deep mine shafts. Very occasionally, the unborn arrived at the surface of the earth in the form of merciless monstrous killers — then returned to the tunnels of Uku Pacha once their mission was fulfilled.

Although, according to Spanish priests and researchers, this demonic kingdom bore all the hallmarks of hell, in reality this was far from the truth. No dead souls were tortured there: this was a governed society of creatures whose sole purpose was to perpetuate evil. This is where everybody ended up upon their death because the Christian notion of heaven was totally alien to the Incas. The unborn constituted an influential caste in the realm of the dead, lording it over all the other dead souls in Uku Pacha; even the gods of evil treated them with respect.

Both Indians and the conquistadors believed in the existence of this shadowy world of the dead.

The Spanish who naturally feared the tricks of the devil and his demons found it easy to transfer their fears onto Uku Pacha. If you think about it, the Christian tradition, too, has demons who clamber out of hell in order to sow unrest and temptation amongst believers.

In the end, the Spanish realized that although you couldn't destroy the local evil, you could starve it of blood. Which means that if the conquistadors had indeed blocked all the passages to Uku Pacha, the unborn have been starving for some hundreds of years. Later cliques which worshipped Uku Pacha could only offer very occasional sacrifices to them which in any case bore no fruit because, having been cut off from all sides, the underground dwellers *were only capable of fulfilling petty wishes like sending ethereal spirits to bring the supplicant bags of gold.*

Which is why, according to today's Indian priests, the unborn crave blood so much they would do anything in their power for an occasional treat.

Miguel heaved a sigh. He rummaged through the cemetery of dirty cups, chose one and greedily gulped the dregs of the coca brew still left at the bottom.

It was all pretty clear to him now. The Artist and his sidekick spilled blood on the ground on purpose, leaving the dolls at the ancient sacrificial sites. Previously, both Incas and conquistadors would descend into Uku Pacha themselves; now, the murderers wanted the unborn to break their bonds and emerge into the world, attracted by the smell of blood and flowers.

What did the Artist want in return? Power? Gold? Eternal life? Actually, it was irrelevant. It had to be something grandiose, otherwise he wouldn't have taken the trouble. His prize must be something unobtainable in any other way.

That excluded money straight away because he had to be rich in any case. That little was apparent.

Miguel cast his eye around the gray room.

Deputy Minister Juarez, sweating and miserable, was still complaining on the phone. A clerk sorting through papers; a photographer; a loitering police patrol; a bored driver awaiting his orders. The place reeked of boiling corn, steeped coca leaves and sheep's milk. This was the kind of force he was supposed to catch a serial killer with.

Miguel reopened the book and turned a page.

November 1st was celebrated all over Tawantinsuyu as an "open door day" of sorts. Reminiscent of American and European Halloween, it was feted in a slightly different vein. For that sole day once a year, the creatures of Uku Pacha were permitted to ascend to earth and dwell in Tawantinsuyu cities for a duration of up to two weeks.

To ensure that people weren't scared of the dead, the Inca Emperor issued a decree according to which the whole population was obliged to don masks of monsters whenever they came out onto the streets. In so doing, nobody could tell the difference between demons and human beings.

This festival is still partially preserved within the Peruvian and Bolivian Indian tradition where it is called La Diablada, or the Dance of the Devils. As a rule, the festivities begin with a procession of some tens of thousands of dancers disguised as Satan, dressed in pink pants, horned masks with long fangs and the crowns of the Great Dragon and the Biblical Beast of 666 fame. The dancers cuss constantly, come on to the girls and drink copious amounts of moonshine, trying to portray themselves as sin incarnate.

ZOTOV

The festivities last for three days, terminating in a dramatized battle between the forces of evil and Archangel Michael who pours holy water over the devils, causing them to disperse screaming. Such processions mimic the ancient ceremonies once held by the Quechua Indians to honor all gods - from Tivu, the patron god of lakes and springs, to Anchanchu, the ugly patron demon of the underground caves.

Miguel stood up sharply. He then sat down, then stood up again, only to sit back down.

My God. Everything clicked. Now he knew. The Artist was preparing his last sacrifice to take place in the next three days to coincide with the approach of La *Diablada*, in order to summon not only the unborn but also some creatures possessing a much more powerful magic. Although malicious and merciless, the unborn were little more than cattle: they were only interested in food and were prepared to grant you any wish if the prospect of blood was in sight. This kind of demon that once was a stillborn child didn't have any particularly esthetic demands. They contented themselves with human flesh and blood thrown to them a bit like feeding swill to pigs.

There was another consideration. If the faces of the unborn only had a mouth but neither eyes nor a nose, how were they supposed to detect the finest aroma of Magnolia Amazonica? And even if they did smell it, for them it was but a minor addition to their meal of human flesh. But the magnificently crafted dolls which not only whetted a discerning demon's appetite but also prickled his olfactory senses — that was a totally different level. Indeed, this was like a rare delicacy served at one of King Balthasar's legendary feasts: the sacrifice of the King of Kings, a meal served on a gilded platter.

The Artist wasn't summoning any bloodthirsty demons from Uku Pacha.

He was summoning the gods.

The unborn were basically only cannon fodder: a brute force which could lay down a path for their leaders, helping them to ascend back to earth. Lured by the dolls and the blood, the gods would arrive in our world on November 1st soon after *La Diablada* had begun.

Which meant he should expect the next sacrifice within hours. Possibly, the last one.

Then, upon the Artist's beckoning, an Entity would arrive in Lima. It could be Tivu. Or Anchanchu. Or some other monster king.

For the whole of last week, the City of Kings had been experiencing minor tremors and earthquakes. Nothing serious, no significant damage. But if the book were to be believed, the Incas considered this a sure sign of demonic armies trying to break out of the underworld.

As if in confirmation, the room started to shake.

Dust, blackened with age, fell from the ceiling. Clinking cups started to slide along desktops. Lightbulbs began to flicker.

Juarez dropped the telephone receiver. The cops hurried outside.

Miguel didn't flinch. Two corporals headed toward him.

"Señor Capitan," they gently took him by the elbows, "We're very sorry but it's time to get out."

STANDING OUTSIDE on the sidewalk, Miguel was taking in lungfuls of the fragrant sea air. The cops were all making frantic signs of the cross, calling for help from the Virgin Mary. A whole crowd of Indian women in their colorful shawls and bowler hats had already gathered outside. They too were crossing themselves.

Miguel chuckled. In the 17th century, the Viceroy of Peru had ordered all Indians to wear European dress under threat of imprisonment. The Indians had obeyed; the problem was, they didn't know the difference between men's and women's clothes. From then on, village girls started wearing men's hats.

The crowd's religious fervor didn't last. It began to pour with rain, prompting the people to change from praying to cussing. Luckily, by then the tremors had subsided. The cops returned to their workplaces just as fast as they'd left them.

Upon his return, Miguel noticed immediately that the phone was ringing — or wheezing, rather.

"Speaking."

"Señor Capitan," the receiver rattled. "Luis

and I have done what you asked us to."

Miguel nodded. "Great. Have you found Enrique? Bring him here ASAP. The floors here at the station have been filthy for a week already. No one here is allowed to slope off work without having a good reason."

The receiver produced a weird crackling noise that sounded suspiciously like sobbing. "My apologies, Señor Capitan," the phone's membrane crackled. "We can't do this. He's dead."

"He's what?"

"We found his body up on the plateau by the Corpus Christi sanctuary. And fifteen more corpses with him, all Indians who used to guard the sanctuary. We've checked all the huts. Someone must have cut their throats. It must have happened at night when they were asleep. What do we do, Señor Capitan?"

Without replying, Miguel hung up.

Now he knew exactly what he had to do. And he had to do it alone.

CHAPTER SEVEN

Hallucination

(Late August — Early October 2015)

THE FOLLOWING SCENE is filmed using the shaky-cam technique so popular today. The color is toned down: it's not quite black and white but neither is it polychrome. The characters are slightly blurred, their outlines glowing the way they appear in today's movies whenever the director wants to portray a feverish hallucination or a drug-induced trip. It's just a tad too slow to be real although not as slow to qualify as slow motion. This is how the movies' main characters usually remember a dream they had a long time ago.

MOSCOW AIRPORT. It could be either Domodedovo or Sheremetyevo — something very generic. The holiday season is in full swing. The check-in booths are absolutely heaving with crowds of sweaty people in shorts and floral shirts dragging their children along together with their squeaky suitcases.

Announcements for arrivals and departures thunder overhead.

The camera pans onto a rosy-cheeked tourist with a pair of shades and a rucksack on his back, waiting to check in. He perfectly merges with the crowd in his Bermuda shorts and Hawaiian shirt with green palm tree print.

The audience recognizes Oleg Smolkin, our reluctant hero.

The camera switches to the next frame as if fast-forwarding through time.

We see Oleg on board the plane, fidgeting in an uncomfortable economy class seat. Air hostesses with bored smiles push trolleys down the aisle.

Oleg drinks tomato juice from a plastic beaker. The stewardesses ask the passengers if they prefer chicken or fish. The majority go for the chicken although it's virtually indistinguishable from the cellophane-wrapped, microwaved fish.

Next, we see the changeover hub. Judging by the giant hams complete with trotters hanging from hooks in the duty free shops, it just has to be Spain.

Oleg stumbles from one shop counter to the next, buying two serrano hams and a bottle of tequila. He undecidedly picks up a box of chocolates, then puts it back on the shelf.

Next, he speaks over his cell phone, his voice barely discernible over the noise of a big airport.

"Hi Sasha. No, I'm officially on holiday... Not in Cuba, no. I'm fed up with it. This time I decided

to go on a South American tour, just for kicks.
Venezuela, Rio de Janeiro, Bolivia, Peru... Too cool,
yes. Costly, I agree, what with the crisis and all.
But I've been planning it for the last three years.
We only live once, you know. What's money? You
can't take it with you. No, Vicky didn't come. You
know her. She's too afraid of the Ebola virus. Yes, I
know it's in Africa. She doesn't. Her geography's not
up to much. What did you say? No, it's a full four-
week tour. I'm gonna post some pictures on
Facebook. Vicky'll go green with jealousy. She's
never been further than Turkey. Okay, I'm off,
byeeee!"

Click. This is a different airplane, larger and
more comfortable. The stewardesses are wearing
green uniforms.

Oleg is fast asleep, his head nodding on his
shoulder.

A couple of empty plastic beakers roll over
the fold-down table. They definitely weren't filled
with juice. Which Russian tourist could resist the
temptation of making a long trip a little shorter?

The plane makes its descent, approaching
the landing strip from the direction of the deep blue
ocean. Palm trees and yellow buildings in the so-
called Mauritanian style flash past the porthole.

Oleg yawns his head off next to a passport
control booth. He receives a pink stamp in his
passport, retrieves his suitcase (after a bit of
running around the luggage conveyor trying to
catch up with it), then meets the hotel

representative who takes him for a race around the towns' streets in an old rust bucket.

All the traffic cops here are women. Apparently, in 2004 exclusively women were recruited for Lima's transport police and to everybody's surprise, drivers never managed to bribe them. As it turned out, Peruvian women took their policing much more seriously than men.

Oleg stares out of the shabby old car's window, ogling bronze-skinned Señoritas in their pretty olive-colored tunics.

The hotel — apparently, a three star — is equally shabby but still decent.

The camera focuses on Oleg breathing noisily in his sleep on a hotel bed.

Then it fast-forwards to the evening and the hotel bar. Oleg meets a girl, talks to her, then hugs her. Her brightly painted mouth resembles a rifle target.

Oleg leans to her ear. She nods and laughs. Oleg rummages through his wallet and produces a fifty-dollar bill.

They're back in the hotel room. The girl is astride the man, moving rhythmically, her hips glistening with sweat. The camera shows their coupling from every possible angle, although rather demurely: the girl's breasts and butt are blanked out with black strips.

Morning. Oleg throws a pill into a glass of water. The water begins to bubble. He drinks greedily, holding his head, then drops back on the bed and promptly falls asleep next to the naked girl wrapped in a blanket.

CUT TO BLACK

THE NEXT SCENE appears to be the start of a new episode.

Oleg is out on the ocean, against a backdrop of penguins and roaring sea lions. A sign saying *Pisco City and Island Excursions* hangs from the boat's planks.

Oleg again, sitting next to the pilot on board a two-seater plane sporting the sign *Naska Airlines* on its wing. The Nasca Desert is a plateau in Peru famous for its giant figures of animals, people and other creatures. Some researchers believe that they served to summon the gods of rain; others are convinced these are alien landing pads.

Oleg again, looking pleased as Punch, taking a selfie with his iPhone by the walls of an imposing colonial cathedral. Him again amid the greenery and the ruins of Machu Picchu, much less smiley this time, his forehead and cheeks covered in numerous mosquito bites. A small herd of llamas is grazing nearby; you can see that Oleg is trying to get closer to them for the sake of the picture.

Evening. Oleg at the chemist's, buying some mosquito repellent and pills for altitude sickness (known here as "soroche").

A dark bar room. Oleg drinks Cusqueña beer from a narrow-necked bottle while scratching everywhere, cussing the insects.

Daytime. Our hero walks down the street between majestic medieval buildings based on foundations made with blocks of flat black stone. Surprised, he studies a mural inside a Catholic church: Jesus and his apostles with Indian faces eating fried guinea pigs at the last supper. This mural does exist in the Cusco Cathedral, you can see it here.

Oleg's camera flashes. He argues with the temple guard who says photography is prohibited, then shoves him a colorful banknote. Him again, sorting through the souvenir stalls at the Plaza de Armas. Back at the airport yawning his head off, overcome by jetlag, then flying off in a new direction.

A snow-white beach; bronze-skinned girls in floral dresses gyrating to the beat of drums. Two bodies, dark and white, entwined in a hotel bed.

The picture begins to strobe: a boat on turquoise water; parrots on palm trees; coconuts; a sea plane bouncing over the cresting waves; cocktails complete with paper umbrellas; crisscrossing laser lights over a dance floor; the silent bubbling of an Aspirin pill in a glass; a sunburned shoulder being smeared with suntan oil.

Another giant airplane. Oleg is fast asleep. The camera takes a close-up of his sour face as he leaves the airport. A raging snowstorm assaults his suntanned cheeks; swirling snowflakes land on him.

ZOTOV

He takes a taxi home and predictably gets stuck in one of those unbearable Moscow traffic jams. The car wheels spin in the thawing snow, black water trickling down the tires.

Oleg's back at work, dishing out presents: souvenirs, figurines, and bottles of rum. He speaks to his boss, then calls Vicky. Judging by the expression on his face, it can be nothing good.

It's evening now. Oleg's on his couch watching porn on TV. Next to him is a coffee table crowded with beer bottles. A plateful of translucent slices of serrano ham from the duty free sits on the couch within his reach.

Fast forward a couple hours. The plate is now empty. Oleg gets up and goes to the kitchen to slice some more ham.

The knife slips and cuts his finger. Lots of blood, cussing and Band Aid. Oleg returns to the room and sets the plate down. In doing so, he knocks over a beer glass which smashes to smithereens on the floor.

Oleg cusses some more. Grudgingly he cleans up the mess, then rummages through a shelf by the television in search for a new glass. He zaps the remote and watches sarcastically as two men are working hard trying to satisfy a peroxide blonde. Beer bottles are emptying one by one, predictably replaced by a flask bearing the famous logo of a white horse.

The party's over. Oleg's head droops to one side, a limp arm hanging off the armchair. He's fast asleep.

SUDDENLY all the lightbulbs in the room begin to flicker: the floor lamp by the armchair, the chandelier on the ceiling and even the wall lamp in the corridor. Their flashing is powerful and scary.

Then they explode all at once, filling the air with shimmering iridescent dust which doesn't settle but remains hanging in the air, gradually enveloping Oleg's sleeping body. As it penetrates his skin, his face starts to glow with every color of the rainbow. His head and his entire body merge with the glittering dust which starts swirling toward the ceiling, rushing in every direction like a swarm of bees trying to find a way out.

It freezes momentarily in front of the dead TV screen. Then the swarm comprised of bits of broken glass, droplets of beer and Oleg's moleculized body begins to work its way into the television screen, covering it with what appears to be an iridescent film.

The camera focuses on a clock on the wall, its hands traveling from 10 p.m. to 12 p.m.

The mysterious iridescent film has disappeared. The TV screen is just as smooth and dark as before, like a morass which has swallowed its victim.

A loud rattling noise shakes the room. Cracks spread over the TV screen, gradually forming a complex web of thin strands.

Something explodes inside the TV. A

shadowy outline escapes a hole in the screen, its blurred silhouette thrashing around the deserted dark room. The shadow seems to be struggling, trying to break free, but is sucked back in.

The room turns pitch black. A single surviving lightbulb keeps flickering, its flashing reminiscent of death throes.

The movie screen turns black.

END OF FILM SPOOL

CHAPTER EIGHT

The Head

Lima, Barrio de Chino
October 27 1931

THE ARTIST was in a hurry. He had to complete the last doll before evening, otherwise he might be late for his date. His love didn't like waiting; she always set up their dates for a certain time. He couldn't afford to be late, otherwise he might not see her for a very long time.

Whenever he had to look at her, he always squinted one eye trying to jealously catch the Apprentice's stare. Their love was crafty; she was playful and cynical. She acted in different ways. Sometimes she seemed to choose both men at once and was prepared to go to bed with them, indulging in her orgies like the Inca Emperor's wife. Othertimes, she'd admire the Artist alone only to start luring the Apprentice into her nets, just like a seasoned Barrio de Chino whore. She was both hot and cold, fickle but faithful — and this was exactly what aroused him, driving him wild, making his heart tremble in his chest.

He loved her madly like he'd never loved before.

Both the Artist and the Apprentice were beside themselves with desire. They were frustrated from all the waiting.

He'd already got so used to the stench of blood at the slaughterhouse that he didn't notice it anymore. The most important thing was that he could wash himself properly. The murderer made sure he had some boiling water once he'd finished his manipulations. He added some lavender oil to the bath water. Usually he entered the house as a rich don clad in a suit and tie; sometimes he also used the disguise of a homeless man. Still, the person who left the slaughterhouse was invariably dressed up as a gentleman, wearing clean brand-new clothes he always bought in advance, elegant, scrubbed clean and fragrant with perfume.

A dead female arm splashed into the brine.

He studied the dead girl's nails. All of them seemed perfect but for the ring finger. He'd have to replace it. How many models had the two friends been forced to destroy in order to put one doll together? Hard to say.

It had taken them a lot of practice; most of their first attempts had gone straight in the bin, so to say. Forty girls? Fifty? It made no difference. Nobody would have started looking for them, anyway, had they not left their dolls in the most public places of Lima.

Luckily, they'd nearly made it. There was very little time left until La Diablada, and then...

The thought gave him goosebumps.

He looked down straight into the giant tub filled with dismembered bodies. Heads, arms, feet, breasts of every size floated in the pinkish liquid smelling of sea salt. The Artist yanked them out one by one and tried to fit them together, all businesslike, as he envisioned his future doll, then squeamishly threw the unnecessary parts into a steel box by his feet.

Holy Virgin Mary, so much waste this time!

But at least he was going to produce perfection incarnate. The Uku Pacha dwellers were going to appreciate his offering. A new entity would enter this world during La Diablada, one upon whose help the Artist depended greatly.

He wasn't as dumb as his Apprentice who had taken a lot of coercing and convincing. He was probably still thinking that it was the Artist who'd buried the pot of gold in his vegetable patch. As if he didn't have anything better to do! The ugly subterranean demons were only their powerful king's entourage; they were his pages, waiters and servants.

Come to think of it, what did the unborn have to offer? They could give him fame, power and riches, even a ghostly army of the undead — but they couldn't work miracles. And in order to obtain true love, you needed a miracle, performed by an experienced inhabitant of Uku Pacha, a true professional of his trade.

There, in his underground tunnels, he was almost impotent, unable to use even a fraction of his magic. But the victims' blood was going to seep through the ground, filling his heart with power. For this, the monster was bound to repay his humble worshippers in kind. Really, it was no big deal for him to create a miracle.

And the two friends had a thing or two to offer him in return. Like making him stay on Earth for many long years, offering him a daily recompense of human flesh and blood.

The Artist smiled, remembering the archeological digs in Cusco. Those useless Spaniards who'd faced a supernatural force for the first time had been petrified, especially once they'd begun dying one by one. Panicking, the Viceroy had ordered the blocking of all the passages leading to Uku Pacha. What an idiot.

Where was his Spain now, once a luxurious fairy-tale empire on which the sun never set? They didn't even have a king now after the poor bastard Alfonso had been dethroned and fled the country, leaving Madrid to the republicans.

Just think that everything could have turned out differently! Had they bothered to sacrifice a meager thousand girls to feed the unborn, the Spanish might have conquered not only South America but the rest of the world as well.

Himself, he didn't need a king's power. Nor the money. Money was dust; power was a toy for generals and impotents.

The only thing that ruled this planet was love, and love alone. In his history lessons in high school, the Artist had studied the story of Genghis Khan, a Mongol warlord. The tale had forever stuck in his heart. Already a very old man, the general fell madly in love with his youngest concubine, Khulan Khatun. Just think of it: a powerful conqueror who'd let oceans of blood from China to Europe — and there he was, at the feet of a girl with bitten nails whose clothes stank of camel sweat.

The Artist was no worse than him, was he? Who would have thought that he'd be infatuated by this woman? That every night he'd fall asleep with her name on his lips? That he'd be kissing her portrait? And even (although he was ashamed to admit it) that he'd be self-gratifying himself under the sheets imagining how she'd straddle his body on the very first night of their physical coupling?

The Artist squeezed his eyes shut, sensing the stirrings of an erection.

He lowered his hand into the pinkish brine, moving his fingers smoothly and dreamily through the liquid like a musician about to put his bow to his instrument.

Life was fleeting, the pieces of his models being the saddest confirmation of this notion. Any woman was only a combination of flesh and bones. Plus a bundle of rather stinky guts which you can't see in her stomach under that pretty dress as you're flirting with her over a glass of wine. But as soon as you fell in love with her, she became your treasure, your sweetheart, your precious baby. You turned to stone in the mad heat of passion, realizing that you couldn't even breathe in her absence, that life wasn't worth jack without her.

That's exactly how he felt about it. Uku Pacha was the only place capable of healing his disease. They could do absolutely everything there.

You shouldn't think he was going to try to force Her to love him back. That would have been wrong and sacrilegious. All he wanted from the demons was to bring them together. And then we'd see who'd be the lucky one — the boorish Apprentice or the sophisticated esthetics-loving Artist.

Oh yes, Señor, then we'd see.

Having said that, the Apprentice had been a good sport.

When the Artist had told his accomplice that he had to take out all of the Incan temple guards in Corpus Christi, the Apprentice hadn't batted an eyelid. He didn't even ask why they had to do it so early. He must have realized that the Artist knew better, not to mention elementary precautions. It hadn't been for nothing the Russian detective had visited the sacred village.

And as for Enrique... They'd been seriously considering approaching him with their grandiose plans as they'd first started out, but they'd stopped themselves just in time. He wasn't a real priest. All the sacrifices in Corpus Christi were nothing but a theater show. They didn't kill anyone; they didn't shed human blood. He'd brought disgrace on the Incan religion by feeding pigs to the gods of evil! The renegade had deserved his death, and so had his spies.

The Apprentice had arranged their execution rather well. He'd brought along five thugs he knew, promising to pay them well. And once it was all over, his two revolvers had done away with his helpers nicely. At short range, quick firing weapons made it light work: ten seconds, twelve slugs and five bodies.

Enrique had only himself to blame. Having strayed onto the path of fake sacrifices, he'd been doomed. The platform by the magnolia tree near the Corpus Christi altar was indispensable for their final ritual, and it was easier to seize it than to ask the renegade's permission to use it.

Although the Artist would have never admitted it, his friend had been right. They should have done away with the Russian when they'd had the chance. Unfortunately, drunken on his success, the Artist hadn't thought about it early on his journey. And now it was already too late. The detective's house was under police protection, and they couldn't very easily start a shootout at the police station: there were too many people around, so the two friends were bound to be caught. And the wretched Russian didn't ever go out for walks.

ZOTOV

The two had been seriously thinking about hiring a professional (seeing as the slums teemed with them, anyway) — but what if the murderer got caught in the act and started singing? Then they could kiss the whole thing goodbye.

Oh no. It was even more interesting this way. The Artist wasn't looking for an easy ride; he wasn't going to just slap some color on a canvas like a street painter; he fully intended to come up with the masterpiece of the century.

Very well. Let the Russian live to witness his triumph. He was going to see what would happen during this Diablada and realize his total insignificance compared to his opponent's brilliant genius.

Because the Artist never doubted his own genius. Everybody in his family had told him so, even more often than was necessary. Both his parents had doted on him. His late father had a desperate desire to see him devote his life to studying the legacy of their ancestors. He may have not followed in his father's footsteps but he'd had a lot more success as an amateur. He'd indeed been a great scholar of their ancestral legacy — so much so that these days, the whole of Lima was quaking with fear at night.

He found it rather flattering. He'd known from the start that the Incan religion was the real thing. Let those educated 20th-century cynics laugh at those who still believed in the unborn and the ghostly armies of Uku Pacha. Being the product of their era, they couldn't think otherwise. The last laugh would be on him.

These days, you couldn't surprise anyone with the mystery of a telephone when you'd pick up the receiver and hear a voice coming from North America or even as far as Europe. No one even stopped to ponder how this happened. Automobiles, airplanes, radio, electricity... there were all sorts of weird and wondrous things that humanity took for granted these days without considering them madness or witchcraft. But when it came to the dead and unborn demons in their underground tunnels — of course they didn't exist! Sure they were only a fantasy, a figment of crazed Quechua priests' imagination provoked by too much coca smoking.

But don't forget that the Incan civilization used to be far richer than all those Spanish ragamuffins in shiny armor who'd come here from the other side of the world brandishing the sign of the cross. They used to pray, begging Jesus in heaven to fulfil their desires, while the Incas had by then already known that all the dreams of wealth, power and conquest were quite fruitful provided you were prepared to pay the price. The dead Uku Pacha dwellers would grant you all this, even though you wouldn't be able to enjoy the fruits of your endeavors for very long, because they would come to get their dues.

Those pompous 20th-century people believed themselves too modern to realize that the Incan mythology was no fantasy at all.

The Artist picked a head out of the brine. The most beautiful he could find.

Strands of hair crusted with salt. Clouded eyes. An open mouth with a white residue covering the lips.

Good enough.

He took the head by the hair and carried it downstairs into his workshop. Descending the steps, the Artist stooped and entered a small cave. It had once been used to store pigs' guts, its floor drenched in filthy brown blood.

In a niche in the wall, flanked by two black candles, stood an effigy of his King. As soon as he'd entered, the Artist knelt facing His Majesty. Holding the dead head in his outstretched left hand, the Artist began to sing a Quechuan dedication chant, rocking to and fro like a Chinese figurine in one of those shops in Barrio de Chino.

The song, just as melodious as it was mournful, was supposed to express the unity of joy and grief upon seeing the King. The statue's eyes watched him in silence but he knew that the King could hear every word.

He bent to the floor and grabbed a knife, its blade fashioned from tinted gray glass. Jumping to his feet, he unhesitantly cut himself with the knife just under the left nipple, right into the tattooed face of the Granter of Wishes.

Blood trickled down toward his crotch, painting his tattooed skin red.

He cut himself again, deeper this time.

Oh, how sweet. Please, I want more.

He pressed the dead girl's head to his chest, sensing her nose and soft lips, wiping his blood away with her hair as if it were a towel, its strands now soaked with blood. He began to gyrate rhythmically, springing high in the air as if almost flying.

The Artist was singing the Great Song of Uku Pacha which the Inca priests had sung many centuries ago.

I swear my allegiance to You.
I bring you my sacrifices.
Here, I pay with blood for my desire.
Arise and come to me.
Let's have a dance; answer my plea.
I'll give you whatever you desire.
Do grant me that which I desire.
I beg you!
I beg you!
I beg you!

This was the original 17th-century lyrics of La Diablada. Later, the Spanish had forbidden singing such songs during dances (as well as the ceremony itself) although the Indians still sung it until the present day.

This was the dance once performed by both the Inca Atahualpa and the Inca Manco. We still don't know whether Francisco Pizarro or Diego de

Almagro had danced it too. But we do know that they did address the spirits of the unborn, summoning the armies of the dead, and even turned to the Incan semi-gods for help ("semi" being the operative word), bringing them sacrifices of ordinary meat.

The Artist, however, was presenting the King with a work of art, so he had little doubt that the god would grant his wish. Of course, you couldn't really tell whether a creature who'd been living for millennia in the dark amongst the dead could appreciate true beauty — but in any case, he was about to arrive.

Soon. Very soon.

The Artist thought he heard the sound of far-off drumbeats.

He closed his eyes. He could see gold-painted Incan legions in their feathered helmets and leather armor, clutching short swords in their muscular hands. Praising Viracocha, priests laid still steaming freshly-ripped human hearts onto their altars. Blood hissed like a serpent on the square stones.

More prisoners were shoved toward the altars, and they walked toward them with the passive gait of the doomed, offering their chests to the knives without a struggle.

The whole thing resembled a conveyor belt.

In one swift motion, a prisoner's chest is cut open; blood fountains upward; a priest's strong hands rip the chest cavity open; the crowd cheers as another heart is torn out. The gods receive their breakfast as they have done since time immemorial.

The Emperor Atahualpa whose golden throne rests on the shoulders of the strongest warriors raises his head and sees a black eagle soaring high in the heavens. This is an omen — a sign from the gods of Uku Pacha that they're thirsty.

In a short wave of his bejeweled hand, the Emperor sends a crowd of female prisoners — the choicest and most beautiful — toward a cave. You couldn't scrimp on these things. The gods saw everything. If you left some sweet morsel for yourself, they would always know.

And they'd punish you.

The girls' clothes are being ripped off. The Emperor smiles.

Knives. Blood. The smell of magnolia.

Oh yes...

The drums stop all at once.

The Artist opened his eyes. Staggering, he fell back to his knees, offering the severed head to the statue.

The air around him began to ripple as if from great heat. For yet another time, he clearly saw both of the King's eyes light up, casting a soft glow into the room.

... HE MET THE APPRENTICE around midnight, drained, exhausted, and at the end of his tether.

ZOTOV

The fourth doll had completely depleted him — but God his witness, this was going to be something special.

There was only one last touch left before La Diablada began. They needed to take a drink from the divine spring, sampling happiness and mustering the powers they needed for the last push.

The Artist was close shaven and dressed in a pressed suit with a chrysanthemum in his buttonhole. The Apprentice too had smartened himself up. Although not quite as expensive, he was wearing a good-quality suit and hat just like a noble don. He was clutching a bouquet of burgundy roses. You could tell he was nervous.

The Artist had a little chuckle: this thug, a murderer, a butcher, was anxious like a nun before her first kiss. He walked over to his friend,

"Buena noche."

"Buena noche, compañero."

They exchanged a hug, slapping each other on the shoulders.

"Today we're installing the fourth doll," the Artist said. "Once that done, neither of us goes home. We're gonna sit it out in our usual hidey hole until La Diablada. It's only a few days. Once the festivities are over, nothing will matter anymore because by then, we'll get what we need. In the meantime, let's savor every moment. This is our last meeting with her in this guise."

The Apprentice chuckled. "You could say

that. Only you know... She always looks at me."

"That's only your imagination, compañero," the Artist replied coldly. "I think she likes me more. Still, it's pretty academic. Very soon we'll find out which one of us is right."

"True," the Apprentice agreed. "Although I think I already know."

The Artist laughed in his face. "You're incorrigible, amigo. Let's not waste time. She hates waiting."

They approached an old colonial mansion and disappeared behind a wrought-iron door.

BACK AT THE SLAUGHTERHOUSE, a candle expired. There was nothing to light there anymore. The pit where the Artist had kept his victims was now empty. Their body parts floated in brine. The last of his dolls rose at the center of the room, stunning in her beauty, her dead crystal eyes glistening.

CHAPTER NINE

The Rat

Glitz City
The movie set of modern Moscow
The Citizens' Advice Bureau

THE MOVIE RESUMES with the same prospective of an old fan on the ceiling of a shabby room. Same view from above; the room is easily seen through the fan's rotating fins.

Four people have frozen below, like a screenshot from an isometric computer game. Two of them are dressed as Red Army soldiers, one aiming his rifle at the other's back. Opposite them is a Wehrmacht officer in a dusty uniform, pointing his Walther at a petite girl with cropped hair. The scene is shot in slow motion; you can see specks of dust float in the sun. The gun in the German officer's hand quivers; the Red Army soldier's grin widens as he presses the butt of his Mosin rifle to his shoulder.

The picture is accompanied by some boring

mournful Hitchcock-style music. The audience clench armrests and lean forward.

A loud noise makes them startle. A girl in the eighth row squeezed her eyes shut, peeking at the screen through the safety of her eyelashes. Something very bad is about to happen.

"PETROV," Oleg says without turning. "That's a surprise. You can't be German, surely?"

"I am," the soldier replies eagerly. "What's wrong with that, *mein bruder*? Haven't you heard about the Brandenburg 800 special regiment?"

Oleg remains silent.

Petrov laughs. "I knew you hadn't. Just so that you know, my dear brother in arms, it's made up of *Volksdeutsche* — German expats who are native speakers of other languages. French, Russian, an so on. I'm a scout, a spy, or a 'ratte' as we call it: a rat. Take your pick."

"I saw you killing Germans," Oleg says dryly.

Petrov grins. "So what? Spies have to wriggle themselves into other people's confidence, *mein lieber freund*. We're trained to be despicable unprincipled bastards. That's our job description. One professional agent is worth more than a whole company of nameless soldiers. But listen, bro — oops, *bruder*, you can't imagine how it works! You didn't even know what hit you. Okay, so I might have smoked a dozen of my own compatriots but just think how useful I've been!"

Oleg winces. Another movie cliché. The

"good" agents in movies are inevitably handsome, noble-minded and good family men. And as for their German counterparts, they're always scumbags — and you can't even be a hundred percent sure they aren't having it off with their German Shepherds. Such a movie character wouldn't think twice about shooting his own or killing some stupid girl who's fallen in love with him.

So yes, okay, he's been stupid. He should have seen through Petrov's fake identity. This is a classic, really: a typical murder-mystery killer who's on no one's suspect list. Here too, he was a perfect decoy with his freckled Russian face and jug ears. He could even have had some plastic surgery on the Abwehr's budget.

Petrov shoves him with the barrel of his gun toward the officer.

"Let me be completely honest with you," the soldier heaves a sigh. His soft village lilt has already disappeared, replaced by a guttural German accent. "I even liked you, even though you're not Aryan. I've spent a lot of time amongst you, so I'm used to mixing with lower races. But I'm a soldier and I obey orders. When our radio man sent me a coded message that I had to deliver you to Glitz City, I obeyed even though I still don't know what they meant by Glitz. So goodbye, brother, don't hold a grudge. I'm gonna tell the commissar we'd gone out to snatch a Kraut canary but walked into an ambush so you got yourself heroically killed by taking out a whole German platoon with a grenade while shouting, "Long live Comrade Stalin!"

"You're a real bastard, Petrov," Oleg says slowly. "I don't blame you though. That's the role you have to play. You're the bad guy. You're obliged to be a scumbag. Your job is to make the audience hate you with abandon and wait for you to finally get your just desserts. Then the whole theater will applaud. Like when they shoot Mrs. Carmody in *The Mist*. When she finally got a bullet in the guts, I was the first to cheer!"

"Who's Mrs. Carmody?" Petrov asks from behind him, anxious.

"What the fuck do you care?" Oleg snaps. "*Mein Kampf* is probably the only book you've ever read in your life! Just believe me there's this writer called Stephen King..."

"Is he an Aryan?" the agent asks.

The German officer finally breaks his silence. "*Genug,*[16]" his voice sounds like a shot out of the blue.

"*Jawohl,*" Petrov says, clicking his heels. "*Kann ich shon gehen, herr Oberst?*"[17]

The officer gives an indifferent nod.

The audience can't see his face because the girl is standing in front of him. Either the German has stooped on purpose or he is unnaturally short.

---

[16] Enough (German)

[17] Yes, Sir! Can I go now, Colonel, Sir? (German)

ZOTOV

All we can see is the glistening of his dark glasses and the silver wire of his epaulettes.

Petrov lowers his rifle butt to the ground and goose-steps toward the exit.

The Colonel raises his Walther like a robot and mechanically points it at Petrov. Oleg's eyes open wide as the officer pulls the trigger. A shot rings out.

The bullet hits Petrov straight in the back of the head. Convulsively he swings round, his face a mask of surprise.

The Colonel shoots him twice more in the chest. The faces of Oleg and Joan are showered with beadlike droplets of blood; their cheeks seem to be covered in freckles.

The rifle clatters to the stone floor, followed by Petrov himself who slumps softly to the ground like a cuddly toy. A pool of dark liquid starts to form around his body.

Joan squeamishly steps aside to avoid the mess. She looks surprised but death doesn't really frighten her: she's seen it all before in the porn world.

Oleg is even less likely to faint: he's been at the front a long time, under fire every day. But naturally he can't contain his curiosity: what the hell is going on in here?

The officer holsters his gun. "I'm sorry," he says softly in very good Russian with just a hint of an accent. "I had no other choice but to try and get you out of here with the help of the now-defunct

Private Petrov. It wouldn't have been a very bright idea for all three of you to try to cross the frontline. It was safer for you to split up and cross on your own and then meet in a safe place. Mr. Petrov has done his job enviably but I won't be needing him anymore. Between us, the scriptwriters didn't conceive him as a very nice person. Please don't get me wrong, I know you shouldn't kill anyone without warning, no matter how bad they are. But you have to agree you don't feel very sorry for them."

The German speaks very politely, apologetically even. You can tell he's embarrassed by both the shooting and the body on the floor, and also by having to upset the other two. Just like a college lecturer who quietly explains his subject to his recalcitrant students who didn't bother to do their homework.

Oleg peers to one side and sees that the officer has no face. A woolen balaclava hugs his head, the dark glasses looking admittedly bizarre over the eye slits.

How strange. The late Private Petrov didn't seem surprised by the Colonel's appearance. At least he didn't pose any questions — even though, judging by war movies, Germans were total control freaks. In which case it makes perfect sense. Petrov received an order from the radio operator to deliver Oleg to Glitz City and hand him over to a Wehrmacht colonel. That was it. It wasn't the person's face that mattered to the movie Germans but his epaulettes.

ZOTOV

Oleg feels a terrible temptation to pick up the rifle from the floor, but... the Jerry will surely shoot him before he can get to it. This is a movie, after all, where all the characters are as hard as nails and even a lethal wound could prove to be a mere scratch.

The problem is, Oleg is a newcomer to this world. He's no superhero. So he has no idea how fate will play out. The movie script might be performed as it's being written, with him playing the bit part of one of the disposable soldiers who get killed in droves in the first ten seconds of any major blockbuster.

Better not to risk it. Had the German wanted, he'd have already killed both of them. But it doesn't look as if he's going to do that.

"What do you want from us?" Oleg says.

The German holds up his gloved hands melodramatically. "Actually, what I need is you."

What a shame he can't see the German's face. Or eyes.

"But first I wanted some proof," the German continues, "that you were the guy who arrived here from another world. Because of this, I set up video surveillance in your room in Sex City. I wanted to be sure. It had happened quite a few times before but as a rule, all those people died before I could get to them. But you're a very special case. I was afraid of scaring you off because you're my last hope of getting back to Earth. I'm here already far too long. You need to know that none of us can get out of here on our own. To open the portal back to Earth, there needs to be three of us. You, I and a local girl. In order to teleport, we need to be together. Sorry if I'm rambling a bit. I'm quite overcome by our meeting."

The officer nods at the rifle lying next to the dead man. "You can pick it up. I'm not going to hurt you. We're all in the same boat. My apologies for keeping the lady here by force and for making her come here. I know I've frightened you. Now we need to leave this building and hurry to another movie. Petrov, may he rest in peace, has brought you to the period-drama district which means that very soon this place will be crawling with police trying to track down German spies. Come with me. You can't go home without me."

"Why?' Oleg asks dimly.

The Colonel shrugs. One of his silver-wound epaulettes crimps. "Because otherwise you'll be stuck here for good."

FROM ABOVE, the camera shows us three people who are exiting the citizens' advice bureau: two men and a woman. They walk toward a vehicle parked next to the building. It appears to be an 1940s German car — an Opel Cadet or something similar.

The three climb into it and leave, raising clouds of dust which conceals the luggage rack and the car's wheels. After a short while, a cavalcade of lorries and black cars arrive at the building,

ZOTOV

disgorging soldiers holding burp guns. They professionally surround the area and start throwing hand grenades in through the windows.

The building shakes from the explosions; its broken windows billow flames and black smoke.

The credits start to roll but they're so tiny that you can't read the cast list.

The screen darkens, then goes black.

CHAPTER TEN

Iluminación

The town of Callao, 10 miles from Lima
October 28 1931

IGUEL HAD ALREADY regretted countless times that he'd agreed to a meeting in this particular tavern. This was the nastiest kind of drinking establishment, packed with whores and stevedores from the port. It reeked of puke and stale fish. The ocean breeze was so strong the shack's walls creaked, so flimsy they let in wind through their numerous cracks.

The detective raised his jacket collar and brought a mug of dubious grog to his lips. The waitress — a huge dark-haired Indian woman in a filthy apron — placed a scruffy bowl of soup in front of him, splashing some of it onto the table. The red tails of "carabineros" — large Peruvian prawns — peered up sadly from the bottom of the bowl.

"Here you are, Señor."

"Thanks, gorgeous."

ZOTOV

"Gorgeous" smiled back, the fat folds around her mouth reminding him of a sea lion. On her way back to the bar, she turned and leered at Miguel, very nearly barging into a tableful of drunken sailors.

If his contact hadn't arrived now, Miguel would be a finished man.

Luckily, the contact did arrive just as Miguel had finished his brief but sad ruminations. A small lean man with a cap pulled over his eyes slumped onto a chair next to him, choosing the one nearest to the wall.

"We could have just as well met up at the tip," Miguel smirked. "The smell is the same, and the food quality is also not far off. It took me a lot of hassle to shake off my ministerial bodyguards. I even had to lie to them about seeing my foxy mistress behind my wife's back before they'd let me go. The funny thing is, I'm not even married but our police force is trained to believe what you tell them.

The little man didn't appreciate the humor. "Here at least nobody knows either of us," he whispered, leaning across the table. "And in Lima, everybody knows who I work for. Had we been noticed in the city together, we'd have both had problems. Anyway, it won't hurt you to taste some humble soup. It gets better after the fifth sip. The prawns aren't the freshest but you won't die from them. At least it's cheap."

Miguel cringed and pushed away the prawns' mass grave. "Have you found out what I asked you to?" he said, unable to contain himself any longer.

"Have I ever not done it?" the man replied with his own question. "Have you got the money with you?"

Miguel produced an envelope from an inside pocket and shoved it across the table. His contact didn't open it, just covered it with his hand, crumpling it.

"It's in five-sol notes," Miguel said. "Just like you asked me."

This inconspicuous fellow had been working for him for quite a while. Every time Miguel needed to dig up some information that required clearance from the National police, he could count on Officer Diego Mariscos from the Internal Investigation Department.

Burdened with a huge family like all Indians, Mariscos suffered from an acute lack of money but unfortunately, his job didn't afford him many bribes. Mainly his money came from petty shopkeepers whose premises were "under police protection" as well as smarmy pimps from Barrio de Chino.

Apart from the doubtless vice of corruption, Mariscos had one other useful quality: he could obtain almost any secret information from police sources provided the money was right. Miguel had used his services on numerous occasions and had never regretted it.

Beaming, Mariscos crumpled the envelope yet again to feel the amount of banknotes inside.

ZOTOV

His face exuded a satisfied and rather orgasmic expression.

"I'm waiting," Miguel interrupted his nirvana.

"Excellent," Mariscos smiled, revealing a mouthful of rotting teeth. "You won't be disappointed."

They quickly got down to business in a barely audible whisper, their heads touching. Mariscos handed Miguel a stack of photographs as he replied to his questions, giving him what seemed to be the right answers.

Miguel looked pensively at the ceiling, then turned back to Mariscos and leaned in toward his ear. The informer nodded. He then rose and left the tavern without looking back.

The waitress walked over to pick up the already-cold soup. "Something else, Señor?"

"Yes, my lovely," Miguel said without looking up. "A glass of pisco."

The very first swig of the stinking brew (by the same token, the vodka they used to serve in Russian taverns hadn't smelled of roses, either) warmed Miguel's body up. He hated pisco with abandon — but you couldn't very easily order champagne or Armagnac in a port tavern.

He really wanted to say, "That's exactly what I thought!"

We all like saying things like that. When a decision has dropped into our lap, we like to think that we knew it all along and it was just hanging around at the back of our heads.

That's only partially true. Once the police had checked out all of the cars of the rich and famous, he'd been so lost for ideas that he'd ordered them to search the city's taxis. Which again had brought up zero results.

That got Miguel seriously thinking. You had to agree that it was physically impossible to hide a good car in Lima, especially because good cars were very few and far between here.

That's when he'd had the bright idea to get Mariscos to run a secret check of all the vehicles belonging to the Ministry of Interior as well as those of the National Police Department.

That was a true eureka moment — a real *iluminación*. Now Miguel knew perfectly well that there were two murderers involved. But that implied that there were two cars, as well.

IT WAS IN THOSE cars that Mariscos had discovered minute traces of blood on the seats. They'd been thoroughly cleaned — but luckily, blood is impossible to get rid of completely. He'd also discovered traces of brine mixed with blood as well as dozens of long dark hairs.

For some reason, Miguel was convinced that they'd fallen from the heads of the Lima dolls.

Just this morning, they'd found the fourth and last one.

Admittedly, the Artist had done a fine job. He'd truly exceeded himself. It was a real work of art (if you disregarded the materials it had been made with, as well as the reason for its existence).

It had taken him nine girls to create his masterpiece — one of them having only been used for her ears and the small toe of her right foot. He'd used two different hair types. Her arms were also different, the left one put together from three separate limbs. He'd also sewn a new skin onto her back.

He'd dressed her in the most expensive robe of red brocade made to order. Doubtful they'd ever locate the dressmaker: it looked as if the Artist had bothered to buy the robe a long time beforehand. The doll's cheeks and nose were covered with more gold than usual; the murderer hadn't even scrimped on some mountain crystal for her eyes.

The doll was shaped as a vase, symbolizing a precious vessel. The Artist had poured the mixture of thickened blood and magnolia petals into her hollow body and attached a fine silver crown to her head. He seemed to have carried out his work with passion and inspiration.

He desperately needed to appease someone down in Uku Pacha. Who exactly it was, Miguel didn't yet know.

Never mind. At least now the bond between the Artist and his Apprentice was clear to him. Deep under the third doll's nails, they'd discovered tiny fragments of human skin: Teresa must have attacked her killer, scratching him. And after having slain her, the Artist had completely forgot to clean under her nails. Artists! He'd been too impatient to begin crafting his present for the gods of the underworld.

Diego was worth every penny he'd been paid. He'd not only found the two cars with the traces of blood and women's hair but also tracked down their owners and taken pictures of them. They'd never seen the tail on them; they hadn't even noticed the bright flash of the camera. This was the work of a truly professional sleuth.

Miguel slightly lifted one of the photographs and peered into the face of a young man. His left cheek was covered in Band Aid whose white strip did little to conceal the dark traces of the three scratch marks under it.

Oh my God.

All his doubts were instantly dispelled. He ordered another pisco and brought it to his lips but wasn't in a hurry to drink. The case was basically closed. If he gave the order now, he could arrest the two of them within an hour, but...

You needed to understand which kind of country you were living in. The blond boy on the photo was very well connected.

Now Miguel realized how the murderer and his accomplice had managed to stay abreast of the investigation and why they'd done away with Enrique at the slightest suspicion. From the very start, those two had had access to all the results of the ongoing investigation, sometimes having stood right before his eyes.

It was still a mystery to him why they hadn't

bothered to do away with him too, considering the ease with which the two of them had murdered dozens of people. Oh yes, sir, this story would come to figure in Peru's history. Or rather, would have come to figure, had it not been for one small detail: the murderer's status.

Miguel had little idea of how he could have appeared in the murderer's family home with a squad of cops in tow. He wasn't even sure there were any cops in his precinct that would be brave enough to comply with the order. He very much doubted it.

Which meant there were only two options left. Either he had to track the Artist down himself, then gun him down when he tried to resist arrest (because Miguel had little doubt that he would resist). Alternatively, he could try to arrest his accomplice and through interrogation, make him show them the location of their workshop where they'd put the dolls together.

Miguel might not have been good at many things, but interrogation was his forte. He'd been through hell in Russia; he still remembered the Vladivostok secret police and how they used to beat Red Army prisoners to a pulp, burning their fingers with cigarettes in order to extract the necessary information. The Red Army had been no better with his fellow White Army officers, drowning them in ice holes or tying them to trees in a frost-bound forest.

Very nice. The good old days.

And what would that give him?

Nothing but problems. Once his assistant had been arrested, the Artist was bound to flee and use his connections to arrange his accomplice's death. Even if they put him in solitary confinement, there'd always be a cop eager to earn five hundred greenbacks for doing away with the main witness.

He wasn't even sure the two were still in town. They'd been watching Miguel all this time, planning their next moves and minimizing the possibility of being arrested. Having unveiled the last doll, they must have gone into hiding for the three days left until La Diablada. They'd completed their mission: a dark overlord was about to rise from the depths of Uku Pacha, bringing them their coveted love on a silver platter.

Oh, yes. The whole police department knew about the two young men's infatuation. Everybody used to laugh at them: of course, they were only snot-nosed youngsters, barely eighteen years old.

Who would have thought.

Never mind. Miguel remembered his own first crush — Anyuta Belozersky, the most ethereal, breathtaking beauty, she of heavenly eyes and fluffy eyelashes. She'd been a high school student courted by some military brat from a neighboring cadet school. Would Miguel not have killed for the prospect of her favors? Absolutely. He would have unhesitantly smoked the wretched cadet for one single interested glance from her. How he'd hated his fortunate rival who would exchange dignified bows with the object of his desire! Miguel had imagined challenging the miserable bastard to a duel with rapiers, stabbing him to death in a well-choreographed attack like d'Artagnan in *The Three Musketeers.*

Youth is merciless in the pursuit of its goal; young wolves won't stop at anything in order to assuage their hunger. The two young men were a couple of social rungs down the ladder compared to the object of their desire; they'd never be able to cross paths with her in real life; for her, the likes of them were only part of a faceless crowd which merited a condescending smile but which would never have been in the running as a suitor or husband.

So the murderers went all-out. And they seemed to be winning.

"Another pisco, Señor?" the waitress returned to the table in her elephantine gait.

Miguel smiled. "No, beautiful. I've gotta be off. How much do I owe you?"

Once again he picked up the photographs and studied them. A dark-haired young man, apparently with a good dose of Indian blood, leaned against a car door with a certain panache, as if posing to an invisible photographer.

Rodrigo Fuegos, the Interior Ministry driver who two weeks ago had driven him to the site of the first doll's discovery. What a sangfroid: to first transport a concoction of four bodies to the magnolia tree, then use the same vehicle to drive the police investigator. He'd even had the cheek to ask Miguel naïve questions en route. No wonder Miguel couldn't breathe with the stench of cheap cigars: the driver had filled the car with smoke on purpose, to block out the smell of the herbs in the doll's belly. It's common knowledge that tobacco is the best thing to camouflage a smell.

It had been Alejandro de Castillero, Fuegos' childhood friend, who'd found him this cushy position. Alejandro was the adopted son of the Deputy Minister Juarez, the Quechua Indian who'd had a marriage of prestige to a beautiful white woman, the widow of a professor of archeology, Alejandro's biological father.

As far as Miguel knew, Alejandro was studying to become a surgeon. He'd love to have known whether the young man had entered the medical faculty before he'd thought of the whole Uku Pacha thing, or if his studying medicine had been part of an already-preconceived plan?

Miguel laid a banknote on the table.

La Diablada was almost upon them. There was no other solution but to sort it out himself.

CHAPTER ELEVEN

The Masquerade

The B-Movie City
Late at night

THE CAMERA SEEMS to be soaring over the city in some sort of bird's eye view, occasionally descending low enough to offer a glimpse of residential areas. They're all different: some dark and gloomy like a parody of Gotham City, others bright and gaudy like a clown's face. Some of the film sets are shamelessly unfinished: slap-dash brickwork with crumbling plaster, leaky roofs and lopsided stairwells, in the style of "Potemkin villages"[18] with their cardboard facades

---

[18] Potemkin village: a fake front of a non-existing house or other structure built to create the impression of a finished habitable building. Named so after Prince Potemkin, the favorite of the Russian Empress Catherine the Great, who, having embezzled the money given to him to build new villages, had fake house fronts built along the Empress' way to pull the wool over her eyes. The expression can also be used figuratively.

built for show and their dusty cobwebbed framework left out of view.

It looks so confusing you can't even tell at first which city the film is set in.

Finally, the bird's eye pans down to a street café window, showing Oleg's profile. He's sitting at a table, typing away on his laptop. A steaming tea cup is sitting on the table to the left of him. He's not wearing the Red Army uniform anymore; he's got a T-shirt on printed with an elephant and a caption below saying, *Thailand.* That, plus a pair of shorts and some flip-flops. He looks like a regular holidaymaker and is even a bit sunburnt.

A waiter walks up to him and leans over with a smile. Oleg shakes his head, looking annoyed.

The bird's eye camera pans back out, showing us that the whole scene is set in a film studio, one that's been quickly slung together and is already falling apart.

As I've already mentioned earlier, it feels so good to finally be able to carry on with my diary. When you speak to yourself out loud, everybody considers you to be a schizophrenic; but if you write your thoughts down in your diary or publish them on the Internet, you're considered a cool dude.

I have very little time to write. Joan has slept a couple of hours in our hotel room, then with my permission she went into town with our new friend. And I'm sitting here, waiting for them to return at any moment.

ZOTOV

They're trying to find out how to set up a teleportation portal. Our new friend has quite a bit of experience in the movie world; he has some useful connections, some local money and a few necessary acquaintances. He's not quite as simple as he seems. He can't get one over on me though, I've been around the block once too many times. Still, we're on the same team. He dreams of getting out of here just as I do. I might have called him a friend, but he doesn't exactly fit the bill.

Never mind. It's not that important.

We dumped the car as soon as we arrived. Only complete dumbasses drive such ancient rust buckets here where they're the laughingstock of the whole town. Having said that, they do laugh a lot overall. Then we moved to the Russian B-movie district: all those budget thrillers, cheap comedies and mediocre crime dramas. Everything's so slapdash it's as if this city's never seen a good film budget. You know what I mean, don't you? You turn the television on, and all you get is a bunch of crap, the acting is atrocious, the humor and the story are straight out of a kindergarten — but this is the only thing you've downloaded, you're too lazy to switch it off, you've got nothing else to do, so you just carry on watching it. You just sit there and stare at the screen, supping beer.

And this is the main problem. If you don't stop watching crap, they'll carry on filming it for the rest of your life.

What is the B-Movie City like? It's a

nightmare. Worse than Stalingrad. Firstly, they're all the same faces from one film to the next. They're mainly the relatives of two or three directors plus the producers' mistresses (at least the latter are changed quite often). Secondly, nothing is made new specially for the film — it's all rented. Like now the waiter has brought me some water: there's nothing else on the menu. The café tables are nicely decorated with props of plastic food. The locals are starving; they travel to nearby villages to swap their possessions for some food because the only things available here are water, root vegetables and herbs. And weed — you can neither shoot nor watch our films without it.

The houses are built in such a slapdash fashion that they often collapse and their roofs fall in, burying the inhabitants. Some high-rises are here just for the show: a single wall with windows in it and it's your problem how you wanna live in it. Funeral processions pass here every day, with much cheering and laugher, similar to those in New Orleans.

Women here are a bit funny. They're stupid, they scream for no particular reason and sleep with all and sundry, flashing their tits often (because today's movie needs to attract the audience somehow). The local men are normally drunk as skunks because it's considered funny. When you come across three drunken thugs in a dark alley in real life, you wouldn't be laughing, but in the movies it's considered a big joke. The table I'm sitting at is made of Chinese plastic but judging by the maker's tag, it's "antique red wood"!

I'm not surprised. Our government doesn't scrimp on the development of the Russian movie industry which is why film crews aim to shoot their pictures on a shoestring (preferably at the seaside just to have an excuse to swim with female actresses) and split the rest between the management. A lot of these films don't make it to theaters at all and are released directly on DVDs. The directors couldn't care less because they've already had their cut, had a swim in the sea and a few leg-overs. That's the reason why the city's population is so pale, gray and mothballed: their films have lain too long gathering dust in the archives.

About a dozen of the people around me, the waiter included, are crude copies of Hollywood actors. Our waiter is the spitting image of Brad Pitt if you see him at night with a hangover. And that girl who's heading for the ladies' room over there looks remarkably like Sharon Stone who's been in an accident.

The problem with our low-budget flicks is that we don't seem to have any of our own ideas. We just copy Hollywood to a T: why would we bother to come up with ideas of our own if someone's already has done so before you?

That's why everything comes out as if it's been rehashed. I take a look out of the window and I see a clone of Schwarzenegger's Commando; not far *away, there's a group of puny special-forces men from our version of* Homeland... *and over there, there's yet another "Brad Pitt" wearing a doctor's white coat, pretending to be a sorry copy of Dr. House.*

What have I done to deserve so much hatred from the powers of evil? The Game of Thrones *I would have understood. A normal guy would have ended up in a normal movie, something like the original* Dr. House, *or* Jeeves and Wooster *or in the worst-case scenario,* Castle. *True, they weren't so perfect, either. Today's TV format in Russia (not counting the cable) is a lot of murders and zero nudity. Because that's how the TV gods of our times view it: killing people is good and beneficial for the young while sex is dangerous and subverting for the young generation. I'd love to know how many people the average person kills in his or her lifetime compared to how many times they have sex?*

Oh... sex... I think I'm gonna be sick. It's been quite a while since I left the porn world but I still suffer from phantom pains.

The waiter has just approached me again — slowly, giving me a chance to take a good look at him from all angles. They're so narcissistic.

"Some more water, Sir?"

"No, thanks, I told you already."

This particular version of Brad Pitt seems to have escaped the drunken dreams of a street sweeper who'd fallen asleep in an abandoned quarry. He speaks in a very theatrical manner.

ZOTOV

Despite me not wanting to remember the porn world, quite honestly they're better actors. Soap directors tend to cast first-year drama students who forget their lines and speak in an overly dramatic manner. A street bum could have done better.

A guy stumbles next to me (looking like a well-worn version of Robin Williams) and ends up with his face in his Caesar salad. Bits of plastic lettuce fly everywhere. The whole room explodes in unnatural laughter with their mouths wide open. Another guy in the corner tumbles down the stairs, triggering another bout of guffawing. Then a girl slips up, revealing her knickers and causing the room to thunder with hilarious laughter. This is our B-movie humor: there's no money for special effects, so just let them all go ass over tit like Charlie Chaplin used to, seeing as we haven't come up with anything new.

But the worst things in the B-Movie City are the cameo appearances of well-know stars who get bit parts with a couple of lines in the style of "Dinner is served". While quite a few of the city dwellers get the chance to broaden their vocabulary, learn new expressions and even hold a conversation, those poor stars are like overage cretins unable to learn new words. Just like the war movie extras I'd met when I first came here.

Just imagine you walk over to a copy of Meryl Streep and try to strike up a conversation:

"The weather's really good today, isn't it?"

"Dinner is served."

"How about a little glass of wine?"

"Dinner is served."

"Just fuck off, will you?"

"Dinner is served."

The city's old-timers like to tell the following legend to any newcomers. According to them, once upon a time in a certain kingdom high in the mountains far far away, there is a high wall surrounded by moats, woods and mine fields. The wall is protected by an electric fence topped with barbed wire and guarded by snipers.

Behind it lies Silver Screen City. It's very small, only a few narrow streets. They have Andrei Rublev, Ballad of a Soldier, White Sun of the Desert, Stalker, The Irony of Fate (the original 1976 one, naturally)[19]... *And others, of course:* Papillon, Apocalypse Now, The Seventh Seal, One Flew Over the Cuckoo's Nest, Seven Samurai... *Not many people live there but they're all happy, intelligent and pleased with each other — even those who play the most despicable bastards. Silver Screen City changes you, improving your taste, and adds a touch of humor and healthy nonchalance to your outlook. There, all girls are alive and not like heartless plastic dolls. The men there have a nice sense of humor and have no problem engaging others in conversation, showing them the entire world in a one-minute speech.*

Many a B-Movie City dweller tried to get there

---

[19] The names of some of the best award-winning Russian movies

ZOTOV

only to perish without a trace, gunned down by
snipers' bullets, drowned in the raging rivers, blown
up in the mine fields or dropped screaming to their
deaths from mountain cliffs. It's common knowledge
that beauty has to defend itself, otherwise it would
be swallowed up by tons of crap. Here too, every
year the B-Movie City population sends out
expeditions to find the legendary place. All those
plastic dolls, good-for-nothings, tongue-tied stars
and other nincompoops set off in search of their
fortune, making the surrounding landscape echo
with the screams of "Dinner is served!"

Could any of them have ever reached their
destination? No one has ever returned to tell the tale.
They either died on the way or realized what kind of
BS they were filming and croaked of
embarrassment. It's a bit like if the characters of
today's Russian cartoon industry had stumbled into
Disneyworld, they'd have to commit mass hara-kiri
on the spot.

Funny, isn't it? We Russians can make decent
vodka as well as tanks, we seem to be able to make
decent clothes; we have some of the most beautiful
women. But the moment we touch something like
cars or movies, everything fucks up. Must be some
divine punishment.

My laptop's battery is almost flat already.

Which is a good thing. I need to stop writing.
Joan and our new friend must already be on their
way.

He explained to me why we had to join forces.

Apparently, Joan is a crossbreed born of a liaison with a human being. She is some sort of key between the two realities who can, under certain circumstances, open a portal to our world.

O god, if I'd only known beforehand! I would have already tried it. Unfortunately, this too requires artifacts. The man in the balaklava is gone off to look for the Dark World district: a penny mix of Meyers' Twilight barring the vampires, dark street culture fantasy and totally unscary horror with terrible (literally) actors. We have no choice: this is the only place where you can find a witch with a half-decent assortment of powders, potions and artifacts required for the opening of portals.

The man did warn me though: we might simply end up in another movie.

Oh well. It's more fun with three people. After the world of porn, nothing can faze me anymore.

There they are! I can see them through the window. They're already coming: Joan and our mysterious friend. By the way, I completely forgot to mention that before entering the Dark World, the stranger had removed his mask. Apparently, there's no need to hide your identity in the B-Movie City. There're no street patrols checking your ID here like there are in Stalingrad.

And you know what? He wasn't some fanged monster. He turned out of be a normal guy, friendly and well-mannered, extremely young. He still keeps apologizing for having frightened Joan and myself —apparently, he feels very bad about it.

ZOTOV

There he is, smiling and talking to the girl.
He's carrying a big plastic shopping bag sporting a
picture of a skull. Judging by his mood, procuring the
artifacts hasn't been a problem.

I need to hurry to finish this while the battery
still holds. I hope this time everything will work ou-

THE MAN BEHIND the table closes his dead laptop.

Two more people enter the café, a man and a woman. We can only see their backs. The film's hero stands up and proffers his hand to the man who shakes it firmly. He then sets the plastic bag on the table and waves his hands in excitement.

The camera moves to one side. We can see the man's blond hair and friendly smile. Still, something in the way the camera films him prevents us from seeing him clearly, blurring all his outlines.

The girl with cropped hair looks at her watch and points at the exit. Both men nod, pick up the plastic bag and leave the café. The waiter shouts angrily from the other side of the room. The man with the bag slaps his forehead, walks back and lays some money on the edge of the table.

The camera turns to focus on his face. The women in the audience gasp.

They're beholding the Artist.

Only this time he's not smiling at all.

CHAPTER TWELVE

Danza de Los Diablos

Lima, Peru
November 1st 1931

T HE BANGING OF THE DRUMS didn't let up for
one moment. Miguel felt as if the musicians
had moved into his head all together and
were rattling their drumsticks on his brain. A mile-
long procession of dancers in blue and white cloaks
with frilly black wings and pants that imitated
goats' hairy legs stretched along the street not far
from the Plaza de Armas. Predictably, their faces
were masked.

Miguel was inconspicuous within the crowd
in his red medieval doublet, crimson velvet
leggings, fancy alpaca-skin shoes and a mask. The
mask was the main attribute of La Diablada, with
giant raspberry-red lug ears, long twisted horns
(which could easily serve as a clothes hanger),
bulging eyes, a pig's nose and a green serpent
entwined around the spikes that protruded from

his forehead.

What a handsome fellow! It was slightly reminiscent of Chinese demons even though at this point you couldn't really tell whether it was due to the Chinese influence or that of Latin America.

Miguel was dressed quite modestly by local standards compared to the bacchanalia that reigned around him. Skeletons embroidered with gold; breastplates symbolizing ancient Incan armor; belts made from clinking coins and enormous orange cloaks. All this was rattling, shouting and dancing — a true hell on Earth.

A water bomb exploded next to him. Miguel startled. Damn their tradition of throwing bottles of holy water around! Flower petals fluttered down from balconies overhead (Miguel wasn't at all surprised to smell magnolia); women were singing and shaking their hips; medieval cannons were firing off strips of colorful fabrics. La Diablada was in full swing.

Miguel was sweating buckets under the weight of his disguise. People around him didn't seem to tire at all; they kept on dancing, giving in to the rhythm.

Just think that only three days ago they had all been petrified by the Artist's atrocities. The streets of Lima had been deserted in the evenings as everybody hurried to hide away in their houses. And tonight they filled the city's avenues, not giving a shit about *la muerte*.

A dancer skipped past him, wearing a mask

painted with a picture of two palm trees. Miguel dipped his horns slightly in acknowledgement and received a respectful nod back.

A fellow cop. There were about fifty of them helping him tonight: he'd asked them to turn up at the Diablada for any emergencies that might arise. Which was about as precise as he wanted to make it. The situation was too unpredictable.

Everything had happened exactly as he'd expected. Both Alejandro de Castillero and Rodrigo Fuegos were nowhere to be found.

Palm trees began to bend as masked people climbed them to pluck the coconuts.

"Demons of Uku Pacha! Come out, we're waiting for you! We have plenty of treats for you!"

The whole day the City of Kings had experienced tremors in various places. If you listened to the old folk, this is how it had always been during La Diablada. Streams emitted jets of steam, boiling fish alive, while volcanoes began to ooze lava. The unborn of Uku Pacha had sensed the smell of blood and were bound to arrive.

They might already be here.

What exactly did Miguel want to find? He didn't know. Both Castillero and Fuegos were bound to be here somewhere but they too were wearing masks. Like any Russian worth his salt, Miguel had this strong gut feeling. Something bad was about to happen, which was why he preferred to keep a police presence on the streets.

Gloomy crimson thunderclouds hung leaden

above the city. Still, the streets were as light as day from all the thousands of torches in the dancers' hands.

Miguel had to be honest with himself. He'd both won and lost.

He'd managed to work out the Artist's identity as well as that of his associate. He'd also sussed out their motive. Still, he'd only managed to work it out after the fact, when the fourth doll had already been discovered.

Caramba! Miguel was well and truly pissed that he'd let the murderers get away — and at the very last moment, too.

In the meantime, rumors had begun to circulate in their department. Apparently, Deputy Minister Juarez — Castillero's adoptive father — was about to be removed from his post for lack of loyalty to El Presidente and for the apparent failure of the investigation.

The mind boggles. Miguel had spoken to Fuegos countless times whenever the driver had delivered letters from the Ministry of Interior. He was a pleasant young man, helpful and polite, and very economical with his words.

Castillero also had been to the station several times but Miguel had never spoken to him, only seen him.

Where were they now? The two killers had to be lurking around somewhere, awaiting their meeting with the monster they'd summoned from Uku Pacha. So where exactly were they going to meet up? And how were they going to recognize each other?

Jesus.

The street was rattling, roaring and screaming.

Women doused themselves in red paint which was supposed to symbolize blood. Fake "devils" reached their clawed hands out to the laughing girls who slipped out of their satanic embrace.

Long ago in Cusco, this is how the Indians had been dancing, worshipping the powers of darkness: the entire city, including the Great Inca and the chief priest, because this was what they'd imbibed with their mothers' milk: evil shouldn't be rejected.

Enrique had been right: there was more evil in this world than there was good, so it paid to be on the safe side and bow to the unborn creatures of eternal darkness.

The only thing missing was a sacrifice. Before the arrival of the Spanish, the Incas used to slaughter thousands of prisoners and hundreds of the finest girls sent to the capital city by their vassal tribes, all to appease the insatiable subterranean gods. They threw their hearts onto altars and poured the blood on the ground by ravines from where it flowed down special drainpipes straight into the mouths of the undead.

Miguel leant against a dirty-yellow wall. It was hot. Horribly muggy. He was desperate for a smoke but he couldn't remove the mask because the murderers knew his face.

Maybe it was wishful thinking but... can't a man dream now and again? So many nasty things happened during La Diablada every year. Like a confrontation between a jealous lover and his girl's random dance partner. You can't imagine how many machetes and guns there were amongst the crowd. All it takes is three shots: one for the hapless rival, another for the Señorita and the third one when the unfortunate tearful Romeo puts a bullet through his own head. These kinds of cases were all too common. Every year, up to a hundred people died during the carnival to honor the demons of Uku Pacha.

Nobody in the police would pay any attention to another two deaths. No one would be the wiser. After the fact, Miguel could offer all the evidence of the part the dead men had played in the terrible series of murders that had shaken the whole of Lima.

Because Miguel had a funny feeling that the four dolls were only the tip of the iceberg. How many girls had the two discarded as unfit to suit their artistic design? Forty? Fifty? And that's erring on the side of caution as not all families had reported their daughters' disappearance.

The place was crawling with police. They were ordered to shoot first and ask questions afterward whenever they saw anything even remotely suspicious. The mentality was the problem: all the celebrations tended to make the police lax. From where he stood, Miguel could see a masked man — a cop, judging by his secret marking — dancing away with abandon. And when you're completely consumed by dancing, you're not going to worry about doing your job. That was the essence of Latin Americans.

The crowd roared with laughter as someone exploded a whole series of water bombs. The air smelled of hot sweaty bodies, running body paint, the omnipresent magnolia petals, rum and pisco. Alcohol always flowed freely during carnivals.

Miguel double-checked the gun in his pocket. It wouldn't be bad to get away from this wall at last and shake off the apathy.

He had a splitting headache. All week, he hadn't slept more than three hours every night. The first thing he intended to do once he'd shot those two scumbags, was go straight home and collapse into his bed.

In his mind, he saw Enrique: calm and smiling, explaining to him step by step the intricate mythology of the long-gone empire.

All the dead girls. The slaughter of the village. Could he have prevented it at all?

It was unlikely the murderers had started only recently. They'd trained and prepared themselves — possibly, going to far-off high-altitude Quechua villages to take part in the remaining rituals of human sacrifice. At the time, they can't have been more than fourteen years old. So what?

ZOTOV

For Indians, twelve years of age was already maturity, the time when the boys started to learn the art of war and the girls began to prepare themselves for their future marriages.

Had anyone bothered to take stock of all the women who'd gone missing in the vicinity of Lima over the last three or four years? He didn't think so. Here, they could kill for a pinch of coca leaves in a boy's pocket; prostitutes were beaten to death and their bodies drowned in mud during the rainy season so that only their mummified remains could be found later.

The city of death. The city of night. The city of horrors.

It had taken someone like the Artist to create a stir, scaring the local society out of their wits and angering El Presidente.

Still, Miguel had little doubt that by Christmas, people would forget the dolls bathing in a sea of blood. The dolls which were stuffed with magnolia petals and lovingly sewn together with silk thread.

The City of Kings had seen things much worse than that in its time.

Enrique... Once again Miguel remembered him: the meek, humble janitor and the stern, commanding priest. The ancient Incan tunnel leading to Uku Pacha. The conversation between them, both stoned from the toxic fumes, under the old Magnolia Amazonica. Miguel's vision of Francisco Pizarro performing a mass sacrifice...

he'd seen the old Spaniard as clearly as if he'd been standing next to him. He could hear the clanking of his rusty armor and could smell the blood... finally, he'd seen him return from the kingdom of the undead and kill his own brother.

Wait a sec.

The thought exploded in his mind, illuminating the dark nooks and crannies of his brain.

What if the Artist and his Apprentice hadn't even known that Enrique had contacted him? What if they'd wiped out the village for a different reason entirely? What if they needed the ancient sacred place — the old magnolia and the secret tunnel to Uku Pacha — in order to perform their last ritual?

While a good fifty cops were searching around Lima trying to hunt them down, desperate to guess their identities from under their masks, the two could already be high in the mountains by the huts of the Indians they'd killed, humbly awaiting the arrival of...

Miguel ripped off his horned mask and threw it to the ground.

Dammit! The streets were blocked by tens of thousands of people. There was no way he could get a cab or even a horse-drawn carriage. The best-equipped policemen were busy patrolling the city. The only thing he could realistically do was run the six blocks to the Ministry of Interior and beg them for a car which would take him absolutely ages.

Still, he had no choice. There was nowhere

he could even make a phone call from. In this part of town, telephones were few and far between: only one house in thirty had one. And you wouldn't knock at a stranger's door, anyway. You can just imagine someone in a stupid carnival costume turning up on your doorstep and begging to use the phone because he's a policeman trying to track down some criminals.

So Miguel started running.

STANDING UNDER the magnolia tree, Alejandro and Rodrigo took turns to slit the throats of the remaining three girls, the last prisoners of the slaughterhouse in Barrio de Chino who'd already lost the last vestiges of their sanity.

Blood snaked its way toward the tree roots. Consumed by the ritual, the murderers ignored their victims' last gasps. Scooping up the viscous liquid, they smeared it over their tattooed bodies, then dunked a tiny dark-stone figurine of an idol into it.

They'd done everything by the book. They'd explained to the idol what was expected of him. He was going to arrive at this exact place.

Swaying on the spot, they both started singing a song — the same one that Atahualpa used to sing before striking up a deal with the Uku Pacha demons. Soon after that, he'd taken the throne still wet with the blood of his brother.

The two kept singing, pledging their obedience. They begged the creature to grant their wish. They promised to become his slaves for eternity and make it worth his while.

Having finished singing, they prostrated themselves by the roots, submerging their faces in the hot blood, and took a generous gulp. They lay like that for about half and hour, motionless, as they awaited the monster's reaction.

Nothing.

The Apprentice was the first to rise to his knees. Appalled, he wiped the bloodied mud from his face.

"Is that it?" he asked the Artist with badly concealed sarcasm. "You should get a medal! Now I'm almost sure it was you who buried that pot of gold in my vegetable patch. We've wasted a whole bunch of time on this shit. We're wanted by the police. We've cut up a whole lot of bitches. And is this our reward, amigo? A thirty-minute mud bath?"

The Artist rose and shrugged noncommittally, trying to conceal his disappointment. "We might have done something wrong. I did warn you it was a complex procedure. But don't start moaning now. At least we've had a lot of fun. Or did you want to spend your whole life driving a cop car with the police department? A dream job, sure! You pour yourself into your leather pants and jacket, you put your cap on, you creak like an old leather sofa — all the slum girls are yours for the taking! But just think about it: you're basically just a cart driver like everybody else. The only difference being, you have neither a horse nor even the oats to feed it with."

Rodrigo's eyes glistened with malice. His right hand unconsciously clenched into a fist.

The black and red heavens of the sunrise were rent asunder by a bolt of lightning. Thunder rumbled non-stop, renewing its claps every few seconds, loud and terrible. Still, not a drop of rain fell to the ground.

The earth shuddered. Dozens of chasms opened up, releasing pillars of steam. The underground tunnels emitted a terrifying guttural roar which ended on a pitiful note.

The magnolia tree split into two. Both the Artist and his Apprentice froze, open-mouthed, at the sight of human faces concealed within the tree trunk, the eyes of the sculptures oozing blood.

In terror, the Apprentice raised his hand to his forehead, whispering a prayer.

The dead Indians' huts began to combust until they exploded in flames. Ten pillars of fire rose to the sky, encircling the murderers.

From under the roots of the bleeding magnolia tree, a crimson bubble began to form. Not a bubble even but rather a clot of bright-red plasma which continued to grow at a frightening speed.

A hand began to form, its long-nailed fingers dripping blood.

A lipless mouth gaped on the flat face. Pointy ears twitched.

The creature reared up on its hind legs, the

hump on its back writhing. One eye opened, then the other, flooding the scene with a deathly pale light.

Alejandro's lips began to shake. He dissolved into hysterical laughter. Rodrigo couldn't drag his eyes away from the monster.

"*Close your eyes.*"

The creature said it in a soft but strangely commanding voice. The two killers obeyed unquestioningly. They stood unseeing, listening to the claps of thunder, the crackling of fire on the huts' roofs, and the guttural groans of Uku Pacha birthing its ugly child into our world.

The men's souls filled with ecstasy. The Artist's heart was dancing.

They had no idea how long they'd stood like that but finally, the same voice ordered,

"*Very well. You can look now.*"

The Artist opened his eyes and froze in disbelief. A man sat on the ground before him, clad in a medieval doublet and a pair of high boots. He was about fifty years old, stocky and muscular, with an aquiline nose and a goatee.

Judging by the guttural sounds emitted by the silent Rodrigo, he'd completely lost the plot.

"Did you call me?" the stranger asked amicably. "I'm at your service."

The Artist was the first to regain his wits. "Most illustrious Señor Shadow," he said in Quechua, bowing profoundly. "Thank you for the unprecedented honor of accepting our sacrifice and revealing yourself to us."

Señor Shadow waved a dismissive hand. "Please. If it's all right with you, let's drop the politeness until later. What is it exactly you want?"

"We want to be loved, Señor," the Apprentice echoed.

"A *woman*?" a furrow formed on the Shadow's brow. "Very well. It's not at all difficult. But why? All this complex sacrifice to grant such a petty request? Any of the unborn could have-"

The Artist gave him the smile of a connoisseur. "Our request, dear Señor Shadow, is quite out of the ordinary. Which was why we dared turn to you for help. You're the only being who has the power to help in questions of unrivaled and unparalleled love. Actually... it would probably be easier for me to show you. Do you mind?"

Señor Shadow nodded, his face a picture of curiosity. Alejandro gestured to Rodrigo. Both of them stepped aside toward an old film projector lying on the ground next to a folded sheet.

Part Three

Cine Commerciale

You can see her with her dark veil
As she walks in the bewitched wood;
Wolves sing when she passes,
Earth bleeds under her foot.

Theatres des Vampires, *Lady In Black*

CHAPTER ONE

The Dead Guests

Night. A corn field.
Something's not right there

FINALLY, THE SCREEN lights up. The audience cheer and lean forward, clutching their armrests. Some guy in the sixth row spills his popcorn which patters to the floor from its paper bucket. Everybody's already fed up with watching the incessant adverts and trailers of potential blockbusters. They can't wait for the movie to restart.

At first, the screen remains dark; all we can hear is some rustling sounds and heavy breathing. That's followed by sobbing, whispers, and the patting of pockets — someone seems to be looking for something.

A lighter flickers, its weak light illuminating three people: the blond youth, the man whom we know as Oleg and the girl with cropped hair. Darkness closes in behind them. They look alarmed; the camera focuses on their faces as they cast anxious glances around.

The young man raises the lighter in his hand. Wherever he points it, all the audience can see is towering stalks with broad leaves.

It's a corn field.

The camera retreats, showing all three surrounded by a dark heaving mass. The speakers play an appropriate soundtrack.

"Where are we now?' Oleg asks sadly.

"Not the slightest idea," Alejandro de Castillero replies. "If I'm not mistaken, this is a corn field which is a crop popular with the peasants of my country. We've still to find out whether we've managed to get back to earth or whether this is just yet another film world. So just in case, compañeros, I suggest you keep your eyes peeled."

Oleg heaves a sigh and nods. It's not as if he has much choice. To begin with, even their return to the real world might cause a whole bunch of new problems. Like, what if they resurfaced somewhere abroad? Like Cuba or Peru where he's seen loads of corn fields like this one? He has neither his passport nor a single penny on him. What's he supposed to do then? No idea. Is he supposed to turn up at the Russian consulate and say, "Sorry guys, I was watching some porn back in Moscow and suddenly got dragged into the television, that's why I've come to you with only the shirt on my back?" Unfortunately, this doesn't sound like a good option.

Not that he gives a shit. By now, he's quite prepared to milk camels, feed on frogs and sleep on the grass, as long as it's all in the real world. Escaping back to reality is the only thing that matters. The rest is irrelevant.

The girl kneads a corn leaf. "We still need to go somewhere."

Both men turn to face her.

"We can, of course, stay here and argue the toss about which world it is — mine or yours — but it's not gonna change much," she continues. "Had this been the porn world, this would have been a perfect excuse to have an orgy which would have been a natural solution to the problem. But somehow I don't think this is Sex City."

The young man gives her a look of respect. "No, Señorita," he says. "Thank you for your words of wisdom. So where are we supposed to go?"

"What difference does it make? Let's go straight on. Sooner or later we're bound to get out of this field."

They continue straight on, each thinking their own thoughts. After a quarter of an hour of struggling through the stalks, Alexandro asks Oleg a question which seems to bother him a lot,

"Why are you so bent on returning to our world?"

"Because I was being surrounded by porn for six months," Oleg snaps. "I've no idea which other worlds you've been to but trust me, reality is a whole lot better. Although I have a funny feeling you've forgotten most of it already."

"Who knows," Alexandro says evasively. "What if our reality is somebody else's blockbuster movie? Have you never thought about it? Life on Earth might be a bad movie but at least you don't feel it, just like Joan doesn't. Haven't you ever met someone whose life seems to be predetermined? They might want to make a career but they can't because of a ton of inner barriers. A person like that is afraid of everything: of offering their ideas at a briefing or taking a stand against their boss. They keep on busting their hump for peanuts day in day out, never leaving their office till the day they die. Don't you think their life is sort of fated, preventing them from making any drastic changes? A guy like that is just like a movie extra playing a bit part in his or her own life. Possibly, we even have directors up in heaven who write their lines for us, making us do whatever's required by the script."

Mud squelches underfoot. Oleg stops.

"I don't give a shit," he says. "Even if it's so, I want back into my own film. Why do you ask? Don't you feel like escaping?"

"Oh yes I do," Alejandro heaves a sigh. "But I've been here for eighty-three fucking years compared to your eight months. I keep wandering from film to film, so now I have a pretty good idea of the state of modern cinematography. If you ask me, black and white movies were the best, and silent ones, even more so. It's true it feels a bit spooky crossing the streets which don't have a single speck of color on them. Or be constantly surrounded by men and women with heavily made-up eyes. Whenever they want to speak to you, they have to reach into their pockets for pieces of cardboard with their lines written on them. Sometimes I'd stand in a group of people at a cocktail party where every lady would have a servant waiting next to her, holding a stack of cardboard prompts in his hands. She'd pick one out and silently wave it in the air, like she was busy socializing. All those characters are terrible drama queens. They're so theatrical. They roll their eyes wildly, they gesticulate, they make a whole show of dying... but you know, it's so charming, so naïve and adorable. One day I left them hoping to find my way back to the real world and since then, I haven't been able to get back. If I had the choice right now, I'd much prefer to forever stay in silent movies. Hollywood makes me sick."

Oleg snaps a stalk of corn and cracks a cynical smile. "You're just a product of your time, Alejandro," he says. "You were born in the beginning of the 20th century, that's why you believe black and white flicks to be the best and our modern blockbusters, a toxic degrading waste of time. Sorry! Chaplin I can understand. I find him funny. A mustachioed man in a bowler hat falling into a cream pie with his tongue stuck out — it's still quite funny, you know. But it all ended with Chaplin, I'm afraid. Overall, their acting was atrocious. School kids do better in amateur plays. All those bulging eyes, curly black mustaches, not to even mention all the gesticulations... At the time, no one watched the movies for the acting but because they were a novelty. No words were really necessary — it was enough to pull a face just like kids do."

Alejandro grabs at his head, clutching his temples. "What do you know about art?!" his voice rings with fury.

"Sorry guys," Joan butts into their conversation. "I have a suggestion to make."

The two men turn and stare at her quizzically.

"We keep walking and walking with nothing to show for it," she explains, shifting from one foot to the other. "It's dark now. We've no idea which way to go. What if we split up? That way at least one of us might-"

Oleg turns pale. "Wait," he says slowly. "I think I've heard that before."

He spins around, trying to take in his surroundings, then raises his hands.

The corn leaves rustle. It begins to drizzle. Crickets are rasping. A slice of yellow moon peeks bashfully from behind the thunderclouds.

Now Oleg knows.

"I see," he says bitterly. "We haven't escaped from anywhere."

"How do you know?" Alejandro asks in surprise.

Oleg heaves a sigh. "This is a classic. Three people, moving across a field in the dead of night. A gloomy corn field. They don't know where to go. It's dark. It's scary. Any old noise sounds like a threat. They keep on walking but there's no end to it. Finally, the girl suggests that they split up after which they all go their own way. Now evil can have its way with them. And one more thing. Joan, you're a virgin, aren't you? Shit. Now it all makes sense."

Alejandro frowns. "What are you driving at?"

Oleg claps his hands, the sound echoing through the night. "We're in a horror film, amigo," he says sadly. "Can't you see?"

The other two have no answer to that.

The corn stalks part on three sides of them, revealing three giggling people wearing clown's masks: red noses and curly ginger temples. Each is holding a machete used for harvesting sugar cane.

"Wanna play?" the first clown offers, his voice a mocking parody. He's shorter than the other two and stooping, a machete clutched in his hands.

Oleg chuckles. "Yeah right! Do you want us to play chase?"

"First we must toss a coin," the second clown says. "To decide which one of you is the first to die."

"You only have two options," Oleg informed them lazily. "Joan is a virgin, so she can't die, according to the unwritten code of horror movies. She's gonna survive and kill you all."

The clowns are noticeably taken aback.

"So what are we supposed to do?" the third clown asks in a thin squeaky voice.

"That depends on who you are," Oleg explains calmly. "Whether you're just psycho friends going on a killing spree *Scream*-style, or you're triplets born of a nurse that's been raped in a psychiatric hospital for lunatic prisoners, or you're a nuclear mutated family of cannibals like in *Hills Have Eyes*.

The clowns shut up. The first one scratches his head.

"Dunno," he doesn't sound too sure. "Would a group of psycho circus artists do?"

Oleg snorts. "This sounds too much like arthouse. Or a 1980s low-budget B-movie. They used to make tons of them, like *My Bloody Valentine*. Judging by your machetes, this is a typical slasher with a $50,000 budget. I saw hundreds of them on a VCR when I was at school. It looks like you're even wearing your own clothes and not from a props department which says something about the movie's economy. Oh well, all the worse for us. Low-budget slashers were notorious for their gore. Mind telling us, guys, what you're planning to do with us? Just curious."

Alejandro and Joan follow the conversation open-mouthed.

"Honestly," the thin-voiced clown sighs, "by now you were supposed to have split up. So now, unfortunately, we'll have to ad lib."

Oleg casts a meaningful glance at Joan.

"First," the clown continues, "we're gonna do the blond dude in. Then we'll chase after you.

You're gonna fall and break your leg. You'll keep crawling, overcoming the pain, and the last thing you'll see in life will be the machete coming down on you. After that, we'll follow the girl and cut her head off. We'll lift it by the hair and fill the field with satanic laughter."

"What if you don't?" Joan asks cautiously.

The clown sighs. You can see even through the mask that he sympathizes with her.

"Sorry, sweetheart," he says apologetically. "I'd have loved not to. But I can't. My Mom was sort of psycho and my Dad was a serial killer. I grew up surrounded by dead bodies. Whenever we had guests, they were already dead. So if you don't terribly mind, I'd rather kill you now and then I can continue this conversation with you. Or rather, with your head. I'll put dried tulips into your empty eye sockets, and then..."

"Ah, this sounds like a Norman Bates rip-off. It's pure *Psycho*. So basically, guys, I've no idea what kind of film you've got going here but I've heard enough. You can shoot them."

Three shots ring out. Alejandro lowers his Walther.

THE CAMERA soars over the corn field, showing a trampled clearing toward the north. Three dead bodies are sprawled on the broken stalks.

As the camera approaches, we can see the red blotches covering the white clown's smocks, their dead hands still clutching their machetes.

ZOTOV

The two men and the girl are seen exiting the corn field. The blond man points to a nearby hill, shouting something excitedly.

The camera follows the direction in which he's pointing, revealing a battered car standing on the hill.

FREEZE FRAME: a key in the ignition.

CHAPTER TWO

A Little Princess

Suburbs of Lima
November 1 1931

"**W**OULD YOU LIKE a glass of water, Señor Capitan? It's very hot here."

Miguel looked up. A cop leaned over him with a courteous smile.

"No, thank you, Augusto," he replied. "I can do without."

Sitting on the ground with his back leant against the reeds of an Indian hut, Miguel struck a match, lighting up yet another cigarette.

He'd lost them again. The two had escaped from right under their noses, leaving behind more girls' bodies, the ground drenched in blood, an old movie projector and some sheets covered in black and red spots.

He'd never see the two again. An Uku Pacha demon had granted the Artist and his Apprentice their wish. Both were probably now heading for either the Brazilian or Bolivian border.

The murderers had slipped through his fingers like sand. He could forget all about his career now.

The silhouette of the Magnolia Amazonica was imprinted on the black sky.

He should have realized it earlier. Both Alejandro and Rodrigo were crazy about the movies. They hadn't missed a single new release. They'd always dressed to the nines whenever they went out to the best theater in town. They'd bought the most expensive tickets and laid gorgeous bouquets against the screen.

Both men favored the same actress, literally since childhood. A Good Little Devil, The Pride of the Clan, The Poor Little Rich Girl, Tess of the Storm Country, Daddy-Long-Legs, the Hoodlum... They watched her every movie countless times.

Rodrigo had a pin-up of her in his car, a cutting from a fifteen-year-old issue of the Theatre Magazine. A rosy-cheeked, golden-haired girl in a pink dress with white flowers. An eternal child who'd played in dozens of films and who'd received a prestigious American prize for movie actors last year. What was it called now? Oscar or something?

Mary Pickford.

The thirty-nine-year old American actress, old enough to be their mother, had become the object of their love and adoration — because the film industry had made her forever young and eternally desirable. They'd fallen for a picture on the screen. A mad love which had no chance of fruition.

In reality Mary Pickford, the idol of millions of movie goers, was already a woman of a certain age married to Douglas Fairbanks who likewise was the idol of millions of teenage girls. Both Rodrigo and Alejandro hated Fairbanks with a vengeance, as did most Pickford's fans.

However, he wasn't their main rival. Mary Pickford was petite — and Russians have a saying that "a small dog stays a puppy all its life". But even despite the saying, she was gradually growing old — and her doting admirers were still stuck in the films of 1914-1920, ogling a sweet little lamb, a poor orphan with the smile of a benign god.

The problem was, they didn't seek the love of the actress but that of her screen characters. They wanted the little lamb to leave the silver screen and bestow happiness on one of them. They daydreamed about it. They were dying of love, quite prepared to pay with their lives for one small kiss.

But in the end, they'd paid with the lives of others.

Their idea of turning to the demons of Uku Pacha for help was quite predictable. Even if you didn't believe in them, they were still your last resort: their black magic was the only means of obtaining the object of your desire. It did cost you — but why would you bother about such petty details?

Why the hell hadn't they asked the demon to

provide two copies of Mary Pickford? That would have simplified matters greatly. Having said that... probably not. Rodrigo and Alejandro weren't the kind who would have agreed to such an underhand maneuver. Mary could only belong to one of them; the loser would have had to either commit suicide or retire into voluntary exile.

So what kind of creature had visited them from Uku Pacha? What great demon had it been, capable of granting wishes? Enrique could have told Miguel about it, had he not been lying in the police morgue.

Well, well, well.

Miguel seemed to have forgotten something. The smoke from the seeds that Enrique had burned, allowing Miguel to meet Francisco Pizarro just before the conquistador's descent to Uku Pacha. It was some sort of local drug akin to the cheap cocaine which Miguel was only too familiar with. His sophisticated fellow White Army officers used to stuff it up their snouts by the fistful, as had the local prostitutes from the port of Vladivostok. The drug didn't allow you to travel in time, of course; all it did was pull images from the deepest recesses of your subconscious. It gave your fantasy the fleeting ability to explode, creating a tangible, colorful hallucination which you could almost touch with your own hands.

Miguel's eyes opened wide. And what if...

What, here, in front of all the cops? Then again, why not? He was their boss, after all.

Miguel sprang to his feet. "Make sure I'm not disturbed," he snapped over his shoulder as he headed toward Enrique's ritual hut.

The small bag containing the seeds was still lying next to the totem pole. The murderers' hadn't touched anything here.

Miguel struck a match, starting a fire, and poured a handful of seeds onto the embers. With a hissing sound, a wave of sickly sweet smoke floated around the room.

MIGUEL CAME ROUND in complete darkness. Still, somehow he could see everything: it was as if he'd acquired some sort of feline eyesight.

He could make out winding corridors and enormous stone cellars without a drop of light. He sensed tens of thousands of creatures inhabiting the pitch blackness. One of them crawled past him: an eight-legged spiderlike monster which had neither nose nor mouth; it moved sideways trying not to touch all the others.

The cellars were filled with sounds. Munching, crunching, chewing, rustling, howling, groaning and incessant screaming — a wild cacophony capable of driving one mad within ten minutes. But these things seemed to have been living here for millennia.

A blood-curdling howl resounded very close. What was it?

A whole pack of black dogs was running toward him, the kind that helps the dead to cross the hair bridge after their funerals. The dogs' eyes glowed yellow in the gloom. They were fat with a healthy sheen to their coats but no one reached out to pat their hackles.

Dead men ambled past him: half-rotten faces, crumbling clothes, their flesh crawling with maggots. They'd been buried during the times of the Incas and taken to Uku Pacha.

And still these were the poor ones. Further on, a mummified group of the landed Incan gentry with painted smiles and red cheeks were feasting at a large table whose legs were fashioned out of tree roots. They ripped dead moles apart and devoured them, their skin so dry it split with the slightest movement. Still, in their airless space they would preserve for centuries to come.

The unborn, however, gave the deadmen a wide birth. They were the highest caste of the local dwellers: servants to demons, they were almost demons themselves. They kept their own company: tall, skinny, eyeless monsters, their nails as long as those of the Chinese Empress. They had huge mouths as round as an apple with black, needle-sharp teeth, long slithering tongues and wrinkled skin.

And those were positive angels compared to their bosses. The noble-born subterranean demons were abominable in their ugliness, the spidery creature by far not the worst of them.

Driven by self-preservation, Miguel pressed his back to the wall every time they passed him even though he knew they couldn't see him. The spawn of the underground kingdom were blind just like the unborn and used their long snouts to sniff their way around in the dark like an ant eater. Some were covered in thick fur, other were hairless; some were tiny, others huge, but all of them kept moving, crawling and running along the smooth granite corridors past the lowest castes of the deadmen.

But even those monsters lowered their heads in respect upon seeing the pompous underground gods. Their skin was spotted like that of a jaguar, horns crowning their crocodile heads, spittle drooling from their open jaws. They never spoke but conveyed their orders by gestures because Uku Pacha is considered to be the land of the mute.

Every now and then the gods would raise their heads and look greedily at the ceiling, their dry gray tongues licking their lipless mouths. In the old days, blood used to drip toward them down the roots of the plants. In their worship of Uku Pacha, the Incas used to slaughter domestic animals daily — mainly alpacas and guanacos, but every now and again the gods would get an abundant treat of human blood. Such as mass killings of prisoners on the altars of Cusco or human sacrifices in order to secure a good harvest. In order to avoid famine, priests would collect ten-year-old children from each family because they were considered the most precious thing their doting parents had. In fact, historians drew parallels between this custom and that of throwing first-born babies alive into the red-hot metallic effigy of the god Baal in Carthage.

Miguel could see that the gods were thirsty. He had no doubt they were enjoying the celebrations in the Lima streets where they could have plenty of hot red liquid.

What kind of calendar did they have in Uku Pacha? What month and which year was it? What time was it there? Unfortunately, he couldn't possibly know this.

He came to a hall full of wooden statues lying on the floor, dressed in all sorts of clothes from the richest to the poorest.

What on earth was that? He had a funny feeling they were people that the Indians wished ill upon. A neighbor, a wife's lover, a governmental official. All you had to do was slaughter a dozen guinea pigs, steal a scrap of one's enemy's clothes, drench it in the animals' blood and wrap it around a wooden figurine. Then you had to spit on it, curse it and throw it down a mine shaft, leaving your enemy to the mercy of the demons, always too happy to yank the guts out of someone.

This looked admittedly similar to the Haitian voodoo cult which used special dolls for the same purpose. It's hard to say now who'd plagiarized whom.

Miguel crossed the hall and headed down a corridor with signposts depicting a crown: a flat gold circle with a horn on each side. He seemed to be floating in mid-air even though there couldn't be

322

any air here. Demons didn't need to breathe.

Closer to the royal halls, he started coming across demons with blood-curdling smiles on their rat-like faces. These were the thieves of cheer who were responsible for people's bad moods.

The place indeed resembled the Christian hell even though no one tortured its inhabitants. This was a simple existence similar to that on earth: some governed, others served. The dead of the Incan hell were all normal members of their underground society. Without them, this world would have ceased to exist.

Miguel passed yet another hall and peeked curiously inside. Hundreds of deadmen stood motionlessly there; their legs had transformed into thick knobbly roots, with branches growing out of their heads and shoulders, reaching up. According to Incan beliefs, the dead could climb out of the underworld by turning themselves into plants which would wriggle their way through the underground passages up to the surface. There, they'd come back to life: a wheel of rebirths similar to that of the Chinese and the Indians.

Still, Miguel could see that their roots had long since withered; these weren't going to make it to the surface anymore. The Spanish had blocked the underground passages, walling the dead up inside.

Having passed all the main halls, Miguel was now at the end of his journey. A spacious room lay before him, its ceiling covered in cobwebs and bats which hung head down from them: terrible creatures stinking of deadmen's guts.

At its center rose a throne built with skulls, the seat of the immortal ruler of this kingdom of the dead.

Miguel forced his way through the kneeling crowd of demons, gods and cadavers surrounding it. The creature sitting on the throne was infinitely more powerful, his magic stronger, his might awe-inspiring.

Ninety-nine steps led up to his throne. Miguel squinted, trying to make out the monstrous king's face.

All in vain. The throne was empty.

Still, the inhabitants of Uku Pacha didn't seem to notice it. Bending in an ecstasy of subservient loyalty, they used their tongues to clean the dirt around the throne.

But their king wasn't there anymore.

Miguel cursed himself with every profanity under the sun. He'd thought that Rodrigo and Alejandro had turned to one of the higher-ranking demons — or one of the gods, even. They didn't want an ordinary deadman who wasn't even capable of healing his own splitting skin. Their sacrifices showed enough worship and respect while teasing the only creature capable of breaking the Spanish seals that secured the passages.

Only the greatest of demons, drunk on his victims' blood, could muster all his forces and use the countless armies of the undead to escape Uku

Pacha during the festival of La Diablada which had been held in their absence in Lima and other Peruvian towns for the last four hundred years.

And it looked like the fourth doll had granted him the freedom he so wanted. The King of the dead was about to repay his liberators in kind by granting them the miracle they craved. A demon wastes a lot of his magic powers on having to break through to earth and stay here — but still he has plenty left.

This was Supay, or "the Shadow" in Quechua — the ruler of the kingdom of the dead — the one the Spanish believed to be Satan incarnate. But still, this wasn't the Prince of Darkness as we know him in Europe.

Supay was much, much worse.

Miguel closed his eyes.

What was this — some kind of hallucination within another one? He squeezed his eyes ever tighter. Reluctantly at first, his mind offered him the blurred but still recognizable images of Rodrigo and Alejandro.

They were walking down the street guided by some mysterious man who looked like a Spanish hidalgo from the Middle Ages. The man sashayed proudly without looking around him while the two friends scampered subserviently after him, heading toward a majestic old colonial building with a colonnade and heavy wrought-iron doors.

Of course. Which meant...

It looked like their attempt to stage a movie

show in Corpus Christi had failed. Possibly, the projector had broken down. It didn't matter, anyway. The two killers only needed the village to birth Supay and explain the meaning of their request to him. The plan itself had to be carried out in the city.

MIGUEL WAS SNAPPED back into reality just like the last time. He rose coughing from the floor and staggered out. Obeying his orders, the cops crowded near the entrance, not daring to come inside.

Miguel didn't even want to ask them how much time he'd been unconscious. He motioned to a police Lieutenant to approach.

"Señor Capitan?"

"I want you to send all our men to Casa de Cine. I want it surrounded."

"The biggest theater in town? But why-"

"Don't ask questions, just carry it out."

"At once, Señor!"

CHAPTER THREE

Skull Hunters

*The very scary district of
the City of Nightmares*

THE FILM BEGINS showing the medieval streets of a Western European city. It appears to be deserted. The cameraman indulges in long shots of shabby buildings, focusing the audience's attention on the graying cobwebs enveloping the window frames and on the roots that are entangling the houses' front steps.

As required by the genre of suspense, the sky is gloomy with thunderclouds. There's nobody around: not by the bus shelters nor even in the kids' playgrounds. Abandoned driverless cars line the streets. Thick white flakes are falling from the sky but it isn't yet clear to the viewer whether these are snowflakes or ash.

The camera moves into one of the side alleys where we see our lead characters — the two men and the woman — walking unhurriedly toward us.

ZOTOV

They're now dressed differently. Alejandro is wearing special-forces camouflage kit. Slung behind his back are fuel tanks. He's holding a long nozzle of what the audience recognizes as a flame thrower.

Joan is clad in leather with two large-caliber pistols on her belt. Oleg's wearing his civilian clothes with an army-issue bulletproof vest over his shirt. An AK-47 hangs from his shoulder.

ALL THREE of them stop. A blonde bare-footed girl of about ten years old is standing next to a defunct traffic light by a crossroads. The cameraman shows her from behind. She's wearing a white dress trimmed with lace.

Oleg takes his AK from his shoulder. The two others are indignant.

"Are you nuts?" Joan snaps. "She's only a child!"

"Have you seen *Silent Hill*?" Oleg replies. "In all horror movies, children are the most dangerous creatures. They're always up to something. They can either see the dead or they're dead themselves. They often can foretell tragic events — and in any case, they always mean trouble. Especially girls! She's gonna lure us to our deaths in a dark forest, or abduct us into another reality, or simply eat us alive. And neither of the three scenarios make me happy, you know."

"Please come to me," the girl sobs. "Please. I'm so cold! I'm freezing."

Unable to resist his urge to help, Alejandro

steps forward.

"You know, don't you, that it's 90 F here?" Oleg asks.

Alejandro stops in confusion. Greasy flakes of ash continue to float to earth.

"Please help me," the girl ups the ante. "I got lost! My mom's disappeared."

"Girl, you'd better get going already," Oleg says not so subtly. "We're not buying bullshit today."

The girl waves her hands in dismay. "Shit! I knew it!"

She opens her mouth wide, disgorging an uncoiling mass of purple tentacles lined with suckers.

Oleg nods to Alejandro who takes a better grip of his flamethrower. A jet of hissing fire spurts toward the monster who ignites like a haystack. Joan presses her hands to her ears, trying to block out the terrible screams which border on the ultrasonic.

The air smells of roasted octopus. Oleg begins to salivate, remembering his vacation in Greece.

The creature collapses onto the tarmac, its tentacles spasming.

"What the hell was that?" Joan asks fearfully.

"An alien, by the looks of it," Oleg says. "They invade human bodies and control them. This is a very important and expensive part of horror movie industry. Unlike the cheap slashers, just running around with a knife won't work here. They need computerized special effects. Think about *The Beast, Dreamcatcher, The Astronaut's Wife, The Faculty* by Robert Rodriguez, not to mention the *Alien* saga. They are basically parasites in our bodies. Alternatively, they use their hosts to brood their eggs or as surrogate parents for their embryos."

Joan shudders. "Why the hell would you watch something like that?"

"We have our needs," Oleg explains, unable to take his eyes from the smoldering tentacles. "You come home after a day's work, turn the TV on and admire some good guys smoking a horrendous monster which looks just like your boss. Sometimes you need to feel scared. Adrenalin hits your blood, providing the mother of all highs."

"Don't you have enough nightmares in your life?" Joan asks, surprised. "Didn't you tell me that an apartment in Moscow costs three hundred thousand dollars? With the euro costing almost a hundred rubles, the wages keep shrinking, there's been a wave of layoffs, isn't all that horrible enough for you? Do you absolutely have to stare at some fucking uncharismatic monster just to feel scared?"

"Er," Oleg pauses, sensing that the discussion has taken a wrong turn for him. "You know…"

The conversation dies away naturally as they hear a menacing hissing sound. An abominable bluish black monster leaps from somewhere up on the roof and crawls down toward them along the wall of a nearby building. It resembles a centipede with the thick skull of a hammerhead shark and the long scaly tail of a crocodile.

Oleg heaves a sigh. "Here we go. This is an Alien. We need to watch out. They normally hunt in packs. Their queen must be lurking underneath us somewhere. They're a nasty bunch, they've acid coursing their veins. They like nothing better than to jump at your face and inject their embryos into you. Honestly, I wish I were still stuck in the porn world surrounded by vibrators and cream. Much safer that way."

The Alien freezes on the wall, peering at its prey.

Slowly so as not to scare it off, Oleg raises his AK-47 and takes aim. Alejandro points his flame thrower at the monster. Joan reaches for her gun.

"Excuse me," the Alien begins mild-manneredly. "Do you mind telling me what you intend to do?"

Oleg is so surprised he very nearly pulls the trigger. "Can you talk?"

"Of course," the Alien replies nonchalantly, fanning itself with its tail. "Not that anyone in this fucking city is interested. They just don't want to know. As soon as they see us, all hell breaks loose. Some start screaming, others just start shooting. Life is so predictable, Sir. We just sit on our nests, hatch our eggs, feed on the local townsfolk... don't even have anybody to discuss literature with."

ZOTOV

"Are they sentient?" Alejandro whispers in Oleg's ear.

"No, not normally," Oleg replies in a similar feverish whisper. "Then again, we've no idea what type of movies we're in. This might be an amateur torrent translation. They like adding these sorts of insider jokes just for kicks. I wouldn't be surprised if it even had a Russian name. Like in that British Plebs series about Ancient Rome. There's that slave there called Grumio. Our translators renamed him Grigory!"

Alejandro bursts out coughing. "Don't you guys have anything better to do on Earth these days?"

"On the contrary," Oleg explains quietly. "It's just that we have a very specific type of humor. And when our government finally croaks from eating bad mushrooms, that's when we'll have a real good laugh."

Alejandro casts him a gloomy glance but says nothing.

"What kind of literature exactly do you like?" Oleg asks the Alien.

"Well, how can I say," the monster replies courteously. "Cookbooks mainly."

"Meaning that you still intend to eat us?" Oleg asks, relieved.

"I wouldn't put it so plainly," the Alien replies mildly. "Then again, why does nobody ever ask what we're supposed to eat here? Vegetarian? Or muesli? Gluten-free bread or cherry tomatoes? I'd have really loved some, Sir. I've been living in this city for decades now, but not a single swine has thought of opening a vegetarian restaurant here! But it's not even about food. We need to procreate and you're the perfect embryo hosts. I personally don't know why but we really like to procreate. It's the best thing going. The moment we see a human, we absolutely have to screw."

Joan shudders. "That's disgusting. You've got slime dripping from your mouth."

"If you'll excuse me, Ma'am," the Alien replies with the utmost gallantry, "it's not as if you've got roses growing out of your gob, either. You really need to stop and think how you present yourselves to us: tailless stinking creatures who are so lacking they're obliged to use their two legs for walking! You're basically cattle. Still, you can eat cows but we can't eat you. What kind of double standard is that? To tell you the truth, the only reason I haven't attacked you yet is because I feel intimidated by your presence, Ma'am."

"My presence?" Joan asks, uncomprehending.

"Yes, lady, yours!" the Alien snaps. "That's pretty stupid of you to ask, isn't it? Human females are deadly. We know! We've met one of your species already. She's a monster. The woman's unkillable. She burned our base, destroyed our hatchlings and ripped our queen apart, and still she won't stop! Abominable creature. We even tried to send a delegation to tell her we wouldn't come anywhere near her provided she stayed away from us too. As if! She just won't leave as alone. Wherever she sees us, she kills us, sending bits of our acidic flesh flying in all directions."

"He's talking about Sigourney Weaver," Oleg explains to the other two. "Incredible woman. She starred in *Alien,* in all five parts of it. She's supposed to be a space pilot. She got herself wounded, burned, crushed, even drowned in liquid metal where she supposedly died. Not that it helped the alien invaders. I'm not surprised they're so scared of her. If she sees us here, she'll make quick work of us too."

In the meantime, about half a dozen more Aliens come out onto the nearby buildings, listening curiously to the conversation. Oleg has a bad feeling about it.

He's right. The first Alien stops his story mid-word and emits a hissing sound which sounds just like the one in the movie. The other monsters reply in a hoarse scream, shaking their spiky tails in unison.

"My apologies, dear friends, but I'm afraid you're toast," the first Alien says graciously. "Can't help it. We've got to procreate. We'll try to kill the lady first — we don't trust her gender — and then we'll sort out the rest of you."

The next ten minutes are filled with the roaring of flames, machine-gun bursts and occasional but precise pistol shots. Oleg sprays an Alien who tries to leap onto him, then dodges the acid spewing from his exploded head. Alejandro has torched two of the monsters who attempted to attack them from the rear. Joan buries a slug right in the center of the last monster's forehead, triggering a fountain of acid.

They linger, waiting, but if there'd been any more monsters, they'd already made themselves scarce.

"I don't recognize you," Joan says, her voice ringing with suspicion. "Not so long ago you were a miserable, nervous, fucked-up individual. You were constantly pale due to the lack of fresh air; your eyes were always watering from the bright lights. And now look at you! You're like an action movie star."

Trying to stay true to his new role, Oleg cracks a condescending smile. "You didn't look surprised when we came to the edge of the corn field and found a car packed with weapons and camo fatigues, did you? Because that's an absolute must in Horror movies. Firstly, the main character is obliged to lay his hands on a weapon, and secondly, it's always the wuss who becomes the tough guy. He's the one who sprays the undead with his machine gun, gets the best girl, saves everybody and even gets himself out of the shit. So my awesomeness is absolutely predictable. We seem to make a classic horror-movie cast. Alejandro is the haughty pretty boy who dies first. I am the wuss who turns into a superhero and thus gets a decent chance of surviving almost until the final credits. And you, Joan, have nothing to worry about. Virgins don't die very often in horror movies. Unless, of course, you..."

"No, thank you. I'm not going to."

"Excellent."

A blonde woman, her eyes glazed over, walks out of a side street toward them. She comes on down the road, tramping down the glass underfoot like a soldier on parade. She walks past a broken shop window on the corner and heads for them with an unwavering confidence.

Unhesitantly Oleg raises his gun and shoots her between the eyes. The camera switches to slo-mo. The air fills with a mixture of blood and gore.

"Why?" Joan asks cautiously. She doesn't panic anymore.

"Just to be sure," Oleg explains. "It never hurts in horror movies. I could never understand it when a character behaved suspiciously and instead of killing him, everybody pretended they didn't see evil even though it literally chattered its teeth like a hungry wolf until it did away with them all. And very often it's a blonde that's the culprit."

As if confirming his words, long iridescent maggots begin creeping out of the dead girl's face. Alejandro lights them up with a burst of his flame thrower. The three give the burning body a wide berth and head off into town.

There, in a narrow but picturesque lane between white Venetian-style buildings, they meet another girl. This one is dark-haired with spikes lining her spine like that of a stegosaurus. She's completely naked.

This time Joan is the first to shoot.

"Well done," Oleg agrees, stepping over the body. "This one is from *Species* which is a totally different story. She's looking for someone to mate with and have offspring. Not to plant an embryo in the host's body but simply have sex with them."

"In that case, we shouldn't have killed her," Alejandro says with regret.

"She would have killed you later, anyway," Oleg snaps. "All these monsters are programmed to have sex simply in order to reproduce. They don't get off on human emotion. The Alien was right: why do extraterrestrials in these films have to breed like rabbits? They don't seem to be doing much else apart from spreading their genes. Strange creatures. What the hell has happened to the good old aliens, cute and cuddly? Why are we constantly visited by these maggot-spreaders, skull hunters like Predator, monsters in huge starships, mad with their own malice, who seek to either enslave or destroy the human race? All those cannibals and body snatchers, you know what I mean. And the funny thing is, they're all so primitive. They're smart enough to build a state-of-the-art spaceship to cross the Universe in, but in everything else they have less brains than a cockroach."

Alejandro smirks. "Are you still trying to convince me that your movies are the best while ours are past their prime? Jesus Christ, can't you realize for one moment that a lot of what you're shooting is crap! I'm not surprised that Bela Lugosi films are still considered horror classics. Your blood just seems to freeze when you watch them. All your horrors and monsters are made of plastic, they wouldn't scare a baby. If you want real horror, you need to watch black-and-white Bela Lugosi and Boris Karloff. If you want to laugh, you need to watch the silent Charlie Chaplin movies. If you want true love, that's Mary Pickford. And please don't argue with me," Alejandro's face contorts into a mask of fury.

Oleg knows better than to argue with him. "Okay," he nods. "I agree. Black-and-white movies are the best thing since sliced bread. And now that I've confessed my love for it, let's try and think how to get out of here. This is our second unsuccessful portal jump. Do we have any other options apart from magic and artifacts?"

Alejandro struggles for an answer. "We'll come back to it," he finally says softly, making sure Joan can't hear. "Just not now."

THE CAMERA FILMS the three from behind. The audience sees them heading into the sunset between rows of empty houses with gaping broken windows and streets lined with burnt-out cars. They momentarily disappear from view. All you can hear is hissing, screaming and the roaring of flames interspersed with bursts of automatic gunfire and the claps of single shots.

Soon Joan and Oleg re-emerge, their weapons at the ready, and head toward a burned-out control post made of stone blocks. Alejandro lags slightly behind, covering his friends.

He stops in order to light up a cigarette. The burning match illuminates a close-up of his face. He stares hard and long at the backs of his companions in misery.

CHAPTER FOUR

Casa de Cine

The center of Lima
November 2 1931

ALEJANDRO WAS SITTING in the movie theater as quiet as a mouse. He'd never been so obedient even with his parents when he was a child.

He was sat next to the Shadow, so afraid that he didn't even dare move. His throat was so dry that his tongue was stuck to the roof of his mouth. Just think: the murderous Artist who not so long ago had reduced the whole of Lima to quaking in their boots, the master and executioner of dozens of young girls whom he'd turned into elaborate dolls, was now afraid of uttering a single word for fear of disturbing the peace of Supay, the King of Uku Pacha.

In the seat to his right lay a dead girl, her arms hanging listlessly. Blood dripped to the floor from her little finger. Alejandro's fashionable shoes were also stained red as the entire carpet underfoot was drenched in blood.

Every single person in the theater was dead — at least five hundred of them, if not more. Alejandro had never seen people being killed so fast and in such numbers...

THE MOMENT Supay had entered the theater, he'd grinned and thrown both hands theatrically in the air like the conductor of an orchestra. The air filled with buzzing of what appeared to be a beehive. Hundreds of tiny razor-sharp bits of metal showered down from the ceiling, piercing eyes and slitting throats.

Their agony had been brief. All of them had died within thirty seconds without even realizing what had happened.

Supay had removed his hat and waited for their croaking to subside, then walked toward the empty seats in the center of the room, glancing curiously at the screen.

"Excuse me, Sir," Rodrigo mumbled. "Why did you do that?"

"For the simple convenience of our experiment," the demon said, focusing his empty eyes on him. "We don't need any witnesses, do we? We would have had to ask all these people to leave and they, in turn, might have started to panic and protest. We don't want any disturbance, Señors. Make yourself comfortable, I implore you."

For the first time, it had occurred to

Alejandro that he and Rodrigo might have done something wrong.

He'd thought that Supay had killed all these people in order to drink his fill of blood, like the ancient Incan legends had forewarned. Still, the demon showed no inclination to gorge himself; in fact, he didn't appear thirsty or starved at all. He didn't even hate all these strangers; he'd only killed them because they'd prevented him from watching the movie.

For him, it was like swatting flies. One doesn't hate a fly simply because it's annoying in its persistence, does one?

The underground demon made himself comfortable in the theater full of dead bodies and prepared to watch his very first show.

Rodrigo had gone upstairs to the projector room. Alejandro heard a shot being fired at the ceiling; then Rodrigo must have arrived at some sort of agreement with the projectionist. Alejandro could almost envisage his Apprentice aiming his gun at the man's head, the barrel almost touching it, as the projectionist was reloading a new pan into the machine, his hands shaking like a leaf...

A DEAD MAN two rows away leaned to one side and slid to the floor. With childish curiosity, Supay stared at the spot of light which had appeared on the screen.

Once again Alejandro realized that he felt like a young schoolboy facing his gray-haired professor.

Supay's very appearance commanded respect: a middle-aged gentleman in medieval Spanish attire complete with a rapier and pair of high leather boots. The carnival was still in full swing, so nobody would raise an eyebrow at such a disguise: there were plenty of them today on the streets of Lima.

The screen showed the title: *A Little Princess*, a 1917 film starring Mary Pickford. It lasted 62 minutes and was arguably one of her most successful appearances which had secured her status as a movie superstar.

Seeing people moving on the screen, Supay raised his eyebrows in surprise. He was visibly shaken —scared even, if you could say that about a subterranean demon. It's one thing to watch an amateur production on a crumpled sheet (because back in Corpus Christi they'd only managed to run their dilapidated projector for barely half a minute before it had broken down) — but watching it on a giant screen was something totally different.

The demon made a slight movement as if trying to get out of his chair.

Oh no, Alejandro thought, suspecting the demon might just jump up and run out of the theater.

But nothing of the kind happened. Supay simply leaned his hand on the shoulder of the dead girl next to him and stared at the screen.

If the Artist had thought that watching the demon's reactions would be more interesting than following the movie, he was mistaken. The moment the adorable Sara Crewe with her headful of the cutest curls had appeared on the screen, Alejandro forgot everything around him. He could barely breathe whenever he saw her. Mary's acting skill was amazing, allowing Alejandro to once again relive the most tender love that could exist.

My God, wasn't she beautiful! She was the eighth wonder of the world.

Alejandro must have seen the film a hundred times, but every time he followed the little girl's story (because Mary tended to play little girls due to her short stature) with bated breath. His eyes welled with tears; he pressed his hands to his chest whispering the lines he'd long known off by heart.

The beauty of the Casa de Cine was, they had regular shows for Mary Pickford's aficionados, screening films shot when she'd been twenty years of age and in her prime. Alejandro's heart filled with anger and pain as he watched the poor Sara being hurt and humiliated by a bunch of swine who later were put to shame by her triumphant transformation once she'd found the treasure her father had bequeathed to her, becoming a noble and a very rich lady.

In the entire course of the movie — which was just over an hour — Alejandro hadn't uttered a word.

Supay was also quiet. Even after the caption saying *The End* had appeared, he couldn't take his eyes off the small spot of light on the white fabric.

Only after about five minutes had passed, did Supay turn to the Artist. "Have you had this thing for a long time in your world?"

"Just over thirty-five years, Señor," Alejandro replied unhesitantly. "Ever since in Paris the Lumière brothers first showed the 50-second *Arrival of a Train.*

Supay tut-tutted. "Already when I saw it in Corpus Christi, I thought that this was real magic. Why do you need me here, my boy? Even the most powerful demons in the whole of Uku Pacha wouldn't be able to work the miracle you've just shown me. And here, it seems perfectly mundane! Can't your science fulfill your dream?"

"Unfortunately it can't, Señor," Alejandro sighed. "Science can't do everything. Trust me: had I had the chance to do it by other means, I would have done so. But I'm afraid I had no choice. I know that you can open gates to other dimensions and travel between worlds. So we're desperate for your help. Both of us are dying of unrequited love for Señorita Mary. Without her, our lives have no purpose. Had it not been for the benevolent fate which brought you here to us, we would have already committed suicide. But... Señor, please tell us you can do it, won't you?"

"I can," Supay agreed easily. "As far as I understand you, you want this Sara girl to come out from over there," he nodded at the screen, "in her human form?"

Alejandro was dumbstruck. "Yes," he said

hoarsely. "That's exactly what I mean, dear Sir."

The very thought that his and Rodrigo's dream might be about to come true made him weak at the knees. Just think of all the suffering and horrors they'd had to go through! What a nightmare it had been! They could have been discovered and arrested at any time — or even shot in an attempt to escape.

Luckily, it was all over now. Mary was about to leave the silver screen and step out into the actual theater. True, there was no telling what her reaction would be to the blood-soaked floor and all the dead bodies but it was already irrelevant.

The main thing was, he was about to enter eternal bliss. It was almost upon him.

Supay gave him a long studious look. His eyes lit up red: a color so familiar to the Artist from the demon's statue in the slaughterhouse cellar.

The monster smiled. Alejandro shuddered, smelling the stench of rotting meat that emanated from the creature's large yellowed teeth.

Supay pushed the girl's body aside and rose to his feet without taking his eyes from the screen.

"I know how you feel," the demon said. "This Sara girl is very beautiful. But doesn't she exist in your world? As far as I understand it, these moving pictures are some sort of theater played by actors. Wouldn't it have been easier for you to just seduce her prototype? This kind of magic is much easier for me than you think. If you wish, tomorrow she could be begging at your feet, dying of love for you."

Alejandro struggled to come out of his stupor and shook a desperate head. "I'm afraid it's not that easy, Señor. She's thirty-nine now; she's old enough to be my mother. In this film, she was barely twenty years old which makes us roughly the same age. Besides, I love Miss Pickford too much to suppress her will. I'm dreaming about lying prostrated in the dust at her feet. I want her to love me of her own free will, the way I am now."

Supay gave him a long look, then burst out laughing. "You're something, you," he said, choking on his laughter. "First he does away with a good forty girls, and then he sits here winging that he doesn't want to force his lover to sleep with him. He wants her to appreciate his haughty and exalted nature! You want her here now? Very well. I'll do as you wish. Go and call your friend now."

"Rodrigo!" Alejandro shouted, ecstatic. "Come back here, quick!"

"Are you going to watch another movie?" Rodrigo's voice came from the booth.

Supay gave a magnanimous nod and sat back down.

"Yes, please!" Alejandro shouted. "Don't kill the projectionist! Just come down here, quick! The master's waiting!"

Rodrigo arrived almost straight away even though it must have taken him some time to strap the projectionist into his chair. He came running toward them, splattering blood all over the floor with his shoes, and jumped to attention as if Supay were some kind of general. Once a cop, always a cop. His face betrayed ecstasy and absolute veneration.

He's so used to obeying authority he doesn't even care whether they wear epaulettes or a crumbling Spanish doublet, Alejandro thought with a sudden dislike. You can't change a slave.

"Señor," Rodrigo bowed to the demon. "I await your orders."

The monster stretched out in his seat, placing his feet on the back of the chair in front. "I understood and appreciated your wish," he said. "Frankly, I've never done anything like this before. How low must your society have stooped if it attempts to attain such an elevated feeling as love by such abominable means. But admittedly, I found this show quite impressive too. It's basically the witchcraft of this new age — a new religion, even, if you think how easily it takes hold of the souls of millions of people and how quickly it turns them into its worshippers. All it takes is showing them the moving picture of a woman turning into a goddess — and all and sundry, young and old, will fawn at her feet. This is life's irony for you! Some four hundred years ago, all you needed to attain the status of a god was to perform miracles unsurpassed in their scope and grandeur. And now all you need in order to join the ranks of divine dwellers is play a couple of roles in a movie! So you two have fallen for a screen idol and want me to bring her from there to here? Piece of cake. Off you go."

"Off we go where?" the two young men asked in unison.

"What do you mean, 'where'?" the demon sounded surprised. "You have to duel now. One of you has to kill the other. The winner takes all, including the beautiful Sara and her tender love."

Silence fell.

"Excuse me, Señor," Alejandro said politely but firmly. "I'm not sure I quite understood you. I thought that Señorita Mary was supposed to choose between the pair of us."

Rodrigo, unwilling to argue in the demon's presence, nodded energetically.

"Why?" the demon inquired calmly. "Wouldn't it be easier if the Señorita were the prize for the winner? Doesn't it make perfect sense to you, my dear Sirs? A choice like this is hard to make, and this way she wouldn't have to hesitate. So what I suggest is very straightforward, really. This way the loser wouldn't have to leave the theater with a broken heart. He'd be lying on the floor with a broken neck. What's wrong with that?"

He watched them, grinning like a Roman emperor in anticipation of a gladiatorial fight. It finally occurred to Alejandro that their wish would only be granted at the cost of the demon's reveling in the demise of one of them. You can't just lure the King of Uku Pacha out of his underground realm: you can summon him but he's by no means his summoners' servant. He wouldn't grant their wish unless there was something in it for him too. Otherwise, what would be the point? He wanted his fun, too, and he would have loved to see the two friends fight each other for the right to win their woman's hand.

Alejandro and Rodrigo walked down the theater aisle toward the first row. They stood there silent, not knowing what to do. The demon watched them expectantly from above.

Alejandro met his friend's gaze. Rodrigo blinked miserably as if saying: *Has it all been in vain?*

Alejandro stepped toward him and draped his arms around Rodrigo's neck in a sudden bout of affection, pulling his friend's head to his shoulder.

Rodrigo sobbed. The Artist stroked his hair, then kissed his cheek. His lips still pressed to Rodrigo's skin, he buried the tinted-gray dagger in his friend's chest.

Rodrigo's ribs crunched as the Artist turned the blade, pulled it out sharply, then stabbed the Apprentice twice again in the heart.

"Ahhhh," Rodrigo gasped. A tear rolled down from his left eye.

"I'm so sorry," Alejandro replied, suppressing his own sobs.

Rodrigo stared at his face with unseeing eyes. Holding back a bout of nausea, Alejandro tried to wipe the specks of blood away but only smeared them over his cheeks, turning his face into a crude crimson mask.

The Apprentice collapsed backwards, spattering blood. He lay on his back, his legs shaking as if he were walking somewhere.

In one last effort, he reached out to the screen as if trying to touch Mary Pickford's sweet face one last time, then froze.

Alejandro wailed, hating himself. He flung the knife away into the darkness, burying it in blood.

A loud laughter and the sound of applause came from behind him. The Artist took a step back and saw Supay clapping his hands in appreciation.

"Bravo, my boy," the demon laughed. "It looks like I underestimated you. Well, thank you. I've thoroughly enjoyed the show. Now the winner will indeed take all."

The skin on the demon's face began to split and crack, dropping to the floor in large flakes. A red haze filled his eyes. Disintegrating flesh hung from his elbows.

His doublet split at the seams and fell apart. His mouth gaped, dripping saliva, as his crooked yellowed teeth began to grow, revealing a forked serpentine tongue.

The demon was shedding his guise of a Spanish grandee like an anaconda does its old skin. Two pulsating spots appeared on his forehead, quickly turning into horns. His nails began to grow and curl, becoming razor-sharp.

Soon Alejandro was facing a beast with pointed hairy ears, large black wings and scarlet skin.

The monster arched his back, leaning on his front legs, and twitched his nose which now resembled a pig's snout. His eyes lit up.

Alejandro stepped back.

"It's okay, Señor," the beast chattered his teeth. "Your dream is on its way."

CHAPTER FIVE

The Bladed Glove

The City of Nightmares
The district of Popular Serial Killers

THE BREAK IS OVER, and the viewers hurry back to their seats. They're holding sugary drinks, bucketfuls of popcorn, and boxfuls of nachos with cheese sauce. Someone's dropped his packet of chips which crunch their weak protest underfoot as the chipless guy cusses the loss of his precious snack.

Finally, the lights dim. The screen lights up, revealing a blurred, murky image. Is the film damaged?

The picture comes into focus. It's a two-story house, nice and neat, very new, with a good roof, an obligatory manicured lawn, a garage and a tarmacked driveway.

Then all of the house windows illuminate from the inside, bathed in a bright electric light. The already-familiar spooky music starts to play.

ZOTOV

The picture continues to blur and quiver like an old VCR tape, distorted by occasional bad tracking.

We can hear breathing and a barely audible whisper, followed by a vile giggle and a sharp clicking sound reminiscent of the opening of a switchblade knife.

A man is sitting in a room on the second floor, typing on a typewriter. He pulls the finished sheet of paper out, lays it onto the table and feeds a new one into the mechanism, then pushes the lever back. The clattering of the keys resumes.

This is the biggest doubt that's eating through me now: does a perfect movie even exist? First those murderous clowns, then a squad of Aliens, and now a crowd of extraterrestrial Predators — Sex City sounds positively safe compared to these! The porn world is hell on earth, no doubt about it, but at least it didn't have machete-brandishing clowns or aliens wanting you as a host for their precious embryo. I've been struggling with sleep for forty-eight hours now because, judging by the setting, this is a typical American 1980s town. Which can only mean one thing. The moment we made it here from the alien-infested district, things went funny. For some reason, we'd run out of ammo and our weapons didn't function anymore, so we had to dump our guns and the flamethrower. Secondly, it's either night or twilight here. Five times we tried to escape but every time we ended up at the same old town square.

Also, we're very sleepy which is pretty understandable.

Sleep is something we can't afford. Because the first person we met in this little town was a man with a scarred face and a stripy sweater: Freddy Krueger.

By then, our weapons were already defunct. Alejandro tried to stab the monster but failed. Although our new friend has already gotten some grasp of modern cinema, he's not a big expert on the 1980s VCR period — all those Terminators, Emmanuelles *and* Nightmares on Elm Street. *For this reason, he doesn't yet realize that characters like Freddy are unkillable. Even if you do kill one, he's bound to be back with no logical explanation for his resurrection.*

When that gloomy monster grinned and started clanking his bladed gloves in anticipation of easy prey, I stepped forward, snatching the initiative from him.

"Excuse me," I said, "but do we look like teenagers?"

He was taken aback by my aggressive approach. "But-" he tried to say.

"But what?" I interrupted him. "Your target victims — and your target audience — are schoolkids. And we're all grownup people in our thirties. You're encroaching on other serial killers' territory. What would the screenwriter have said to that? What are you going to do next — attack an old folks' home? You're losing your knack, I'm afraid."

ZOTOV

Freddy looked embarrassed. "But this is what I do," he said, twitching his blades. "You see, my job is to slash people in their dreams. Mainly teenagers, true. Girls usually, even though they're a very troublesome bunch. Some of them manage to kill me too. You have only one girl here, so I thought..."

"I like this attitude," Joan said who'd immediately known who she was dealing with. "In porn-free worlds, women are powerful beings who exterminate whole armies of monsters and serial killers. A woman is a force to be feared and reckoned with."

"That's because you haven't been to the world of romantic melodrama yet," I replied, then turned back to Freddy. "I'm sorry, Sir, but we've just been passing by. We don't mean any harm. What if you just leave us alone?"

I must have overdone it because Freddy seemed to dislike my last lines.

"And do you think I'm just enjoying a stroll?" he snarled. "I'm on a mission, sort of."

I raised my eyebrows in fake amazement. "You don't mean it! Your mission was completed a hundred years ago. You killed the children of those bastards who'd burned you alive in the boiler room. You eliminated their friends. You did away with their extended families. You made short work of everyone living within a hundred miles of Springwood, including the director Wes Craven and the entire film crew! And you even had the audacity of getting your name on the cast credit list: "Freddie Krueger as himself"! *Your game is up! What's the point?"*

I could see Freddie was really embarrassed, so I pressed the point. I started consoling him, like he had a great future in front of him, he had a huge following. You have to admit that movie monsters have it easier than real-life serial killers. Do we know of many Chikatilo fans? That particular Russian predator was disgusting in his vileness. Nobody in their sane mind would love him, not even the scum of the earth. But Freddie Krueger, oh! That's a different story entirely. An abominable killer with knives for fingers and a face only a mother could love, in his signature filthy sweaters — and think of all those girls who had his poster on their bedroom walls.

So I tried to explain to Freddie that he could change his own destiny. He could give master classes to novice murderers, teaching them how to slash, stalk and snatch their victims from reality into a dream. If that didn't appeal to him, he could always start his own cooking TV show. He was a perfect man for the job: who could peel apples or chop meat faster than he could?

Also, considering the current craze for political correctness, he could just sue the filmmakers and demand compensation. Because if you remember, the back story to The Nightmare on Elm Street *was as follows: Freddie Krueger was a real-world serial killer who was arrested but then released on a technicality. The parents of the murdered children took the law into their own hands, locking Krueger in*

ZOTOV

the boiler room where he worked, then burning him alive.

How's that for a human rights abuse? True, it would have been much better for him had he been a hunchbacked handicapped homosexual African American, but even so, his chances were quite high.

On hearing all this, Krueger scratched the back of his head, shaving off entire strips of skin from his neck. It all sounded interesting, he said, and he needed to give it some thought. He might actually drop in and kill us later.

I agreed that it was an excellent idea.

Then we awoke on the lawn next to this nice neat house, realizing it had only been a dream. The thought made our blood run cold.

Unfortunately, as we were leaving the place of our impromptu stopover, another murderer attacked us. This guy was wearing a white ice hockey mask, brandishing a huge machete (nothing like the cutlery the clowns had been playing with). No points for guessing this was Jason from Friday 13.

That was one dangerous dude. Still, I allowed myself a sigh of relief. At least this was reality and not a dream.

"Why does everybody want to kill us?" Joan asked in surprise.

"And why does everybody in your world want to screw me?" I snapped back.

She shut up angrily.

Without saying a word, Jason headed toward us. He was dead, after all, so he couldn't speak.

EL DIABLO

Just think about the story behind Friday 13*:
An eleven-year-old boy who'd drowned in a lake
while his counselors were drinking and having it off
in the woods, resurrected on the anniversary of his
death, looking strong and powerful like a twenty-
year-old man. What I find strange is that apparently,
there're no schools or colleges training future serial
killers at the bottom of the lake. Horror films make it
so simple. When the astonished movie goer finally
dares ask, "How the hell is that possible?" the
filmmakers reply, "It just is."*

*But this Jason flick took this primitivism to
new heights: whoever the camera pointed at, he was
going to do away with.*

*It was basically the same as porn, only with
murders and gore. And still we loved watching it, so
much so that we were afraid to visit the bathroom at
night.*

*Alejandro backed off. I could quite understand
him. We'd had a gutful of faces like Jason's. There
was no telling what they might do the next moment.*

*Luckily, unlike Freddie, Jason could be
momentarily distracted. I took a baseball bat (of
which there're plenty lying around here for some
reason) and very nicely but resolutely hit Jason right
in the middle of his mask.*

*The bastard dropped to the ground. Alejandro
snatched the machete from him.*

*Then we carried on as we'd previously
agreed. While we held both his hands (with him
trying to struggle out of our clutches in complete*

silence, making it even scarier), Joan jumped into the nearest car (because starting a car without a key is piece of cake in all these movies) and rammed it into Jason.

With a crunching of bones, a dark pool of blood spread from under the car's wheels.

I warned the others that it wouldn't hold him back for more than five minutes. Seeing as Jason was undead, sooner or later he'd be able to push the car off himself and resume his chase. This was how it always was with him.

My friends in misfortune knew better than to object.

Alejandro and I picked up a baseball bat each and went running. Personally, I got out of breath almost straight away but Alejandro was quick on his feet like an Olympian. Joan, she was as fast as a deer.

Worst of all, it was night time — horror films' stomping ground.

I was the first to stop and beg the others to take a breather. I'm no marathon runner which is bad news: in horror movies, one has to run fast. Everybody seems to be constantly on the run in them; the only exception being Japanese horror flicks with dead girls — but their looks would freeze anyone to the floor.

By then, I'd already realized that I was beginning to get the knack of it and that our situation wasn't as bad as it had first seemed. True, a quiet American town with its homegrown serial killers is all Mickey Mouse stuff compared to the latest Japanese offerings.

We were standing there, me gasping for breath. On an empty lot in front of us towered a white three-story building.

We ran inside. Immediately I got a nagging feeling that this had been a very wrong move. Creaking flaky doors; broken lightbulbs with their shards grinning; rusty beds squeaking ominously in the corridors. The wind wailed. I could hear the clanking of locks on cell doors with tiny barred observation windows.

Oh shit. Everything was clear now. This was a mental hospital; all I had to do was guess which film it was supposed to be.

The single surviving light bulb bathed everything in its weak glow. I saw a man in a white mask standing right at the end of the corridor. Not an ice hockey mask like Jason's but just a thin plastic one with huge holes for eyes. He stood there calmly, twiddling with a wide kitchen knife. The mask looked as if it was glued to his face.

At this point, I calmed down a bit. This was Michael Myers, the serial killer from Halloween*. Like Jason, he was also a silent killer — but at least he was alive. Then again, could you really call him alive by now? He'd been stabbed in the forehead, shot with half a dozen bullets, burned alive and even beheaded — but nothing seemed to kill him. Had real-life killers been as robust as him, then they'd have to execute the Washington sniper at least once* *every week — provided they could catch him. Because movie murderers are usually strong as hell so that even an entire police squad can't subdue them. With the honorable exception of* Saw *with its terminal-cancer protagonist: apparently, by the mid-2000s, the new generation had gotten so fed up with all-powerful predators that a handicapped killer was just the ticket.*

That's not to mention the "old fart" trend which allows the casting of geriatric stars like Schwarzenegger who still performs in action thrillers well into his seventies. I wouldn't be surprised if they made a new Terminator *movie, with the robot's dentures chattering as he brandishes his two machine guns mounted on his Zimmer frame.*

I cast a cautious look around me, half-expecting a good guy with a loaded gun. No such luck.

With a heavy step, the guy in the white mask came toward us, holding his knife at hip height. Joan screamed, shaking her head in desperation.

"What's wrong with you?" I asked her.

"Dunno," she sounded puzzled. "I thought I was supposed to do this."

"I see... actually, yeah, you're right."

"This one, is he also a woman killer?"

"That's just the nature of horror movies. They kill a whole bunch of cute blondes even before the opening credits have rolled."

"Why can't they kill men?"

"They're just not as funny to watch when they

scream and try to scamper away in their stilettoes."

Joan took offense and fell silent even though I was telling the truth.

Myers was getting closer.

Alejandro heaved a long-suffering sigh and got a better grip on his baseball bat. The events of the last hour had just been too much for him.

I gestured to him to wait. This kind of serial killer was best shot on the spot. Unfortunately, we didn't have firearms. Had this been a computer shooter game, we could have frisked a dead special-forces man. There're always plenty of them lying around there, complete with ammo, grenades and a first-aid kit.

If only the ceiling would just cave in on him! I looked up but the ceiling didn't show any inclination to fall anytime soon.

Then I heard gunshots. One after the other, six in total.

Myers stopped with his arms spread wide like he'd been crucified, then slowly (it always happens in slow-mo in these kinds of movies) fell on his back, raising clouds of dust.

Joan was standing in a police firing stance, holding the revolver with both hands.

"Thanks."

"You're welcome."

"Couldn't you have told me earlier that you had a gun? Actually, where the hell did you get it from?"

"In the car's glove compartment. I checked it

just in case. You did tell me that you could find guns in the most unexpected places just when the going gets tough and the good guy needs one. And the going's not tough now?"

"Absolutely."

"So you see."

I decided not to tell Joan how disappointed I was. Just imagine: a serial killer in a white mask is chasing us up and down the mental asylum with a knife in his hand, trying to break doors down as he hunts the girl. One of us might try to find shelter under a bed; he lies there holding their breath and watching the murderer's feet as the latter prowls around the ward. How cool is that?

And she just shot him down, end of story. You really couldn't explain to her that a five-minute horror film would crash at the box office. Imagine a serial killer who walks out into the moonlight twirling his knife as he grins predatorily — and the good guys just come and shoot him down? That would be the end of the film industry.

Never mind. I was pretty sure we'd still have our fun. The story wasn't over yet. We were yet to meet Leatherface with his chainsaw, the spoiled wuss Psycho wearing rollers and his Mommy's housecoat, and even the monster from Hellraiser with his pin-studded head. It certainly wouldn't get boring, that's for sure.

We kept going for another half-hour, following our noses until we came to an empty house which looked quite suitable for human habitation. It even had electricity, hot and cold running water and a kitchen with a plateful of pancakes.

While we were staying there, Alejandro swanned off to see if he could procure a teleport artifact capable of taking us back home. He hadn't kept his word and left without telling me about the other way of escaping the movie world.

Joan doggedly kept boarding up the windows at the back of the house, thinking to make us safer. She could be forgiven for her ignorance of the horror movie industry. She had no idea that even the most stupid serial killer could easily penetrate any locked room so all her hard work was in vain.

And me, I'm now typing this on a typewriter I discovered in the library, trying to stay awake. Because Freddie promised to come back for us — and as far as I know, he always follows through on his threats. Plus all those guys with their knives and chainsaws who're out to get us as well. As some idiot author said in his old psychedelic book The Seal of the Moon, *"In a good horror novel, evil never dies". This is absolutely true.*

Jesus, I'm so sleepy. My eyelids feel leaden... but I must keep going. I drink coffee by the bucket and keep writing in my journal. Let me think... what else can I tell you?

THE CAMERA zooms out and starts to spin, showing us the deserted streets. Not one passerby; the streetlamps are barely glowing; the wind is whipping up the dry leaves.

ZOTOV

Then all the windows start to go out one by one, in a complex pattern as if someone's playing naughts and crosses, until it reaches the house where Oleg is sitting. In a split second, everything's submerged into darkness.

The audience exchange indignant whispers. A couple of people throw fistfuls of popcorn at the screen. Still, others don't share their protest and even grumble angrily at the culprits who whisper their apologies.

Finally, a rattling noise comes from the speakers, followed by a woman's scream and the sounds of fighting. We can hear two heavy blows and the thud of a body falling to the floor.

The girls in the audience scream instinctively. An old lamp lights up above the house's front door, hissing and sparking.

A stranger walks out onto the front porch and carefully closes the door behind himself. He reaches for a cigarette from a red and white pack, clicks his lighter and lights up. The smoke twists upward as the stranger peers up at the moon.

The audience don't know what to think. This person is none of the three heroes. As far as we can judge by his face, it's not a human being at all.

CHAPTER SIX

Hell

Lima, the Casa de Cine movie theater
November 2 1931

MIGUEL FROZE stock still in front of the movie theater's main entrance.

He was so livid his face had turned blood-red. There were only three bullets left in his revolver. He didn't dare peek inside because he had no idea what he might see.

Out of the fifty cops who'd been patrolling the city center, he was the only survivor. The demons of Uku Pacha had been waiting for them.

When one of the cops had been snatched by a dreadful creature, everybody had laughed. This was La Diablada: you couldn't surprise anyone with a trick like that. The passersby must have thought that the cop's head was made of papier-mâché and the blood, from tomato sauce. No one seemed to have realized that they weren't painted masks but the real faces of the unborn. When Supay had risen to the surface, the ancient underground evil had risen together with him.

And now the demons were quenching their hunger, on the days when they'd traditionally been allowed to walk the Earth. They'd spent the last four hundred years in their subterranean tunnels so naturally, they were as thirsty as hell.

Miguel dreaded to even think of how many cadavers they'd have to collect from the streets of Lima the next morning. He wasn't even sure he'd live to see it.

Predictably, firing at demons had proved to be a waste of time. Bullets just didn't seem to harm them. The sign of the cross hadn't worked, either. Not even holy water had done the trick (because Miguel had picked up a small bottle of it at the nearest church).

The spawn of Uku Pacha were immortal, and all the Indian legends would sadly confirm this fact. It might work in Europe where you could indeed defeat demons with the sign of the cross, vampires with stakes and werewolves with silver bullets. These demons, however, would only leave on their own accord — and not before they'd had their fill of human blood. It wasn't even about feeding themselves on human flesh — the thing was, the blind monsters of Uku Pacha hadn't killed for quite a while. And killing people was their only raison d'être.

One of the cops had loosed off an entire clip into an unborn who'd only laughed, screwing up his eyeless face. Another demon had sprung like a dog onto a cop's back and ripped a piece of the man's skull away from the back of his head. The resulting fountain of blood had caused a roar of laughter from the pisco-happy dancers which drowned out the rattle of the drums: just look at those two dragons attacking each other!

Cops were being dragged into gateways which then echoed with their screams and the demons' hungry growling. Miguel's men were being ripped apart and devoured right there in the square, to the catcalls of the inebriated townsfolk. The entire police special force had been eliminated within minutes as the demons couldn't be fooled by masks and could pick them out immediately in the crowd.

Miguel had had no desire to die like a hero on the battlefield. He'd used four slugs to knock two demons off their feet and run off before they could recover. The Casa de Cine was only a couple of blocks away.

Its doors were opened beckoningly.

Miguel walked in and very nearly fell on his back when he slipped on the blood. The bodies of the security guard and "el conductor" — which is how they call ticket controllers in Peru — were lying right in the middle of the vestibule. The guard was now eyeless, with just two bloody holes in his face. The conductor had been even less lucky: his entire head had gone walkabout. The bodies of the waitresses lay beside the bar next to five moviegoers who must have turned up late for the show.

Miguel ran up to the door into the theater and froze in hesitation. He could see a weak light coming through a crack in the door: apparently, the show was on.

His fingers closed around the useless revolver.

Shit. What was he supposed to do now?

"Come in," a calm voice came from the depths of the theater. "I know you've been standing there for quite a while."

Miguel had no intention of resisting. The invitation sounded like an order uttered by a smiley welcoming host.

Miguel stepped inside. Immediately he sensed the familiar squelch of blood underfoot which he remembered from his initial visit to the first crime scene.

A shiver ran down his spine. Not again.

His premonition hadn't betrayed him. The theater was packed with dead bodies.

Miguel scanned the room, his gaze alighting on some of the corpses. A bespectacled elderly man; a girl in a frivolous hat, her eyes rolled with only the whites showing, her lips pulled back, exposing her teeth as if she were about to bite. A family with three children, their mother clumsily trying to shield them with her own body; a group of school truants with unnaturally white faces...

It looked like most of them had died instantly

before they'd realized what was happening. The dead were sitting, staring at the screen, as if they were still enjoying the show.

Aha. This seemed to be one of Mary Pickford's most famous films: *A Little Princess*. And it was being watched by somebody who was sitting surrounded by the corpses without taking his eyes off the screen.

If Miguel had secretly hoped to see Alejandro or Rodrigo, his hopes had been dashed. He hadn't recognized the voice that had invited him in. The creature spoke Spanish with a perfectly cultured Castillano accent.

"Actually, I didn't expect you to come," Supay said melancholically.

The horned monster turned his crimson face toward him. The King of Uku Pacha was uglier than any monster ever conceived by any film director.

The creature smiled. A string of viscous saliva glistened as it clung onto his fangs.

Miguel heaved a sigh and stuffed the revolver back in his belt.

"Good," the monster said. "You've managed to surprise me twice today. You know who I am, don't you? What a shame we're not back in the times of the Incas. Before, my servants used to wreak havoc in Cusco and all over Tawantinsuyu and they always got away with it. Then later the Spanish — talk about the devil! — tried to confront my people and sever the link between Uku Pacha and the world of the living until they realized this was pretty much undoable. So they blocked all the tunnels and passages — simple! Cheap and cheerful. Had it not been for those two sweet young men who so kindly summoned me, I'd have never gained enough strength to emerge. But I knew that my escape from Uku Pacha might make a lot of people unhappy which was why I asked my servants to accompany me through the Corpus Christi passage and secure my safety during my exchange with those two very nice young men — and to enjoy a good meal as well. Having said that, the fact that you somehow found your way here means my entourage didn't do their job properly. Still, today is a very special day and I'm not going to punish them. Trust me, human, when I say that today Supay is the most merciful and benevolent creature that has ever trodden planet Earth."

Miguel looked around, taking in the roomful of corpses. "This I can believe."

A gentle smile touched Supay's lips. "I like you."

"You're flattering me," Miguel replied nonchalantly.

His gut feeling told him that this was the right attitude to adopt with the demon. If he behaved calmly and independently, there was a slim chance the monster might spare him. He knew perfectly well that he could die at any given moment.

"Mind telling me what you've done with those nice young men who so kindly summoned you?" he asked.

"You mean those?" Supay nodded at the stage. "Go and take a look."

Miguel walked over to the screen. Both bodies lay on the stage: Rodrigo sprawled on his back, one hand reaching out toward the screen. The blood covering the large wounds in his chest had already congealed.

Alejandro lay on his side next to him, his head unnaturally twisted to one side. Miguel couldn't see any wounds but he had little doubt this one too was as dead as a doornail.

Despite the gravity of his situation, Miguel couldn't help smiling at the irony. The Artist and his Apprentice had killed dozens of young girls, successfully avoiding the police and sacrificing everything for the sake of their only love, only to be murdered by the very creature they'd summoned to help them.

Indeed, demons never played by the rules. You never knew what they might do next.

At that moment, neither did he.

Miguel crouched next to Alejandro's body and turned his head to face him. The young man's glazed-over eyes stared at the ceiling. There was no fear in them, only submission.

"How funny," he said, standing up.

The demon smirked. "You think?"

"They bent over backwards to please you. They killed all those girls. They worshipped you like a new Jesus. And what did they get?"

"Jesus? Who's that?" Supay asked curiously.

Miguel shrugged. "Doesn't matter." He wasn't prepared to go into involved religious discussions right now.

"If you say so," Supay agreed with ease. "So regarding your question. To tell you the truth, human, it's always been like this. Those who turned to the creatures of Uku Pacha for help never received anything but death. Firstly, because we hate being disturbed about petty stuff, even when they offer us sacrifices of human blood. Because the problems of this world *are* petty in our eyes. And secondly, the only reason we accept their sacrifices is to avoid coming to the surface to kill humans. So it's in their own interests really to keep us well fed. What makes you think we've ever fulfilled the wishes of those who offered us sacrifices?"

Miguel's head went round. He felt queasy. "Are you sure?" he asked weakly. "How about the Emperor Atahualpa? And Inca Manco? Or Francisco Pizarro and Diego de Almagro? All of them offered blood sacrifices to the denizens of Uku Pacha, and they did it by the book. In return, they were all granted power, no matter how short-lived. All of them had time to enjoy their reign — *then* they died. Am I correct?"

Supay rose from his seat. He turned out to be much taller than Miguel had imagined him.

The demon headed for him, kicking dead bodies out of his way, until he loomed over Miguel,

374

his jaws gaping open, like an anaconda about to devour its prey. Miguel smelled the stench coming from the demon's mouth which dripped long, viscous threads of spittle.

"Atahualpa?" the monster repeated. "Oh yes, he visited Uku Pacha once. But human, you don't understand. Any person who comes to see us becomes a guise for us, our passport to your world. We put on their body like you put on clothes; we receive their face, then do whatever we please. We love competing on earth in our new guises, it's just a kind of sport we have. Once we escape from Uku Pacha, we start by killing all their friends and relatives to make sure they don't notice the change. That's how one of us usurped the throne as Atahualpa, killing his brother first. And that's what I did to Francisco Pizarro's brother. The problem is, our demonic power tends to run out on earth, gradually turning us into perfectly normal humans. I donned Pizarro's body to destroy the army of the unborn at Cusco commanded by Inca Manco — or rather, by a fellow demon who'd snatched his body. My triumph didn't last though. Very soon I was defeated at Cusco by Diego de Almagro, who too was possessed by a fellow demon. I made quick work of him though and had his head cut off in the city square. Not that it helped me much: in three years' time, I was killed by my own kind in a palace coup. And when our human bodies die, our spirit goes back to Uku Pacha. We can even keep our host's appearance, that's why I've been walking around like Francisco Pizarro for the last four hundred years. Why do we need your world, might you ask? Well, for one, there's no life in Uku Pacha, is there? It's the world of the dead, after all. Here on earth, you have scheming, intrigue, power, love, entertainment... and what do we have? We're dying of boredom, never mind that we're already dead. And now they," he nodded at Alejandro and Rodrigo's bodies, "I don't care what kind of a wondrous future they'd dreamed up for themselves and what kind of wish I was supposed to grant them in return for the pretty dolls they'd made. Although admittedly, they were quite an eye-opener. I had no idea back in my moldy tunnels that you'd invented such an incredible thing as the cinema!"

The demon turned to the screen. "This is awesome," he growled. "The best invention in all the thousands of years of my existence. Human beings have learned how to convert their fantasies into visual form, and the result has surpassed all expectations. Before, my experience was limited to earth and Uku Pacha. And now I've received the ability to travel between all kinds of magic worlds! I spared the projectionist and I'm on my fifth film now. The choice is incredible. I can follow Frankenstein to the realm of dead monsters; I can take a stroll with Charlie Chaplin or enjoy the company of," his clawed finger pointed at the screen, "of this charming lady. The moment I saw her, I sensed something snap within my heart. This is so unlike me, don't you think? I've surprised myself. I even wanted to... how can I put it... to *touch* her. Not the actress but the character herself. I wanted to feel her for real. Mary Pickford and I have only known each other for a few hours but I have this feeling as if I've known her my entire life. I've no desire to stay here nor do I want to summon her like those two sweet young men, may they rest in peace. I'm going to pay her a visit myself. You're about to become witness to a new miracle as I will enter the world of movies and stay there for as long as I can."

The demon stepped toward Alejandro's body.

His horrendous face began to change, its quivering outlines blurring. His clawed hands hung listlessly. His two horns dropped to the ground like two dead snakes. His snout deformed and was sucked into his face; his sharp teeth disappeared behind his lips.

His entire body began to lose shape until it turned into weightless substance which headed for Alejandro's body and began pouring into his mouth.

Miguel watched as the body showed signs of life. Alejandro's eyes glistened; his eyebrows arched, his legs twitched.

The Artist stirred and sat up, swaying. He ran his hands over himself like someone rearranging one's clothes, then reached into his vest pocket, produced a small mirror and opened it with a flourish, admiring his own reflection. He gave his cheeks a light pull, readjusted his left eyelid and made some chewing motions with his teeth.

It had all taken less than a minute. Now Miguel was facing Alejandro de Castillero, very real and perfectly alive. It was undoubtedly him — but still not quite. It was a bit like staring at a mannequin in a badly fitted business suit.

The deadman's face scowled and fell to one side as Supay tried to crack a smile.

So that's how one loses one's mind, Miguel thought. Not that I care. This is my death.

"I'm not gonna kill you," the demon said. "You're free to live and tell everyone about our meeting. No one's gonna believe you, anyway, apart from a couple nutcases. It's time for me to go. I need to find her. I want to reunite with her in the wondrous world of ecstasy," he sprang onto the stage in front of the screen.

The demon reached his hand toward the white fabric which acquired a soft glow. Color drained from his clothes and even his body which turned a glowing gray — or rather, black and white.

The demon turned his face toward Miguel and smiled like a human — a happy, toothy grin. Miguel half-expected him to say something haughty befitting the occasion but the demon said nothing. His body was simply sucked into the screen as if it were a vortex.

Mary Pickford threw her head back in a bout of cheerful laughter. A column of raging fire erupted from her mouth. The screen began to shrink, engulfed in flames. The curtains caught fire.

Stumbling over the dead bodies, Miguel made for the exit. He paused by the projector room's door, pulling the door handle as hard as he could as the projectionist screamed inside, begging for help.

Still, the fire was already upon him.

"I'm sorry," Miguel whispered, then scrambled out into the cinema lobby. Behind him, the fire roared, spreading the stench of burned flesh as all the bodies caught fire.

Miguel staggered outside and slumped onto the steps, his lungs bursting with bouts of coughing. Behind his back, the Casa de Cine was ablaze.

A blood-covered police corporal ran over and leaned over him. "Señor Capitan... there's nobody left... all our men our dead. You and I are the only ones alive. Have you found the Artist?"

Miguel shook his head. "No. I'm afraid, he escaped."

"Where to?"

Miguel looked up at the corporal. "Far from here. Very far."

His eyes welled with madness. He exploded in a bout of uncontrollable hoarse laughter.

CHAPTER SEVEN

The Heart

The City of Nightmares
An abandoned house in a dark alley

THE MOVIE SCREEN lights up slowly and weakly. The picture is blurred, similar to that of a night-vision camera. We can make out the outline of a man strapped to a chair against a gray background. His hands are bound behind the back of the chair. From time to time he tries to struggle free but his captors did a good job restraining him.

The camera zooms in on his sore wrists which he must have rubbed raw as he tried to escape the bondage.

Opposite him, another man leans comfortably back in his chair, a glass of wine in his hand. Or at least it appears to be wine. They're talking in the dark without seeing each other, their voices so low we can't really hear anything they say.

The audience exchanges disappointed

whispers. Some guy in the twentieth row stands up, shrugs and heads out to get some beer. Before the theater's disappointment rises to indignation, subtitles begin to run.

"So that's how you got here?" the captive says.

"Exactly. I've told you everything now. I've been perfectly honest with you."

"That's interesting. So you claim you're an Incan demon?"

"Not exactly. I'm the King of demons."

"Of course. That changes everything. You sure you're not a nutcase?"

"In that case, you're a nutcase too. Or do you think it's normal to travel to a porn world, escape that into a war-movie setting, only to end up in a horror film?"

"Okay, let's presume you're indeed an underground monster who fell in love with Mary Pickford and used his magic powers to penetrate the movie world. Why would you try to escape it, then? Hasn't your dream come true?"

The demon sighs. "That's what I thought. The problem was, I too used to be an all-powerful force capable of dethroning kings, snatching human bodies and leading armies of ghosts to victory. Once I entered the movie world, my magic was gone. Here I became an ordinary human being. So ordinary that Mary Pickford — or rather, little Sara Crewe — didn't want to know me."

His voice rises a notch, filling with fury. "She

didn't even want to talk to me, can you imagine? And there was nothing I could do about it! Later, I had the chance of visiting a few more Pickford films but with the same result. She showed no reaction to my presence whatsoever. You see, the thing is, those period movies were very clichéd and it took a very specific type of hero for Miss Pickford to fall for. He had to be young, penniless but noble-minded. Unfortunately, even in my Alejandro guise I didn't quite fit the mold. But that wasn't the main problem. Pickford's heroines' relationships with the opposite sex were limited to light kissing as any sex scenes were unthinkable in 1917 movies. So all I gained with my persistence was that I was branded a bad guy which is a terrible thing to be in a silent movie. There, all bad guys are terrible bastards with a face that begs to be punched. Just like they portray Russians in Hollywood today."

The captive shuddered. "I know what you mean."

"So basically, it didn't work. I was so disappointed in the whole thing I wanted to go back but it turned out I didn't know how to do it! Because here I didn't have my magic abilities anymore, did I? I wasn't the great subterranean demon any longer — I was just an ordinary guy. Having said that, even in those silent movies I noticed a few characters that used certain artifacts to travel from one flick to the next. I've no idea what they are... but if you think about it, there're some magic experts in almost every movie who look suspiciously alike. So I too started traveling. You can't even imagine where I've been these last eighty years... In *Casablanca* I've been... And in *Quo Vadis*... And in the *Invasion of the Body Snatchers*... I've been to each and every one of the Bond films... and even in *Twilight* and other such vampire flicks."

"My commiserations."

"Yeah right. I don't even want to mention Bollywood."

"Oh. That's tough. But at least they're a happy bunch."

"They can dance, that's for sure. So to cut a long story short, at a certain point I realized I was stuck. There was no way I could go back; all I could do was travel between movies. And travel I did. For decades. I learned several more languages: French, English, Russian and Hindi. I drank the best French wines with Gerard Depardieu, I fought shoulder to shoulder with Schwarzenegger, I even slept with Kim Cattrall from *Sex and the City*."

"No way!"

"Why not? She's not the picky type."

"So why do you want out?"

"I'm so tired you can't imagine. This world is fake, you understand, don't you? It's like a crooked mirror which has nothing to do with reality. I'm so fed up with cutesy romances about billionaires falling for factory girls. I can't watch another action movie where the good guys never run out of ammo. All those Goth teenagers making out with vegetarian vampires and spoiled rich brats using bondage on homely secretaries to awaken their carnal side... I'm fed up with flying superheroes who wear their underpants on the outside. I wanna go home."

"It still doesn't explain why you had to bash me on the head and bring me here."

"Oh, that's the easy part. I already told you: it takes three people to escape back to earth. But there's something else I haven't told you yet. It's about Joan. We need her to get out. Without her, we're doomed to forever travel between films. But it's more than that, I'm afraid. If she continues traveling with us, she can help us open portals between movies, but that's the extent of it. The only way we can get back to our world is by sacrificing her. There's just no other way."

A long pause hangs in the air.

"What did you say?!" the prisoner struggles in his bonds.

"Exactly. That's exactly why I had to restrain you. I made a good job of it, too. This isn't a movie: you can't wriggle yourself free from my tenets. I knew you were going to do that. I expected you to fake indignation, whatever's left of it, and that's something I can't afford at the moment. And I haven't finished yet. Just sacrificing her isn't enough. I've brought my ritual knife. We'll have to eat her heart."

Silence.

"You're sick."

"Look who's talking. I worked her out a long

time ago. She's a half-blood. Once I knew that, I sat tight in Sex City just waiting for the third one to arrive. Very few people travel to the movie world on their own accord like I did. Most of them just jet sucked in. I had no idea if it was going to work. But it did. I summoned you. There was a bond between us allowing me to sense your presence anywhere."

"What the hell are you talking about?!"

"I'm telling you the truth. I summoned you here."

Silence.

"Want me to tell you how I did it? Remember the flea market in Cusco? You bought a souvenir there, a funny figurine of an ancient god. Nothing special, just the usual tourist trash. Am I right? Tourists love buying all sorts of gaudy knickknacks. What they don't do, they never ask about their provenance. The black figurine on your TV stand? Remember it?"

"Jesus. The market at Plaza de Armas. That's what the vendor told me: he said it was Supay, the underground King. After some haggling, I managed to get it off him for eight bucks."

"Congratulations. That was one of the ten sacred idols of Uku Pacha which can connect its owner to our world. A cell phone and portal all in one, if you know what I mean. That was the idol used by Alejandro and Rodrigo. They used it to send their messages to Uku Pacha. You activated it by unthinkingly smearing it with your own blood, twice. You cut yourself slicing serrano ham, remember? And then you broke a beer glass and reached for another one off the shelf which was just next to the figurine? So you see. That's how you fed it."

Silence. The demon takes a gulp of wine. "I've been watching you. I wanted you to get desperate. I wanted you to lose hope. And I won. You must hate me now."

"You could say that. You're a scumbag, you know that? Fucking piece of shit."

"Come on, say it. I'm a demon. That says it all. We're not supposed to hand out candy to underprivileged children. I'm doing what I'm supposed to do. I was born like this. I don't give a damn whether it upsets you or not. I'm fed up with walking around in Alejandro's body which is why I dragged you here. I don't think you have a choice. It's either we cut Joan's heart out of her chest or you stay here forever. And then I'll do my best to make sure you'll never leave the confines of porn flicks and bad war movies. Are you quaking yet?"

The demon leans low over Oleg, breathing in his face. "I know, I know. You must feel so proud of yourself, Mister Knight on a White Charger. Now listen to me. This is the movie world. And here, it's the bad guys who usually survive and earn the right to a remake. Like that Spectre guy in the Bond movies, the one with the cat. Or Freddie Krueger. Jason, Chucky, Michael Myers, Leatherface, Death in *Final Destination*... They're cool, clever and charismatic. They have tons of fans because the bad guys are always the best. They always survive. Even when they're showered with bullets, they still scramble back to their feet. And when you think they've finally kicked the bucket, they snap their eyes open. So you can play a hero all you want, compañero, be my guest. Problem is, you're in the wrong movie. You're neither Batman nor Superman. You're not even Iron Man. What makes you think you're blameless? Haven't you dumped your girls? Haven't you cheated on them? How many times did you forget to pay back the money you'd borrowed from a friend? Did you switch off the phone and tell your boss your mother was ill when in fact you were nursing a hangover? You're just an ordinary guy. Are you sorry for Joan? But she's not even real. She's a movie character. Her world doesn't exist. To kill her is like destroying a cartoon image. Trust me. I know what I'm talking about. Once we get out, I promise I'll give you as much gold as you can carry. Or what other commodities do you have over there, oil? I can do oil too. You help me, and I'll help you. Quit playing the hero, man."

The light comes on. The camera focuses on Oleg's face, showing his inner struggle. His face is distorted with pain as he tries to think of a way out.

The demon waits patiently, staring out the window. Finally he downs the rest of his wine, savoring it, smacks his lips with pleasure and turns back to Oleg. "And?"

"No."

ZOTOV

"Ohh. You don't understand nice, do you? I knew you'd play hard to get. I even expected you to fake agreement, then to stab me in the back the way it often happens in movies. But you seem to be more into Disney, Mister Goody-Two-Shoes. You know what? I have no intention of staying here. And I'm fed up with trying to reason with you. I'm gonna bring Joan here now and cut her heart out of her chest right in front of you. And then I'll stuff a piece of her heart down your throat with my knife handle. I'll make you eat it, dammit! I don't dive a fuck about your inner struggle, excuse my Spanish!"

The demon slaps Oleg across the face. "That's it! I'm so pissed with you you can't even imagine. You wanted to save the girl? Idiot. Now you can sit and watch her die."

The demon stands up, walks behind the prisoner and checks the straps on his wrists. You can tell he knows what he's doing.

Smiling, he hurries out of the kitchen and soon comes back, pushing Joan in front of him. Her hands are bound and she's wearing black underwear as a fleeting bow to *Fifty Shades of Gray*.

THE THEATER speakers stop working. The audience watches the demon open his mouth as he apparently says something to Oleg who shakes his head in response. The monster then turns to Joan who spits in his face.

388

The demon grins. He forces her to the floor and reaches for his knife, then raises it high in the air.

End of film spool.

The theater fills with indignant catcalls as the viewers hurl empty Coke bottles and handfuls of popcorn at the screen; someone even flings his cell phone. People stomp their feet and rattle their seats, cussing at the theater staff.

Pointless. The light in the projection room goes out. The theater turns pitch black.

CHAPTER EIGHT

Corpus Christi

Lima, the Republic of Peru
November 2 2014

GABRIEL MARTINEZ was restless and slightly annoyed. Oh no, he couldn't complain, thank God! The Holy Virgin Mary had saved him; she'd protected him and showed him the right way. As soon as he'd have a moment, he'd go to the cathedral and pray his heart out.

Who would have thought? His grandfather, Papa Miguel of all people!

Gabriel remembered him well: a hunched old man, completely gray, who'd never managed to shed his Russian accent. Because of him, the local kids used to tease Gabriel, calling him El Ruso — a moniker which had stuck to him for the rest of his life despite the fact that there was nothing Russian left in him at all. Gabriel's father could still speak Russian after a fashion — simply because Papa Miguel forced him to — but Gabriel couldn't say anything apart from the obligatory "Privet" and "Na zdorovie!" which his father had ordered him to learn just to humor Papa Miguel.

Papa Miguel had died fifteen years ago, one year short of his centenary. He was perfectly lucid until the last, he drank rum by the glass, pouring it with a soldier's unshaking hand, he walked everywhere leaning heavily on his gnarly cane and never complained about his health.

His demise had been quick and unexpected. Only the night before, he'd been reading *The Chronicle of Peru* by Pedro de Cieza de Leon — a 16th-century Spanish priest who'd recorded Tawantinsuyan tribal traditions and mythology. The next morning, they'd found him still crouching over the book with his eyes open. He was already stiff.

Admittedly, Papa Miguel hadn't been the last person in the city of Lima. On certain occasions, he used to wear his uniform with the insignia of a full General, its tunic hung with decorations. Gabriel distinctly remembered one of them, a pretty little cross on a black-and-orange ribbon[20]. It was definitely silver, or at least that's what the dealer had told him when he'd purchased Papa Miguel's decorations. The dealer had been an honest man, there weren't many like him around anymore. He'd bought the tunic too and offered a good price for it.

---

[20] The Russian order of St. George awarded for personal bravery

ZOTOV

But the memory of the figurine still made Gabriel blush. He wanted to give it away for free but the dealer wouldn't have any of it and graciously paid six sols for the useless thing — less than a couple of dollars. The dealer was known to buy up such junk in order to sell it to the tourists at the local markets: those foreign *imbéciles* couldn't get enough of them.

And Gabriel could always use an extra six sols. He was constantly out of a job (not that he was that eager to find one) but he still needed the money to buy drinks in the bar — for his friends as well as for all those pretty *chicas* in miniskirts who'd perch themselves on bar stools next to his. They loved his sky-blue eyes — just like his grandfather's — and his big heart to match, so Russian even though he'd only ever seen Russia on television. Every time they'd showed the vast expanses of that faraway Northern land, its cities and people, Papa Miguel would shout, "Gabriel, come quick!" So naturally Gabriel had to come and watch, even if only to show some respect to his granddad, although the programs bored him out of his mind. What could possibly be interesting about Russia? The country was so cold that even water froze there; it was piled with snow like that place in South Argentina where Gabriel had gone with his friends to celebrate their graduation. That wasn't a country but a fucking refrigerator.

And his grandfather had seemed to miss it. He really wanted to go and visit it once. Every year he kept saying, "This time, I'm gonna go, I swear." He'd even bought a plane ticket just before his death.

He hadn't made it though. At least the airline had had the decency of refunding his money.

Papa Miguel had never spoken much about his past. According to Gabriel's father, he'd arrived in Peru without a pot to piss in and started his service as a traffic cop, then worked his way up through the ranks, retiring as a General. Regardless of the force in power (because coup d'états here bred faster than Amazon piranhas), each and every one of the country's presidents and tyrants had treated Papa Miguel with the utmost respect, ending with Alberto Fujimori who'd personally awarded him another decoration during the celebrations marking Papa Miguel's 95th birthday.

The old man's career had taken off when he'd managed to catch the Trujillo Predator and climaxed when he'd burned alive the Artist and his Apprentice, the two most notorious serial killers in the history of Peru and probably in the whole world if you didn't count the Nazi. They were a student and a car driver who'd killed over fifty whores in Lima plus forty cops and fifteen villagers from some place called Corpus Christi. But the pinnacle of their murderous career was the Casa de Cine massacre where those two butchers had managed to slay five hundred people. Papa Miguel had locked the theater doors and burned the two scumbags to a crisp, so that no one could even identify them later in those pre-DNA days.

Papa Miguel had become a national hero. El Presidente had invited him to a general assembly of the junta and granted him the Grand Cross of the Sun of Peru. Few Peruvians had ever earned the honor, let alone Russians, or so the dealer had told him when he'd generously paid three thousand American greenbacks for the cross.

Still, catching the two monsters had apparently left its stamp on Papa Miguel.

Gabriel had heard his share of rumors — which his own father never confirmed and which Gabriel would have never have found the courage to ask Papa Miguel about. According to them, his grandfather had spent the next couple of years in a mental asylum. Plainly speaking, he'd gone nuts. The rumors claimed that Papa Miguel, feverish and beyond himself, had tried to convince the cops that he'd seen Supay, the King of Uku Pacha and the god of evil, who'd apparently come to the theater to meet with the two killers who'd summoned him with their blood sacrifices.

No one had believed him, of course, but his words hadn't surprised anyone. After what he'd been through, losing his marbles was perfectly understandable.

But even after the local doctors had fixed his troubled head, Papa Miguel was never quite the same afterwards. He appeared perfectly normal but... for example, he spent every vacation away from Lima on archeological digs studying the ancient sites of the Tawantinsuyu Empire. He'd traveled all over Peru north to south and even gone to Bolivia: there was just no stopping him. He had an absolute passion for old ruins and bones, worse than the love for a girl.

The things he'd found! In those days, nobody bothered about authorizations and such. Papa Miguel used to bring back all kinds of crazy stuff from his trips — ancient pots and figurines, and even a slab of stone which had a picture of what appeared to be an astronaut — or maybe a guy with a horned head.

Still, Gabriel had never thought much about the Supay figurine. It was definitely a fake. The craftsmanship was too poor and the stone itself filthy. Only after he'd sold it to the dealer had it dawned on him what a blooper he must have made. Papa Miguel had never kept useless junk.

Gabriel had immediately hurried back to the dealer and offered him ten bucks, like, he wanted to keep the figurine as a memento of his grandfather.

Too late, wasn't it? The dealer had already gotten rid of the statuette. According to him, he'd sold it to some traveling peddler from Cusco, the kind that amble from one place to the next loaded like llamas with everything from women's bowler hats and shawls to cheap souvenirs and bottles of Inca Cola.

In other words, he'd lost the figurine. But this loss gave Gabriel an idea.

ZOTOV

What if there were other figurines like that one? There must have been a reason for Papa Miguel to keep it on display encased in a glass cube. He'd never touched the wretched thing, allowing it to gather dust and dirt — but the moment Gabriel got anywhere near it, his grandfather would frown and start yelling at him.

Not that Gabriel cared. Old people are all like this, never willing to part with their sagging beds and crumbling cupboards.

And not just old people. Take Gabriel's father, for instance. The man had zero commercial sense. About five years ago, Gabriel had started hinting heavily about going through Papa Miguel's archives. You never know, they might find something worth their while.

As if! His father just didn't want to know. He kept saying they had to give it all to the museum in accordance with Papa Miguel's last will. Problem was, Papa Miguel had never had the chance to instruct them which artifacts were destined to which museum. So in the end, it had come to nothing.

Then last month father had died from a heart attack. He'd been driving when it had happened, resulting in him flying off the road. His body was so badly burned they'd had trouble identifying it. He was the only person who knew the exact location of Papa Miguel's archives — but he'd never told Gabriel anything about it, no matter how hard Gabriel had begged him. "I'm busy, son, you'll have to wait, I'll tell you tomorrow." And as they say, tomorrow never comes.

Now Gabriel had to rack his brains trying to guess where Papa Miguel had hidden his treasure. Was it in a special bunker or a bank vault or in some secret stashes scattered all over Lima?

Please don't laugh. He wasn't mad yet.

He knew there were several figurines. Papa Miguel used to bring lots of them from his travels. And honestly speaking, his hidden treasure was indeed Gabriel's last resort. He had no source of income. True, his father had left him the house and the garage (minus the gutted car). So what? You couldn't smear them on bread. How was he supposed to buy drinks and party with the *chicas*? His father's funeral had consumed every single penny left on his father's bank account. The money Gabriel had gotten for his grandfather's tunic and decorations (and that wretched figurine) had only lasted him a couple of months. What a shame. And now of all times, just as he'd finally got some chance with Linda! Beautiful Linda with her coffee-table backside which looked so nice and round in Gabriel's bed. But Linda wanted a diamond ring and threatened to leave him for José next door.

He needed the money, dammit. He could sell his grandfather's furniture, all his paintings and Persian rugs, but that would only last him a week, if that.

He had to think hard. Where would Papa Miguel have secreted his hoarded artifacts to keep them away from prying eyes? The cellar? They didn't have one. The garage? He'd checked it already, with zero results. Gabriel had no desire to dig their entire garden up although he'd already been seriously considering it.

He was wallowing in desperation when it finally dawned on him.

Papa Miguel had been a cop, hadn't he? And those police pen-pushers were crazy about paperwork. They wouldn't have had a cup of mate tea without first logging it into a book. Papa Miguel was no different. He must have kept a logbook of his archeological finds somewhere. He simply must have.

Driven by the sudden epiphany, Gabriel climbed up into the attic and started going through Papa Miguel's papers.

When he'd seen the sheer amount of boxes, he'd very nearly had a heart attack himself. The old photographs depicting his grandfather as a young man of barely twenty, fresh as a daisy, in a tunic and a peaked cap, saber at his side, standing under the Russian flag embroidered with the two-headed eagle. Another picture showed him with a girl, a pretty little item with a charming nose and stern eyes. Neither of them was smiling.

Of course. It was during the Civil war in Russia, wasn't it? Some communists had seized power there — a bit like Sendero Luminoso fighting the government here in Peru. Russian communists had been more successful though. They'd made quick work of all the nobles. Papa Miguel had been lucky he'd made it out of the country in time.

More photos... here, Papa Miguel in his police uniform in Lima. He'd been really lucky with his career. Gabriel would have never become a cop, not in a thousand years. Why would he want to? Two generations of cops in one family was well enough. Their job left no space for the family. Papa Miguel's wife had run off with a street artist; Gabriel's own mother had found a job in the US and had never come back. Gabriel didn't remember her at all: he'd only been two years old when she'd left them. His parents were already quite old when they'd had him: his Dad had married when he was forty-five, and so had Papa Miguel.

To cut a long story short, Gabriel kept sifting through all those tons of paperwork when he came across a thick notebook bound in black oilcloth.

Problem was, it was all in Russian.

Gabriel had very nearly pulled out all his remaining hair in dismay. Why hadn't he listened to his father when he'd forced him to learn the language? So he just stared at a large title followed by lots of drawings of figurines and things, each with a detailed description in Russian.

Over two hundred items. Just what the doctor ordered. But the main thing was, at the end of the notebook there was an address in Spanish next to a map ripped out of a road atlas.

Jesus and Holy Mary, glory be to you! Gabriel went as far as promised to have the biggest candle, the size of a ship's mast, made in Our Savior's honor and light it in Lima Cathedral.

The rest was paperwork, if you'll excuse the pun. Gabriel rented a car, loaded a shovel and a pick in it and headed off to the mountains. And there...

Papa Miguel had been a very smart man, oh yes, sir. Why would he want to keep all those expensive artifacts at home? All he'd done, he'd bought a useless plot of land far from Lima and hadn't even bothered to fence it off. Without knowing the address, no one would have ever found it. And even if they had, they would have been none the wiser. Just a small plateau high in the mountains.

GABRIEL STOOD facing a magnolia tree: split in two, it was black and dry with age. Some hundred and fifty feet from it stood a small square house, lopsided and crumbling.

That was the extent of it.

The cliff near the tree sported a deep crevice which had been filled with concrete and blocked with enormous boulders, each almost the size of an elephant. No idea who and how had delivered them here from the foothills below.

Not that it baffled Gabriel. Old men and their whims! It was very possible that the crevice had emitted some toxic gases which was a common thing in the mountains.

He entered the crumbling house. It was

empty with the exception of a large fire site at its center, complete with a tall blackened pole. It must have been one of those Indian totems like the one Papa Miguel used to have in his room, topped with a red-faced beast. The totem was still gathering dust in the room as the dealer had refused point blank to take it.

Gabriel opened the map. Easy! The treasure was hidden in the right corner of the hut, ten feet deep. Digging for it would be a job and a half though.

Still, Gabriel had decided against hiring an assistant. In treasure hunting, eyewitnesses are lethal. This was Peru and not some cozy Switzerland where apparently there was no crime at all. South America was different: here, your best friend could become your gravedigger if he found out he could make a few thousand dollars selling the figurines.

As he kept digging, his head was crowded with thoughts.

What if the figurines were pure gold? From what Gabriel had heard, the Emperor Inca Atahualpa had kept the bulk of gold he was supposed to pay the Spanish. Here, everybody had heard about the magic land of Eldorado. What if Papa Miguel had found it?

Gabriel kept puffing, wiping sweat off his brow. Like most town dwellers, the future millionaire had little idea of how to use a shovel. Soon the palms of his hands were covered in bloodied blisters but he ignored the pain and continued to dig fast and hard without taking breaks. He knew that his efforts would be rewarded.

He was right. Finally, his spade hit a chest lid.

Yes! He'd done it!

Still, Gabriel was far from drooling over his find. He'd seen plenty of films where the main character chased after a treasure only to discover a cuddly toy in the coveted chest as the grandfather's last practical joke.

Gabriel flung the shovel aside, then secured a steel hook by the pit's edge and slung a rope through it. The hook seemed to hold.

Indiana Jones, eat your heart out!

The lid of the capacious coffin-like wooden chest had split from the blow of his shovel. Gabriel began to gingerly break off pieces of the wood with his bare hands. Finally, the rusty nails gave way and the planks fell apart.

Yes. Glory be to all the saints in heaven and all the demons in hell, this was it!

Refusing to believe his eyes, he sifted through the figurines, each fitted with a small description on a plaque.

Inti the Sun God. Pariacaca, the God of thunderstorms, with the head of a falcon. The terrible Paricia who killed peasants with water from the sky. The figurine of Urcaguary, the God of precious metals, made — surprise! — from solid gold.

Jesus Christ almighty, this was millions of dollars' worth!

Why had Papa Miguel collected it all? Why had neither he nor his son told anything to Gabriel? Their family had never been that poor — in fact, they were quite middle-class — but they could have been stinking rich!

Old men and their frugal habits! Why? He couldn't have taken it with him, could he?

Gabriel spent a long time studying each and every figurine, bringing them to his eyes and looking at them against the sun.

When he'd finally finished, it was already dark. He carefully laid the figurines into the crates he'd brought with him, wrapped them in thick blankets and loaded them in the car.

His heart thumped hard against his ribs, threatening to jump out of his chest.

WHEN HE RETURNED home, it was well past midnight. Gabriel locked the house and drew all the curtains, then took a shower to wash away all the dirt and sweat. His hair still dripping, he took another stock of the figurines.

He just couldn't believe it. He was a millionaire. The prettiest girls. A Rolls Royce. Hundred-dollar cigars. The best brandies instead of this gut rot pisco. A penthouse in Manhattan. Lots of things.

Exhausted, the freshly-baked treasure

hunter collapsed on the bed but was too excited to sleep. Blindly he reached for a book from the bedside table. A short story collection by Stephen King: good enough.

The book opened at *The Mist*: a novella about giant insects from another dimension killing people in a grocery store. Gabriel began reading but cussed seeing his bloody thumbprint on the page. He'd completely forgotten about his blisters.

Dammit. He really didn't feel like climbing out of his comfortable bed in search of some Band Aid. Did that mean he'd left bloody prints on all the figurines? Never mind. Tomorrow he'd have to clean them up with a brush and some tissues, that's all.

Gabriel staggered to his feet and headed for the bathroom in search of the first-aid kit and some scissors. Band Aid... yes.

Why was his head spinning? The world seemed to be crumbling. No wonder: he was dead on his feet. At least he'd never have to work hard for the rest of his life.

Gabriel took good aim and cut off a short strip of Band Aid.

His grandfather's notebook lay on the desk, still open on page one. Big block Russian letters were perfectly legible:

MY LAST WILL AND TESTAMENT. I WANT THE GODS TO BE BURIED WITH ME.

Gabriel grabbed at the bathtub's edge, wide-eyed, staring at his fingers which were crumbling like sand down the tub.

He opened his mouth to scream.

THE FINAL CHAPTER

Vampirism

Moscow, a café next to the
Alexeyevskaya metro station
December 2015

OLEG BROUGHT Joan's hand to his lips and gently kissed her palm. "I still can't believe it," he admitted.

"*You* can't! How about me, then?" the girl said.

She looked out of the café window at all the people bustling past with bagfuls of presents. Flurries of snowflakes whirled over the Christmas trees in a small street market. The cars stuck in a traffic jam tooted half-heartedly. This was winter Moscow as usual, the standard scene just before New Year[21].

---

[21] Traditionally, Russians don't celebrate the Western Christmas of December 25 (religious Russians celebrate the Orthodox Christian Christmas which is January 7) so the

Oleg turned to the window too, following her gaze. So beautiful. Like a fairy tale, really. Just think that he used to ignore it all like a typical busy Muscovite. Those amazing rosy-cheeked girls, their necks cuddled by soft fluffy scarves. Grim businessmen in black great coats lugging their briefcases. Laughing young men. A couple of drunks — you couldn't escape them — but even they were full of good cheer as the season required. A wonderful time when all people seem to be better and kinder to each other.

"This is so strange," Joan continued. "Your world is so magical but I still can't get used to it. Some guy can be ogling me in the metro but still he won't come over and suggest a blow job. Even though it would probably be more honest that way. Women aren't ashamed of wearing underwear under their clothes in public transport. Virtually all of them wear panties — but other women don't laugh at them. And where are your sex shops? Aren't they legally obliged to take 95% of all retail? These people seem to buy cucumbers and sausages to actually eat them. Your shops are full of different foods, not just yogurt which we use to imitate you-know-what. You can actually get jailed for rape here. Oh sweetheart... this is so strange and scary. If you remember, I used to take pills for vertigo

---

peak of the season festivities in Russia falls on the New Year's night.

every night. I've no idea how you survived in our world."

Oleg chuckled, pleased. "I still can't get used to it, either. So many girls in this café and not one of them has walked over to me and cast a meaningful glance at the ladies' room.

Joan laughed.

"There're no serial killers lurking behind every bush," Oleg continued, "and no one here pretends they're movie superstars clad in soldiers' fatigues. Although when I saw the new dollar exchange rate, I did think this was some psychedelic arthouse flick with a five-thousand budget."

Joan raised her eyebrows. "Talking about that, you've been away for almost a year — and no one has reported you missing. People are so indifferent here. They lack consideration. Back in Sex City, when someone has a heart attack in the street, he'd be immediately surrounded by women. Okay, so they would all want to screw him but still..."

Oleg shook his head. "You don't understand. This isn't a movie. Time flows differently here. In the movies, you can show a gap of thirty years in the matter of a couple of seconds. It depends on the genre, of course, because sci fi is different from drama and a murder thriller isn't the same as a romance — but I was only absent for a week. True, I got fired because I couldn't explain my absence. Vicky wasn't worried because she must have thought I'd just decided to take a break from her and gone on a last-moment vacation to Turkey or somewhere. And as for my friends... you've no idea of the kind of hectic lifestyle we have here in Moscow. I could have gone for a hundred years and no one would have been the wiser. So you might be right, actually. People aren't that considerate here," he broke out in a quiet relieved laughter.

"I'd like to thank you," Joan said grimly.

Oleg rolled his eyes. "What, again? Don't you think you've said it enough times?"

The girl clasped his wrist. "I had no idea someone was capable of such things. You refused to eat my heart and I'll never forget it. Let's face it: we barely knew each other. All we'd had was a few tête-à-têtes. And you were quite prepared to give your life for me. Here in Moscow, I've begun to realize that people tend to promise things far too often. When you ask your god for something, you always promise him to lead a pious life. But the moment your god does what you ask him to do, you forget your promises all too lightly. Had I been a god, I would have left your planet a long time ago. You guys aren't real believers. Scammers, more like."

"Supay had been stuck in the movie world for eighty years but still he failed to understand one thing," Oleg said, innocuously fiddling with her fingers. "Movies have their own laws which are laid down by film directors. It's true that virgins never get killed in horror movies — but normally, the charismatic male lead survives too. You and I, we made one such pair. We were technically unkillable — but Supay had failed to realize this despite all his cunning and wisdom. So just as he'd herded you into the room, I suddenly felt that my tethers had slackened. After that, I only worried about having enough time to break free and save you. But you tripped the bastard up, didn't you? He fell and dropped his precious dagger. I wriggled out of my bonds which skinned my wrists quite badly, grabbed the dagger and stabbed him, then released you. Remember his eyes? He really couldn't believe he was dying. It's true that bad guys often die simply to resurrect in a sequel. But for Supay, there'll be no sequel. You and I, we both know why..."

They fell silent, warming their hands on their coffee cups.

"Were you shocked when I cut off his head?" Joan asked with a smile.

"A bit, yeah," Oleg admitted. "I still liked to think of women as those ethereal creatures, sugar-and-spice-and-all-things-nice, and there you were cutting him up like a seasoned butcher. But then I understood you. In horror movies, you have to destroy evil once and for all, tear it apart, otherwise it will respawn. Much better to get covered in blood than walk into the sunset hand in hand while the monster rises silently from the floor behind your backs. Beheading him at least guaranteed a couple hours of peace. Not that we were in any real danger. Supay had turned into an ordinary guy, don't forget. In the real world he may have been a demon — but not there. What shocked me much more was what we did later."

Joan lowered her eyelashes. "Sorry."

"It's all right. Don't apologize. You explained it well. We had to drink his blood, I understand."

"I still feel embarrassed about it. Just please don't consider it vampirism or cannibalism. Supay may have looked like a human being but he wasn't one. Remember what Great Mother said? Artifacts can curve space and change its direction. They can either send you home or to another movie. The demon was right about one thing: the ritual takes three people and requires a bloody sacrifice. Two of the travelers have to sacrifice the third one and taste his flesh or blood. So we had to drink from the dead demon's veins. Just as Great Mother thought, in order to travel between worlds we needed either a half-blood born of the incestuous union between our races, or a creature of your world which wasn't human. At least that's what she told me. This is an old rule which exists ever since the first travelers from earth graced our world with their presence which probably happened soon after motion pictures had been invented. You are just a human being but both me and Supay answered the requirements. So it's simple, really. Drinking blood is disgusting but sweetheart... we simply had no choice. Just a mouthful, and only to stop this nightmare."

ZOTOV

"I still remember its taste, you know," Oleg said pensively, staring at the café ceiling. "It was like nothing I'd ever tasted before. It's honey sweet with a touch of brine and it stung my tongue like pepper. At first it made me sick; but then I felt us being teleported. It's such an incredible feeling I still can't get over it. If you'd told me all these things in August, I'd never have believed you. Some obscure Latin American demons, for crissakes! Everybody thinks they're just cute souvenirs for tourists — who would have thought that they have absolute power over the Peruvian underworld. There're so many things we still don't know about our world but we have the audacity to think we do. If we could transcend reality and enter the movie world, what other worlds and dimensions do we travel to without even knowing? Books, computer games, famous paintings? Each of them could be a universe in itself with its very own set of rules. It might take me a while to get over it."

Joan chuckled. "You could say that. How you attacked Supay's figurine by your television! Chopped it to a thousand little pieces, you. But I understand. There're too many things I need to learn too. And cooking is one of them. That's one thing they don't teach you in the porn world!"

"Well, there're other things as well. And you learned them pretty quickly," Oleg gave her a wink.

Joan laughed. "I'm surprised you're so cool about it! I thought you might have joined a friary immediately after you left Sex City."

Oleg leaned over the table and kissed her on the lips.

"I want you to screw me," Joan said. "Let's go back to your place. Leave the car here. It's much faster by metro."

Oleg pulled out his billfold and flung a banknote on the table without even looking how much it was. Laughing and holding hands, they walked out into the street and dove into an underground crossing.

Please God, don't let anything bad happen now, Oleg thought. Happy endings do exist in real life and not just in the movies.

They burst into the metro and kissed on the train all the way back. Oleg's apartment was a twenty-minute walk through the crunching snow. The two were all over each other in the elevator, then barged into the apartment. Without even locking the door, they began ripping the clothes off each other with all the passion of young lovers.

Nothing bad happened. Nothing at all.

Because this *was* the happy ending, dammit.

EPILOGUE

SUPAY WATCHED the frozen figures of Oleg and Joan share a kiss on the movie screen. Finally, the picture faded, replaced by the closing credit roll. To his left and right, people started rising to their feet, picking up their wrappers and colas and heading for the exit. The demon alone stayed put; he lounged in his seat munching on his popcorn.

Just think that those two idiots really thought this was a happy ending!

Never mind. It was better this way. They were yet to realize they weren't back in Moscow at all.

They were in their own biopic. A very popular movie genre these days. Whoever was unlucky enough to end up there could continue living their own life albeit slightly jazzed up for the screen. And Oleg had one hell of a life story that simply begged to be made into a movie: an ordinary Russian sales rep wh'd teleported to another dimension, killed a monster, rescued a beautiful girl and brought her back to Moscow. If that wasn't a readymade blockbuster, what was?

Supay had at some point ended up in the

Biopic City too. At the time, it had taken him a lot of effort to realize that he wasn't back in Uku Pacha but in its illusory imitation. He'd managed to escape by a sheer miracle — but Oleg might need some time to realize the terrible truth. And as for Joan, she'd never be able to tell the difference between the real Moscow and its silver-screen rendition. Lots of pretty girls? It could happen in real life, too. Cheerful happy drunks? During the Christmas season, why not? Lots of advertisement in the streets? Hey, you couldn't surprise a Muscovite with *that*!

Supay leaned back in his seat. He'd studied Moscow — the *real* Moscow — pretty well in the two months he'd spent here. He wasn't in a hurry to go back to Uku Pacha. One day, sure, but not now.

He was going to enjoy this city. He was going to bleed it dry.

Then he'd move on, sampling one megalopolis after the next, gradually making his way back to Peru where he'd find the old *huaca* passage and reclaim his throne resting on heaped-up skulls.

His subjects must be missing him by now.

There had always been only one thing required in order to return from the movie world back to earth.

The traveler had to be sacrificed.

Two human beings — one a half-blood, the other a fellow traveler — had to open up your chest with an ancient ritual knife and drink your blood.

Once that done, you could return back home; otherwise, you'd simply travel to yet another movie.

That was a very old ritual that few knew and even fewer used.

He couldn't even remember who'd invented it. Was it the first zombie movies, monochrome horror flicks or sci fi thrillers with clockwork cardboard aliens? Whatever it was, Supay had always known he could do it. Even stripped of his magic powers, a demon never quite becomes an ordinary human being. So he could still do a lot, even after having been stripped of his immortality.

Supay's cold lifeless laughter echoed through the empty theater. That guy — Oleg, wasn't it? — thought he was a movie hero. Yeah right! It had been Supay who'd loosened his bonds. He'd made sure that Joan's tethers were slack enough for her to easily wriggle out of them.

He'd spent ages planting the idea in Great Mother's stupid blind head. Ditto for Joan: who did she think it was who'd kept whispering the right thoughts in her little ear as she was prowling the streets of the B-movie world in search of the right artifacts? If she didn't want a demon to rise from the dead, he'd instructed her, she had to stab him three times in the heart, then cut off his head and drink his blood...

They were all puppets, bit actors in a play staged by a talented director. It was him who'd chosen those two. He'd brought them together. He'd masterminded their love affair. And it was he who'd

416

manipulated Oleg and Joan into sacrificing their reluctant traveling companion.

Did he deserve an Oscar for the best screenplay or not?

Then again, Supay didn't need much. He was perfectly happy with what he already had. They were about to celebrate Christmas here: apparently, festivities would abound. Supay loved festivities. They always required sacrifices.

If Muscovites didn't know anything about Uku Pacha — well, it was about time they learned.

The thing he loved best about the real world was that here, evil always triumphed. The world of stinking-rich scumbags quite prepared to cut each other's throats for an extra dollar; the world of heartless criminal politicians; the world where voiceless amateurs competed for their fifteen minutes of fame on national TV while truly talented singers performed in shabby roadside cafes. The wonderful world of treachery and injustice, perfect for Supay to show what he was worth.

He would get thousands of followers — gazillions of fans -especially female fans! — and maybe even temples. His raison d'être, like that of any Incan god, was competition — and if he'd managed to become the god of the underworld, becoming a god on earth would be a piece of cake.

Still, he had to hurry. His demonic powers were inevitably going to dwindle on Earth. He could count on at least a couple of years of fun before returning to his underground lair.

ZOTOV

And now he even had a new attire. He'd been wearing Alejandro's body for the last eighty years and had got pretty fed up with it.

"Excuse me!" a theater cleaner's voice cut through the demon's musings. "Are you leaving or are you gonna stay here all night?"

Supay rose, headed for the indignant old woman and looked her right in the eye. The cleaner made a sobbing sound and grabbed at her heart. Ignoring her collapsed body, Supay walked out of the theater.

He wrapped his greatcoat tighter around him and offered his face to the floating snowflakes. He walked past a giant movie poster depicting a girl in a young man's arms and the outline of a fiery-eyed monster looming over the two.

El Diablo, the poster said.

This frozen rain is beautiful, the demon thought. He used to think that you could only get snow high up in the mountains but here it was falling from the sky in city streets. The real world was so amazing — much better than anything made at the dream factory.

A smartphone buzzed in his pocket. Clumsily the demon pulled it out, nearly dropping it in the process. He still wasn't used to this weird thingy despite the fact that he'd seen it hundreds of times in the movies.

"Hello," he mouthed an unfamiliar new word.

"Oleg!" a girl's moaning voice exploded in the phone. "You coming or not?"

418

"Sorry, Vick, I'm stuck here for another couple of hours," Supay said in a soft apologetic tone. "Tonight will be special, I promise. I've got a present for you."

"No way!" Vicky squeaked, making Supay jump and rub his ear. "In that case, I promise you a very special night. I've already bought some great lacy underwear. I'm gonna send you a picture now. You're gonna *love* it."

"Leave the underwear out," the demon said calmly.

In less than a minute, he was studying Vicky's nude pic. "Excellent," he chuckled smugly. "I had my doubts, you know. But now I can see you're a perfect fit."

"Pardon?" Vicky said nervously. "Oleg? Anything wrong?"

"Oh no, sweetheart," Supay reassured her. "Everything's fine. I'll see you in the evening. Kisses. I'll bring my surprise along."

The demon hung up and stared at his own reflection in the phone's glossy screen. He took himself by the chin and turned his face aside, studying his profile.

Oleg's body suited him fine. Had he been transferred into Joan's, that would have been quite a predicament. But the victim always received the body of the person who had been the first to stab them. So in this respect, he'd been lucky. Oleg wasn't the cover boy type, but still quite presentable. Also, he had enough money and a

ZOTOV

place to live.

The first thing Supay had done once he'd teleported to Moscow was call Vicky and apologize. Back in the City of Nightmares, Oleg had told him they'd fallen out. Humans were funny creatures in this respect: they loved pouring their hearts out to complete strangers, oblivious of the fact that the chatty fellow traveler on the train might in fact be evil incarnate.

So the demon had made Vicky part of his plan... and tonight she was going to play her role. It had been a while since he'd had a good ritual like those held by Alejandro and Rodrigo. He was getting hungry... and he had no intention of going cold turkey for much longer.

He'd tried to drink blood back in the movie world but that was a surrogate, a fake, a bit like making love with a condom. Everything was fake there, even Dracula who'd turned out to be a boring pop-culture wuss.

The demon walked over to the car, opened the door and got in.

Back in the movie world, he'd worked out how to operate these things. He started the motor and pulled out, then proceeded toward Arbat Street slowly and gingerly, as a learner driver should, grinning apologetically to traffic cops.

He still lacked a certain item he'd ordered for the evening ritual; the delivery had taken two months and now he was about to pick it up. Vicky had no idea that the slow courier service had added two more months to her useless little life.

Having reached his destination, Supay left the car at the paid parking as any law-abiding citizen would. He hated this new idea of paid parking so much he'd have gladly added a couple of town hall workers to tonight's sacrifice.

Still, the time wasn't right yet.

He opened the brand-new briefcase he'd bought two hours ago and headed past all the souvenir stalls and street artists toward an inconspicuous little antique shop. He rang the bell, nodded at the activated CCTV camera and walked down the steps into a well-lit basement room.

A bored middle-aged man in a black suit was waiting for him at the desk. He resembled an undertaker rather than an antique dealer. Two equally bored burly guys with crew cuts sat on a sofa by the opposite wall: this line of business required adequate security. Well done.

"I've got the money," Supay slapped the empty briefcase.

"Excellent," the dealer said bleakly. "In which case..."

"Show me the item," the demon said. "I can tell a fake."

The dealer took offence. "We're a serious business. Here, take a look."

He gingerly set a handmade narrow mahogany box onto the desk, opened it and unfolded the velvet cover.

Inside lay a flat knife with a blade made of

rock glass.

"A sacrificial knife, as you ordered," the dealer said. "It's believed to have been owned by Atahualpa, the last Incan emperor. One of a kind. Two hundred thousand dollars is a rather modest price, I assure you. I never go over the top my clients."

Supay lifted the knife. It felt warm in his hands.

Oh, yes.

"Thank you so much," he said wholeheartedly. "This is exactly what I was looking for."

ONCE BACK IN THE CAR, he lovingly sat the briefcase with the knife on the seat next to him. There were no traces of blood on his jacket: his magic was still enough to make the two bodyguards break each other's necks. The panic-stricken old man had been easy prey.

Supay started the car, waiting for the frozen motor to warm up.

His phone rang again. Women!

"Are you gonna be long?" Vicky nagged. "I'm already in bed, waiting for you."

"It might take me a while," the demon admitted. "But I'm on my way."

"Don't forget to bring your surprise."

"I won't, sweetheart. It'll be the first thing you'll see when you open the door. I promise."

He turned the wheel, steering toward the

Sadovoe ring. According to the satnav, it might take him an hour and a half to get to the apartment.

One thing you couldn't buy here was fresh magnolia petals.

Never mind. He'd have to make do without.

CREDITS START ROLLING

About the Author

GEORGY ZOTOV WAS BORN on March 1 1971 in Moscow.

The future bestselling author was a very bad student. His teachers struggled to push him up through the classes. He hated studying and barely finished high school. Looking back, he now wishes he never did. Working turned out to be much harder.

He found college a whole lot easier though, mainly because they taught him what he enjoyed learning: the history of the Byzantine and Roman Empires. But by the time he graduated as an archivist historian specializing in ancient civilizations, the fall of the Soviet Union had rendered his new job pretty useless. "You couldn't have fed a cat on my wage, let alone a big sonovabitch like myself," the future author admitted.

So he did a straight swap for journalism. At least journalists had fun, or so he thought. Zotov interviewed the dictator of Pakistan as well as Presidents of Moldova and Latvia (the latter interview proving so scandalous it even earned its own Wikipedia mention). He reported from war-torn Abkhazia and Tajikistan, then visited the fronts of Iraq, Afghanistan and even Syria –

where he was arrested and spent three days in prison without food or water. He still remembers it fondly. He was deported from both Syria and Iran in his capacity as a journalist and still enjoys his *persona non grata* status there.

This was his third arrest abroad which makes Zotov the only modern wordsmith who under the unwritten code of prisoners qualifies as an incorrigible felon. He received a shrapnel wound as well as a prestigious national journalism award for his investigative report on the Nazi Lebensborn project.

Zotov has published fifteen books whose combined print run exceeds half a million copies. He prides himself on a reader's review he saw on the Net,

"The guy is a total nutcase. He's completely off his head. Still, the book is very funny."

Want to be the first to know about our latest LitRPG, sci fi and fantasy titles from your favorite authors?

Subscribe to our **NEW RELEASES** newsletter:
http://eepurl.com/b7niIL

Thank you for reading *El Diablo!* If you like what you've read, check out other LitRPG, sci fi and fantasy titles published by Magic Dome Books:

An NPC's Path LitRPG series by Pavel Kornev:
The Dead Rogue
Kingdom of the Dead

Level Up series by Dan Sugralinov:
Re-Start
Hero

The Way of the Shaman LitRPG series by Vasily Mahanenko:
Survival Quest
The Kartoss Gambit
The Secret of the Dark Forest
The Phantom Castle
The Karmadont Chess Set
Shaman's Revenge
Clans War

Dark Paladin LitRPG series by Vasily Mahanenko:
The Beginning
The Quest
Restart

Galactogon LitRPG series by Vasily Mahanenko:
Start the Game!

The Bard from Barliona LitRPG series by Eugenia Dmitrieva and Vasily Mahanenko:
The Renegades
A Song of Shadow

The Neuro LitRPG series by Andrei Livadny:
The Crystal Sphere
The Curse of Rion Castle
The Reapers

The Expansion (The History of the Galaxy) series by A. Livadny:
Blind Punch
The Shadow of Earth
Servobattalion

Point Apocalypse *(a near-future action thriller)* **by Alex Bobl**

The Sublime Electricity series by Pavel Kornev
The Illustrious
The Heartless
The Fallen
The Dormant

You're in Game!
(LitRPG Stories from Bestselling Authors)

You're in Game-2!
(More LitRPG stories set in your favorite worlds)

The Game Master series by A. Bobl and A. Levitsky:
The Lag

Moskau by G. Zotov
(a dystopian thriller)

El Diablo by G.Zotov
(a supernatural thriller)

More books and series are coming out soon!

In order to have new books of the series translated faster, we need your help and support! Please consider leaving a review or spread the word by recommending *El Diablo* to your friends and posting the link on social media. The more people buy the book, the sooner we'll be able to make new translations available. Thank you!

Till next time!

www.ingramcontent.com/pod-product-compliance
Lightning Source LLC
Chambersburg PA
CBHW071636260626
47170CB00001B/130